PENGUIN  CLASSICS

EXPLOSION IN A CATHEDRAL

ALEJO CARPENTIER (1904–1980) was one of the major Latin American writers of the twentieth century, as well as a classically trained pianist and musicologist. His best-known novels are *The Lost Steps*, *Explosion in a Cathedral*, and *The Kingdom of This World*. Born in Lausanne, Switzerland, and raised in Havana, Cuba, Carpentier lived for many years in France and Venezuela before returning to Cuba after the 1959 revolution. A few years later he returned to France, where he lived until his death.

ADRIAN NATHAN WEST has translated more than thirty books from Spanish, Catalan, and German, including Benjamin Labatut's *When We Cease to Understand the World*, a finalist for both the National Book Award for Translated Literature and the International Booker Prize. He is the author of *The Aesthetics of Degradation* and the novel *My Father's Diet*, and his essays and literary criticism have appeared in *The New York Review of Books*, *London Review of Books*, *The Times Literary Supplement*, and *The Baffler*. He lives in Philadelphia.

ALEJANDRO ZAMBRA is the award-winning author of numerous novels and other works of fiction, including *Chilean Poet*, *Ways of Going Home*, *The Private Lives of Trees*, *Bonsai*, *Multiple Choice*, and *My Documents*. His short stories have been published in *The New Yorker*, *The New York Times Magazine*, *The Paris Review*, *Granta*, and *Harper's Magazine*. Born in Santiago, Chile, Zambra lives in Mexico City.

ALEJO CARPENTIER

Explosion in a Cathedral

Translated by
ADRIAN NATHAN WEST

Foreword by
ALEJANDRO ZAMBRA

PENGUIN BOOKS

PENGUIN BOOKS

An imprint of Penguin Random House LLC
penguinrandomhouse.com

Originally published in Spanish as *El siglo de las luces* by
Compañía General de Ediciones, Mexico City

LIBRARY OF CONGRESS CATALOGING-IN-PUBLICATION DATA
Names: Carpentier, Alejo, 1904-1980, author. | West, Adrian Nathan, translator. |
Zambra, Alejandro, 1975- writer of foreword.
Title: Explosion in a cathedral / Alejo Carpentier;
translated by Adrian Nathan West; foreword by Alejandro Zambra.
Other titles: Siglo de las luces. English
Description: [New York] : Penguin Classics, [2023] | Includes bibliographical references.
Identifiers: LCCN 2022056085 (print) | LCCN 2022056086 (ebook) |
ISBN 9780143133889 (paperback) | ISBN 9780525505679 (ebook)
Subjects: LCSH: Hugues, Victor—Fiction. | LCGFT: Biographical fiction. |
Magic realist fiction. | Novels.
Classification: LCC PQ7389.C263 S513 2023 (print) |
LCC PQ7389.C263 (ebook) | DDC 863/.64—dc23/eng/20230320
LC record available at https://lccn.loc.gov/2022056085
LC ebook record available at https://lccn.loc.gov/2022056086

Printed in the United States of America
1st Printing

Set in Sabon LT Pro

For Lilia, my wife

Words do not fall into the void.
The Zohar

Contents

Foreword

Alejo Carpentier's Second Language

I.

I like to think of literature as a second language—especially the second language of the monolingual. I'm thinking, naturally, about those of us who never systematically studied a foreign language, but who had access, thanks to translation—a miracle we take for granted all too easily—to distant cultures that at times came to seem close to us, or even like they belonged to us. We didn't read Marguerite Duras or Yasunari Kawabata because we were interested in the French or Japanese languages per se, but because we wanted to learn—to continue learning— that foreign language called literature, as broadly international as it is profoundly local. Because this foreign language functions, of course, inside of our own language; in other words, our language comes to seem, thanks to literature, foreign without ever ceasing to be ours.

It's within that blend of strangeness and familiarity that I want to recall my first encounter with the literature of Alejo Carpentier, which occurred, as I'm sure it did for so many Spanish speakers of my generation and after, inside a classroom. "In this story, everything happens backward," said a teacher whose name I don't want to remember, before launching into a reading of "Viaje a la semilla" (Journey to the Seed), Carpentier's most famous short story, which we would later find in almost every anthology of Latin American stories, but which at the time, when we were thirteen or fourteen years old, we had never read. The teacher's solemn, perhaps exaggerated reading allowed us, however, to feel or to sense the beauty of prose that was strange and different. It was our language, but converted into an unknown music that could nonetheless, like all music, especially good music, be danced to. Many of us thought it was a dazzling story, surprising and crazy, but I don't know if any of us would have been able to explain why. Because of the odd delicacy of some of the sentences, perhaps. Maybe this one: "For the first time, the rooms slept without window-blinds, open onto a landscape of ruins." Or this one: "The chandeliers of the great drawing room now sparkled very brightly."

Although our teacher had already told us that everything in the story happened backward, from the future to the past, back toward the seed, knowing the trick did not cancel out the magic. The magic did come to an end, though, when the teacher ordered us to list all the words we didn't know and look them up in the dictionary—each of our backpacks always contained a small dictionary, which, we soon found, was not big enough to contain Carpentier's splendid, abundant lexicon.

Was that how people in Cuba spoke? Or was it, rather, the writer's language? Or were we the ones who, quite simply, were ignorant of our own language? But *was* that our language? We discussed something like that, dictionaries in hand, while the teacher—I don't know why I remember this—typed some numbers into a calculator laboriously, perhaps struggling with his farsightedness.

I reread that story just now, and I again find it extraordinary, for reasons I presume are different. But I get distracted by the melancholic attempt to guess which of those words I didn't know back then: embrasure, denticle, entablature, scapulary, daguerreotype, psaltery, doublet, gnomon, balustrades, licentious, gunwads, matchstaff, epaulet, sentient, décolleté, tricorne, taper, tassel, calash, sorrel, benzoin, sophist, crinoline, ruff, octander . . .

To read Carpentier entailed, first of all, listening to him, and then translating him. First, listening to him the way we listen to a song in a language very like our own but that we don't understand entirely, and enjoying the echoes and contrasts. And then translating him; translating before we knew how to translate, or even that we were translating. Translating him in our own language. For someone who grew up with the Spanish of Chile, reading Carpentier was, of course, to travel to the island of Cuba, but above all it was to travel to the island of Carpentier.

II.

The foreignness of his own language was clear to Carpentier from the start, as the son of a French father and a Russian mother. Throughout his life, he affirmed the official story that he had been born in Havana, but a few years after Carpentier's death, Guillermo Cabrera Infante leaked the juicy tidbit that he had actually been born in Lausanne, Switzerland (a bit of gossip that was never disproven, perhaps because it was supported by a birth certificate).

The hypotheses about this lie—or, to put it more kindly, this slight displacement of the truth—are numerous, of course. Carpentier probably wanted to minimize his foreignness, for reasons we do not know, though contemplating them is fascinating. Listening to him in interviews on YouTube, any Spanish speaker would agree that this is a person who speaks the language with unusual dexterity and mastery, with his guttural pronunciation of the r as the sole, though conclusive, mark of his foreignness. And so it isn't hard to believe this new version of his biography, which presents him to us as a Cuban whose mother tongue was not Spanish, though he mastered the language very quickly, with extraordinary proficiency, when he arrived in Cuba with his parents at four or five years old.

There is no disputing that Carpentier was born on November 26, 1904, which is not relevant in and of itself, of course, except for readers who are interested in astrology. But I mention it because that is also the birthday of Esteban, one of the protagonists of *Explosion in a Cathedral*, who in fact becomes a translator—significant, since the book is often understood as a novel about the "translation" of the ideals of the French Revolution to the Caribbean. Although we later come to realize that the beautiful and terrible initial section foreshadows Esteban's importance, the figure of that orphaned, sickly boy seems, in the first chapter, less relevant than his cousins, Carlos and Sofía, with whom he lives as one more brother in a big house in Havana.

The novel opens with these three teenagers in mourning after the death of their father, a well-to-do plantation owner who had been widowed years before. Instead of returning to the convent where she has been educated so far, Sofía chooses to stay home with her brother Carlos—who is destined, or more like condemned, to take over the family business—and her cousin, whom she tries to care for and protect. The three young people cope with their pain even as they discover the joys of this shared life, "absorbed in interminable readings, discovering the universe through books." Grief becomes, as well, "a fitting pretext to stay aloof from all commitments or obligations, ignoring a society whose provincial intolerance tried to bind existence to ordinary norms, to appearing in certain places at certain times, dining in the same modish pastry shops, spending Christmas on the sugar plantations or on estates in Artemisa, where rich landholders vied with each other over the number of mythological statues they could place on the verges of their tobacco fields . . ."

They are distracted from this intense and entertaining life of seclusion by Victor Hugues, a trader from Marseille of indeterminate age ("thirty or forty perhaps, or maybe much younger"), whose seductive irruption on the scene opens up a promising space attuned to revolutionary idealism and enthusiasm. Rounding out the group is Doctor Ogé, a mestizo physician and Freemason and a friend of Hugues's, who tries to help Esteban as he is in the throes of an asthma attack. There is a crucial scene in which Sofía refuses to give her hand to the doctor, betraying racial prejudices that are typical of her class and time ("No one would trust a negro to build a palace, defend a prisoner, arbitrate a theological dispute, or govern a country"). But Victor Hugues replies categorically, "All men are born equal." And it turns out that Ogé not only treats Esteban's asthma attack, but also cures him completely. This miracle leaves an indelible mark on the characters' values and prospects, especially Sofía's and Esteban's; the latter, now free of illness and faced with the racing speed of history, dares to embark on a different life.

I don't want to give anything away here about the fate of certain characters who go on to engage directly with the changing and bloody era in which they live. Perhaps it will suffice to say that Victor Hugues and Esteban set out for France, from where Hugues—a historical character adapted by Carpentier from diverse and elusive sources—returns to the Caribbean in a position of power, on his way to becoming the "island Robespierre," while Esteban, after discovering Paris and feeling "more French than the French, more rebellious than the rebels, clamoring for peremptory measures, draconian punishments, exemplary retribution," and moving to Bayonne to translate ineffective revolutionary pamphlets, also returns to the Caribbean, having now become the narrator who, almost without realizing, we met in the novel's preamble. Increasingly disillusioned and guilt-ridden, Esteban finds the appreciative contemplation of nature to be practically his only consolation. As for Sofía, her marriage to Jorge seems to set her up for riches and insignificance, but widowhood and her later reunion with Hugues turn her into the surprise protagonist of the novel's last stretch; her decisions, motivations, and fate have for decades fed an interpretive debate that is today perhaps more current than ever.

III.

"I think I am one of the few Cubans who can boast of having visited almost all of the islands in the Caribbean," said Carpentier in an interview in which he emphasizes that none of those islands is like any other. That cult of the specific inundates each of the minute and vivid descriptions that abound in his work. The beauty of Carpentier's prose can never be emphasized enough, and here it rises to incredible levels, especially in the descriptions of marine landscapes: "Esteban saw in the coral forests a tangible image, an intimate yet ungraspable figuration of Paradise Lost, where the trees, still badly named, with the clumsy and quavering tongue of a Man-Child, were endowed with the apparent immortality of this luxurious flora—this monstrance, this burning bush—for which the sole sign of autumn or springtime was a variation in tone or a soft migration of shadows . . ."

This exuberant prose, which is proudly and decidedly baroque, still manages not to compete with the story. We are carried forward, it seems to me, at a fluctuating speed, and we even, at times, laboriously change ships; the pace is remarkable, as are the pauses, the tricky overall tardiness that opens up emotional spaces and unsuspected storylines. The narrative inhabits us, so to speak. At times we don't really know what we are reading, and, more importantly, for long passages we forget that we *are* reading. Carpentier works his style in such a way that it is still possible to read this book as a historical novel, even as an adventure tale, although of course he problematizes the idea of adventure ("Esteban knew well the tedium the word *adventure* could conceal," the narrator says at one point).

It's possible that a pessimistic reading, one that is grounded in the brutality the novel relates so bluntly, is more persuasive than one that fully validates the idea of progress. The world of this novel is—much like our own, in fact—complex, protean, ambivalent, filled with characters who fluctuate between feeling fascinated and repulsed by the present, between heroism and mediocrity, between opportunistic conformity and radical idealism. It occurs to me that, as much for Spanish-speaking readers as for English-speaking ones, the change in title is useful. The original title, *El siglo de las luces*—something like *The Century of Lights* in English—is ironic in a way that hangs over the book like a disturbing shadow, while the English title highlights the crucial recurrence in the novel of *Explosion in a Cathedral*, the painting by François de Nomé that depicts a halted movement, an "endless falling without falling," and, along with the repeated references to Goya's *The Disasters of War*, gives the novel a constant and powerful visual counterpoint.

Since it was first published in 1962, the novel was initially read, naturally, in light of the Cuban Revolution, with Carpentier already en route to becoming an emblem of a successful revolution, as he was until his death. I don't think that the novel, in and of itself, allows for some of the unequivocal expert readings it was subjected to: there are some critical commentaries that seem to understand it as a collection of the author's badly disguised opinions, which is particularly unfair given its complexity, ambition, and reach. Does this novel express a real hope in revolutionary processes, or rather a radical skepticism? "Esteban's journey is not circular but spiral," notes Roberto González Echevarría in his stupendous book *Alejo Carpentier: The Pilgrim at Home*, a particularly illuminating reading that attends to the nuances of *Explosion in a Cathedral*'s striking monumentality.

IV.

Explosion in a Cathedral is a novel that, just like Italo Calvino said about classics, has never finished saying what it has to say. Especially to us, who in a way inhabit the future that it foresees or prefigures. Read today, some sixty years since its original publication, at the end of a pandemic, amid wars and totalitarian governments and a radical climate crisis, a novel like *Explosion in a Cathedral* continues to accompany us, to question us, to challenge and move us, and ultimately to help us in the arduous and terrible exercise of reading the world.

Contrasting the novel with the present could open many a debate, and I imagine them all as vibrant and impassioned. What happens to us when we realize that there are others for whom *we are the others*? Do we ever truly become aware of such a thing? Is it possible to change history without violence, without thousands of innocent dead? What does this novel have to tell us about colonialism, globalization, feminism, human rights, the rights of nature, transculturation, migration, war?

Perhaps the somewhat irrational wish that Spanish were his mother tongue led Carpentier to build his astonishing version of that language, which takes on, even for Spanish speakers, a music that is old and new at the same time, one that allows past, present, and future to coexist. Literature, at the end of the day, is a complex form of consciousness, which allows us to imagine what we would be like if we were bilingual, or multilingual. And of course that includes imagining what we would be like had we learned the languages that were wiped out in our own lands and in the territories of neighboring countries, the languages that were savaged and erased to create the illusion of monolingualism. Perhaps if we respond to the challenges raised by this novel, if we undertake the countless discussions it permits and induces, it will help us become more humble, less dumb, less deaf.

ALEJANDRO ZAMBRA
Translated by Megan Mcdowell

A Note on the Translation

It's hard enough to get a book translated into English the first time. Why bother translating it again? One reason might be a lack of recognition; and it's true that Alejo Carpentier, despite the range and breadth of his body of work, is only barely, or maybe, canonical in English, and most people who do know him have read a single book, 1949's *The Kingdom of This World*. But another, more germane reason might be that the book has in some sense not been translated at all. *Explosion in a Cathedral*, in the version published in 1962, was translated not from Carpentier's *El Siglo de las luces*, but from René Durand's French translation, *Le Siècle des Lumières*. Such relay translations were common at the time, and more than one author—Witold Gombrowicz comes to mind—has overseen the translation of works from a less-known mother tongue into an international language from which subsequent translations are meant to proceed. I'm probably less of a purist about this than most, but the fact remains that this is now looked down upon and that, as anyone who's played telephone knows, the further the remove from the original source, the more distortions are likely to creep in.

Let's start with the title: *El Siglo de las luces* means "the century of light," not "explosion in a cathedral." The *Encyclopedia of Latin American Literature* says a literal translation would have sounded "totally pedestrian and flat," and praises translator John Sturrock's title, taken from a painting that plays an important role in the novel, as capturing "the spirit of the work." Whether this is true is irrelevant: the title is here to stay, like Kafka's *Amerika* or Stieg Larsson's *The Girl with the Dragon Tattoo*.

The change does elide something, though: "el Siglo de las Luces" is a common term in Spanish for the Enlightenment or the Age of Reason. That Carpentier chose this for his title is in part ironic, pointing to the ease with which reason may be bent to the ends of barbarism; at the same time, it is an expression of sympathy for the prophecies of the late-eighteenth-century Freemasons, who played a significant role in the diffusion of the Enlightenment past Europe's shores and who foresaw a century of light (*siglo de luces*), of superstition cast out by science and reason, but failed to imagine that it would be accompanied by the Reign of Terror, the horrors of colonialism, and the cycles of upheaval and suppression that extended from the Napoleonic Wars through the revolutions of 1848 and onward.

Then there's the first sentence: "Esta noche he visto alzarse la Máquina nuevamente." John Sturrock writes, "I saw them erect the guillotine again tonight." Problem one: to the great frustration of second-language learners, "esta noche" can mean both "tonight" and "last night." A person who's slept badly will most likely say, "Esta noche he dormido fatal." Carpentier's intention here is uncertain, but scholars and native speakers I've consulted concur with my sense that "last night" feels more correct. The *them* seen erecting the guillotine is an intervention, a typical resort for the translator dealing with Spanish's often frustrating impersonal reflexives; in Carpentier's words, the device seems to rise ominously, on its own. Sturrock lets the cat out of the bag when he tells us it's a guillotine. Carpentier prefers to write "la Máquina," the Machine—capitalized, to indicate its stature, but with its nature unspecified: a machine among many, cousin of the steam engine, the flying shuttle, and the power loom, a single instance in a far-reaching movement toward the rationalization and mechanization of human endeavors. (It should be mentioned in passing that Guillotin, the machine's inventor, was a physician and Freemason, founder of a Lodge called *La Verité*, and lived through the French Revolution and the bloody years that followed it.)

Sturrock's translation generally makes things easier for readers; Carpentier's long paragraphs are broken up, his labyrinthine sentences chopped down, his ornate, often antiquated vocabulary brought up to date. Comparatively, I have been more conservative: visually, my text resembles the original, and Carpentier's flourishes have left me free to indulge that vice which Fowler censures as "the love of the long word." Still, literalism has its limits. In his exuberance, Carpentier gets the occasional thing wrong: he speaks early on of "black retinas" when he must mean pupils; he has Cazotte's camel from *Le diable amoreaux* vomit a greyhound rather than a spaniel, as in the original. Such trivialities I have silently corrected. The question of style is thornier; the author's peculiarities demand respect, but different languages have different degrees of tolerance for prolixity and ambiguity, and there are bits of bombast I have overruled when I did not think English would well bear them. At one point, Carpentier writes, "horrified at the impossibility of escaping the trial of confronting a storm"; most English speakers will struggle to see how this is superior to the simpler "horrified of the storm." A tic of writers in Spanish generally is their preference not to say someone *did* something when they might instead say he began to do it, managed to do it, was able to do it; another is to say something occurred suddenly when it cannot have occurred otherwise (we need not be told that a lightning strike or the explosion of a shell is sudden). In these minor matters, I've relied on my judgment.

While not so vain as to suppose I've done everything right, I am confident this new translation of *Explosion in a Cathedral* is substantially more correct than its predecessor. Just browsing for errors in the Sturrock translation, I've found enough to presume there are many more, not all of them inconsequential. A few examples: the Spanish *acabar por*, to wind up doing something, is routinely translated as *to finish*; the War of Palmares, which occurred in the Brazilian Maroon settlement of Quilombo dos Palmares, is translated as the "War of the Palm Trees"; the spiders Sturrock has descend from the ceiling of the magic castle of Gottorp are almost certainly chandeliers; though the sound of drums was common in nineteenth-century skirmishes, in many cases, Carpentier must mean "artillery" when he uses the word *batería*; and so on and so forth.

Explosion in a Cathedral reappears at a time when the effects of slavery and colonialism and the legacies of nineteenth-century liberalism are being reexamined and reevaluated. Carpentier's vision of these matters is trenchant, but immune to simplification and dogmatism. In his account of the northward migrations of the Carib people, he underscores the brutality of life in the pre-Columbian Americas, not to excuse the ravages of the conquistadors, but to hint at an inclination to cruelty and plunder universal in the human heart. His portrayal of the corruption of the revolutionary idealists, who abhorred slavery and embraced self-determination only so long as it was politically expedient, is a sour reminder of how easily self-interest eclipses virtue. The chronicle of Maroon settlements and revolts retold in these pages by the Swiss Sieger, who speaks of "a Great Emancipation that began in the sixteenth century," will be of interest to anyone hungry for counter-narratives that official history tends to overlook.

All this would run the danger of didacticism were it not for *Explosion in a Cathedral*'s language, its lush sensuality, its attempt to render world-altering events in the tones of private experience, to explain the fervor that ignites revolutions and conquests as fruit of an inalterable human compulsion toward new shores and new feelings. As in Goya's *Disasters of War*, which is quoted throughout, reason is the agent of emotion and instinct, and human undertakings are destitute of vision. This is equally true for the broad movements of revolution and reaction that shaped the nineteenth century and for the philosophical and sentimental education of the book's protagonists. On its own, Carpentier's sweeping tableau of French colonialism in the Americas would be an accomplishment; but his prose, alternately precise and baroque while unstintingly poetic, makes this a masterpiece. I hope that the present translation will convey to contemporary readers something of its beauty and grandeur.

ADRIAN NATHAN WEST

Explosion in a Cathedral

Last night, I saw the Machine rise up again. It stood on the prow like a door opened against the vastness of a sky that was already carrying the scent of land across a sea so placid, so assured in its rhythms, that the ship, slightly elevated, seemed to drift off to sleep as it pressed on, poised between a yesterday and a tomorrow that traveled with us. Time froze between the North Star, Ursa Major, and the Southern Cross. I don't know, it's not meant for me to know, if these were indeed the constellations, so copious that their vertices, points of light on orbital paths, grew confused and glissaded over one other, shuffling their allegories around a full moon frosted by the pallor of the Way of Saint James . . . The Door-without-hinges rose up on the prow, a meager frame with a set square, an inverted gable, a black triangle, and fixtures of cold beveled steel. The structure, naked and abrupt, loomed like an apparition over the dreams of men—a warning to each and all. We had left it on deck, far off in the April mistrals, and now it soared up once more on that same prow, at the fore, like a way-finder, like (in its implacable geometry, in the requisite exactness of its parallels) a giant apparatus for navigating the sea. No longer was it encircled by pennants, drums, or rabble; it knew neither excitement, nor furor, nor grief, nor the drunkenness of those who, back then, back there, had closed in on it like the chorus of an ancient tragedy as tumbrils creaked toward the thundering of drums. Here the Door was alone, face turned to the night, vertical over the tutelary figurehead, diagonal blade shimmering in the wooden casing that opened onto a panorama of stars. The waves rose in attendance, sundered and stroked the ship's flanks, and closed again behind us with a sound so measured and continuous that its permanence soon resembled the silence a man believes to be pure silence when he

*hears no voices like his own. Living silence throbbing, uni-
form, not yet resonant with severation and rigidity . . . When
the blade dropped, diagonal, with a transitory whistle, and the
lintel was painted as scrupulously as a proper threshold should
be, the Vested One, whose hand had set the mechanism in motion, murmured through clenched teeth, "We need to protect it
from the salt air," and he sealed the Door with a broad tarpau-
lin lowered from above. The breeze smelled of earth—humus,
manure, resin, ears of grain; of the soil of that island placed
centuries before under the protection of a Lady of Guadalupe.
Her figure, held aloft by an archangel in Cáceres in Extremadura, and in Tepeyac in the Americas, floated above the arc of
the moon.*

*I had left behind an adolescence whose family landscapes,
after three years, had grown as remote to me as the wounded,
prostrate self I had been before Someone came to us on an evening ringed by a racket of door knockers—as remote as the
witness was remote from me now; the guide, the illuminator of
days past, predecessor to the sullen Sovereign who, reclining
on the gunwale, was meditating—beside the black rectangle in
its inquisitory envelope, quivering like a balance to the rocking
of every wave. Now and then, the water flashed with the gleam
of scales or an errant wreath of gulfweed.*

CHAPTER ONE

I.

Behind him, in mournful diapason, the Executor turned once more to his reckoning of the exequys, cross-bearer, oblations, vestments and tapers, cloths and flowers, requiem, registration of the death—and who had come in pomp, and who had wept, and who had said that we were nothing . . . And yet the idea of death seemed not quite so glum aboard that ship that crossed the bay beneath a torrid midafternoon sun, the light of which, nourished by foam and bubbles, reflected off of the waves and flared under the awning, penetrating eyes and pores, tormenting the hands seeking rest on the gunwales. Draped in makeshift mourning, smelling of old dye, the adolescent looked at the city, which bore, at that hour of reverberations and long shadows, a strange resemblance to an immense baroque candelabrum; its windows—green, orange, and red—shed their colors on a motley rocaille of balconies, archways, spires, belvederes, and glassed-in galleries with drawn blinds—all of it resting on scaffolds, crossbeams, gallows, and poles, from the days when building fever had overtaken the residents, grown rich after the recent war in Europe. It was a country indentured to the air that swept through it, thirsty for the winds that blew from sea to land and back, shutters, shades, jalousies, hollows all open for the first cool draft. Then came the clink of chandeliers and girandoles, fringed lamps, bead curtains, unruly weathercocks, announcing the occasion. The fans—of palm, painted paper, Chinese silk—would suddenly fall still. But at the end of this momentary respite, the people would return to the task of thrashing the inert air, dormant again inside the rooms' high walls. Here, light congealed into heat, the hasty sunrise thrust it into even the remotest bedchamber, where it seeped through curtains and mosquito nets; even more so now that the rainy season had come, and the brutal midday showers—a veritable deluge, with thunder and lightning—hurriedly voided their clouds, soaking the roads, which fumed when the torrid heat returned. However much the palaces flaunted their incomparable columns and blazons sculpted in stone, in those months they abided in mud that clung to their bodies like an incurable illness. If a carriage should pass, they were immediately soiled, doors and barred windows spattered from the puddles sinking all round, washing away the dirt beneath the pavement and emitting new fetors as one drained into another. Though adorned with precious marble, mosaics, coffered ceilings with rosettes—with grillwork so distinct from crude bars, it was as if lucid iron vegetation were clinging to the windows—not even the mansions of the wealthy could escape the silt that rose from the former marshlands no sooner than the roofs began to drip. Many of the attendees, Carlos thought, would have had to cross at the street corners on boards laid in the mud, or jump over large stones to keep their shoes from sinking into the hollows and getting stuck there. Foreigners praised the color and good humor of the population, after spending three days at their dances, gambling dens, and bars, where the bands enlivened the spendthrift sailors and set the women's hips aflame; but those who suffered life there for a year knew how the dust and grime and saline breezes left a verdigris sheen on the doorknockers, ate into the iron, made the silver sweat, spread mildew on old engravings, and clouded the panes of glass in frames over drawings and aquatints at whose centers the figures, warped by humidity, seemed swathed in fog brought in by the north wind. On the San Francisco wharf, a North American vessel had just moored, and Carlos spelled its name out mechanically: the *Arrow* . . . And the Executor went on painting his picture of the funeral, which had been magnificent, no doubt, fit for a gentleman of such virtues—with plentiful sacristans and acolytes, finery, solemnity; and the workers from the warehouse had wept discreetly, manfully, doing honor to their sex, from the psalms of the Vigil to the Mass for the deceased . . . but the son remained as though absent, vexed and fatigued, after riding since dawn over royal roads and shortcuts that never seemed to end. No sooner had he reached the estate, where solitude gave him the illusion of independence—there, he could play his sonatas till daybreak, by candlelight, bothering no one—than he heard the news that forced him to turn around, pushing his horse to extenuation and still arriving too late to attend the burial. ("I don't want to enter into embarrassing details," the other man says, "but we couldn't wait any longer. Your blessed sister and I kept vigil, and we were so close to the coffin . . .") And he thought about mourning; about that mourning that would, for a year, condemn his new flute, purchased where the finest instruments were manufactured, to lie still in its case lined with black oilcloth, while he was forced to respect, in others' presence, the idiotic notion that where there was pain, there should be no music of any kind. His father's death would deprive him of much that he loved, alter his plans, expel him from his dreams. He would be condemned to administer the firm—he who understood not the first thing about numbers—in a black suit behind an ink-stained desk, surrounded by bookkeepers and wretched underlings too well acquainted to bother uttering a word. And he bemoaned his fate, swearing he would escape in the coming days, without qualms or valedictions, on any vessel fit for a fugitive. Amid his lamentations, the ship moored by a bollard where Remigio was waiting for him crestfallen, a mourning ribbon on the brim of his hat. When the carriage turned onto the first street, throwing mud to the left and right, the scent of the sea vanished, swept away by the breath of vast buildings filled with leather, salted meat and fish, wax and brown sugar in cakes, and onions left so long in the cellar that they sprouted in dark corners beside green coffee and cocoa that had spilled from the scales. A clangor of cowbells filled the afternoon, accompanied by the usual migration of the newly milked cows to the pastures outside the city walls. Everything smelled powerfully at that hour, on the edge of a twilight that would brighten the sky for a few brief minutes before dissolving into night: the poorly lit firewood, the trampled manure, the wet canvas of the awnings, the saddlers' leather, and the birdseed in the canaries' cages hanging in the windows. The damp roofs smelled of clay, the still-moist walls of moss, the corner stalls of fritters and French toast, of

boiled oil left too long in the fryer; the coffee roaster smelled of
bonfires in the Spice Islands, giving off dun smoke that wheezed
and belched toward the austerely classical cornices, lingering
between wall and wall before dissolving like a warm mist
around some saint on a bell tower. The salt beef, though,
smelled unmistakably of salt beef; stored in every basement and
backroom, its acrid stench reigned over the city, invading palaces, impregnating curtains, overpowering the church's incense, seeping into the opera halls. The salt beef, mud, and flies
were the curse of that emporium, visited by ships from across
the globe, a place where—Carlos thought—only the statues
could be at ease, immobile on their pedestals splashed with rus-
set mud. As though an antidote to that stench, there suddenly
emerged, over a dead-end street, the noble aroma of tobacco
piled in lean-tos—bound, packed, bruised by the knots that
cinched the bales in their palm bark wrappings, tender bits of
green still in the dense leaves, bright gold eyes in the supple layers, still live and vegetal amid the meat. Breathing an odor that
for once he welcomed, that alternated with the smoke from a
new coffee roaster nestled in the sloping walls of a chapel, Carlos thought with anguish of the routine life that awaited him—
doomed to live in that city across the sea, an isle on an isle, his
music stilled, the closed ocean holding any possible adventure
at bay. He would find himself enveloped, a corpse in its death
shroud, in the reek of salt beef, onions, and brine, the victim of
a father he reproached—however monstrous it was to do so—
with the crime of having died prematurely. In that moment, the
young man suffered as never before from the sense of captivity
borne of living on an island; of being in a land without roads to
other lands a man could reach on wheels, on horseback, on
foot, crossing borders, sleeping every night in a different inn,
wandering with no sense of north beyond one's inclinations, the
fascination felt for a mountain scorned once you've caught sight
of another mountain—or for the body of an actress encountered in a city you'd never heard of the day before, then followed for months from stage to stage, sharing the desultory life
of the entertainer . . . After tilting to round a corner presided
over by a cross stained green by the sea breeze, the carriage

stopped before a studded door with a black ribbon hanging from its knocker. The alcove, the vestibule, the courtyard were carpeted in jasmine, spikenard, white carnations, and house-leeks with sagging crowns and stems. In the great room, hag-gard, twisted—draped in mourning clothes a size larger than her own that seemed to immure her like a paper prison—waited Sofía, surrounded by Clarist nuns filling decanters with water scented with lemon balm, orange blossom, salts, herb infu-sions, in a sudden show of industry for the new arrivals. The chorus raised its voice, commending valor, obedience, resigna-tion to those left below while others came to know a Glory that never failed nor ceased. "Now I will be your father," the Execu-tor moaned from the corner where the family portraits hung. The bell of the Church of the Holy Spirit struck seven. Sofía took leave with a gesture that all present understood, withdrawing to the vestibule in rueful silence. "If you need anything . . ." Don Cosme said. "If you need anything . . ." the nuns chanted in turn. Every latch on the main door was locked. Crossing the courtyard where, in the midst of the eddo, the trunks of two palm trees rose like columns, clashing with the architecture surrounding them, crests mingling in the incipient night, Carlos and Sofía walked to the room by the stables, the darkest and dankest in the house, perhaps, and yet the only one where Esteban could manage to sleep a full night now and then without suffering one of his crises.

But there he was anchored, hanging on one of the window's uppermost bars, writhing gauntly from the effort, crucified, crestfallen, torso stripped bare, ribs rippling in relief, his lone garment a shawl curled around his waist. His breast exhaled a dull whistle, oddly tuned to two simultaneous notes, which died off at times in a groan. His hands searched the grating for a higher bar to hang from, as if his body, marked by violet veins, wished to stretch itself ever thinner. Impotent before an affliction that defied all potions and poultices, Sofía passed a cloth soaked in cool water over the sick man's forehead and cheeks. Soon his fingers released the iron, slipping down the bars, and Esteban, aided by brother and sister in his descent from the cross, tumbled into a wicker chair, staring through dilated black pupils, absent despite their fixity. His nails were blue; his neck vanished into shoulders raised so high they almost hid his ears. Knees splayed, elbows thrown forward, the texture of his anatomy waxen, he looked like an ascetic in a painting by one of the Flemish or Italian primitives, entirely absorbed in some monstrous mortification of the flesh. "It was the goddamned incense," Sofía said, sniffing the black garments Esteban had left in a chair. "When I saw him start choking in church . . ." But she fell silent, recalling that the incense, the scent of which the sick man couldn't bear, had been burned during the solemn funeral rites of a man the Parish Priest had described in the eulogy as a dearly beloved father, an exemplary gentleman, the very image of benevolence. Esteban threw his arms over a sheet knotted into a noose between two rings set into the wall. His sorry plight grew crueler there amid the things Sofía had tried to use since childhood to distract him from his fits: the little shepherdess atop a music box; the band of monkeys with the broken cord; the balloon with the aeronauts hanging from the roof that rose and fell when you tugged on a string; the clock with the frog that danced on a bronze dais; and the puppet theater, its stage like a Mediterranean port, where Turks, gendarmes, waitresses, and bearded men lay scattered—one with his head askew, one with his hairpiece chewed away by roaches, another without arms, the butcher's boy vomiting termite dust from his eyes and nose. "I won't go back to the convent," Sofía said, shifting to let Esteban rest his head in her lap; he had fallen to the floor softly, seeking the frigid safety of the flagstones. "This is where I need to be."

II.

Their father's death had certainly affected them. And yet, alone in the light of day, in the oblong dining room with the blackened still lifes—pheasants and hares nestled in clusters of grapes, lampreys with wine bottles, a pastry toasted to a golden brown a person could sink their teeth into—they might well have admitted that an almost sybaritic sense of freedom had overcome them during that meal ordered from the neighboring hotel because no one thought to send the servants to market. Remigio brought back cloth-covered baskets filled with almond-crusted seabream, marzipan, squab à la crapaudine, truffled this and confited that—a far cry from the minced meats and stews that generally graced the table. Sofía came down in her robe, eager to try a bit of everything; a Grenache that Carlos proclaimed excellent helped Esteban get his color back. The house, which they had always looked on with eyes accustomed to its character, at once familiar and strange, took on a novel and singular significance, imposing myriad demands now that they realized they alone were responsible for its stewardship. It was evident that their father—so taken with his business that he even went out before Mass on Sundays to close contracts and buy wares straight off the boat, outflanking those who waited for Monday to make their purchases—had left in a state of pitiful neglect the dwelling their mother abandoned long before, victim to the cruelest flu epidemic the city had ever known. Pavers were missing in the courtyard, the statues were covered in grime; mud rose up from the road and splashed into the vestibule; the odds and ends of furnishings in the sitting rooms and bedrooms seemed better suited to a rag-and-bone shop than to a mansion for decent people. Years back, the fountain with its mute dolphins had run dry, and panes of glass had been missing from the French doors. And yet, certain paintings, of varied subjects and dissimilar in style, lent dignity to those walls mottled with dark spots from the damp—pieces that had found no buyers at an auction of foreclosed properties and were sold off as a single lot. They might have been valuable, if they were the work of masters rather than forgers, but it was impossible to say in this city of merchants, which lacked experts able to discern the signs of a modern hand or distinguish the grandeur of a historic style beneath the craquelure of the mishandled canvases. Beneath a *Slaughter of the Innocents*, quite possibly by a disciple of Berruguete, and a *Saint Denis*, quite possibly by an imitator of Ribera, lay an open, sun-kissed garden of masked harlequins that captivated Sofía, even if, in Carlos's estimation, those fin-de-siècle artists had abused the figure of the harlequin as a mere pretext for playing with color. His own preference was for realism, scenes of reaping and grape harvests, though he recognized that several of the pictures of static subjects hanging in the hall—a cauldron, a pipe, a fruit basket, a clarinet resting next to sheet music—did not lack for a certain beauty owing to the excellence of their execution. Esteban favored the imaginary, the fantastic, and dreamed awake before the works of contemporary creators, with monsters, spectral horses, impossible perspectives, a tree-man sprouting fingers, a wardrobe-man with empty drawers projecting from his abdomen . . . His favorite was a large piece from Naples, the product of an unknown hand, that negated every law of plasticity: an apocalyptic catastrophe in indefinite suspension. *Explosion in a Cathedral* was the title of that vision of a portico strewn in shards through the air—laggardly dissevering its parallel lines, hovering all the more dramatically to fall—poised to heap its tonnage of stone over the masses cowering in dread. ("I don't know how you can just stand there looking at that," said his cousin, but she too was oddly fascinated by that inert earthquake, that soundless tumult, that illustration of the end of time within reach and yet latent, dreadfully deferred. "It's to grow accustomed to the idea," Esteban answered, without knowing why, with that reflexive persistence that leads a person to repeat the same unamusing pun in the same circumstances for years on end without ever making anyone laugh.) At least the French master a few steps away, with his invented monument in the middle of an abandoned square—a kind of Asiatic-Roman temple, with arcades, obelisks, and finials—offered a sense of peace, of stability in the wake of tragedy, before one entered the dining room, which announced itself in costly still lifes and furnishings: two china cabinets of abbatial dimensions, impervious to termites and woodworms; eight upholstered chairs; and a long table on Solomonic columns. But as for the rest—"remains of a rubbish sale" was Sofía's verdict as she thought of her narrow mahogany bed, she who had always dreamed of a mattress where she could toss and turn, sleep sideways, curled up, or with her arms and legs outspread, according to her whims. Her father, true to the customs inherited from his peasant grandparents, had always slept on a canvas cot presided over by a crucifix in a room on the second floor, between a walnut chest of drawers and a chamber pot of Mexican silver that he would empty at dawn into the drain in the stables with a sweeping gesture that suggested a farmhand nobly mowing wheat. "My people were from Extremadura," he had often said, as though that explained everything. He was proud of an austerity alien to hand-kissing and soirees. Dressed in black as always since his wife's untimely death, he'd been brought back by Don Cosme from the office, where he'd gone to endorse a document, after an apoplectic fit had left him lying in the ink of his own signature. Even in death he retained the hard, impassible expression of a man who had never asked for favors and never performed them for others. Sofía hadn't seen him in recent years, apart from the odd Sunday, at the compulsory family luncheons that took her away from the Clarist convent for a few hours. As for Carlos, after grammar school, he was constantly sent off to the plantation with orders to fell, clear, or harvest. These could just as well have been issued in writing, for the lands were modest and almost entirely employed in the cultivation of sugarcane. "I rode eighty leagues to bring twelve heads of cabbage," the young man observed, emptying his saddlebags after another journey to the country. "That's how you raise a Spartan," replied his father, who had a penchant for associating Sparta with cabbage, much as he accounted for the portentous levitation of Simon Magus with the bold hypothesis that the Samaritan had some knowledge of electricity. Carlos's father's plan of sending him off to study law was indefinitely postponed due to his fear of the new ideas and treacherous political enthusiasms that thrived in the halls of universities. The old man spared little thought for his weakly nephew Esteban; an orphan since boyhood, he'd grown up treating Sofía and Carlos as his siblings and never received less than they did. And yet, for the old merchant, who worked all year from sunup to sundown, there was something vexing about a man in frail health, especially in his own family. He would occasionally peek into the invalid's room, furrowing his brow with disgust when he found him suffering one of his attacks. He'd grunt something about the damp, about people who were determined to sleep in caves like the Celtiberians of old, and, with a wistful recollection of the Tarpeian Rock, he would offer him grapes just in from the north, evoking the figures of illustrious cripples before departing with a shrug of the shoulders, muttering condolences, words of encouragement, proclamations about new medicines, and excuses for his inability to go on caring for those whose ailments left them stranded on the margins of a life the purpose of which was productivity and progress. After dawdling in the dining room, trying this and that with no concern for order, eating first a fig and then a sardine, or marzipan with olives and raw sausage, *the little ones*, as the Executor called them, opened the door to the adjoining building where the firm and warehouse lay, a door which had been sealed for three days of mourning. Past the desks and strongboxes, open roads cut through piles of sacks, barrels, and bundles of numberless provenance. At the end of Flour Street, with its fragrance of overseas mills, was the Avenue of Wines of Fuencarral, Valdepeñas, and Puente de la Reina, dripping red from the spigots in the barriques and exuding the aroma of cellars. The Road of Ropes and Riggings led to the fetid corner of cured fish, white flakes sweating brine onto the floor. Returning via Deer Leather Road, the adolescents found themselves back in the Spice Quarter, with its cabinets that conjured up, no sooner than you'd opened them, scents of ginger, laurel, saffron, and Vera Cruz pepper. Wheels of Manchego cheese reposed on parallel boards leading to Vinegar and Oil Court, past which, under vaults, the most miscellaneous items were kept: piles of playing cards, barber's utensils, bundles of padlocks, green and red parasols, cocoa mills, Andean blankets brought over from Maracaibo, heaped dyers' sticks and books of gold and silver leaf from Mexico. Nearer by were the platforms with their sacks of bird feathers—soft and swollen, like serge counterpanes. Carlos leaped over them abruptly, mimicking the motions of a swimmer. An armillary sphere, symbol of commerce and navigation, stood in the midst of that universe of things arrived on countless ocean routes, and Esteban spun its rings with a distracted hand. Everything, even here, was swathed in the stench of salt meat, but it was bearable now, as the meat was stored in the building's furthest rooms. The siblings followed Honey Street back to the writing tables. "What garbage! What garbage!" Sofía murmured, her handkerchief pressed into her nose. Standing now on sacks of barley, Carlos contemplated the horizon below the roof, thinking with trepidation of the day he would have to set about selling, buying, reselling, negotiating, haggling, ignorant of prices, incapable of distinguishing one grain from another, forced to locate their purveyors in thousands of letters, receipts, invoices, proofs of purchase, appraisals all tucked away in drawers. A scent of sulfur constricted Esteban's throat, swelling his eyes and bringing on an attack of sneezing. The effluvia of wine and smoked herring made Sofía faint. Giving her arm to her cousin, who was on the verge of another fit, she hurried home, where the Clarist Mother Superior was waiting for her with an edifying book. Carlos returned last, carrying the armillary sphere, which he placed in his bedroom. In the half-light of the salon with its covered windows, the nun spoke softly of the lies of the world and the solace of the cloister, while the men of the house amused themselves shifting the tropics and ecliptics around the terraqueous globe. A new life was beginning in the torpor of that afternoon, which the sun made unusually warm, lifting fetid evaporations from the puddles in the street. Gathered again for dinner among the fruits and fowl of the still lifes, the young people began making plans. The Executor counseled them to spend their mourning period on the estate while he took care of the deceased's affairs—as was the custom, all instructions had been conveyed to him personally, with no record of the arrangements made apart from what was preserved in his memory. Carlos would find everything in order on his return, when he would embark formally on an apprenticeship in the ways of commerce. But Sofía recalled that previous attempts to take Esteban to the country "to breathe the clean air" had only aggravated his torments. Where he suffered least was, in the end, in his room with its low struts beside the stables . . . There was talk of other journeys: to Mexico with its thousand domes, which glimmered from the other end of the Gulf. But the United

States, with its unceasing progress, fascinated Carlos, who longed to see the New York harbor, the battlefield at Lexington, and Niagara Falls. Esteban dreamed of Paris, its exhibitions of paintings, its intellectual cafés, its literary life; he wanted to take a course at the Collège de France, where they taught Oriental languages, the study of which—while not especially useful from a pecuniary perspective—must be invigorating for a man like him, who aspired to read the manuscripts of recently discovered writings from Asia. Sofía imagined performances at the Opéra and the Comédie Française, where the eye could admire a thing as beautiful and celebrated as Houdon's Voltaire right there in the vestibule. In their itinerant imaginings, they gazed at the doves on Piazza San Marco and the Epsom Derby; visited Sadler's Wells Theatre and the Louvre; stopped at storied booksellers, legendary circuses, the ruins of Palmyra and Pompeii, saw Etruscan miniature horses and mottled vases on display in Greek Street, yearned to take in everything and settle on nothing—and the men, their senses inflamed, were secretly attracted by a world of licentious diversions, and would know where to look and how to indulge when the young lady was out shopping or visiting monuments. After their prayers, without yet taking a decision of any kind, they embraced each other and wept, feeling alone in the universe, defenseless orphans in an indifferent, soulless city, estranged from everything that spoke of poetry or art, captive to the business, to fidelity. Overcome by the heat and the scent of salt meat, onions, and coffee coming from the road, they climbed to the attic wrapped in their robes, taking blankets and pillows with them, and fell asleep, their faces turned toward the sky, after a discussion of habitable and likely already inhabited planets where life might be better than it was on this earth, which was subjugated permanently to the workings of death.

III.

Surrounded by nuns who urged her—tenaciously, but without haste; softly, but insistently—to make herself a maidservant to

God, Sofía quieted her reservations by exerting herself on Esteban's behalf, adopting the role of surrogate mother. Absorbed
in her new profession, she didn't hesitate to undress him and
give him sponge baths when he was incapable of doing it himself. The afflictions of that young man she'd always looked on
as a brother made her presence a necessity, and strengthened
her instinctive resistance to retiring from the world. As for Carlos, he feigned to ignore his own rude good health, taking the
least cough as a pretext to climb into bed, sending for boozy
punches that put him in a superb mood. One day he strolled
through the house's several rooms, pen in hand—with the mulatta servant trailing behind him, holding the inkpot aloft like
a sacrament—to take an inventory of useless debris. He drew
up an exhaustive list of all that was needed to furnish a proper
dwelling and passed it to the Executor—himself ever disposed
to play the "second father" and satisfy any and all of the orphans' desires . . . Just before Christmas, boxes and bales
started arriving and were placed as they appeared throughout
the rooms on the lower floor. From the salon to the carriage
house stretched an invasion of items which were left resting in
crates, a few slats torn away, cushioned by straw and shavings,
waiting for some eventual imposition of order. A heavy wardrobe, carried in by six black porters, stood untouched in the
vestibule, while a lacquered screen, set down next to a wall, remained nailed in the container in which it was shipped. The
porcelain cups sat in the same sawdust that had cushioned them
during their passage, while the books meant to form a library
of new poetry and new ideas were unpacked, a dozen here, a
dozen there, and left all round in piles, on armchairs and nightstands still redolent of fresh varnish. The baize of the billiard
table was a prairie outstretched between the moon of a rococo
mirror and the stern silhouette of a desk of English marquetry.
One night, they heard gunfire in a coffer: the strings of the
harp, which Sofía had ordered from a factory in Naples, were
snapping in the humid air of their new clime. The mice from
neighboring buildings made nests across the house, and cats
came, filed their claws against the exquisite woodwork, and un-
raveled tapestries of unicorns, cockatoos, and harriers. The

disorder reached its culmination in the artifacts of the Cabinet of Physics Esteban had ordered, intending to replace his automata and music boxes with entertainments that would instruct as well as delight. There were telescopes, hydrostatic scales, bits of amber, compasses, magnets, Archimedes screws, miniature hoists, communicating vessels, Leyden jars, pendulums and balances, tiny machines to which the manufacturer had added, to substitute for a few missing pieces, mathematical instruments of the most advanced sort available. On certain nights, the adolescents would devote themselves to the building of strange contraptions, lost in the pages of instruction manuals, calling theories into question, waiting for dawn to test the functioning of a prism, marveling as they saw the colors of the rainbow paint themselves across a wall. They had grown slowly used to living in the nighttime, following Esteban, who slept best during the day and preferred to stay up till dawn. The worst of his crises tended to come in the final hours of the night, waylaying him just as he was falling asleep. Rosaura, the mulatta cook, set the table for lunch at six in the evening and left out a cold dinner for midnight. From one day to the next, a labyrinth of boxes had filled the house, and each of the young people had a private corner, a stretch of floor, a place for solitude or discussion on the subject of some book or physics mechanism that had begun all at once to function in the most unexpected way. A sort of ramp or Alpine trail emerged from the doorway in the salon, scaled an armoire placed on its side, rose over the Three Crates of Crockery, one laid over the other, past which you could contemplate the landscape below before ascending, through craggy byways of broken boards and battens like nettles, to the Grand Terrace, made up of the Nine Crates of Furnishings, atop which the expeditioners felt the roof beams graze the napes of their necks. "What a beautiful sight!" Sofía would shout with a laugh, pressing her skirt into her knees when she reached the heights. But Carlos swore there were other routes, riskier ones that attacked the parcel massif from the other end, that required a mountaineer's knack until the climber surfaced all at once on his belly, hauling his body up with the noble wheeze of a Saint Bernard dog. On paths and plateaus, hideaways and bridges, they read what their fancy dictated: newspapers from another era, almanacs, travel guides, a Natural History, a classical tragedy, or a new novel they kept stealing from each other, the action of which took place in the year 2240—unless Esteban, from some summit, was scornfully aping the tirades of a well-known preacher, elucidating a verse from the Song of Songs and savoring Sofía's irritation as she plugged her ears and shouted that men were swine, the whole lot of them. In the courtyard, the sundial had transformed into a moon clock and marked the inverse of the hours. The hydrostatic scale allowed them to confirm the weight of the cats; the little telescope, poked through a broken pane in the skylight, gave a view of things in nearby houses that elicited equivocal laughter from Carlos, the solitary astronomer standing on an armoire. The new flute was drawn from its case in a bedroom lined in mattresses, like a madman's cell, so the neighbors wouldn't hear. There, head cocked at the music stand, sheet music scattered over the carpet, the young man gave long nocturnal concerts that grew steadily more sonorous and skillful unless he gave in to the urge to play a rustic dance piece on a recently acquired fife. Often, suffused with tenderness for one another, the adolescents swore they would never part. Sofía, whom the nuns had inspired at an early age with a fear of men's natures, angered when Esteban jokingly—and possibly to test her—spoke of her future matrimony, blessed by a gaggle of children. A *husband*, any husband brought into that household would have seemed an abomination—a transgression against the flesh they regarded as property held in common that must remain intact. They were going to travel together, and together they would know the wide world. The Executor was the one best suited to take care of "the stinking rubbish next door." Moreover, he seemed favorably disposed to their yearned-for travels, assuring them that letters of credit would follow them wherever they went. "You must go to Madrid," he said, "to see the Correos building and the dome of San Francisco el Grande. Architectural marvels of that kind are unknown in these parts."

In their century, the speed of communication had made distance a thing of the past. It was up to the young people to choose, after the last of the countless Masses purchased for their father's eternal repose—Masses Sofía and Carlos attended every Sunday before bed, traveling on foot through still-deserted streets to the Church of the Holy Spirit. They hadn't yet found the resolve to open the crates and bundles and arrange the new furniture. The task overwhelmed them before they'd begun—particularly Esteban, whose illness made strenuous physical activity impossible. Besides, a morning invasion of upholsterers, varnishers, and other strangers would have ill-suited their habits, which flouted all ordinary sense of time. It was early if one of them started the day at five p.m., rising to receive Don Cosme, who was more paternal and obsequious than ever, sending out orders, anxiously acquiring any and everything, unconcerned with costs. The warehouse business was flourishing, he said, and he always made sure Sofía had more than enough money to maintain their home in grand style. He praised her for taking on the responsibilities of a mother, keeping a close eye on the young men, and in passing tossed a subtle but spiteful dart at the nuns who convinced distinguished young ladies to lock themselves away so the church could get its hands on their property—and one was free to say as much while remaining a pious Christian. The visitor would depart with a bow, announcing that, for now, Carlos's presence wasn't needed at the firm, and the young people would return to their domains and labyrinths, where an arcane nomenclature reigned. They dubbed the pile of crates threatening to tumble "The Leaning Tower"; the chest that bridged two wardrobes was known as "The Druids' Way." Whoever spoke of Ireland meant the corner with the harp; whoever said Mount Carmel referred to the sentry post of half-unfolded screens where Sofía customarily retired to read her spine-chilling mystery novels. When Esteban set all his scientific apparatus in motion, they said Albertus Magnus was at work. Everything was transfigured in this perpetual game that marked new distances from the outside world through the arbitrary counterpoint of lives unfolding on three distinct planes: Esteban remained in the

terrestrial, as his ailment inclined him little to ascension; he en-
vied Carlos, who would leap in the heights from box to box,
dangle from the girders of the Moorish-style ceiling, or sway in
a hammock from Veracruz spanning the roof beams exposed
between the plaster; Sofía's existence proceeded in an interme-
diate realm, some ten palms' lengths from the floor, her heels at
the height of her cousin's temples, where she shifted books to
and fro among their assorted hiding places, their "warrens" as
she called them, spreading out at ease, unbuttoning her blouse,
removing her stockings, pulling her skirt up over her thighs
when it got too hot . . . For the rest, their dinners took place at
daybreak, by candlelight in a dining room invaded by cats,
where, in rebellion against the rigidity always observed at family meals, they behaved like barbarians, each carving the meat
more carelessly than the other, snatching the best morsels,
breaking poultry bones to see what they augured, kicking each
other under the table, snuffing the candles to better pilfer a pastry from their neighbor's plate—slovenly, slumping, slouched
on their elbows. When not hungry, they would eat while playing solitaire or building houses of cards; if in bad spirits, they
would bring along a novel. When the two boys conspired to get
under Sofía's skin, she cursed like a mule driver; but in her
mouth, a seedy interjection took on a surprisingly chaste air,
shedding its meaning to become an expression of defiance—
vengeance for the many, many meals in the convent, taken with
eyes lowered to her dish after saying grace. "Where'd you learn
that?" the other two asked, laughing. "At the whorehouse," she
replied naturally, like a habitué. Weary, after a time, of bad behavior, of trampling urbanity, of shooting bank shots with walnuts over a tablecloth stained from an upturned tumbler, they
would say good night at dawn, taking to their chambers a piece
of fruit, a fistful of almonds, a glass of wine, in an inverted twilight rife with proclamations and morning prayers.

IV.

This always happens.

GOYA

The year of mourning passed, and the year of half-mourning began, but little changed in the lives of those adolescents, who settled deeper into their new habits, absorbed in interminable readings, discovering the universe through books. They never left home, grew oblivious to the world, and found out the events of the day by chance, through some foreign newspaper that reached them months after the fact. Hearing word of the presence of a "good catch" in the locked mansion, certain people of standing had tried to approach them through overtures of all sorts, alleging sorrow for those orphans living in solitude; but their offers were met with cold evasion. The house's inhabitants took mourning as a fitting pretext to stay aloof from all commitments or obligations, ignoring a society whose provincial intolerance tried to bind existence to ordinary norms—to appearing in certain places at certain times, dining in the same modish pastry shops, spending Christmas on the sugar plantations or on estates in Artemisa, where rich landholders vied with each other over the number of mythological statues they could place on the verges of their tobacco fields. They emerged from the rainy season, which filled the streets with new mud, and one morning, half-asleep, at the start of what he called his night, Carlos heard the loud thud of the knocker against the front door. He wouldn't have paid it mind had another not come moments later, this time from the door to the coach house, and then more of them afterward, at each and every door to the building—and at last, the hand returned impatiently to the place it had begun, and the thundering repeated, door by door, a second time and then a third. It was as if some would-be intruder were running around his home in circles, in search of a crack he might slink into—and that impression of someone or something in orbit grew stronger the more the knocks resounded, echoing in the most recondite of corners, in places that offered no egress to the street. Being a holiday, Holy

Saturday, the warehouse—often sought out by visitors in search of information—was closed. Since no one answered, he assumed Remigio and Rosaura were at the Mass of the Resurrection or else shopping at the market. "He'll get tired of knocking," Carlos thought, sinking his head into his pillow. But when the blows continued, he threw on a robe in fury and descended to the hall. He looked outside just in time to glimpse a man turning the nearest corner with a hasty step, an enormous umbrella in hand. On the ground lay a card, slipped beneath the wings of the door:

> **VICTOR HUGUES**
>
> Négotiant
> à
> Port-au-Prince

Cursing this unknown character, Carlos lay back down, not giving him any more thought. When he awoke, his eyes came to rest on that square of paper, tinted an odd green by the last ray of sun passing through the transom light. The *little ones* were gathered around the boxes and bundles in the sitting room, Albertus Magnus absorbed in his physics, when the same hand from that morning lifted the knockers again. It must have been ten at night—early for them, but late according to the customs of that city. Sofía grew suddenly afraid: "We can't have a stranger in here," she said, noticing for the first time the peculiarities of what had come to form the natural setting of her existence. Accepting an unknown party into the family labyrinth would have been like betraying a secret, handing over a relic, dissipating a spell. "Don't open, for God's sake!" begged Carlos, rising with an angry expression. But it was too late: Remigio, roused from the early hours of his slumber by a knock at the door to the coach house, guided in the foreigner, holding a candelabra aloft. The visitor was a man of indefinite years—thirty or forty perhaps, or maybe much younger—his face frozen in that imperturbability etched into every face when the wrinkles sink prematurely into the

forehead and cheeks, molded by the movements of a physiog-
nomy used to brusque transitions—as the first words he uttered would make evident—from extreme tension to ironic
passivity, unrestrained laughter to hard willfulness, reflecting
an overmastering dedication to imposing his ideas and convictions. His skin was leathery from the sun, his hair combed in a
careful pretense of carelessness in keeping with the latest fashions, and altogether this gave him a look of robust health. His
clothing clung too tightly to his vigorous torso, the swelling
muscle in his arms, the sturdy legs that trod with certain steps.
If his lips were loutish and sensual, his very dark eyes gave him
an imperious and almost arrogantly intense glow. He was a
man of bearing, but his first impression as likely aroused aver-
sion as sympathy. ("A brute like that," thought Sofía, "only
pounds on people's doors if there's something inside he wants.")
After greeting them with effusive courtesy that hardly ex-
punged the discourtesy of his loud, insistent knocking, the visitor started speaking swiftly, leaving no time for others to
interject, saying that he had letters for their father, and had
heard wonders about the old man's intelligence; that the time
was ripe for new agreements and new transactions; that the
merchants here, entitled to trade freely, should establish relations with the other Caribbean islands; that he had brought
with him, as a modest gift, a few bottles of wine, of a quality
not to be encountered in the local marketplace; that . . . When
the three of them shouted that their father was long since dead
and buried, the stranger—who expressed himself in an amusing patois, with some Spanish, a good deal of French, and a
sprinkling of English turns of phrase—stopped short with an
Oh! so wounded, so deceived, so inimical to his flowing verbiage, that the others burst into cackles, not even stopping to
think how shameful it was to laugh just then. Everything happened so quickly, so unexpectedly, and the now disconcerted
trader from Port-au-Prince joined in with their mirth. Sofía,
coming back to reality, uttered the words For God's sake! and
everyone turned immediately downcast. And yet the tension
from before was dispelled. The visitor walked forward without
being asked, seemingly unaffected by the reigning disorder or

Sofía's extravagant dress—for a laugh, she'd donned one of Carlos's shirts, the bottom hem of which grazed her knees. With an expert's air, he tapped a porcelain vase, stroked the Leyden jar, praised the manufacture of a compass, twisted the Archimedes screw, muttered something about levers that could lift the world, and embarked upon the tale of his voyages, which began with him as a cabin boy in the port of Marseille, where his father—very much to his honor—had been a master baker. "Bakers are of great use to society," Esteban remarked, pleased to be in the company of a foreigner who did not, upon setting foot in their land, set to boasting of his high birth. "Better to pave roads than make porcelain flowers," the other said, availing himself of a classical quotation before mentioning his Martinican nursemaid, black, a true negress and a sort of omen of his future wanderings; though in his tender years he had dreamed of Asia, all the ships that took him on were bound for the Antilles or the Gulf of Mexico. He spoke of the coral reefs of Bermuda; of the opulence of Baltimore; of Mardi Gras in New Orleans, in no way inferior to the one in Paris; of the mint and watercress liqueurs of Veracruz; and so on, descending to the Gulf, passing Pearl Island and remote Trinidad. Promoted to First Mate, he had reached as far as distant Paramaribo, a town that might well be the envy of people given to bluster—at this, he pointed at the ground—for its broad avenues lined with orange and lemon trees, their trunks beautified with inlaid seashells. There were regal dances aboard the foreign vessels that dropped anchor at the foot of Fort Zeelandia, and the Dutch women, he said, with a wink to the young men, were prodigal with their favors. All the world's wines and liquors could be tasted in that iridescent colony, served at banquets by bejeweled negresses in necklaces and anklets and clad in skirts of Indian textiles, their nearly transparent blouses cinched to their firm, throbbing breasts—and to calm Sofía, who was already furrowing her brow at the image, he dignified it with an opportune snippet of French verse alluding to Persian slave girls in similar garments at the palace of Sardanapalus. "How genteel of you," the girl hissed in acknowledgment of his graceful volte-face. In any case—the man

continued, now changing latitudes—the Antilles were an archipelago filled with wonder, where the strangest things existed: giant anchors abandoned on solitary beaches; houses
held to the rocks by iron chains to keep the cyclones from dragging them off to sea; a vast Sephardi cemetery in Curaçao; islands inhabited by women who stayed alone for months and
years on end while the men were off working on the mainland;
sunken galleons, petrified trees, unimaginable fish; and in Barbados, the sepulcher of a grandson of Constantine XI, last emperor of Byzantium, whose ghost appeared to solitary travelers
on windy nights . . . Then Sofía asked the visitor with great
seriousness if he had seen mermaids in the tropical seas. Before
the stranger could answer, the young woman showed him a
page from *Les délices de la Hollande*, a very old book that told
how some time after a storm had broken the dikes of West
Friesland, a sea-woman appeared, half-buried in the mud. She
was taken to Haarlem, where they clothed her and taught her
to sew. She lived for years without learning the language, her
instinct driving her always toward the water. Her moans were
like the plaints of a woman on her deathbed. The visitor, un-
moved by the tale, spoke of a mermaid found in the Maroni
River years before. Major Archicombie, a highly esteemed soldier, had described her in a report delivered to the Academy of
Sciences in Paris. "An English major cannot be mistaken," he
added, with almost tedious gravity. Carlos, noting that the visitor had risen somewhat in Sofía's esteem, turned the discussion back to the subject of voyages. But all that was left to
speak of was Basse-Terre in Guadeloupe, with its fountains of
flowing water and its houses that recalled those of Rochefort
and La Rochelle—had the young people not visited Rochefort
or La Rochelle . . . ? "They must be horrible," Sofía said, "I
suppose we'll be *forced* to spend a few hours in such places
when we leave for Paris. Why don't you talk to us of Paris,
which you must certainly know from one end to the other."
The stranger looked at her askance, and instead of responding,
said he had left Pointe-à-Pitre for Saint-Domingue with the
aim of opening a shop, but had finally established himself with
a prosperous general store in Port-au-Prince: a warehouse full

of merchandise, leather, salt meat, and fish ("How awful!" Sofía exclaimed), wine barrels, spices—"More or less *comme le vôtre*," he said, accompanying the French with a thumb pointed toward the parting wall, which the young lady considered the height of insolence: "We don't deal with all that personally," she told him. "It can't be *easy* or *leisurely* work," the man replied before telling them he'd come from Boston, the capital of big business, an excellent place to procure wheat flour for better prices than in Europe. He was waiting for a large shipment now, which he would sell part of in the square, dispatching the rest of it to Port-au-Prince. Carlos was about to dismiss the intruder, who had followed his interesting autobiographical prologue by straying into the odious subject of buying and selling, but the latter, rising from the armchair as if he were in his own home, walked toward the books piled in a corner. He grabbed one, and was emphatically pleased when the author could be somehow connected with advanced theories in politics or religion: "I see you all are very *au courant*," he said, weakening their resistance. Soon they were showing him editions of their favorite authors, which the stranger handled with deference, sniffing the grainy papers and calfskin bindings. Then he approached the contraptions in the Cabinet of Physics, putting together an apparatus whose parts lay scattered across various pieces of furniture: "This is useful for navigation as well," he said. Because it was hot, he asked permission to strip down to his shirtsleeves, astonishing his hosts, who were unnerved to see him penetrate so familiarly a world that had now turned tremendously strange with this addition of an unaccustomed presence in the midst of the Druid's Way and the Leaning Tower. Sofía considered inviting him to eat, but was ashamed to tell him lunch was served at midnight in their home, with dishes better suited to midday; but the foreigner, adjusting a quadrant they'd had no notion of the purpose of before, winked toward the dining room, where the food had lain on the table since before his arrival, saying, "I've brought *my own* wines." And after searching out the bottles he'd left in the courtyard upon entering, he placed them noisily on the tablecloth, telling the others to sit. Again, Sofía was scandalized at this impudent

intruder who had burst into their home, arrogating the functions of the *paterfamilias*. But already the men were savoring
an Alsatian wine with such abundant signs of gratification
that, thinking of poor Esteban—who had been very sick recently, and seemed quite taken with the new arrival—she
adopted the pose of a standoffish, courteous lady of the house,
passing the dishes to the man she called "Monsieur Hyug"
with a reedy accent, *Huuuuuuuug*, the other corrected her,
putting a verbal circumflex on each U and ending in a curt G,
with no appreciable effect on Sofía's pronunciation. Rather
than try to utter his surname correctly, she took malign pleasure in deforming it further, saying "Yug," "Yuk," "Ughez,"
and concluded with a series of tongue twisters that degenerated
into laughter chortled out over the pastries and marzipan Rosaura had brought for Holy Week, reminding Esteban all at
once that today was Holy Saturday. "*Les cloches! Les cloches!*"
the guest bellowed, pointing up with a quivering index finger
to suggest how long the bells, small and large, had resounded
in the city that morning. Then he went for another bottle—this
time from Arbois—and the boys, somewhat tipsy, greeted it
uproariously, blessing it with the sign of the cross. Their glasses
drained, they walked out into the courtyard. "What's up
there?" Monsieur Hyug asked, stepping toward the broad
stairway. He took the stairs two by two, and made it soon to
the second story, looking out from the gallery beneath the roof,
where a wooden balustrade ran between the pillars. "If he
dares enter my room, I'll send him out with a kick," Sofía murmured. But the indifferent visitor did approach this last door,
half-closed, and push it softly. "That's a kind of attic," Esteban
said, holding his light up, and entered a room he hadn't visited
for years. Trunks, crates, chests, and suitcases were pushed
against the walls, their order marking a comical contrast to the
disorder reigning below. In the back stood a sacristy cupboard,
and its splendidly veined wood caught Monsieur Hyug's eyes:
"Sturdy . . . exquisite." To boast of its hardiness, Sofía opened
it, showing him the thickness of the doors. But the stranger was
more interested in the old suits hanging from a metal rod: garments that had belonged to members of her mother's family,

who had built their home; to the academic, the prelate, the ensign, the magistrate; grandmothers' dresses, faded satins, austere frocks, festive lace, muslin gone green from the salt air, percale, calico; costumes worn once and put away: of a shepherdess, a card reader, an Incan princess, a distinguished lady of old. "Wonderful for play-acting!" Esteban exclaimed. And taken all at once with the very same idea, they took down those dusty relics, amid a great whirl of moths, hurling them downstairs over the waxed mahogany handrail. Not long afterward, in the Great Room transformed into a theater, they took turns mimicking and guessing the object of each other's buffoonery: it was enough to change out the different pieces of outfits, to pin up parts of them with needles, to don a nightshirt as a Roman peplum or an ancient tunic, and they embodied heroes from history or novels, with escarole woven into a laurel crown, a pipe for a pistol, a cane slid into a mended belt making do for a sword. Monsieur Hyug, evidentially a lover of antiquity, played Mucius Scaevola, Gaius Gracchus, and Demosthenes—a Demosthenes identified swiftly when he hurried off to the courtyard in search of stones. They all recognized Carlos, with flute and cardboard tricorne hat, as Frederick of Prussia, despite his protests that Quantz, the flautist, was who he had in mind. With a toy frog brought from his bedroom, Esteban parodied the experiments of Galvani, but cut his performance short when the dust from the clothes brought on a severe attack of sneezing. Sofía, sensing Monsieur Hyug's scant acquaintance with things Spanish, gave mean-spirited renditions of Inês de Castro, Joanna the Mad, and the Illustrious Kitchen Maid, making herself as ugly as possible, her features twisted into moronic semblances to bring life to a last, unidentifiable personage who turned out, amid shouts of protest from her audience, to be "a Bourbon princess, whichever one, take your pick." When dawn was near breaking, Carlos proposed a *great massacre*. Hanging the suits from delicate threads on a wire stretched between the trunks of two palm trees, adorning them with grotesque faces drawn on paper, they threw balls at them and tried to knock them down. "Attack!" Esteban shouted, calling them to the charge. And prelates fell, and captains, ladies of the court and pastors, amid laughter bellowed in the narrow courtyard, which could be heard all along the street . . . Day surprised them in the midst of this, in a trance of rabid joy, far from sated with their play, hurling paperweights, tureens, flowerpots, encyclopedias at the suits they hadn't managed to fell with stones: "Attack!" Esteban shouted, "Attack . . . !" At last, Remigio was obliged to bring out the carriage and take the visitor to his nearby hotel. The Frenchman took his leave reluctantly, with great shows of affection, promising to return that evening. "He's quite a character," Esteban said. But now the others had to dress in black to go to the Church of the Holy Spirit, where another Mass would be spoken for their father's eternal repose. "Suppose we didn't go?" Carlos ventured with a yawn. "Either way, they'll still deliver it." "I'll go myself," Sofía replied sternly. But after some hesitation, alluding to the imminence of a perfectly routine indisposition, she pulled the curtains to her room and got into bed.

V.

Victor, as they called him, came every evening to their home, and proved adept at the most startling tasks. One night, he sank his hands into the kneading trough and molded croissants that revealed his skill as a baker. At other times, he blended magnificent sauces from combinations of the strangest ingredients. He turned cold meat into a muscovite delicacy with the addition of fennel and ground pepper, and boiled wine with spices to dignify any and all comestibles, consecrating them with ostentatious names in honor of illustrious chefs from the past. The discovery of *El arte cisoria* by the Marqués of Villena among a shipment of rare books from Madrid produced a week of medieval repasts, with pork loin standing in for the fruits of the hunt. He built the most complex contraptions with the Cabinet of Physics—nearly all of them were now assembled—to illustrate theories, analyze the spectrum, and raise sparks that enchanted the eye, and he expatiated upon

them in that picturesque Spanish he'd acquired on his travels
through the Gulf of Mexico and the Caribbean isles, rich with
novel words and turns of phrase. At the same time, he had the
young people practice their pronunciation in French, reading
aloud a page from a novel or, better still, a comedy for several
voices, as if they were in the theater. Sofía laughed a great deal
one twilight—which for her was the same as dawn—when Esteban declaimed, in that marked southern accent he owed to
his new teacher, the following verses from *Le Joueur*:

> *Il est, parbleu, grand jour. Déjà, de leur ramage*
> *Les coqs ont éveillé tout notre voisinage.*

On a stormy night, they allowed Victor to stay in one of the
bedrooms. When they awoke the next day at nightfall, not long
before the neighborhood cockerels tucked their beaks beneath
their wings, they were party to a spectacle hardly to be believed: bare-chested, shirt torn, sweating like a black stevedore,
the Frenchman had pulled out all that was sitting in the boxes
more or less untouched, ordering, with the help of Remigio, the
furnishings, tapestries, and vases to his liking. At first, the impression they gave was melancholic and disconcerting. An entire choreography of dreams had collapsed. But slowly, the
adolescents began to delight in that unexpected transformation, finding the spaces airier, the lights brighter—discovering
the supple depths of an armchair, the fine inlay of a credenza,
the warm tints of the Coromandel lacquer. Sofía went from
room to room, as if in a new home, looking into unfamiliar
mirrors which, placed one facing the other, multiplied her
image into the inscrutable foggy distance. Climbing a ladder,
Victor touched up certain corners here and there where
humidity had left ugly blotches, and the paint stippled his eye-
brows and cheeks. Possessed by a sudden fever for order, the
others leaped on what was left in the crates, unrolling carpets,
unfolding curtains, pulling porcelain from the sawdust it was
packed in, and throwing whatever had shattered out into the
courtyard—regretting, perhaps, that there weren't more shards
for them to hurl against the parting wall. That morning, there

was a lavish dinner in the dining room, which in their minds took place in Vienna, as Sofía had for some time been reading articles praising the marble, crystal, and rocaille of that incomparably musical city watched over by Saint Stephen, patron saint of all those born on December 26 . . . Afterward, they held an Ambassador's Ball before the beveled mirrors in the salon to the sound of Carlos's flute, and he didn't worry what the neighbors might think, in the midst of this extraordinary celebration. Foamy punch sprinkled with cinnamon, prepared by the Crown Minister, was served on trays, while Esteban, playing the haughty, decorated dauphin, noticed that each guest at the party danced worse than the others: Victor, because he hurtled around like a sailor on deck; Sofía because the nuns hadn't taught her how to caper; Carlos, because he spun to the tune of his own music, like an automaton mounted on an axle. "Attack!" Esteban shouted, bombarding them with hazelnuts and birdshot. But the dauphin's pranks came to a bad end; the whistling sounds from his trachea signaled the onset of a fit. In minutes, his face was furrowed, aged by a rictus of travail. The veins swelled in his neck, and he spread his legs and splayed his elbows, lifting his shoulders and clamoring for air that even in the vastness of his home he couldn't find. "We need to get him somewhere cooler," Victor said. (Such a thing had never occurred to Sofía. When her father, austere as she, was still alive, he would not have stood for anyone leaving the house after the hour of the rosary.) Lifting the asthmatic in his arms, Victor took him to the carriage while Carlos unhooked the horses' harnesses and collars. And at last, Sofía found herself outside, between mansions that grew larger in the night, their columns higher, their roofs broader, their eaves stretched out over the grillwork capped by a lyre or a mermaid, or the heads of goats silhouetted against an iron coat of arms rife with keys, lions, and scallop shells in homage to Saint James. They emerged onto the Alameda, where some of the streetlamps were still lit. It looked strangely empty, shops closed, arcades in shadows, the fountain mute and the ships' beacons swaying on the tops of the masts behind the jetty, tightly packed like trees in a forest. Over the murmur of the calm waters, broken against the pilings on the docks, there rose an aroma of fish, of oil and marine decay. A cuckoo clock sounded in some sleepy house, and the watchman called out the hour, announcing that the sky was clear and cloudless. After three slow turns, Esteban told them he wanted to go further. The carriage drove toward the Shipyard, where the vessels under construction recalled gigantic fossils with their rows of exposed ribs. "Not that way," Sofía said, seeing they were already past the docks and the husks of ships, in a place where people of dreadful aspect were beginning to appear. Victor, paying her no mind, lashed the horses' hindquarters softly with his whip. There were lights close by. And when they turned a corner, they found themselves on a street packed with seamen, where dance halls with open windows were bursting with music and laughter. Couples shimmied to the rhythm of drums, flutes, and violins with a licentiousness that brought blood into Sofía's cheeks. Scandalized, dumbstruck, she couldn't take her eyes off that tumult inside, presided over by the acid accents of clarinets. Mulattas wagged their hips, showing their haunches to their many admirers, then scurrying away from the fevered gestures they had provoked a hundred times over. Onstage, a black woman, skirts raised over her hips, tapped out the rhythm of a Cuban folk song that kept returning to the capricious chorus: *When, my darling, when?* One woman showed her breasts for the price of a drink, another one next to her lay back on a table, flinging her shoes toward the ceiling, her thighs emerging from her slip. Men of all colors and conditions walked to the backrooms of the taverns, hands buried in the dough of buttocks. Victor, who moved with a coachman's finesse among the drunks, seemed to relish that depraved racket, distinguishing the North Americans by their stagger, the English by their songs, the Spanish because they sipped red from wineskins and *porrones*. At the doors to the shacks, the whores clutched at passersby, letting them paw, hug, and grope them; one woman, pressed into a pallet by the weight of a black-bearded colossus, hadn't even had time to shut the door. Another stripped nude a bony cabin boy too drunk to manage it on his own. Sofía was about to shout from disgust and indignation, but more for Carlos and Esteban than for her. That world was so strange to her, she saw it as a vision of Hell unrelated to the worlds known to man. The promiscuities of the port denizens, who knew no creed nor law, were deeply alien to her. But in the expressions of her brother and cousin, she saw something murky, strange, expectant—acquiescent, even—that incensed her. It was as if *that* didn't repel them as deeply as it did her; as if there were a glimmer of understanding between their senses and those foreign bodies, those inhabitants of another universe. She imagined Esteban, Carlos at that dance, at that house, writhing on those cots, mingling their pristine sweat with the women's dense perspirations . . . Standing in the carriage, she tore the whip from Victor's hands and brought it down so forcefully that the horse galloped away, its breeching upturning a vendor's pots and pans. The boiling oil, the fish, the pastries, and empanadas spilled out, raising howls from a scalded dog that rolled back and forth in the dust, leaving scraps of skin on the broken glass and the bones of sea bream. Mayhem broke out all along the street. Several black women ran behind them in the night, armed with sticks, knives, and empty bottles, throwing stones that bounced off the roofs, kicking up chips of roofing tiles that had fallen from the eaves. The insults proffered, so exhaustive, so insuperable, so blasphemous, and so obscene, nearly moved them to laughter once the carriage had taken them away. "The things a young lady has to hear," Carlos said as they followed a winding route back to the Alameda. Once home, Sofía vanished into the shadows, not even saying good night.

Victor returned, as was his custom, at nightfall. After a momentary reprieve, Esteban's condition had worsened through the course of the day, his seizures turning so severe that they considered calling a doctor—in that house, this was an unusual response, because the invalid, chastened by past experience, knew that the remedies of apothecaries, if they had any effect at all, only ever made his condition worse. Hanging from his bars with his face turned to the courtyard, the adolescent had removed his clothing in desperation. His ribs and clavicles jutting out in relief, seeming to have penetrated the skin, brought to mind the cadavers in certain tombs in Spain, gutted and reduced to taut leather stretched across a frame of bones. Bested in the struggle for air, Esteban tumbled to the floor, slumped against the wall, face purple, nails almost black, looking at the others with eyes on the verge of death. His racing pulse pounded through his veins. A waxy sheen covered him, and his tongue, without a drop of saliva, pressed against his teeth, which trembled in his white gums. "We've got to do something!" Sofía shouted, "We've got to do something!" After minutes of apparent indifference, Victor asked, as if moved to a difficult decision, for the carriage, saying he would go for Someone with extraordinary powers who could treat the disease. He returned after half an hour in the company of a stoutly built mestizo in extremely elegant dress whom he presented as Doctor Ogé, an esteemed physician and distinguished philanthropist he'd known in Port-au-Prince. Sofía bowed slightly before the new arrival, but without extending him her hand. He could well have taken pride in the relative lightness of his skin: it was like a prosthetic hide, stretched over one of those faces with broad nostrils and dense, frizzy hair. But whoever was a negro, whoever had something of the negro about them, was for Sofía synonymous with servant, stevedore, coachman, or itinerant musician—it mattered little that Victor, noticing her contemptuous expression, explained that Ogé, scion of a well-to-do family in Saint-Domingue, had studied in Paris, and had degrees that attested to his intellect. His vocabulary was scrupulous, even affected—with antiquated or obsolete turns of phrase when he spoke in French, and an excessive differentiation of the c and z when he spoke in Spanish—and his manners betrayed his constant desire to preserve the impression of his urbanity. "But . . . he's a negro!" Sofía hissed into Victor's ear, her breath striking him like a soft blow. "All men are born equal," he responded, shoving her slightly aside. The idea he'd expressed only aggravated her revulsion. This was admissible, perhaps, as a humanitarian conjecture, but she could never consider a negro a doctor worthy of her trust, let alone commend the flesh of her kin to an individual of the wrong color. No one would trust a negro to build a palace, defend a prisoner, arbitrate a theological dispute, or govern a country. Esteban, emitting death rattles, cried out in despair, and all of them hurried to his room. "Let the doctor do his work," Victor said, brooking no resistance. "We have to get him through this attack one way or another." The mestizo remained immobile, not looking at the ill man, not examining him or even touching him, instead sniffing at the air in a strange manner. "It wouldn't be the first time," he said after a moment. And he looked up toward a small oeil-de-boeuf window in the darkness of the wall, open high between two roof beams. He asked what lay behind it. Carlos remembered that there was a narrow, very damp lot there, full of broken furniture and rubbish, a sort of passageway separated from the street by a narrow fence covered in ivy, where no one had set foot for many years. The doctor insisted they take him there. After passing through Remigio's room—Remigio himself was out searching for some tincture—they opened a creaking door, painted blue. What they saw at that moment was astonishing: in two long, parallel flower beds grew parsley, broom, nettles, mimosas, and wild herbs, with several clusters of mignonettes in splendorous flower. As though raised on an altar, a bust of Socrates that Sofía remembered seeing in her father's office when she was a girl was nestled in a niche amid strange offerings of a kind benighted people used for their incantations: wooden bowls filled with grains of corn, brimstone, seashells, iron filings. "C'est ça," Ogé said, contemplating the minuscule garden, as though it held some deep significance for him. And moved by a sudden impulse, he began to tear the mignonettes up by their roots and pile them between the flower beds. He then went to the kitchen, returning with a shovelful of lit embers, set a bonfire, and threw on it every bit of vegetation growing in that narrow strip of land. "Most likely we've found the origin of his illness," he said, with an explanation that, for Sofía, resembled a lecture in necromancy. According to him, certain ailments were mysteriously related to an herb, plant, or tree growing in the vicinity. Every human being had a *double* in the vegetable world. And there were cases where this *double* stole the energies of the man it grew in concert with for the furtherance of its own development, condemning him to suffering whilst it flourished and shed its seed. "*Ne souriez pas, Madamoiselle.*" He had seen it many times in Saint-Domingue, where asthma afflicted the children and teenagers, and many died from asphyxiation or anemia. At times, merely burning the vegetation in the sick man's vicinity—in his home or on the land surrounding it—sufficed for a miraculous recovery. "Sorcery," Sofía said, "That's what this is." Just then, Remigio reappeared, deeply upset by what he saw. Seething, out of sorts, he threw his hat to the ground, shouting that they had burned his plants; he'd been growing them a long time to sell them at the market, they were medicinal; they had destroyed his *caisimón*, which it had taken him great effort to acclimate, and which healed disturbances of the male parts when its leaves were applied while saying a prayer to Saint Ermenegildo, whose pudenda were tortured by the Sultan of the Saracens; all this was a grave offense to the lord of the forest, whose *portrait*, as he called it, with his characteristic wisp of beard—and at this, he pointed toward the bust of Socrates—blessed that place, which no one in that house had ever had any use for. And, bursting into tears, he groaned that if the master of the house had placed a bit more faith in his herbs—and he'd offered them when he saw the old man was going down a bad road, obsessed of late with bringing women into the house when Carlos was on the estate, Sofía off in the convent, and the other one too ill to notice—then he wouldn't have died the way he had, hunched on top of some female, likely flaunting a vigor age had diminished. "Tomorrow, you are to leave!" Sofía shouted, bringing the odious scene to an end, dumbfounded, disgusted, incapable of coming to terms with that deafening revelation . . . They returned to Esteban's room, and Carlos—who had not yet grasped the significance of Remigio's words—lamented the time wasted on this pointless song and dance. But something strange was happening with the invalid: formerly drawn out and high-pitched, the whistling in his throat became intermittent, and now and then died away for a few seconds. It was as if he were drinking in short sips of air, and with the relief they brought him, his ribs and clavicles returned to their place, beneath and not above the surrounding tissue. "Just as there are men who die consumed by fire trees or Saint Benedict's thistle," Ogé said, "he was being slowly killed by the yellow flowers that were feeding from his essence." And now, sitting down, squeezing the sick man's knees between his own, he looked him in the eyes with imperious fixity, while his hands, with an undulating movement of the fingers, seemed to spill an invisible fluid over his temples. A stupefied gratitude crossed the patient's face, a decongested face that went pale in places, leaving visible, here and there, the anomalous relief of a blue vein. Changing methods, Doctor Ogé rubbed the tips of his thumbs in circles around the patient's eye sockets, his hands moving in concert. Then he stopped, bringing them in, drawing them closed and holding them at the height of his cheeks, as if in this way to conclude some ritual. Esteban slumped on his side on the wicker ottoman, overcome by sudden drowsiness, sweat welling from all his pores. Sofía covered his naked body with a blanket. "Give him an infusion of ipecac and arnica leaves when he awakens," said the medicine man, carefully smoothing his suit in the mirror, and saw reflected the probing gaze of Sofía following him with her eyes. There was something of the magician, of the charlatan in his theatrical gestures. But with them, he had produced a miracle. "My friend," Victor explained to Carlos, uncorking a bottle of Portuguese wine, "belongs to the Harmony Society of Cap Français." "Is that a musical association?" Sofía asked. Ogé and Victor looked at each other and burst into laughter. Angered at their unexpected mirth, the young lady returned to Esteban's room. The sick man was sleeping heavily, his respiration normal, and the color was returning beneath his nails. Victor waited for her in the doorway to the great room: "The negro's honorarium," he said in a low tone. Embarrassed at her obliviousness, Sofía hurried back to her bedroom, retrieving an envelope which she handed to the doctor. "*Oh! Jamais de la vie!*" the mestizo exclaimed, rejecting the gratuity with an indignant gesture, and talking of modern medicine, which for years now had been compelled to admit that certain forces, though still poorly understood, exerted an effect on man's health. Sofía glared at Victor. But her gaze was lost in the void: the Frenchman was concentrated on Rosaura, the mulatta, who was crossing the courtyard with her hindquarters swaying beneath a light blue flowered dress. "How interesting," the young woman murmured, as though following along with Ogé's words. "*Plaît-il?*" the other man asked. A palm frond fell in the courtyard with a sound like a curtain being torn. The wind carried in the scents of the sea, a sea so near it seemed to drain into all the streets in the city. "We'll have a hurricane this year," Carlos said, looking at Albertus Magnus's thermometer and trying to convert Fahrenheit to Réaumur. A latent distress filled the atmosphere. Words were divorced from thoughts. All were speaking through foreign mouths, even if the words emerged from above the chins of their own faces. Carlos had no interest in Albertus Magnus's thermometer; Ogé had no sense that he was being heard; Sofía found no relief from the intimate resentment of an irritation turned against Remigio—laggard revealer of something she had suspected a long time, which made her detest the wretchedness of the masculine condition, incapable of the dignity or serene solitude of a spinster or a widow's existence. And her exasperation with her indiscreet servant only grew as she realized the negro's words gave her reason to confess that she'd never loved her father, whose kisses, stinking of licorice and tobacco and planted reluctantly on her forehead and cheeks when he took her back to the convent after those tedious Sunday luncheons, had been odious to her since puberty.

VI.

Sofía felt alien, divested of herself, as if on the threshold of a period of transformations. On certain afternoons, she had the feeling that the light, falling here and not there, endowed things with a new personality. A Christ emerged from the shadows to stare at her with sad eyes. An object, unnoticed up to then, would announce the delicate precision of its manufacture. The veining of an armoire would summon forth a ship. A

painting would speak another language, with a figure in it
looking suddenly restored; with the harlequins emerging more
visibly from the foliage in the parks, while the broken pillars,
blown outward—but suspended interminably in space—of the
Explosion in a Cathedral exasperated her with their arrested
movement, their endless falling without falling. Books she had
coveted months before and ordered impatiently from catalogs
had arrived from Paris but remained now still partly wrapped
on a shelf in the library. She moved from one thing to the next,
abandoning practicalities to tinker with useless things, gluing
bits of broken vases together, seeding plants that wouldn't
grow in the tropics, amused by a botanical treatise, bored by a
reading full of Patroclus and Aeneas, setting both aside to dive
into a trunk of scraps of fabric; incapable of persisting, of seeing her stitching to completion, or the household expenses, or
a translation—utterly unnecessary, as far as it goes—of the
"Ode to Evening" by the Englishman Collins . . . Esteban was
also changed; his character and demeanor had undergone
many alterations since the night of his portentous recovery—
because the fact was, since the destruction of Remigio's hidden
garden, his illness had not struck again. No longer afraid of his
nocturnal crises, he was always first to leave the house and
awoke earlier and earlier each day. He ate when he felt like it,
not waiting for the others. At all moments, a voracity—requital
for all the diets the doctors had imposed on him—drove him
to the kitchen to dig his fingers into the casseroles, to grab the
first puff pastry from the oven, to devour the fruit just in from
the market. Weary of pineapple juice and horchata, which recollected his ailments, he slaked his thirst at all hours with great
glasses of red wine that imparted their color to his face. He
was insatiable at the table, especially when lunching alone, at
midday, sleeves rolled up, open shirt revealing his chest, in
Arabian slippers, pouncing on a tray of shellfish, wielding his
cracker so brusquely that bits of shell flew off toward the walls.
Over his bare body, like a robe, he wore a bishop's cassock
taken from the wardrobe where the family's clothes were
stored; his hairy legs emerged beneath its amaranth folds, and
its satin was delightfully cool beneath the rosary he strung

around himself in place of a belt. This bishop was perpetually in motion, playing skittles in the gallery over the courtyard, sliding down the stair rail, hanging from the balusters, trying to revive the chimes of a clock that had been still for twenty years. Sofía, who had bathed him often during his crises without ever noticing the downy shadows darkening his anatomy, took care now, from a growing sense of shame, to avoid looking out at the terrace when she knew the boy was washing in the open air, then drying himself in the sunlight lying on the brick floor, without even a towel across his hips. "He's turning into a man on us," Carlos said with joy. "A man indeed," Sofía joined in, because she knew that, for several days now, he'd been shaving off his peach fuzz with a straight razor. Restoring the temporal order, Esteban had given back their true meaning to the hours violated by the habits of the house. He rose earlier each day, until he was even sharing the morning coffee with the servants. Sofía contemplated him with astonishment, alarmed at the new figure growing inside that being who had been aching and pitiful a few weeks before; who now, in the air he deeply inhaled and exhaled, free of phlegm and congestion, found an energy still too potent for his bony shoulders, his slender legs, his silhouette, which remained scraggy after his long plight. The young woman felt the unease of a mother noticing the first signs of virility in her son—a son who grabbed his hat more and more frequently, taking any pretext to roam the streets, concealing that his wanderings always led him to the harbor streets or the edges of the Alameda, near the old church that marked the boundary of the Arsenal neighborhood. Timidly, at first, venturing to one corner today, tomorrow to the next, measuring the distance, he arrived slowly to the street with the saloons and dance halls, which was singularly peaceful in the afternoon. Already there were women there, just awakened, newly bathed, in the doorways blowing tobacco smoke and shooting mocking looks at the young man, who fled the most aggressive of them, slowing before others whose whispered overtures only he could hear. As the houses spoke to him, they exhaled a turbid perfume, of soaps and essences, of indolent bodies and warm bedrooms, and his pulse raced at the thought that the decision of a second would suffice to penetrate that world rich with enigmatic possibilities. Between an abstract notion of the physical mechanics and real consummation lay an enormous distance only adolescence could gauge—with the vague sensation of guilt, of danger, of the commencement of Something implicit in the grasping of a stranger's flesh. For ten days, he walked to the end of the street, almost resolving to enter the place where a lazing girl, always sitting on a footstool, had chosen wisely to wait in unbroken silence. Ten times he passed her without daring, but the woman, knowing he had chosen, certain she would have him tomorrow if not today, watched him impassively. At last, one afternoon, the blue door of the house closed behind him. Nothing of what occurred in those warm, narrow chambers, with no adornments but a few petticoats hung on nails, struck him as especially significant or extraordinary. Certain modern novels, unprecedented in their crudity, had shown him that true delectation obeyed subtler shared impulses. And yet he returned every day for weeks to the same place: he needed to show himself he was capable of doing it without remorse or physical impediments—his curiosity to experience other bodies growing—just as other boys his age did quite naturally. "Who sprayed you with that abominable perfume?" his cousin asked one day, sniffing at his neck. Later, Esteban found a book on the nightstand in his bedroom that detailed the horrible diseases sent to man as punishment for carnal sins. The young man put the book away, not realizing it was intended for him.

By now, Sofía was used to spending the long afternoons alone, since Esteban was so frequently out and Carlos was busy with a new diversion, going to the riding school at the Campo de Marte, where a famous horseman gave displays of Spanish equestrian art, spurring the horses to rear up nobly as in statues or to trot by with poise and rhythm, manning the bridle on beasts with manes braided *a la Federica*, that is to say, in the Portuguese style. Victor continued visiting them at nightfall. Sofía would greet him with questions about the flour shipment from Boston, which never made it into port. "When it arrives," he would tell her, "I will return to Port-au-Prince with Ogé, who has some business there." The prospect horrified her, as she feared the reappearance of Esteban's disease. "Ogé is training disciples here," Victor told her to ease her mind, but without specifying where he taught these lessons or the view of them taken by the Federation of Doctors, parsimonious in handing out accreditations. He often spoke ill of Don Cosme, an awful tradesman in his opinion: "He's a *gagne-petit*, he can't see past his own nose." Despite Sofía's antipathy to everything pertaining to the firm next door, Victor began advising her: no sooner than they were old enough, she and her brother should dismiss the Executor, entrusting their affairs to someone more capable, someone who could make the company prosper. He listed all sorts of new goods that could earn them spectacular profits. "This is exactly as if I were speaking with my blessed father, God rest his soul," Sofía said, bringing this tiresome discourse to an end, her voice so airy, so false, that even its timbre was sarcastic. Victor laughed a long time; he did this whenever a sudden change of mood interrupted his monologues; and then he recollected his voyages—to Campeche, Marie-Galante, Dominica—listening to himself with evident satisfaction. He evinced a disconcerting blend of vulgarity and distinction. He could pass from the most florid southern verbosity to extreme reticence, depending on the path their discussion took. He seemed to harbor several individuals within him. When he talked of buying and selling, he would gesture like a money changer, his hands transformed into the plates of a scale. Then, concentrated on the reading of a book, he would stiffen, with a tenacious furrowed brow, his eyelids seemingly immobile over his somber eyes, which bored into the pages with determination. When he chose to cook, he transformed into a chef de cuisine, balancing slotted spoons on his forehead, making a toque of the first cloth he could find, drumming on the pots and pans. On some days, his hands were hard and miserly—with that way of closing his fist over his thumb that Sofía found unpleasantly revealing. Other times they were light and agile, caressing the object of his words as if it were a sphere suspended in space. "I'm a commoner," he would say, as though showing off a blazon. But when he played charades, Sofía noticed his preference for the role of legislator or judge in an ancient tribune. He took it tremendously seriously, perhaps imagining he was a talented actor. More than once, he had insisted on interpreting scenes from the life of Lycurgus, a figure he seemed particularly to admire. Wise in commerce, versed in the methods of Banking and Insurance, a merchant through and through, Victor nonetheless advocated for the redistribution of land and wealth, the adoption of children by the State, the abolition of fortunes, and the introduction of an iron currency, like that of the Spartans, which could not be hoarded. One day, when Esteban felt especially cheerful and hail, he proposed they throw a party to celebrate The Restoration of Normalcy with Regard to Mealtimes. A grand banquet would be held at eight on the dot, with the invitees to arrive from different parts of the house—those farthest from the dining room—just before the final tolling of the bells of the Church of the Holy Spirit. Whoever didn't appear in time would be subject to assorted penalties. They were all expected to wear something from upstairs in the suit closet. Sofía chose the costume of a Duchess ruined by pawnbrokers, and set to unstitching the overskirt with Rosaura's help. The episcopal vestments had already lain in Esteban's room for some time now. Carlos would dress as a Naval Ensign, while Victor donned a magistrate's toga—"*elle me va très bien*"—before going to the kitchen to marinate the squabs for the second course. "This way, representatives of the Court, the Church, the Armed Forces, and the Magistracy will be in attendance," Carlos said. "We're missing a Diplomat," Sofía observed. And with a laugh, they agreed to saddle Ogé with the role of Plenipotentiary Ambassador of the Kingdoms of Abyssinia. But Remigio, sent to retrieve him, returned with disconcerting news: the doctor had left early that day and hadn't returned to his hotel. And a policeman had just been to search his room, with orders to confiscate his books and papers. "I don't understand," Victor said. "I don't understand." "Might someone have denounced him for illegally practicing medicine?" Carlos asked. "That *illegal* medicine of his is what cures the sick!" Esteban yelled, appalled . . .

Dazed, unsteady, searching anxiously for a hat that failed to appear, Victor hurried off in search of information. "It's the first time I've seen something upset him," Sofía said, running a handkerchief over her sweaty temples. The heat was sweltering. The air stood paralyzed between the inert curtains, the withered flowers, and the plants that seemed forged from metal. The leaves of the palm trees in the courtyard hung like wrought iron.

VII.

Shortly after seven, Victor returned. He'd learned nothing of Ogé's whereabouts, but believed he'd been taken prisoner. Or perhaps the accusation had reached him—what the accusation was, he couldn't say—and he'd managed to reach a friend's house where he could hide out for a time. The report was correct: the police had searched his room, taking away his papers, his books, and the suitcases containing his personal effects. "Tomorrow we'll see what can be done," he said, then mentioning something he'd heard on the way back, which people were talking of outside: that night, a hurricane would strike the city. An official warning had been issued. There was great commotion on the docks. The sailors were talking about a cyclone, and taking emergency measures to save their ships. People were hoarding supplies of candles and food, and everyone was nailing planks over windows and doors. Unshaken by what they'd heard, Carlos and Esteban went for hammers and nails. The Cyclone—named in singular, because there never was more than one that did serious damage—was something all the town's residents expected. If it changed course and missed them this time, it was sure to return the following year. What mattered was knowing whether it would hit the city directly, tearing off roofs, shattering church windows, and sinking ships, or would instead veer away and lay waste to the fields. For the island's inhabitants, the Cyclone was looked upon as a fearsome celestial reality that would eventually descend upon all. Every province, every town, every village

harbored the memory of a cyclone that had seemed destined
for it. The most one could hope for was that it would sweep
through quickly without causing too much harm. "*Ce sont de
bien charmants pays,*" Victor complained, reinforcing the
shutters of one of the windows facing the street, recalling
that Saint-Domingue was likewise acquainted with this yearly
threat . . . A sudden, brutal storm sent tremors through the air.
Water fell on the foliage in the courtyard, vertical and dense,
with such ferocity that it knocked the soil from the planters.
"Here she comes," said Victor. A vast roar blanketed the
house, enveloped it, conjuring in unison the distinct tones of
the roof, the window slats, the skylights, with water falling in
sheets or droplets; water crashed, plunging from the sky, vomited by a gargoyle, swallowed by the channel of a gutter. Then
came a truce, warmer, its silence denser than it had been in
the first part of the night. The second rains—the second
admonition—came more belligerent than the first, this time
accompanied by irregular bolts of lightning that clustered together in a sustained charge. Victor stepped out on the gallery
over the courtyard, where the wind passed overhead without
stopping or descending, borne forward by the force that had
brought it there—whirling back on itself, tautening, its revolutions more powerful—from the far Gulf of Mexico or the Sar-
gasso Sea. With a mariner's knack, Victor tasted the rainwater:
"Salty. From the sea. *Pas de doute.*" He made a resigned gesture that said the coming hours would be trying, went to look
for bottles of wine, glasses, and biscuits, and settled into an
armchair, surrounded with books. They arranged lamps and
candles that each wind burst threatened to snuff out. "Better
to stay awake," the Frenchman said, "a door might blow open
or a window crack." A pile of boards and carpentry tools were
still near to hand. Invited to share the shelter of the salon,
Remigio and Rosaura joined together in a prayer, with reiterated pleas to Saint Barbara . . . It was just after midnight when
the full force of the hurricane swept the city. An immense roar
rose up, and with it clamor and destruction. Objects rolled
through the street. Others flew over the bell towers. Splintered
beams dropped from the sky, shop signs, roof tiles, panes of

glass, broken branches, lamps, barrels, riggings. Unimaginable knocking came at every door. Buffet after buffet shattered the windows. The houses shook from the foundations to the ceilings, groans emerging from their timbers. And then a torrent of putrid, muddy water flowed from the stables, the back lot, the kitchen, the street, erupted into the courtyard, clogging its drains with a mess of horse manure, ashes, refuse, and dead leaves. Victor shouted to alert them and rolled up the large rug in the salon. After throwing it onto one of the upper steps of the stairway, he walked toward the flood, which was rising by the minute, and had penetrated past the thresholds of the dining room and bedrooms. Hastily, Sofía, Esteban, and Carlos lifted what they could, piling everything on sideboards, tables, commodes, and armoires. "No!" Victor shouted. "Over there!" And stepping knee-deep into the fetor, he opened the door that led to the storehouse. It too was flooded, and much of the merchandise was afloat, passing softly through the light of the lamp. Shouting, issuing commands, putting order to their efforts, Victor pointed to what should be salvaged, setting the men and the mulatta to work. Bundles of perishables, sections of cloth, bunches of feathers, items of value were thrown over the piles of sacks, where the water wouldn't reach them. "The furniture can be repaired," Victor shouted. "This we can stand to lose." Once it was clear the others understood and were taking care of the most pressing things, Victor returned to the house, where Sofía was curled up on a divan, sobbing with terror. The water stood palm-deep around her. Victor picked her up, carried her to her room, and laid her on the bed. "Don't move. I'll take care of the furniture." And he began running up and down, up and down, with tapestries, folding screens, stools, chairs, and anything else that could be salvaged. By now, the water reached his knees. Then a rumbling sound augured collapse, and a wing of the roof hurled its tiles into the courtyard like a fistful of playing cards. A mountain of rubbish and broken crockery blocked the door to the storehouse. Sofía, peeking over the parapet, shouted in fear. Victor climbed back up, a chest of trinkets in hand. After pushing the young woman firmly into her room, he collapsed,

breathless, into an armchair: "I can do no more." And to calm
the girl, who begged him for succor, he said the worst part of
the cyclone was over; the others were safe in the storehouse
atop the mounds of sacks; there was nothing to be done now
but to wait till dawn. Most importantly, the doors and windows hadn't given. It wouldn't be the first time that sturdy
manse had survived a hurricane. Adopting a cheerful tone, he
told Sofía she looked, quite frankly, repulsive in that dress
soiled with filthy water, those muddy leggings, her damp, unkempt mane speckled with dead leaves. Sofía went to her dressing table and soon returned in her nightgown, after running a
comb through her hair. Outside, the ramming of the cyclone
splintered into gusts of wind, some frail, others brutal, but increasingly sporadic. What now was falling from the sky was
like a fog of water with the scent of sea. The racket of things
pushed, dragged, rolled, cast down from up high now diminished. "The best thing would be to sleep," Victor told Sofía,
bringing her a glass of fortified wine. And with astonishing
aplomb, he removed his shirt and stood there bare-chested.
"Not even if you were my husband," Sofía thought, turning
toward the wall. She was going to say something, but sleep
muddled her words . . . She awoke with a start—it was already
night—with the impression that someone lay at her side. An
arm was resting over her waist. And that arm squeezed and
cinched and weighed more and more. She was baffled, unsure
what to think: after the horror she had been through, it was
pleasant to feel protected, enveloped, sheltered by the warmth
of another being. She was about to fall asleep again when she
shivered, realizing the situation was unacceptable. Turning,
her body encountered the nakedness of another body. A nervous explosion jolted through her, and she struck him with her
fists, her elbows, her knees, hoping to scratch, to wound, keeping at bay that unfamiliar pulsing in her entrails. The other's
hands grasped at her wrists; a pernicious breath heated her
ears, speaking strange words to her in the darkness. They were
bound, knotted, mingled in struggle, and the man failed to get
the advantage. Driven by an unknown, titanic force radiating
from her vulnerable interior, the woman turned tense and

hard, tried to hurt him, never allowing him to pull her toward him or knead her flesh. At last, he gave in, announcing his defeat with a dry laugh that hardly concealed his irritation. But the woman wasn't done struggling, and the protest and recriminations she voiced revealed a shocking capacity to humiliate, to strike where it hurt most. The bed was now lighter by the weight of one body. Walking through the room, the man begged in a puling tone that she not be stern with him. He excused himself, and his justifications stunned the young woman now listening to him, who was doubly victorious, having never suspected a man so consummate and mature, so energetic and self-assured, could ever consider her a lady—her, for whom the years of childhood were still so present. Her flesh was out of danger for the moment, but Sofía felt a perhaps graver danger pulling at her: the danger that the voice alluding to her as it spoke, at times with agonizing sweetness, from within the shadows, was opening to her the doors of an unknown world. That night, adolescent games had ended. Words took on a new weight. What had happened—what hadn't happened—would adopt enormous dimensions. The door creaked and there materialized, over the lights of a greenish dawn, a human form withdrawing slowly, dragging its legs as if in defeat. Sofía remained alone, throbbing, bewildered, unquiet, with the feeling of emerging from a horrifying ordeal. Her skin had a strange scent that she couldn't rid herself of, perhaps real, perhaps imaginary: a dark, animal aroma, which in some way was her own. The light brightened her room. Next to her, in the shadows, lingered a presence that had left behind the imprint of its body. The girl began making the bed, slapping it on both sides to fluff the feathers in the counterpane. Once done, she felt humiliated; that must be how the whores made their beds down there in El Arsenal after they'd lain with a stranger. Or broken, corrupted virgins when they woke after their wedding night. This was the worst of it: the sprucing up, smoothing out, which had a kind of complicity, of acquiescence about it; a shameful restoration, the secret gesture of a lover eager to erase the disorder left behind by an embrace. Sofía lay back down, so weary in defeat that when Carlos found her sobbing, she was too deeply asleep for his calls to wake her. "Leave her," Esteban said, "she needs to be alone."

VIII.

The day brightened slowly, the light dawdling behind the hour, over a roofless city full of rubble and residue, reduced to the skeleton of bare beams. Nothing remained of the homes of the poor but rough-hewn corner posts with rickety wooden floors suspended over mud flats, like stage settings for misery. Acquiescent families picked through the few things left to them—the grandmother rocking faintly in a wicker rocker; the pregnant wife fearing her pains would come to her amid the devastation; the tubercular or asthmatic child wrapped in blankets on the raised edge of the platform, like a fairground actor after the end of the show. The masts of sunken sailboats rose from the filthy waters of the harbor among capsized boats floating aimlessly in clusters. The corpse of the odd sailor washed up occasionally on the shore, hands tangled in a bundle of cords. In El Arsenal, the cyclone had swept in low, scattering the timbers of half-built ships, bursting the thin walls of the taverns and dance halls. The streets were muddy moats. Some of the old palaces, despite their thick masonry walls, had been bowed by the wind, sacrificing their doors and transom windows to the hurricane, which once inside had ravaged from within, leveling porticoes and facades. The furnishings of a famous woodwright's shop—San José Pequeño's, near the docks—had been carried off by the wind, landing in a field outside the city walls, past the orchards, where hundreds of palm trees lay in flooded creeks like the shafts of ancient columns toppled by an earthquake. And yet, despite the magnitude of the disaster, the people, used to periodic visitations from that scourge they viewed as a preordained convulsion of the Tropics, set immediately to sealing, repairing, plastering, diligent as insects. Water covered everything; everything smelled of water; everything got water on one's hands. Drying, baling, draining the water however possible, was the order of the day for all. And in mid-afternoon, once they'd finished restoring their own homes, the carpenters, masons, glazers, and locksmiths offered their services to the others. When Sofía emerged from her torpor, laborers brought by Remigio were in all parts of the house, some covering what was left of the roof with new tiles while others dragged out the rubble lining the courtyard. Mortar, plaster, beams borne on shoulders came and went across the halls and galleries, while Carlos and Esteban, walking from the storehouse to their home, made an inventory of damaged furniture and spoiled merchandise. In the salon, Victor, dressed in a suit of Carlos's too small for his frame, had a pained expression as he paged through the company's books. When he saw Sofía, he sank his face into his hands, pretending he hadn't noticed her. The young woman walked on dutifully to the kitchen and pantries, where Rosaura, who hadn't yet slept, was pulling pots, pans, and utensils from the mud already hardening on the floor. Sofía seemed baffled by her toil, by that singular event that had disorganized all that was organized, introducing again in every room a chaos like that which had reigned before. That afternoon, new Leaning Towers, new Druids' Ways were born, new winding mountain passes between boxes, furnishings, unhung curtains, rolled rugs on the tops of the cupboards—but the odor was not the odor of earlier days. And the incomparable nature, the violence of an event that had torn everyone from their habits and routines, aggravated the endless contradictory sorrows Sofía felt upon waking when she remembered the events of the night before. *That* formed part of the vast disorder in the city, became part of the scenography of the cataclysm. But one thing stood out past the breached walls, the ruined belfries, the sunken ships: she had been *desired*. That was so strange, so unexpected, so unsettling, that she couldn't admit the reality of it. In mere hours, she'd begun to shed her adolescence, sensing that her flesh had ripened in the presence of a man's cravings. He had seen her as a Woman, before she had seen herself as a Woman—when she could not yet imagine others would concede her the status of Woman. "I'm a Woman," she murmured, offended and, as it were, confounded by an enormous weight placed on her shoulders, looking at herself in the mirror as one looks at another, dissenting, vexed by some doing of fate, finding herself long and ungainly, feeble, with her narrow hips, her skinny arms, her asymmetrical breasts, which for the first time made her feel contempt for her own body. She had departed from a path free of dangers to reach another, fraught with disparities between real and reflected image, and setting forth on it would demand she pass through paroxysms and vertigo . . . Soon night fell. The workers left, and a vast silence—the silence of ruin and mourning—overtook the castigated city. Exhausted, Sofía, Esteban, and Carlos went to sleep after a meager meal of cold meat, where they'd said little apart from a few remarks about the damage caused by the cyclone. Victor, self-absorbed, pressing figures with his thumbnail into the tablecloth—adding, subtracting, erasing—asked to stay late in the salon; better yet, until tomorrow. The streets were impassable. There were likely marauders out, brigands engaged in their nocturnal vocation. Moreover, he seemed very occupied with finishing his review of the books. "I believe I've come up with something that could interest you all a great deal," he said. "Tomorrow, we'll talk."

It was not even nine the next day when Sofía, awakened by the blows of hammers, the screech of saws and pulleys, the voices of workers resounding in the house, walked to the salon, where something strange was occurring. The Executor was seated in an armchair grinning, and in front of him, at a certain distance, like judges in a tribunal, stood Carlos and Esteban, frowning, exceedingly serious and expectant. Victor was pacing through the room, hands clasped behind his back. Now and then he would pause before the newcomer, glare at him, and return to his thoughts with a reluctantly groaned *Oui!* Finally, he sat in his own armchair in the corner. He looked into a journal where he seemed to have taken notes *(Oui . . . !)* and began to speak in a loose, indulgent tone, polishing his nails on his sleeve, toying with a pencil, or, taking a sudden interest in some aspect of the little finger of his left hand. He said he was not a man inclined to insert himself in other people's affairs. He praised the diligence of Monsieur Cosme (Coooome, he called him, with a drawn-out circumflex) in satisfying the desires of his charges—in ordering them whatever they wished, in taking care that they wanted for nothing at home. But that diligence—*n'est-ce pas?*—might well serve as a convenience intended to quiet any suspicions in advance. "Suspicions of what?" the Executor asked, as if none of this concerned him, scooting his chair in little hops toward his charges to make his place in the family clearer. But Victor motioned to them, adopting an intimate tone that seemed to make of the other an intruder: "Since we have just finished reading Regnard, *mes amis*, let us recall those verses, which you yourselves could surely recite by heart: '*Ah, qu'à notre secours à propos vous venez! / Encore un jour plus tard, nous étions ruinés.*'" "So now we're at the *Comédie Française*," Cosme said, laughing at his own joke in the midst of an exasperating silence. "Sometimes on Sundays," Victor continued, "while the young ones were asleep" (and he pointed at the door that led to the warehouse), he had entered the adjoining building, looking around, observing, counting, adding, notating. And—his was a merchant's soul, that much he wouldn't deny—he had established that certain of their wares failed to correspond with the inventories the Executor regularly delivered to Carlos. He knew ("Quiet!" he shouted to Don Cosme, who tried to speak) that business was harder now than before; that wiles and artifice were part and parcel of fair trade. But this was no justification (and here his voice swelled fearsomely) to present these orphans with a false notion of their accounts, particularly as it was clear they would never read them . . . Don Cosme tried to stand. But Victor outflanked him, strode toward him in long steps, index finger raised. His voice had turned metallic and hard; the state of the warehouse was a scandal—a scandal begun the day of the death of Carlos and Sofía's father. With a simple look at the books, carried out in the presence of witnesses, he would demonstrate that this confidence man, this so-called protector, this embezzler-executor, was lining his pockets at the expense of unfortunate children, whom he swindled immorally in the knowledge that their inexperience left them incapable of managing their own property. Nor was that all: Victor was apprised of the risky speculations this *second father* had undertaken with his wards' money; of purchases made through go-betweens he described as *canes venatici*, evoking, with deep indignation, Cicero's *In Verrem*. Don Cosme tried to get in a word amid that verbal deluge, but Victor, raising his voice, prolonged his accusation, sweating, formidable, as though he had grown larger in the meanwhile. He had loosened his collar with a gesture so abrupt that its two loose tips hung over his vest, freeing a throat of dense cords, all engaged in the finale of a stentorian peroration. For the first time, Sofía found him handsome, even beautiful, with his bearing of a Roman tribune, with that fist he brought down over the table, marking the paroxysm of a period. He then walked to the back wall, leaning into it. He crossed his arms amply, and after a fleeting pause the Executor failed to make use of, he concluded, drily and peremptorily, in a tone of utter derision: "*Vous êtes un misérable, Monsieur.*"

Don Cosme seemed to have shrunk, huddled over deep in his chair, which was too plush to serve as a frame for his meager person. A tremor of rage moved his lips in silent agitation while his nails scratched the velvet of the armrest. Then he leaped up, barking a single word to Victor that sounded, to Sofía's ears, like an explosion in a cathedral: "Freemason!" The word flared, burned out, and exploded again with magnificent percussion: "Freemason!" He went on repeating it in ever-louder and ever-changing tones, as if it sufficed to quash all accusations, nullify any indictment, exonerate whomever proffered it. Seeing a defiant smile was Victor's lone reply, the Executor mentioned the shipment of flour from Boston that had never arrived and never would: a pretext to conceal the misdeeds of an agent of the Freemasons of Saint-Domingue in league with the mulatto, Ogé, a mesmerist and wizard, whom Cosme would refer to the Federation of Doctors for ensorcelling those youngsters with extravagant artifices Esteban would realize had been useless soon enough, when his illness returned. Now Don Cosme led the charge, circling the Frenchman like an incensed horsefly: "I am talking of men who pray to Lucifer; men who hurl insults at Christ in Hebrew; men who

spit on the crucifix; men who slice open a lamb crowned with
thorns on the eve of Maundy Thursday, its hoofs nailed down,
its body stretched across the table for an abominable banquet."
For that, the Holy Fathers Clement and Benedict had excom-
municated these blackguards, condemning them to burn in the
fires of Hell . . . And with the horrified tone of a man revealing
the mysteries of a Sabbath he himself had attended, he spoke
of these heathens who rejected the Redeemer, who adored a
certain Hiram Abiff, Architect of Solomon's Temple, and paid
tribute in their secret ceremonies to Isis and Osiris, regaling
themselves with titles like King of the Tyrians, Raiser of the
Tower of Babel, Knight Kadosh, Grand Master of the Knights
Templar—as a testament to Jacques de Molay, a libertine
found guilty of heresy and burned alive for adoring the Demon
in the figure of an idol named Baphomet. "These men pray not
to the saints, but to Belial, Astaroth, and Behemoth." They
were a mob who crept into all parts, opposing the Christian
faith and the authority of legitimate government in the name of
"philanthropy," a pursuit of happiness and democracy that
gave cover to an international scheme to destroy the established order. Looking Victor in the face, he shouted the word
conspirator until his voice, weary from the effort, broke into a
fit of coughing. "Is all of this true?" Sofía asked in a timid
voice, astonished and appalled to hear of Isis and Osiris in
such portentous settings as the Temple of Solomon and the
Castle of the Templars. "The one true thing is that this house
is falling into the ground," Victor replied peacefully. And,
turning toward Carlos: "The matter of unfit guardians was already dealt with in Roman law. We shall see him in court."
The word *court* violently reanimated the Executor: "We'll see
who goes to prison first," he grunted. "From what I hear,
they'll soon be rounding up the Freemasons and undesirable
foreigners. The foolish tolerance of earlier days is finally at an
end." And, grabbing his hat, he said: "Throw this charlatan
out of the house before they arrest *you all*!" With a "Good
day . . . to *all*," he bowed, reiterating this threat, leaving the
salon with a slam of the door so resounding it shook all the
windows in the house. The young people waited for Victor to

explain. But he instead began sealing with wax the thick string he had used to tie the warehouse's books: "Keep them here," he said. "This is your proof." Then he strolled pensively out into the courtyard, where workers were finishing their repairs under the watchful eye of Remigio, who was pleased to find himself in the role of foreman. As though in need of some physical release, he picked up a brickmason's trowel, stepped in among the workmen, and set to smoothing and filling in a wall in the courtyard damaged by falling tiles. Sofía watched him climb a scaffold, his face specked with plaster and mortar, and remembered the myth of Hiram Abiff: despite certain aspersions she'd heard in church; despite the lamb crowned with thorns, the blasphemies uttered in Hebrew, and the Popes with their fearsome Bulls, that Secret of which Victor—now envisioned a Builder of Temples—was a repository fascinated her, somehow. She saw him as an envoy from forbidden lands, versed in arcana; an explorer of Asia who had come upon an unknown book of Zoroaster—an Orpheus, traverser of Avernus. And she thought back to when he'd mimicked an ancient architect murdered treacherously by a mallet blow in one of their games of charades. She'd even seen him dressed as a Templar, in a tunic adorned with a cross, enacting the torments of Jacques de Molay. There was reality in the Executor's accusations. But it was a reality that drew her, secret, mysterious, suggestive of occult powers. A life lived in service to a dangerous conviction was more alluring than one spent waiting chastely for a few sacks of flour. Better a conspirator than a merchant. The adolescent yen for disguise, for signs and countersigns, for dead drops, private codes, padlocked diaries, all reawakened with the adventure she had glimpsed. "Can these people really be as horrible as all that?" she asked. Esteban shrugged: defamation had hounded sects and secret societies throughout history. From the early Christians, who'd been accused of cutting children's throats, to the Bavarian Illuminati, whose only crime was to wish for the good of humanity. "Of course, they oppose God," Carlos said; "God is nothing more than a hypothesis," said Esteban. Now, as though yearning to break free of an intolerable oppression, Sofía screamed: "I'm tired of God; tired of nuns; tired of guardians and executors, notaries and forms, robbery and filth; I'm tired of things, like this one, which I can't stand the sight of anymore." And jumping over an armchair pushed against the wall, she took down a large portrait of her father and threw it to the floor so violently that the canvas tore away from the frame. To the feigned indifference of the others, she stomped bitterly on the fabric, sending flakes of paint flying into the air. When the picture was destroyed, wounded, insulted, Sofía fell panting and scowling into a chair. Victor dropped the bricklayer's trowel, a look of surprise on his face: Ogé was hurriedly entering the courtyard. "We must go," he said, and told briefly all he'd found out while hiding in the house of a *brother*: the cyclone, calling the authorities' attention to more pressing matters, had briefly interrupted a planned offensive against the Freemasons. The order to undertake it had come down from Spain. For now, nothing more could be done here. It would be wisest to take advantage of the present disorder. While people's sole concern was restoring walls and clearing roads, they could leave town and observe from a distance what turn events would take. "We have a farmhouse that will do," Sofía said with a firm voice, going to the pantry to prepare a basket of victuals. There, surrounded by charcuterie, mustards, and breads, they agreed that Carlos should remain at home to gather information. Esteban went to take down the tacking for the horses, while Remigio was sent to the line of hacks in the Plaza del Cristo to hire two beasts for remount.

IX.

The carriage rolled on pitted roads, creaking, leaping, hobbling, beneath a late last drizzle that burnished the black oilcloth, seeped into the backseat with the reeling wind, and soaked the attire of Esteban and Ogé, who were seated on the box; at times it leaned so far to the side, it threatened to fall over; it descended in the waters of the ford until droplets splashed the lanterns; there was mud everywhere, and they only broke free of the red earth of the sugarcane fields to sink into

the gray earth of fallow fields marked by cemetery crosses—
and as he passed them, Remigio crossed himself, bringing up
the rear on one of the remounts. The travelers sang and laughed
despite the inclement weather, drinking Malvasia, eating sand-
wiches and shortbread and candies, rejoicing strangely at the
new air that smelled of green pastures, cows with swollen udders, campfires of fresh wood—far from the brine, the jerked
meat, the germinating onions that jousted with their vapors in
the city's narrow streets. Ogé sang a song in creole: "*Dipi mon
perdi Lisette / mon pas souchié kalenda, / mon quitté bram-
bram sonnette, / mon pas battre bamboula.*" Sofía intoned a
beautiful Scottish ballad in English, paying no mind to Esteban, and even affected a hideous accent to irk him. Victor sang
out of tune, but with a very serious demeanor, something that
started with the words, *Oh Richard! Oh mon Roi!* But he never
made it any further, because he didn't know the rest. In the afternoon, the rain grew fiercer, the roads worse; Victor coughed,
Esteban hacked, and Sofía shivered in her damp clothes. The
three men took turns riding in front, and this constant entering
and exiting of the carriage impeded their conversation. The
great question—the great enigma—of Victor and Ogé's doings
remained in suspense; no one had broached the subject, and
perhaps they had sung so much along the way awaiting the
right moment to dispel these mysteries . . . They reached the
house in the depths of night. It was a structure of unworked
stone, poorly cared for, covered in cracks, with numberless
rooms, long halls, multiple archways covered by a sloping roof
sagging between decrepit beams. Despite her exhaustion and
her fear of the bats flapping all round, Sofía arranged the sheets
and blankets on the beds, filled the washbasins, mended the
mosquito nets, and promised more comforts for the following
night. Victor wrang the necks of two chickens, grabbing their
throats and whirling them like feathered pinwheels in the air
before dropping them in boiling water, plucking them bare, and
chopping them into small pieces for a quick *fricassée*, its sauce
dense with brandy and ground pepper—"*pour réchauffer Messieurs les voyageurs.*" After finding fennel grass growing in the
courtyard, he beat eggs for what he called an *omelette aux*

fines-herbes. Sofía bustled about the table, putting together a centerpiece of aubergines, lemons, and wild gourds. When Victor invited her to inhale the fine aroma of the *fricassée*, she felt his hand rest against her waist, but carefree this time, brotherly, neither heavy nor insistent, and she did not take it as an affront. Admitting she found the stew excellent, she whirled away from him in a pirouette and returned to the dining room unflustered. The dinner was merry, the talk afterward merrier still, with the ease, the security they felt under that roof in a house lashed now by harsher rains, which burst against the taro leaves as though striking sheets of parchment, and tore pomegranates and rose apples from the trees in the garden . . . Victor, adopting a more serious tone, spoke expansively of what had brought him to their country. Business, above all: silks from Lyon were subject to high taxes passing through Spain on their way to Havana and Mexico; a better line was shipping them from Bordeaux to Saint-Domingue, then bringing them over covertly on North American vessels that delivered wheat flour to the Antilles on their return. Hundreds of pieces were then taken to market in identical sacks, others through a sophisticated scheme employed by the forward-thinking creole merchants and their contacts in the port authorities as vengeance against the Spanish monopoly's abusive levies. Working through his own firm as agent of the factories of Jean-Baptiste Willermoz (a very important personage, Esteban thought, since Victor forced his accent when pronouncing his name), he had sold great quantities of Lyon silk to shops throughout the city. "It's not an especially honest business is it?" Sofía asked intentionally. "It's a way of struggling against the tyranny of the monopolies," Victor replied. "Tyranny in all forms must be resisted." And a man had to start somewhere, because here the people were dormant, inert, trapped in a timeless world on the margins, tobacco and sugar the only things they could think of. Whereas "philanthropy" held sway in Saint-Domingue, a place in touch with all that was happening in the world. Believing the movement would spread as far in the colonies as it had in Spain, he'd been tasked with establishing relations with local affiliates, to create a conventicle of the kind that existed in other places. But his

disappointment had been great. The philanthropists in this
wealthy city were few and apprehensive. They seemed ignorant
of the significance of the social question. They were sympa-
thetic toward the movement, which was gaining adherents
worldwide, but they themselves did nothing to help it prosper.
From timidity, from cowardice, they let legends circulate about
spitting on crosses, insulting Christ, sacrilege and blasphemy,
all of them disaccredited elsewhere. (*"Nous avons autre chose
à faire, croyez-moi."*) They couldn't grasp the universal importance of events now taking place in Europe. "Revolution is on
the march, and no one can stop it," Ogé said with that impres-
sively noble accent he reserved for certain affirmations. This
revolution, Esteban thought, could be reduced to four lines
about France published between a listing of plays and an adver-
tisement for the sale of guitars in the local newspaper. Victor
admitted that since his arrival in Havana, he had lost all contact with the recent events so passionately followed in Saint-
Domingue. "To begin," Ogé said, "a recent decree authorizes
men of my color (and with a finger, he pointed to his cheeks,
which were darker than his forehead) to take up any and all
public appointments. This is a measure of enormous importance. *E-nor-mous.*" Now, prompting each other, their voices
changing, each interrupting the other's words, Victor and Ogé
dove into an explanation both intriguing and confusing, from
which Esteban extracted a few clear concepts: "We have left the
religious and metaphysical eras behind us; now we are entering
the era of science." "The stratification of the world into classes
is irrational." "We must strip from mercantile interests the horrible power to unleash wars." "Humanity is divided into two
groups: the oppressors and the oppressed. Custom, necessity,
and the lack of leisure prevent the oppressed, in their majority,
from ever recognizing their condition. When they do, civil war
will break out." The words *freedom, happiness, equality,
human dignity* came up repeatedly in that halting exposition as
justification for the imminence of a Great Conflagration that
Esteban accepted that night as a vital purification; as an Apoc-
alypse he yearned to witness, the sooner the better, to begin his
life as a man in a new world. And yet, he seemed to sense that

Victor and Ogé, though joined by the same words, were not in agreement about things, men, methods of action that related to the coming events. The doctor mentioned a Martinez de Pasqually, a noted philosopher, deceased some years before in Saint-Domingue, whose teachings had left a profound mark on men's minds. "A fraud!" Victor said, with ironic reference to Him who attempts to make spiritual connections beyond the earth and seas, his disciples kneeling in unison on the solstices and equinoxes in magic circles traced out in white chalk, surrounded by lighted candles, kabbalistic signs, aromatic smoke, and other Asiatic paraphernalia. "Our intent," said Ogé irritably, "is to cultivate the transcendental forces dormant in mankind." "Start by breaking their chains," Victor said. "Martinez de Pasqually," the doctor replied violently, "has taught that Humanity's evolution is a collective act, and that individual action perforce implies the existence of collective social action: he who *knows* more will *do* more for his neighbors." This time, Victor nodded softly, acceding to a notion not wholly in accordance with his convictions. Sofía expressed her perplexity before this movement of ideas that adopted such diverse and contradictory forms. "Questions this complex cannot simply be grasped outright," Ogé said vaguely, giving her a glimpse of the mists of an underground world whose arcana remained secret. Esteban felt now he had lived as though blind, ignorant of the most stirring realities, failing to recognize the only thing worth seeing in that era. "And there is much we have yet to receive news of," Victor said. "And we shall go on without news, because the governments are afraid, deathly afraid of the spirit sweeping across Europe," Ogé concluded in a prophetic tone. "The time has come, my friends. The time has come."

They spent two days talking of revolution, and Sofía was astonished at how the subject roused them. Talking of revolution, imagining revolution, situating oneself mentally within the heart of a revolution, means making oneself, to some degree, the master of the world. Those who speak of revolution find themselves compelled to wage it. Plainly, this or that privilege must be abolished, and so the people proceed to abolish it;

evidently, this or that oppression is odious, so they draw up
measures against it; clearly, this or that person is a blackguard,
so they condemn him unanimously to death. And when the
earth has been purified, they set to building the City of the
Future. Esteban advocated for the suppression of Catholicism,
with exemplary punishments for all who reverenced those *idols*.
Victor agreed, while Ogé thought differently; as man had
always shown a tenacious aspiration toward something that
could be called *the imitation of Christ*, that sentiment should
be transformed into a drive to overcome, with man seeking to
resemble Christ by raising himself to an Archetype of Human
Perfection. Ill-disposed to transcendental speculations, Sofía
brought the others back down to earth with her concrete interest in the situation of women and child-rearing in the new society. The discussion descended into shouts over whether a
Spartan education was satisfactory and adaptable to the epoch.
"No," said Ogé. "Yes," said Victor . . . On the third day, the
dispute around the distribution of wealth in the new society
had grown so heated that Carlos, arriving at the farmhouse
after an arduous trip on horseback, thought those inside were
quarreling. They fell quiet when he came in. His face spoke of
grave news, and indeed, matters were grave: the campaign
against the Freemasons and undesirable foreigners had begun.
The government in the mother country may have tolerated lib-
eral ministers, but it was determined to uproot advanced ideas
from its colonies. All this had pleased Don Cosme, who informed Carlos he'd had word of an arrest warrant for Ogé and
Victor. "*Décidément il faut filer*," the merchant said, unper-
turbed. And fetching his luggage, he brought forth a map and
pointed to a spot on the island's southern coast. "We're not far
from here," he said. And he told how, in his seaman days, he
had dealt in sponges, coal, and hides around the harbor, and
knew people there. Without another word, he and his companion gathered their things, leaving the others in pained silence.
They would never have imagined they would be so moved by
the departure of Victor, the stranger, the intruder who had
come almost inexplicably into their lives. His appearance, with
a thundering of door knockers, had had something diabolical

about it—with his aplomb as he took over their home, sitting at the head of the table, rifling through their closets. As if in an instant, the contraptions from the Cabinet of Physics had worked; the furnishings had emerged from their crates; the sick had been made well, the inert had begun to walk. Now they were left alone, defenseless, without friends, prone to the depredations of a delinquent, vulnerable magistracy—they who, if they had a poor grasp of business, understood even less of the law. In cases of doubt as to the integrity of a guardian—Carlos had heard from a lawyer—the Courts would name a co-guardian or a Guardian Council who would remain in power until the male children reached the age of majority. In any case, they would have to act, with an appeal to justice. Carlos had an ally in mind in the person of a former bookkeeper, recently let go by Don Cosme, who boasted of knowing a great deal about the man's machinations. While they dealt with these matters, the persecution unleashed on the Freemasons would most likely die down. Summer outbursts of this kind were a known feature of the Spanish administration; then the accusations were filed away, and the eternal torpor returned. They would stay in close contact with Victor. He could return for a few weeks to take stock of the warehouse and propose new directions for the business. It was even possible he might abandon his affairs in Port-au-Prince, which were less promising than those here. They saw in him the ideal administrator, and perhaps, with his talent for numbers, it would profit him to establish himself in a city with a great bustle of merchants. But for now, there was no avoiding reality: Victor and Ogé had to flee. Both were in danger of being captured and "expelled from the Dominions," as other Frenchmen had been with no regard for their long residence in Spanish territories. Sofía and Esteban would accompany them to the harbor town . . . which they reached without incident three days later, thirsty, aching, stomping through dust, with dust in their hair, under their clothes, behind their ears, after a thankless journey through plantations whose hospitality they had shunned, sugar farms that had already finished their milling for the year, and wretched towns hardly distinguishable against a monotonous landscape of flooded savannahs. The fishing village stretched along a filthy strand coated in dead algae and tar patches, where crabs swarmed between broken boards and rotten ropes. A pier of planks, cracked from the weight of marble unloaded days before, led out into a sea that raised no foam, cloudy as though intermixed with oil. Amid the sponge fishing boats and coal barges, fishing schooners were visible, piled high with wood and sacks. One boat, its slender masts rising high over the posts of the other ships, lifted Victor's mood after several hours of wordless weariness. "I know that ship," he said. "We'll have to find out if it's coming or going." And suddenly impatient, he entered a kind of tavern-general-store-ropeyard-inn in search of lodging. All they had were cramped rooms with pallets and washbasins, their whitewashed walls covered in more or less obscene inscriptions and drawings. There was a somewhat better hotel, but at a distance from the harbor, and Sofía was so fatigued that she preferred to stay there, where the floors were clean, the breeze was blowing, and earthen vessels of fresh water were on hand to wash away the dust. While the travelers settled in as best they could, Victor went to the docks in search of informants. Calmer now, Sofía, Ogé, and Esteban gathered around a table, where they were served a dinner of beans and fish beneath a lamp behind the glass of which insects clashed with a dry clatter. And they would have eaten with relish, had a plague of tiny mosquitoes not appeared, brought in from the nearby marshlands by the setting sun. They flew into their ears, nostrils, and mouths, and slid down their spines like cold grains of sand. Impervious to the smoke of dry coconuts laid on a clay oven's grill to keep them at bay, the creatures rose up in clouds, leaving everyone's faces, hands, and legs peppered with welts. "I can't take it!" Sofía said, scurrying to her room and climbing under the netting after snuffing the two candles placed on a stool that served as a nightstand. But still, she heard the humming all around her. Beneath the coarse tulle eaten through with damp, full of holes, the storm continued: the faint sharp whistle from temple to shoulder, from forehead to cheek, with an interlude just before a landing was felt on the skin. Sofía turned, slapped herself, struck herself with the heel of her hand, here, there, on her thighs, between her shoulders, on her knee pits and flanks. Faintly, wings grazed her temple, then came closer with wrathful intensity. Finally, she curled up underneath a thick sheet, coarse as sackcloth, that covered her head. And eventually she fell asleep, drenched in sweat, over a bedspread sopping with sweat, cheek sunken in a miserable pillow soaked with sweat . . . When she opened her eyes, it was dawn; the trimmed and spurred fighting cocks crowed from the pit; the plague had dispersed, but she was so fatigued she believed she was ill. The idea of passing another day—another night—in that place, with its brackish waters, its heat already lurking in the light of dawn, its storms of insects, was intolerable. Wrapping herself in a robe, she went to the shop for vinegar to relieve the swellings covering her skin. She found Ogé, Esteban, and Victor sitting at the same table as the night before, awake, drinking black coffee from small, rough-hewn bowls, with a captain who, despite the early hour, had dressed in his uniform—blue fabric, gold buttons—to come on land. His patchily shaven cheeks bore the fresh marks of a dull razor. "Caleb Dexter," Victor said. And added, lowering his voice, "He too is a philanthropist." In his usual tone, he concluded peremptorily: "Gather your things. The *Arrow* lifts anchor at eight. We are departing for Port-au-Prince."

X.

Now, the chill of the sea. The massive shadow of the sails. The breeze from the north which, passing over land, gathered in the vastness, bringing vegetal scents the sentries could distinguish in their lookouts, recognizing the smells of Trinidad, Sierra Maestra, Cape Cruz. With a tiny net attached to a rod, Sofía lifted wonders from the sea: a knot of gulfweed, the fruits of which popped between thumb and forefinger; a cluster of mangroves adorned with tender oysters; a coconut no bigger than a walnut, of a green so splendid it looked varnished. They passed over beds of sponges that painted dun splotches on the clear bottoms, floated amid cays of white sand, never losing sight of a coast dissolving in mist, which grew increasingly mountainous and craggy. Sofía had been pleased to agree to the voyage, which freed her from the heat, the mosquitoes, the thought of a tedious return to the day-to-day, the monotony—made more monotonous by the absence of him who could transfigure reality at all moments—accepting it as though it were a simple excursion across the waters of some Swiss lake edged with rugged, romantic cliffs; a *promenade en bateau*, unimaginable yesterday, which Victor, in his predicament, had pulled from his sleeve like a conjurer. Finding them places onboard, with a cabin below deck for the lady, Victor's friend had welcomed them onto that vessel in thanks, he said, for the others' affection and generosity. They could spend a few weeks in Port-au-Prince and return on the same ship—with a fellow philanthropist as captain, they had no need of a safe conduct—as soon as the seaman had left Suriname, where he had a shipment to deliver. Viewing it all as an escapade, a return to the happy chaos of earlier days, they had written a letter to Carlos, with a description of this exploit which, for Sofía, was taking on a providential significance after all those dreams of travel, all those itineraries left on paper, all those departures never resolved. This, at least, was something new. Port-au-Prince wasn't London or Vienna or Paris, but it did represent a change. They would land in France's overseas possessions, where they spoke a different language and breathed a different air. They would go to Le Cap Français, to the Théâtre de la Rue Vaudreuil, to see a performance of *Le légataire universel* or *Zemire et Azor*. They would buy the latest sheet music for Carlos to play on the flute, and books, many books that dealt with the economic transformation of Europe in their century and the revolution—the one that was already underway . . . Sofía had lain fishing on her stomach on the prow, the sun reflecting off her skin. But now a clamor of voices roused her: in the aftercastle, nude apart from knee breeches cinched at the waist, Victor and Ogé were in a water-fight, lowering their pails on ropes, each struggling to fill his faster than the other. The torso of the mulatto was magnificent in its vigor, waist lean below shoulders that swelled potently, lustrous and firm. Victor was more robust, and his barrel chest revealed muscles in stiff relief—while those on his back seemed to ripple down his spine—each time he lifted a bucket hauled up from the sea to empty in his friend's face. Esteban said, "This is the first time I truly feel young." "I have to ask myself if we really ever were young," said Sofía, turning back to her fishing. The water was flecked with iridescent jellyfish, their colors changing with the rhythm of the waves; but their indigo persisted, trimmed with red festoons. The *Arrow* clove slowly through a vast migration of medusas oriented toward the shore. Observing the multitude of those ephemeral creatures, Sofía was agape at the continual destruction of all that was engendered, the perpetual luxury of creation; the luxury of multiplying, all the better to suppress; the luxury of incubating in the most elemental wombs as in the lathes of man-gods, only to consign to the future the fruits of a world in a state of perpetual devourment. In sumptuous ceremonial garb, myriad lives emerged from the horizon, still suspended between vegetable and animal, sacrificial victims to the Sun. They would lodge in the sand, where their crystals dried little by little, clouded, shriveled, wizened to a glaucous tatter, a foam, a mere dampness effaced immediately by the heat. She couldn't imagine an annihilation more complete, without trace or vestige—without proof, even, that the living had ever lived . . . After the jellyfish came glassy wanderers—pink, yellow, striped—in a diversity of colors reflecting the dazzling midday light over a jasper sea severed by the ship. Cheeks aglow, hair loose in the breeze, Sofía enjoyed a bodily serenity she had never known before. She could stay for hours below the shadows of a sail, watching the waves, thinking of nothing, servile to the voluptuousness of her entire body—soft, indolent, senses alert to any provocation. The crossing made a glutton of her: in her honor, the Captain had the table laid with fine foods, beverages, and fruits that startled her palate with new savors: smoked oysters, the famous Boston biscuits, English ciders, never-before-tasted rhubarb pies, juicy medlars from

Pensacola, which ripened along the way, and melons from orchards in New York. Everything was different, extraordinary, and this held her in an atmosphere of irreality. When she asked after the name of a strangely shaped outcrop or an islet or canal, her geographical notions, taken from maps of Spanish manufacture, always conflicted with the nomenclature of Caleb Dexter: for him this was Caymanbrack, that the Nordest Kaye or Portland Rock. Even the ship had something enchanted about it, with its philanthropic captain from Victor and Ogé's secret world—world of Isis and Osiris, Jacques de Molay and Frederick of Prussia—who kept in a vitrine with his navigation instruments an apron adorned with the Acacia, the Temple of Seven Steps, the two Columns, the Sun, and the Moon. At night under the awning on the stern deck, Ogé spoke of the marvels of magnetism, the collapse of traditional psychology, or the secret orders flourishing across the globe, with names like the Initiated Knights and Brothers of Asia, the Legion of the Black Eagle, the Elect Cohen Knights, the Philalethes Society, the Illuminati of Avignon, the Hermetic Brotherhood of Light, the Philadelphians, the Knights of the Rose Croix, and the Knights Templar, who pursued an ideal of equality and harmony while laboring for the perfection of the Individual, destined to ascend, with the aid of Reason and Light, to spheres where mankind would be forever freed of fears and doubts . . . Sofía saw that Ogé was not an atheist like Victor, for whom Christian priests were "mere black-dressed harlequins tugging the strings of marionettes," and the Great Architect a passing symbol to be tolerated while science worked to clarify the enigmas of creation. The mestizo referred to the Bible often, accepting some of its mythical assertions, the same way he used terms from the Kabbalah and Platonism and talked often of the Cathars, whose princess Esclaramunda Sofía knew from a captivating novel she'd recently read. For Ogé, the carnal act was not a perpetuation of Original Sin, but its expurgation. In discreet euphemisms, he affirmed that Coupling was a return to Primal Innocence; from total, Edenic nudity came a placation of the senses, a joyous and tender quietude that eternally reenacted the

purity of Man and Woman before the Fall . . . Victor and
Caleb Dexter, respecting each other as colleagues, conversed
about navigation, discussing a Rocky Shoal that various treatises indicated was dangerously hidden four fathoms deep, but
that neither of them had encountered in their travels along the
coast. Mr. Erastus Jackson, the ship's mate, joined the group,
telling horrifying tales of the sea—such as the time Captain
Anson lost his bearings and strayed through the Pacific for a
month, unable to find the Juan Hernández Islands; or when a
schooner was found near Grand Caico without a single crew
member on board, but with the fires in the kitchen still lit,
freshly washed clothing stretched out to dry, soup warm in
its tureen on the officers' table. The nights were sumptuous.
The Caribbean Sea was filled with phosphorescences drifting
tamely toward the coast, visible against the profiles of the
mountains softly lit by a waxing quarter moon. Sofía was entranced by the spectacles this journey offered to her eyes, with
its straying vegetation, peculiar fish, green lightning, and prodigious sunsets throwing allegories across a sky where every
cloud resembled a sculpted frieze—warring Titans, Laocoön,
chariots, fallen angels. Here she marveled at a coral reef; there
she saw the snoring islands, the low deep voice of their caverns
resonant of gravel that would never stop rolling. She was unsure whether to believe the holothurians swallowed sand, or if
it was true that whales descended to the tropics. But everything seemed plausible on this journey. One evening, they
showed her a strange fish, the Sea Unicorn, and it reminded her
of Victor's first appearance in the House with the Door Knockers. She had asked him jokingly back then if there were mermaids in the Caribbean Sea. "That night, I was nearly sent
packing," Victor said. "More than once I was tempted," Sofía
said, letting the phrase remain ambiguous, and not confessing
how painful this realization was now when, each time they
brushed past each other in the narrow hallways or on the steep
stairs, she would slow her pace, waiting absurdly for him to
seize her again. In the end, *that*, brutal as it was, had been the
one truly important thing—the only revelation—she had ever

known. She descended to the cabin and stretched out on her pallet. An irksome sweat soaked her bunched leggings; her blouse twisted aside and tugged unpleasantly at her breasts; the wool blanket on her bed chafed her skin; and she heard shouts and running on deck. Arranging herself as best she could, Sofía hurried to the gunwale to see the nature of the commotion. The ship was passing through a bale of turtles; two sailors, recently lowered in a boat, were trying to trap the largest of those slick swells. But the fins of sharks had appeared in the midst of their opulent carapaces, and now they were ramming the boat. The fishermen returned, cursing bitterly of all they might have had: brushes and combs, costly bookmarks and buckles. They took to hurling harpoons out of spite—as if the deaths of a few sharks could placate their timeworn rage against the species. The sailors bent over the railings, throwing fishhooks on chains, and the beasts bit them voraciously, snagging on barbs that poked through from their eye sockets. Dragged up from the water with tremors and a terrible flapping of tails, they flopped over the gunwales, and the crew pounded them with sticks, staffs, iron rods, even the bars from the capstan. Blood ran from their ruined hides, stained the water, speckled the sails, drained off toward the scuppers. "It's a good thing, what they're doing," Ogé shouted, striking them as well, "those fish are monsters." The whole crew had come out—some straddling the yardarm, others leaning toward whatever their hands could reach, armed with stakes, adzes, saws, brutally whipping chains or jabbing a hand drill, waiting for their chance to strike and wound, to sink in a hook. Sofía returned to her cabin to take off her blouse, stained by oil and bile in the tumult. In the little mirror beneath the window that served as a skylight, she saw Victor coming in. "It's me," he said, shutting the door. Above them, the shouting and blasphemy continued.

XI.

What uproar is this?

GOYA

Victor, leaning on the prow, looked incredulous when the ship dropped anchor in the port of Santiago. He saw the *Salamandre*, the *Vénus*, the *Vestale*, the *Méduse*, vessels that plied routes between Le Havre, Le Cap, and Port-au-Prince. With them was a multitude of smaller craft—hulks, schooners, sloops—which he knew belonged to the merchant fleets from Léogâne, Les Cayes, and Saint-Marc. "Has every ship in Saint-Domingue gathered here?" he asked Ogé, who failed, like him, to guess at the reasons for this unusual migration. Anchors cast, they hurried to land in search of news. What they discovered shocked them: three weeks before, the negroes had revolted in the North. The uprising had spread, and the authorities had lost control of the situation. The city was full of refugee colonists. There was talk of massacres of whites, of arson and torture, of horrifying rapes. The slaves had brutalized the daughters of the families, subjecting them to unspeakable cruelties. The country was given over to extermination, pillage, and lubricity . . . Captain Dexter, who had a small cargo bound for Port-au-Prince, would wait a few days, hoping for news to ease his mind. If the disorder continued, he would go directly to Puerto Rico and Suriname, avoiding Haiti. Victor, worried over the fate of his possessions, was uncertain what to do. Ogé, however, was calm: no doubt, the whole affair had been overstated. The correspondences with other events of far-reaching scale were too many for this to be a simple rebellion of barbarians in a fervor of rape and arson. People had likewise spoken of frenzied mobs, drunk on blood, after a certain July 14 that was now transforming the world. Among the most distinguished officials in the colony was his brother Vincent, like him educated in France, a member of the Society of the Friends of the Blacks in Paris, an esteemed philanthropist; he would have known to contain these insurrectionary masses if they were pouring into the streets and fields clamoring for something other than their just due. Many of these men were like Vincent, steeped in philosophy, conscious of what the times demanded. There was nothing to do but wait a bit; as the days passed, what had happened would become clear. If Dexter was insistent that he wouldn't travel to Port-au-Prince, no matter, the ships now seeking safe harbor in Santiago soon would. A journey to the neighboring island onboard one of them would be a pleasurable jaunt . . . In the meanwhile, they would have to deal with the heat, which seemed to seep up from the orlop, from the hold, from the hatches, from the very timbers of the *Arrow*, when the ship, sails furled, stood anchored in the harbor—the harbor of Santiago, and moreover in the month of September. An inescapable smell of warm tar invaded the cabins and passageways, but not enough to mask the vapors of potato peels, rancid fat, and waste water from washing dishes, which rose up to the deck from the kitchens. Worst of all, there was no way to take refuge onshore. No lodging was available in the city: refugees had filled the pensions, the hostels, and inns, contenting themselves with a billiard table in place of a bed or even an armchair shoved into a corner where they could pass the night. People mobbed the cathedral stairway and defended tooth and nail that stretch of cool stone that served them as a mattress. Ogé and Esteban slept on the *Arrow*'s deck, waiting for dawn to take the first boat to land in the hope of finding relief in the streets and their little houses painted pink, blue, or orange, with wooden railings and studded doors that evoked the early days of colonialism—when Hernando Cortés, still a modest mayor, sowed the first vines brought from Spain in the recently discovered Antilles. They would lunch in some tavern on whatever they could find—even the staples were lacking—before seeking out the picturesque shelter with thatched palm roofs that French swindlers, shrewd in profiting from turmoil, had raised in the port of Santiago like an afternoon fairground. Esteban was surprised that neither Sofía nor Victor cared to accompany him on his rambles through the city. But even with the stifling heat, they chose to stay onboard the *Arrow*, which remained empty otherwise in those days of forced immobility; at the first opportunity, the crew went to shore, returning at nightfall or sometimes well after, drunk and uproarious in their canoes. Sofía said the temperature kept her awake till dawn, when she'd drag herself to bed just as the others were starting to wake. At sunrise, Victor would sit in the forecastle, facing the city, at work on the voluminous correspondence related to his company. And so various days passed—with some on land, others onboard, some maddened by the fetor of the ship, others failing to notice it—until, one morning, Dexter announced that a North American vessel had arrived the night before from Port-au-Prince and informed him that the island was in the grips of revolution. They could wait no more; he would set sail in midafternoon, traveling on without stopping at the island of Saint-Domingue. After gathering their things and lunching on Westphalia ham washed down with beer so warm the foam clung to the glasses, the travelers took leave of the philanthropist captain and the rest of the men from the *Arrow*. Sitting on their luggage at one of the gateways to the port, they considered their situation. Ogé knew of a rickety Cuban sailboat leaving for Port-au-Prince the next morning with a fleet of local merchants to bring back refugees. It would be best for Sofía to stay in Santiago while the three men departed. If the situation was different from what it seemed—and Ogé insisted that the events must correspond to something more complex and nobler than the zeal for pillage—Esteban would return on the same ship and retrieve his cousin. Ogé was confident, moreover, in the authority of his brother Vincent, whom he'd had no word from for months but who held, he knew, a very important post in the colonial administration. For Victor, there was no question of staying: his business, his home, his merchandise were all in Port-au-Prince. Sofía asked them angrily to take her, promising not to be a burden; she wouldn't need a cabin of her own; she wasn't afraid. "It's not a matter of fear," said Esteban. "We can't expose you to the dangers hundreds of women there have faced." Victor agreed. If life was possible on the island, they would come back for her. If not, he would leave Ogé behind to manage his affairs and would return to Santiago to wait out the storm. With all the French refugees in the city, no one would bother to see if the Victor Hugues there was the same one denounced in Havana as a Mason. Santiago was harboring hundreds of members of Lodges from Port-au-Prince, Le Cap, and Léogâne. Accepting the men's judgment, she stayed behind with Victor and their scattered luggage while Ogé and Esteban addressed the problem of finding her decent lodging. On board the *Arrow*—svelte and magnificent, with its slightly slanting rigging, its slender shrouds, its trembling ensigns—preparations were being made to depart, with a great bustling of sailors on deck.

The next morning, an old Cuban sloop with patched sails and a parlous appearance departed the port of Santiago, setting course along a coast where the hills grew ever higher. The ship seemed less to advance than to luff in struggle against the contrary currents . . . An interminable day slipped past, then a night with a moon so full that Esteban, at the foot of the mast in fitful sleep, thought twenty times that it was dawn. The sloop entered the maws of the Gulf of Gonâve, and soon sighted the coasts of an island where, Ogé said, the cascades' water granted women the power of orphic clairvoyance. Each year, they made a pilgrimage to that gleaming altar of the Goddess of Fertility and the Waters, submerging themselves in the foam that fell from the high rocks. Some would begin writhing and shouting in a trance, possessed by a spirit that dictated omens and prophecies—and these prophecies were fulfilled with startling veracity. "I'm surprised a doctor would believe all this," Victor said. "Doctor Mesmer," Ogé replied sarcastically, "has miraculously cured thousands in your cultured Europe, magnetizing water in vessels and inducing a state of inspiration in his patients of a kind the negroes here have known since time immemorial. It just happens he charges a fee for it, whereas the gods of Gonâve work for free. That's the only difference . . ." They traveled on along nebulous coasts as dusk proceeded. Victor, who had been impatient throughout the day, slept heavily—as though needing to recover from his expenditure of nervous energy—after a scant dinner of herring and biscuit. Esteban woke him just before dawn. The sloop was entering Port-au-Prince. The city center was in flames. A giant inferno reddened the sky and hurled ash over the surrounding hills. Victor told them to send down a boat right away, and soon he had stepped onto the fishermen's dock. Trailed by Esteban and Ogé, he crossed streets full of negroes carrying clocks, paintings, and furnishings salvaged from the flames. They came to a bare lot where charred boards stood smoking with scales of ash between tiny bonfires. He stopped, trembling, tense, sweat dripping down his forehead, his temples, and the nape of his neck. "Allow me to welcome you to my home," he said. "That was the bakery; this was the storehouse; behind it was my bedroom." He grabbed a half-burnt oaken board: "This made an excellent counter." His foot tripped against the plate of a scale, blackened by fire. He picked it up and gave it a long look. Then he threw it to the ground, where it clanged like a gong, lifting up a swirl of soot. "Pardon me," he said, and burst into sobs. Ogé left in search of family he had in the city.

The day was born beneath low clouds dense with smoke, embraced by the mountains encircling the gulf. Sitting on the oven from the bakery—the one thing identifiable amid the formlessness—Victor and Esteban watched the city recover its rhythms within the annihilation of the city itself. Peasants came in with fruits, cheeses, cabbage, and sheaves of cane to lay out in a market that had ceased to be a market. They arranged themselves where their posts had once stood, at open-air stands that obeyed an order, a topography now destroyed. The insurgents, after setting everything alight, appeared to have vanished. The calm of extinguished coals, cinders, and embers on the rubble-covered earth gave a bucolic aspect to the men hawking milk from their piebald goats, praising the fragrance of their jasmines and the excellence of their honeys. The giant at the end of the breakwater, holding up an enormous squid for sale, was transfigured into Cellini's Perseus. Several priests, quite far off, were pulling down the singed scaffolds of a church still under construction. Freighted pack mules followed their usual itineraries on streets that were no longer streets, veering off where going straight was no longer possible, pausing at the illusion of a corner where the tavern keeper had arranged his liquor bottles over boards propped on bricks. Victor surveyed and resurveyed with his gaze the site of his annihilated shop, strangely taken, in his suppressed rage, with the liberating feeling of owning nothing, of being left without a single belonging, without furniture, contracts, a book—without a yellowing letter whose words might give him solace. His life was at the zero point, without commitments to fulfill or debts to pay, suspended between a shattered past and an unimaginable tomorrow. New fires had broken out on the *mornes*: "Burn what's left to be burned, everything, and be done with it," he said. And he was still there, at midday, beneath the white splendor of the clouds stretching from hilltop to hilltop, when Ogé arrived. His face was hard, cut through with new wrinkles, and Esteban didn't recognize him. "Well done," Ogé said, his eyes sweeping over the vicinity of the fire. "You got exactly what you deserved." And at Victor's questioning, angry expression: "My brother Vincent was executed in the Place d'Armes at Cap Français: they beat him with iron bars until his body was broken. They say his bones sounded like a hammer cracking walnuts." "The insurgents?" Victor asked. "No. Your people," the doctor responded with eyes of immobile sternness, looking without looking. And in that deserted lot, he told his younger brother's dreadful tale. He had been selected for an important administrative role but had been stymied by the French colonialists' refusal to accept the decree of the National Assembly that had authorized educated negroes and mestizos to carry out public functions in Saint-Domingue. Weary of arguments and petitions, Vincent had taken up arms, leading a squadron of malcontents similarly aggrieved by the intransigence—the insubordination—of the whites. With the aid of another mestizo, Jean-Baptiste Chavannes, he marched on Cap Français. Routed in their first encounter, Vincent and Jean-Baptiste sought shelter in the Spanish part of the island. But there, the authorities took them prisoner, laid them in irons, and returned them under escort to the Cape. Placed in a cell in a public square, they were humiliated for days on end: insulted and spit on by all who didn't throw rubbish and buckets of waste on them as they passed. Soon, a scaffold was raised; the executioner grasped his iron rod, unleashing his fury on the legs, arms, and thighs of the captives. When he'd finished, they brought out the axe. To set an example, the young men's heads were placed on lances and paraded along the road to the Grande Rivière. The passing vultures, flying low, picked at the faces bruised from torture, which soon lost all human aspect—left mere sponges of flesh with scarlet pits, flourished by dissolute guards who stopped for a drink at every inn . . . "There is still far more to burn," Ogé said. "Tonight will be terrible. Leave as soon as you can . . . !" They went to the docks, where the wooden wharfs were charred for long stretches, and stepped across struts of fireproof quebracho. Underneath them floated corpses devoured by crabs. The Cuban sloop, full of refugees, had left without waiting another hour— as they heard from an old negro stubbornly mending his nets, as if even in the midst of this vast horror a tear in the weave were a problem of capital importance. All the ships were gone save one recent arrival whose crew had just learned of the events in Port-au-Prince; it was a frigate, a three-master with high gunwales, and countless boats were rowing toward it from the shore. "This is your only chance," Ogé said. "Go, before they eviscerate you." In a canoe so poorly built they had to bail it out with gourds, the black fisherman rowed them out to the *Borée*, but the captain, leaning overboard and hurling imprecations, refused to let them onboard. Then Victor made a strange sign—a sort of drawing in empty space—that quieted the seaman's oaths. He lowered a rope ladder, and soon they were on deck next to the man who had understood the ruined merchant's abstract imploration. The ship, bursting with refugees—stinking, feverish, sleepless, weary, sweating through their garments, scratching their scabs and lice; one beaten, one wounded, one raped—would set sail immediately for France. "There's no other solution," Victor said, seeing Esteban wavering at the magnitude of this unplanned journey. "If you stay, they'll kill you this very night," Ogé told him. "*Et vous?*" Victor asked. "*Pas de danger,*" the mulatto responded,

pointing at his dark cheeks. They embraced. And yet, Esteban
had the impression that the doctor was less affectionate than
on other occasions. There was a stiffness, a distance, a measure of seriousness between their bodies. "I'm sorry for what's
happened," Ogé said to Victor, as if, of a sudden, he represented the entirety of the country. And with a brief gesture of
leave-taking, he returned to the boat, where the fisherman was
pushing against the body of a horse with an oar, struggling to
shove it away. Soon, a thunder of drums broke out over Port-
au-Prince, rising to the peaks of the *mornes*. New fires grew in
the redness of the twilight. Esteban thought of Sofía, who must
be waiting pointlessly in Santiago—where she had lodged in
the home of some honorable merchants, former suppliers to
her father. But it was best this way. Ogé would get a sense of
what had happened. Carlos would go find her. The strange adventure beginning today was not the kind you could undertake
with a woman on a ship where whoever had to wash up would
do so in the open, in view of everyone—and there were many
other things that, necessarily, would be done in view of all. In
part unsettled, in part remorseful, Esteban was yet thrilled at
the incredible adventure ahead of him. He felt more robust,
more complete, more a man beside Victor Hugues. Back turned
to the city, as though proud of abandoning his past under a
mountain of ash, the Frenchman grew more French, speaking
French with another Frenchman, apprising himself of the latest
news from his country. All of it was interesting, unusual, extraordinary. But nothing was so remarkable, so sensational as
the King's flight and his arrest in Varennes. That was so tremendous, so hard for any mind to grasp, that even the words
King and *arrest* failed to coincide or constitute an immediate,
admissible possibility. A monarch arrested, shamed, humiliated, prisoner to a people he claimed to govern, but was unworthy of governing! The highest crown, the most illustrious
power, the loftiest scepter in the universe, with a gendarme to
either side of him. "To think I was dealing in contraband silks
while such things were happening in the world," said Victor,
bringing his hands to his head. "Just as back there, people were
witnessing the birth of a new humanity . . ." The *Borée*, pushed

by the night breeze, drifted beneath a sky of stars bright where the painted shadows of the Eastern mountains converged with the pure drawing of the constellations. The fires of before were now behind them. In the Orient arose, erect and magnificent, glimpsed by the eyes of understanding, a Pillar of Fire that guided the departed to every Promised Land.

CHAPTER TWO

XII.

The healthy and the sick.
GOYA

When he thought of his birth city, made remote and strange by the distance, Esteban could not help but evoke it in watercolor tones, its shadows accentuated by the prodigious light of all the illuminated things, the skies turning gravid with thunder and storm clouds, the narrow muddy streets where negroes bustled amid tar, tobacco, and salt meat. There was more coal than flames in that painting of a Tropic which from here appeared static, oppressive, and monotonous, with its endlessly reiterated paroxysms of color and its nights falling from the sky so one hurried to fetch the lamps—long nights stretched longer by the silence of people who drifted into sleep before the voice of the sentry chanted the hour, ten o' clock, in the name of most blessed Mary, conceived without sin, pray for us who have recourse to thee . . . Here, in the sumptuous elucidations of an incipient autumn that was portentously novel for a boy from an island where the trees were ignorant of the passage from green to scarlet and sepia, all was a riot of banderoles, a flourish of cockades and rosettes, flowers hawked on corners, thin shawls and skirts worn in civic ostentation, with a prodigious array of reds and blues. Esteban felt—after long years of undisturbed seclusion—that he had fallen into an enormous fair, its characters and adornments the inventions of a stage manager. Everything spun, lured, caught one's eye: the insistent din of chatty womenfolk, coachmen arguing across box seats, colossal foreigners, foul-mouthed lackeys, layabouts, blabbermouths, gossips, newspaper readers, debaters gathered in impassioned huddles with the spreaders of baseless rumors, the knows-better-than-anyones, the has-it-on-good-words, the saw-its, the was-there-and-now-is-here-to-tell-its—not to mention the ardent patriot deep in his cups, the journalist with three articles to his name, the policeman feigning a cold to justify his covered face, the anti-patriot in overdone patriotic dress hoping his attire won't stink of deception—all of them, at all hours, stoking the down-and-out masses with some riotous bit of news or other. The Revolution had suffused the Street with new life—the Street, a matter of enormous importance for Esteban, because that was where the Revolution lived and was observed. "Joy and exuberance of a free people," the boy thought, watching and listening; and he took pride in that title, *Foreign friend of Liberty*, that one and all bestowed on him. Another man might have soon grown used to this; but so suddenly pulled from the torpor of the tropics, he had the impression of being somewhere exotic—yes, that was the word—surrounded by an exoticism far more picturesque than that land of palm trees and sugarcane where he'd grown up, never thinking anything he saw was worthy of the term *exotic*. Exotic for him—truly exotic—were the flagstaffs and banners, the allegories and ensigns, the chargers with their wide rumps, as if pulled from a carousel dreamed up by Paolo Uccello, nothing like the bony, fickle nags—good sons of Andalusians, in the end—of his country. All was spectacle, pleasing to pause and admire: the café decorated in the Chinese manner, the tavern with a flag of Silenus mounted on a barrel. The open-air funambulists who copied the feats of famous acrobats and the dog shearer who'd set up shop on the riverbank. Everything was singular, unanticipated, amusing: the wafer vendor's suit, the display case of pins, the red-painted eggs, and the turkeys praised as "aristocratic" by the woman plucking feathers in the Market. Each shop was a theater, with a window for a stage: of lamb hocks over paper lace; of a perfumer too pretty for one to believe she lived from the few articles on display; of a fan maker, and of another beautiful woman, her breasts resting on the counter, offering revolutionary symbols sculpted in marzipan. Everything was beribboned, swathed, adorned, with candied dyes: Montgolfier balloons, lead soldiers, a print illustrating *The Death and Burial of the Invincible Marlborough*, here pronounced "Mambru." More than a revolution, he was in a gigantic allegory of revolution, a metaphor of revolution—a revolution waged elsewhere, based on hidden polarities, elaborated in underground councils, invisible to those most anxious to know. Esteban, apprised of names yesterday unknown, which moreover would change on the morrow, was unsure who was waging this revolution. In an instant, there emerged obscure figures from the provinces, former notaries, seminarians, lawyers without cases, even foreigners, and their stature grew within weeks. Too near to events, he was dazzled at the many faces newly arrived to the tribunes and clubs where he heard the bellows of youths little older than himself. The assemblies he attended, mingling with the public, offered no further information: unacquainted with the speakers, disconcerted by the torrential extravagance of their words, he marveled at them like a Laplander suddenly seated in the United States Congress. This one he admired for his adolescent impulsivity, the expedient severity of his steely verbiage; that one for the earthy inflections of his booming voice; the other, for an eloquence more caustic and incisive than the others'. Victor Hugues kept him poorly informed in those days, because they hardly saw each other. Both were living in a modest hotel, poorly lit and worse ventilated, where the stench of mutton, cabbage, and leek soup wafted in at all hours, along with the scent of rancid butter emanating from the threadbare carpets. At first, they had given themselves over to the pleasures of the capital, frequenting houses devoted to amusement and leisure, where Esteban, through many excesses and not a few attempts on his money purse, managed to tame the concupiscence typical of the many foreigners who reached the banks of the Seine. But after a while, Victor, bankrupt apart from what little he'd earned in Cuba, began to think of tomorrow, while Esteban wrote to Carlos, asking him for a letter of credit through the mediation of Messieurs Laffon of Bordeaux, purveyors of the Conde de Aranda's garnacha and moscatel. The Frenchman had acquired the habit of leaving early and disappearing until very late. Knowing his nature, Esteban refrained from asking questions; Victor was a man who would speak of achievements only once they'd been achieved and he had gone on to aspire to greater achievements still. Turning inward, Esteban let himself be guided by the rhythm of each day, following the drums of a parade of guards, entering the political clubs, joining impromptu protests, more French than the French, more rebellious than the rebels, clamoring for peremptory measures, draconian punishments, exemplary retribution. His favored newspapers were those of the extremists; his favored orators, the most implacable. Any rumor of a counterrevolutionary complot sent him out to the street, armed with the first kitchen knife he found. To the great irritation of the landlady at his hotel, he appeared one morning with all the neighborhood children in tow, carrying a fir shoot he planted solemnly in the courtyard, dubbing it the new Tree of Liberty. One day he took the floor in the Jacobin Club, shocking all present with the idea that it would suffice to bring the Revolution to the New World if they indoctrinated with the ideal of liberty the Jesuits expelled from the Overseas Possessions and wandering now through Italy and Poland . . . The booksellers in the neighborhood called him "the Huron," and, flattered by this sobriquet that united the memory of Voltaire and the image of America, he flouted the urbane customs of the ancien régime with frankness, coarse words, and pitiless judgments that at times even wounded the revolutionaries. "I'm perfectly pleased to raise hackles, to talk about rope in a hanged man's home," he liked to say, relishing his own intolerable crudeness. And on he went coining huronisms from one assembly to the next, one gossip-mill to the next, even in the clubs where the Spanish in Paris gathered: Masons and philosophers, philanthropists and secularists conspiring actively to take the Revolution to the Iberian Peninsula. They never tired of taking an inventory of cuckolded Bourbons, lecherous queens, and cretinous scions, reducing Spain with its backwardness to a somber assortment of nuns with stigmata, tales of miracles and rags, persecutions and outrages that reduced the territory between the Pyrenees and Ceuta to a pestilent netherworld of reaction. They compared this slumbering, benighted country to enlightened France, whose Revolution had been greeted, applauded, acclaimed by men like Jeremy Bentham, Schiller,

Klopstock, Pestalozzi, Robert Bruce, Kant, and Fichte. "But it's not enough to take the Revolution to Spain; we must also bring it to America," Esteban said in these meetings, to the approval of one Feliciano Martínez de Ballesteros, who had come from Bayonne and amused him with his witty anecdotes and his occasional whim of singing *tonadillas* by Blas de Laserna while playing the tune with panache on an old clavichord resting in the corner. It was a wonder hearing Spaniards gather around the instrument, each shouting over the other to intone the verse that ran:

> In days of yore, Muhammad would take
> His drinks with zeal, shouting one more pour,
> He'd empty his cup and later would wake,
> Hung over on the floor,
> Hung over on the floor.

To a man, they flaunted a vest with the word *Liberty* sewn in its lining with red thread, forbidden by Royal Disposition in Spain and its American domains. There were plans for invasions, uprisings in the provinces, landings in Cadiz or the Costa Brava, the election of enlightened ministers, the printing of imaginary newspapers, the composition of proclamations— all of which filled their nights with discussion and gave each the pleasure of listening to himself prattle, shattering chrismons and hurling crowns to the floor in pure Castilian verbiage, deriding all the members of the Iberian Dynasty as whores and bastards. Some regretted that the Prussian Anacharsis Cloots, Apostle of the Universal Republic, had presented himself at the bar of the Constitutional Assembly as Ambassador of the Human Race without including a single Spaniard in his retinue of Englishmen, Sicilians, Dutch, Russians, Poles, Mongols, Turks, Afghans, and Chaldeans, all in their national costume, and had instead contented himself, as a suitable representative of that neighboring country moaning under the noose and chains of despotism, with a nameless stand-in. And so Spain's voice had not been heard on that memorable occasion when even a Turk had taken the floor. "They can disdain us if they will, that doesn't make us nothing," Martínez de Ballesteros said, shrugging his shoulders. "Our time will come." For now, he knew of very valiant men who were prepared to go to France and place themselves in the service of the Revolution. Among them, young Abbot Marchena, a superior soul, to judge by the tone of his letters and a few poems he had sent translated from Latin . . . But Esteban did more than walk aimlessly through the streets, go to parades and civic celebrations, debate frantically until late into the night. One memorable day, he was initiated into the Lodge of United Foreigners, penetrating the vast fraternal laboring world that Victor had only revealed traces of. They illuminated the Temple for him, resplendent and arcane, where surrounded by the glimmer of swords, he was made to walk, tremulous and dazzled, toward the Columns of Jachin and Boaz, the Delta and the Tetragram, the Seal of Solomon, the Star of the Golden Ratio. There, enveloped in aureoles and emblems, were the Knights Kadosh, the Knights of the Rose Croix, the Knights of the Brazen Serpent, and the Knights of the Royal Arch, the Princes of the Tabernacle, the Princes of Lebanon, the Princes of Jerusalem, and the Grand Master Architect and the Sublime Prince of the Royal Secret; and, flooded by emotion, feeling unsuited to such honors, he initiated his ascent toward their degrees, advanced toward the mysteries of the Grail, the transformation of Rough into Perfect Ashlar, the Resurrection of the Sun in the Acacia conserved, recovered in the heart of a tradition which, regressing vertiginously in time, stretched from the great initiatic ceremonies in Egypt to Jakob Böhme, the Chymical Wedding of Christian Rosenkreutz, and the Secret of the Templars. Esteban had felt One with All, illuminated before the Ark that he now must rebuild in his own being, in homage to the Temple constructed by the master Hiram Abiff. He was in the center of the Cosmos; the Firmament opened over his head; his feet trod the path from Occident to Orient. Emerging from the shadows of the Chamber of Reflection, chest naked to reveal his heart, right leg bare, left foot exposed, the Apprentice responded to the three ritual questions of what Man Owed to God, Himself, and Others. Then, the lofty lights of a Century grew—a marvel he had walked toward blindly, as though borne by a superior will, from the time of that afternoon of Great Fires in Port-au-Prince. He grasped now the exact meaning of his hallucinated voyage—like Percival's journey in search of himself—toward a Future City which, lay not in America, like Thomas More's Utopia or Campanella's City of Sun, but instead in the very cradle of Philosophy . . . That night, unable to sleep, he walked until morning through the old quarters with their patina of damp, over tortuous and unfamiliar streets. Peaked roofs loomed over him on unimagined corners like the prows of giant ships without masts or sails, capped with chimneys that stood out against the sky with the ancient elegance of knights bearing arms. Scaffolds and signs emerged from the shadows, iron letters, drowsing flags in the penumbra, only hinting at the exact nature of their forms. Here stood lines of wagons for the market; there a wheel hung over the tangled wicker of half-woven baskets. The muzzle of a ghostly Percheron twitched in the heart of a courtyard where a cart raised its shafts in a ray of moonlight with the unsettling immobility of an insect aiming its barbs. Following the route of the old pilgrims to Santiago, Esteban stopped at the end of the street. The sky seemed to be waiting for someone to top the hill, bequeathing the scent of reaped wheat, the good augur of clover, the warm, damp breath of wine grapes trampled in vats. He knew it was an illusion; that further up lay other houses, and many more where the suburbs wove together. And so, stopping where he had to stop to retain the privileges of this celestial perspective, he contemplated what men had contemplated for centuries, singing canticles with their scallop shells, pilgrims' staffs, and pelerines, dragging their sandals over this route, feeling the Portico of Glory nearer as the days separated them from the Hôpital à Saint-Hilaire in Poitiers, the resinous Landes, the repose of Bayonne, the convergence of the Four Paths at Puente de la Reina, beyond the Valle de Aspe. They had passed through there year after year, generation after generation, driven by irrepressible fervor, marching toward the sublime work of Master Mateo, who had certainly been a Mason—about this there could be no doubt—like Brunelleschi, Bramante, Juan de

Herrera, and Erwin Steinbach, architect of the cathedral of Strasbourg. Dwelling on his initiation, Esteban felt ignorant and frivolous. An entire literature essential to his perfection was unknown to him. Tomorrow he would buy the necessary books, supplementing for himself the elementary lessons he had received . . . No longer so sensitive to the revolutionary tumult that shook the streets at all hours, he spent long nights studying, learning more of the occult but undeniable transit of the Ternary across time. One day—around seven—Victor found him already awake, dreaming of the star Wormwood from Revelations; earlier he had immersed himself in the prose of *The Coming of the Messiah in Majesty and Glory* by Juan Josafat Ben-Ezra, an author whose name, beneath its Arabic flourishes, concealed an active brother in their cause from the Americas. "Are you willing to work for the Revolution?" a friendly voice asked him. Snatched from his distant meditations, returned to the immediate reality which was, in essence, no more than the first of the Great Traditional Aspirations, he said yes, proudly, enthusiastically; he would brook no doubts as to his fervor, his longing to strive on Liberty's behalf. "Ask for me at ten in the office of Citizen Brissot," said Victor, in a finely tailored suit and boots that still squeaked like sheets of cordovan leather in a storehouse. "Ah! And if it comes up, not a word about Freemasonry. If you wish to join us, you'd best not set foot in another Lodge. We've wasted too much time on that hogwash." At the sight of Esteban's astonished expression, he added: "Freemasonry is counterrevolutionary. This is not open for discussion. Jacobin morals are the only morals." Grabbing an edition of the *Apprentice's Catechism* lying on the table, he broke it along the spine and dropped it into the wastebasket.

XIII.

Brissot received Esteban at ten-thirty, and by eleven he was on a road to the Spanish border, one of the old routes of the Way of Saint James. "Freedom must give me sandals, and a ribbon

shall be my scallop shell," said the young man, satisfied with
that sudden burst of rhetoric, when he learned what was expected of him. In those days, there was a need for men who
wrote well in Spanish and could translate documents from
French so that revolutionary writings could be disseminated in
Spain. Printing was already underway in Bayonne and wherever else there were presses near the Pyrenees. Abbot José
Marchena, who had the ear of Brissot and was widely praised
for his talents and Voltairean sarcasm, advised haste in getting
their doctrine to the Peninsula, to kindle at last a revolution
that was imminent, and would flare up soon in other nations
thirsting to break the odious chains of the past. For Marchena,
Bayonne—not to disdain Perpignan—"was the ideal place to
gather the Spanish patriots wishing to work for the regeneration
of their country," but they needed the collaboration of intelligent people who understood that "the language of regenerated
Republican Frenchmen is not yet suitable for the Spanish," who
would have to "be prepared gradually," respecting, for a time,
"certain ultramontane prejudices, incompatible with liberty,
but too deeply rooted to be destroyed with one blow." "Is that
clear?" Victor had asked Esteban, as if taking responsibility
for his protégé before Brissot. The young man, clutching his
staff, had replied with a brief but credible discourse laden with
Spanish quotations which showed not only that he agreed with
Marchena, but that he could moreover express himself as lu-
cidly in the French language as in his own . . . And yet, after a
few hours, considering his destination, it struck him that the
mission they'd entrusted him with wasn't an especially enviable one: departing from Paris just then was like abandoning
the Grand Theater of the World for exile to the hinterlands.
"This is no time to complain," Victor said harshly, on hearing
the young man's misgivings. "Soon, I will be sent to Rochefort
for a time. I, too, would prefer to stay. But we all must go
where we are sent." There followed three days of carousing, of
lavish meals and dalliances with ladies, and this brought the
two men closer once more. Esteban spoke openly to Victor, incapable of hiding that, despite the Frenchman's admonition to
forget about Freemasonry, his time with the Lodge of United

Foreigners had left him with many pleasant memories. They had dubbed him Young Brother from America and given him a toga at his initiation. Nor could one say a healthy democratic mentality didn't reign in a place where a Charles Constantine of Hesse-Rotenburg addressed as his peers a swarthy patriot from Martinique, an old Jesuit from Paraguay nostalgic for his communitarian mission, a Brabantian typesetter expelled from his country for publishing proclamations, or a Spanish exile, peddler by day and orator by night, who claimed Freemasonry had been active in Avila since the sixteenth century, as attested to by certain images of compasses, draftsman's squares, and mallets found recently—so he said—in the Church of Our Lady of the Assumption, constructed by the Jewish master builder Robin de Braquemonte. They had heard music there by an inspired Mason composer, Mosar or Matzarth or something along those lines, when a Viennese baritone sang his hymns in the initiation ceremony, embellishing with rich fermatas the melodies of *Oh heiliges Band der Freundshaft treuer Brüder* or the invocation: "*Die ihr des unermeßlichen Weltalls Schöpfer ehrt, Jehova nennt ihn, oder Gott, nennt Fu ihn, oder Brahma.*" He had made contact with interesting men who saw revolution as a victory of a material and political order that would culminate in the total victory of Man over himself. Esteban remembered Ogé when certain brothers, Danish and Swiss, spoke of the splendid court of the Prince of Hesse—and Charles Constantine, always a great gentleman, confirmed their accounts—where somnambulists were asked about the Fall of the Angels, the building of the Temple, or the chemical composition of Aqua Tofana. In the court at Schleswig, miraculous cures were effected through magnetism, turning birches, walnuts, firs into streams of beneficent fluids. The doors that concealed the vision of the future were forced open, with consideration of the respective virtues of the oracles yielded by the eighty-five forms of traditional divination, which included bibliomancy, crystallomancy, gyromancy, and xylomancy. Extreme sophistication was reached in the interpretation of dreams. And automatic writing allowed dialogue with the deep self, aware of its former lives, that lay hidden inside every man. This procedure revealed that the Grand Duchess of Darmstadt had wept at Golgotha, at the foot of the cross, and that the Grand Duchess of Weimar had witnessed the Judgment of the Lord in the Palace of Pilate; and for years the philosopher Lavater had been certain he was formerly Joseph of Arimathea. On certain nights, the chandeliers of the magic castle of Gottorp—enveloped in mists that dampened the wrappings of its Egyptian mummies—descended over the tables where, with gentlemanly calm, a Count of Bernstorff, reincarnation of the Apostle Thomas, played cards with Louis of Hesse, who recalled his life as John the Baptist, and Christian of Hesse, who had been the Apostle Bartholomew in earlier days. Prince Charles was frequently absent from these evenings, preferring to lock himself away and *work*, gazing so intensely at a piece of metal the Greeks called the *Electronum* that tiny clouds appeared before his eyes, and he interpreted their shapes as warnings and signs from the Other Shore . . . "Balderdash!" Victor exclaimed, irritated at this talk of portents. "When there are so many *real* things to consider, wasting time on this swill runs counter to the Revolution. We were fortunate to see quickly what lay in back of that Solomonic masquerading: traitors eager to turn their back to the age, distracting the people from their most urgent obligations. Further, the Masons preach moderation in the name of their brotherhoods, and that is a crime. We must look upon all moderates as enemies . . ." Esteban made connections that resolved the mystery of Victor's earlier relations with Freemasonry: his silk supplier, Jean-Baptiste Willermoz, Grand Chancellor of the Convent of the Gauls, a man esteemed by the Princes of Hesse, was the leader of an order that had drifted toward mysticism and Orphism under the influence of the enlightener Martinez de Pasqually, who died in Saint-Domingue. This enigmatic Portuguese Jew had founded chapters in Port-au-Prince and Léogâne, winning over the minds of men who, like Ogé, were beguiled by esoteric speculation; but his hermeticism vexed the former merchant and others more inclined to political subversion. Respecting Willermoz's prestige as a philanthropist and industrialist—he employed thousands of

workers in his factories in Lyon—Victor had acceded to the essential principles of the doctrine and was initiated in accordance with the Grand Orient Rite; but—and this was the
origin of his disputes with Ogé—he doubted Martinez de
Pasqually's spiritualist practices and his boasts of being able to
communicate across great distances with his disciples in Europe using only the power of his mind . . . "Those magicians
and seers were nothing but a band of *emmerdeurs*," Victor
said, and nowadays, he prided himself on being a man with his
feet planted firmly on the ground. Often he took the floor at
the Jacobin Club, where he rubbed elbows with Billaud-
Varenne and Collot d'Herbois, and had even once or twice run
across Maximilien de Robespierre, whom he held supreme
among the revolutionary tribunes, rendering him an homage
so impassioned that Esteban, hearing this immoderate praise
of his eloquence, his notions, his carriage, even his sartorial
grace in the otherwise slovenly and unrefined assemblies,
joked: "I see he's a sort of Don Juan, but for other men." Victor, hostile to such raillery, replied with an irate obscenity,
bringing his hand to the seam of his breeches.

After a long and meandering voyage on muddy roads, with
pinecones crunching under carriage tires, Esteban arrived at
Bayonne and placed himself at the disposition of those who
were preparing to incite revolution in Spain: the ex-sailor
Rubín de Celis, the mayor Bastarreche, and the journalist
Guzmán, a friend of Marat and contributor to *L'Ami du Peuple*. It struck him disappointingly that his unknown face, his
yearning for immediate action, were unwanted in a place
where many professed a Jacobinism hindered by Hispanic scruples, virulent with regard to whatever concerned France, but
tame and wary when their eyes turned toward the River Bida-
soa. They soon sent him off to Saint-Jean-de-Luz, now called
Chauvin-Dragon to honor the memory of a son of the town, a
heroic Republican soldier. The printing press there was small
but energetic, devoted to issuing endless proclamations and
revolutionary texts chosen by Abbot Marchena. Marchena
was a skilled agitator, ever clutching his pen to follow the

rhythm of events, but he rarely made his way to the border country these days and spent most of his time in Paris, where he had
frequent meetings with Brissot. Believing himself friendless on
those shores, Esteban was pleased one night to meet a solitary
fisherman on the banks of the Untxin, and he greeted him with
delight: the intelligent former Mason Feliciano Martínez de Ballesteros, raised to the rank of Colonel and overseeing a corps of
Miquelets known as "the Huntsmen of the Mountains," who
would combat Spanish troops in any eventual incursions and
incite them to join the cause of the Republic. "We must be prepared," he said. "In our country, blackguardism is running ram-
pant: just look at our Godoys and our Bourbon whores." Esteban
took long walks with that jocose man from Logroño through
villages that had changed their names in recent days: Ixtasson
was now called Unión; Arbonne, Constance; Ustarritz, Marat-
sur-Nive; Baigorry, Les Thermopyles. In those first weeks, the
young man admired the rustic Basque churches with their short,
pugnacious belfries, their vegetable plots bordered with slabs of
stone sunken in the dirt. He stopped to watch a herder goad a
team of oxen, a sheepskin stretched over the yoke; they crossed
the bridges with their backs arched, stomping vexed over torrents
of water and snow, pulling up, as they passed, the orange-tinted
mushrooms growing in the cracks between the stones. The architecture of the dwellings charmed him: indigo blue beams, softly
sloping roofs, wrought-iron anchor bolts sunken in the masonry.
The mountains from the Carolingian romances, eroded to
sharp counterforts on paths where harried flocks of handsome
sheep roved around an outcropping the paladin Roland might
have gazed on long before, and the pastureland—above all the
pastureland, damp and soft, the bright green of a green apple
while at the same time resembling nothing but itself—inspired
thoughts in him of the bucolic destiny revolutionary principles
would return to men. And yet, as he came to know them better, the people somehow disillusioned him; these phlegmatic
Basques, with bulls' necks and equine profiles, lifters of stones,
fellers of trees, and navigators in no way inferior to the men
who had searched for Iceland and were the first to watch the

sea harden into floes, were unshakably loyal to their traditions. They could not be outfoxed: they carried wafers in their berets, hid bells in haylofts and kilns, and furtively built altars on farms, in the backrooms of cafés, in a cave guarded by sheepdogs—wherever one least expected—to hold their clandestine Masses. When ruffians shattered the idols in the cathedral of Bayonne, the Bishop found people willing to take him across the border to Spain with his monstrance, cincture, and baggage. It had been necessary to shoot a girl who took Mass at Villa de Vera. Accused of sheltering and protecting recalcitrant clerics, the population of the border towns was deported in its entirety to Landes. The fishermen who lived in Chauvin-Dragon went on calling it Saint-Jean-de-Luz, and Saint Stephen went on protecting Baigorry in the minds of those who tilled its soil. La Soule never lost its zeal for bonfires on Saint John's Eve nor its medieval-looking dances, and no one there would have dared to denounce a neighbor for praying the rosary or crossing themselves when they mentioned the witches of Zugarramurdi . . . Two months Esteban had spent in that alien world, insidious, shifting, surrounded by the Basque language, which he would never grasp and which could never be deciphered by examining the faces of its speakers, when he was stunned by the news of war with Spain. Now he would never cross over to Iberia to witness the birth of a new nation, as he had dreamed when he heard the hopeful words of Martínez de Ballesteros, with his endless predictions of imminent uprisings among the people of Madrid. He was prisoner in a France blocked by English squadrons on the Atlantic side, with no possibility of returning to the country of his family. Before now, he'd never thought of returning to Havana, wishing to play a part, however small, in a Revolution destined to change the world. But the thwarting of this mission was enough to ignite an almost painful longing for home and his people, for different lights and flavors from another world, and a hatred for the tasks assigned him—which were nothing more, in the end, than bureaucratic tedium. It wasn't worth it, coming so far to see a Revolution and then not to see it; to remain the listener in a nearby park overhearing the fortissimos from an opera house he'd been barred from entering.

Months passed, and Esteban tried to make himself useful in his monotonous labors. In Spain, none of what was expected ever occurred. Even the war in that part of France had been languid and mundane, going no further than defensive patrols by the heavy contingents General Ventura Caro had placed along the border and refused to move despite his army's numerical superiority. At night, rifle fire sounded in the mountains, but at most there were a few skirmishes or brief encounters between reconnaissance units. A long summer passed, sunny and tranquil; the autumn winds returned; the beasts went back to the stables with the first winter winds from the north. With time, Esteban found that the distance from Paris filled him with confusion, and he lost sight of the processes of a politics in constant mutation—inconsistent, self-devouring, prone to fits, complicated by committees and mechanisms that could hardly be grasped from afar, with news constantly arriving of unexpected developments, of the rise of unknown personages or the treacherous fall of some notable who only yesterday drew comparison with the great statesmen of ancient days. Regulations, laws, decrees rained down, annulled or contravened by emergency measures no sooner than the province had adopted them. Weeks were extended to ten days in length; the months were named Brumaire, Germinal, Fructidor, and didn't correspond to the old ones; new weights and measures were instituted, disconcerting those accustomed to talking in terms of fathoms, palms, and bushels. No one could say what was actually happening, nor which men they should trust, in a place where the French Basques felt closer to the Spanish Navarrese than to the officials from the remote North who abruptly imposed strange calendars or changed the names of cities. The war would be a long one because it wasn't a war like others, waged to placate a Prince's ambitions or lay claim to foreign territories. "The kings understand," men shouted in the Jacobin tribunals, "that the Pyrenees are no obstacle to philosophical ideas: there are millions of men on the march ready to change the face of the

world . . ." And March came—for Esteban, March would forever remain March, however much he had liked the ring of the
new calendar's Nivôse and Pluviôse. An ashen March under lattices of rain that sheathed the Ciboure hills in diffuse silk, giving a ghostly aspect to the boats returning to port after fishing
in the verdigris sea, shaken and sad, its unhorizoned distances
dissolving in a misty, whitish sky, still entrenched in winter. Deserted beaches were visible through the window of the room
where the young man carried out his duties as translator and
corrector of proofs, surrounded by stakes where the ocean deposited dead algae, broken boards, shreds of sailcloth after evening storms that roared through the gaps in the shutters and
whipped the creaking, lichen-covered weathervanes. In the former Place Louis XVI, now Place de la Liberté, they erected the
guillotine. Far from the stage where it had taken part in a Transcendental Tragedy, far from the square splashed with the blood
of a monarch, the machine, washed with rain—not frightful,
merely ugly; not fateful, merely viscous and sad—gave the sorry
impression, when put to use, of a makeshift theater in the provinces, with itinerant actors struggling to mimic the grandeur of
productions in the capital. Fishermen carrying traps stopped to
watch the executions, or three or four passersby with quizzical
expressions, spitting tobacco juice between their teeth, or a
boy, a maker of rope sandals, a squid vendor; they would go
back on their way at the same pace as before when the body of
whomever it was began to spit blood like wine from the spout
of a wineskin. It was March. An ashen March under lattices of
rain that made the hay swell in the stables, streaked goats' fur
with mud, sent up from kitchen chimneys acrid smoke clouds
smelling of garlic and dense oils. Esteban had heard nothing of
Victor for months. He knew he had occupied, with a cruel
hand, the post of Public Accuser in the Revolutionary Tribunal
of Rochefort. He had asked—and of this, Esteban approved—
that the guillotine be placed in the same hall as the tribunals, to
save time between sentence and execution. Deprived of Victor's
warmth, his rigor, his ardor, of the glow of direct contact with
a Billaud or Collot—with one, with any of the leading lights of
the Hour-he-was-living-through, which was not the same as

the hour where he was stationed—Esteban had the sense he was diminishing, wilting, losing all personality; that Circumstance had absorbed him, and his humble contributions were irremediably anonymous. Feeling so negligible, he longed to cry. In his grief, he yearned for Sofía's soft lap, where he had rested his head so many times, in search of that sustaining, maternal force that brimmed in her virgin entrails as if from a true mother . . . And then he really did start to cry, meditating on his solitude, his uselessness, just before he saw Coronel Martínez de Ballesteros enter his bedroom-office. The chief of the Miquelets of the mountains was agitated, stiff, his hands sweaty and trembling—recent news had evidently shaken him.

XIV.

"I've had it with these frog eaters!" the Spaniard shouted, collapsing onto Esteban's pallet. "More than had it! God damn every one of them!" He closed his hands over his face, remaining a long time in silence. The young man served him a cup of wine, and he drank it in one draft then asked for another. He stood and paced from wall to wall, talking chaotically of what had raised his ire. He had just been dismissed from his military post—relieved, *re-lieved*, by some commissar or other from Paris who had been granted unlimited powers to reorganize the troops in the region. His misfortune was an effect of the hostility against foreigners that had been growing in Paris and was now reaching the frontier: "First they defamed the Masons, now they're trampling the best friends the Revolution has." It was said that Abbot Marchena, in hiding from his pursuers, might find himself in the guillotine at any moment: "He, who did so much for the cause of freedom." The French had overtaken the Bayonne committee, driving out the Spaniards— one for being too moderate, one because he was a Mason, another on account of his suspicious character. "Watch out, my friend, you, too, are a foreigner. In a matter of months, just being a foreigner in France will be a crime." Martínez de Ballesteros continued with his unhinged monologue: "While they were dawdling in Paris, dressing their whores up like the Goddess of Reason, they lost their big opportunity to bring the Revolution to Spain. They were too inept for it, too invidious. Well, they can sit and wait . . . and as for their ideas of universal revolution, all that's gone out the window! Now it seems the *French* Revolution is all that matters! As for the rest . . . let them rot! Everything we're doing here is useless. They make us translate a Declaration of the Rights of Man into Spanish, and every day they violate twelve of its seventeen principles. They stormed the Bastille to free four forgers, two madmen, and a sodomite, then they built a prison in Cayenne far worse than any Bastille . . ." Esteban, afraid a neighbor might hear him, alleged a need to buy writing paper to get the frenzied man outside. Passing the former home of Haraneder, they went to the Librairie de la Trinité, which had opportunely remade its signage and was known now as the Librairie de la Fraternité. It was a poorly lit shop with low ceilings, and from midmorning on, an oil lamp hung lit from its beams. Esteban spent hours there leafing through new books in an atmosphere somehow reminiscent of the back of the warehouse in Havana, with those dusty accumulated objects they'd dug through to find the armillary spheres, planispheres, mariners' telescopes, and physics contraptions. Martínez de Ballesteros shrugged looking at a collection of engravings that evoked the highlights of the history of Greece and Rome: "Today, every scoundrel thinks he's made of the same stuff as the Gracchi, Cato, or Brutus," he murmured. Walking to a battered pianoforte, he leafed through François Giroust's latest songs, published by Frère, which were written in a simple-to-grasp notation and widely sung to the accompaniment of guitars. He showed Esteban the titles: "The Tree of Liberty," "Hymn to Reason," "Despotism Crushed," "The Nursemaid of the Republic," "Hymn to Saltpeter," "The Rousing of the Patriots," "Chant of the Thousand Gunsmiths." "Even music must bow down to reason," he said. "They think now whoever writes a sonata has failed his revolutionary duties. Grétry himself beats us over the head with the *Carmagnole* at the end of his ballets to show off his civic spirit." And in a kind of protest against François Giroust's offerings, he attacked the allegro of a sonata with infernal brio, discharging his fury on the keys. "I'd do well not to play music by a Freemason like Mossar," he said, bringing the piece to an end. "There might well be an informant hiding under the lid." Esteban purchased his paper and left, followed by the Spaniard, who didn't wish to remain alone with his spite. Despite the frozen rain now falling, an executioner in a beret was uncovering the guillotine, waiting for some convict to stretch out his neck without any witnesses on hand, apart from the guards who were posted at the base of the scaffold. "Chop away," Martínez de Ballestero raved, "extermination—in Nantes, in Lyon, in Paris, extermination." "After it's been bathed in blood, humanity will emerge regenerated," said Esteban. "Don't go quoting foreigners to me, I don't want to hear a word about Saint-Just and his reddened Sea (*Sen Yu* he called him, he'd never gotten the pronunciation right), that's cheap rhetoric and nothing more," Martínez replied. They crossed the inevitable carriage, which was carrying a priest, hands bound, to the scaffold. Walking along the quay, they stopped at a fishing boat with sardines and tunas flapping on deck around a grayish ray straight from a Flemish still life. Martínez de Ballesteros pulled out an iron key he carried on his watch chain and threw it scornfully into the water. "A key to the Bastille," he said. "Counterfeit, to boot. The bastard locksmiths forge them by the dozen. These talismans are all over the world now. We've got more keys to the Bastille than there are splinters of the true cross . . ." Looking toward Ciboure, Esteban noted an unusual movement of people on the road to Hendaye. In disorder, in scattered groups, soldiers from the Huntsmen of the Pyrenees regiment were arriving, some singing, but all of them so weary—so eager to climb up on a cart of some kind and rest their feet—that the carolers could only persist under the influence of drink. They looked like a stampede of deserters, undirected, ignored by the officers on horseback who had already reached this part of the bay and were dismounting in front of a café to dry their wet clothes by the heat of a hearth. Visceral fear overtook Esteban at the thought that those troops might be returning in defeat—routed, perhaps, by the enemy forces under the command of the Marquis of Saint-Simon, head of a band of émigrés that had been expected to attack audaciously for some time. Looking closely at the new arrivals, though, he saw mud and damp but little evidence of battle scars. While the sick and sniffling looked for shelter from the drizzle under the eaves or by pressing close to the walls, the rest reveled more raucously, passing around their rations of brandy, herring, and bread. The sutlers were setting up their grills, pulling dense smoke from the wet firewood, when Martínez de Ballesteros approached a cannoneer with a strand of garlic over his shoulder to ask the reason for that unforeseen movement of troops. "We're going to America," said the soldier, drawing out a word that immediately acquired a solar gleam in Esteban's mind. Trembling, anxious, with the almost irritable expectancy of a person excluded from festivities on his own domains, the young man and the decommissioned colonel entered the tavern where the officers were resting. Soon they learned this regiment was destined for the Antilles. Others would arrive there to join an armada being formed in Rochefort. They would depart in small vessels on successive journeys, hewing to the coast; the English blockade made such prudence necessary. Two commissars from the Convention would join the ships: Chrétien and a certain Victor Hugues, who was, they said, an old sea dog, familiar with Caribbean waters, where even then a powerful British squadron was marauding . . . Esteban walked out to the square, afraid to miss an opportunity to flee a place he felt threatened—and aware that the futility of his duties would soon be evident to those paying him. He sat on a stone step, oblivious to the icy wind tautening his cheeks: "Since Hugues is your friend, do what you can to get him to take you. He's a powerful man now that he's got Dalbarade's support—Dalbarade, we knew him when he was commissar in Biarritz. You're going to seed here. The papers you translate are piling up in a cellar. And keep in mind, you're a *foreigner*." Esteban shook his hand: "What will you do now?" The other responded, with a resigned look: "The same as always, despite everything. Once you've waged revolution, it's hard to go back to what you did before."

After composing a long letter to Victor Hugues—copied out several times and dispatched to the Naval Ministry, the Revolutionary Tribunal of Rochefort, and a fellow Freemason he'd once known, whom he urged to pass it along to its addressee wherever he might be—Esteban waited for his pleas to bear fruit. In plain terms, he depicted himself as a victim of administrative indifference, of disunion among the Spanish Republicans, blaming his work's scarce impact on the mediocrity of the men who had succeeded one another in command. He complained of the climate, hinting that it might cause his former ailment to return. Tugging the cord of friendship, he invoked the memory of Sofía and the distant house where they "had lived together like brothers." He ended with an exhaustive enumeration of his abilities and their use to the cause of revolution in America. "You know, moreover," he concluded, "that the foreigner's situation is far from enviable in these days and times." He added, thinking of those who might intercept his letter: "Some Spaniards in Bayonne, it appears, have lapsed into deplorable counterrevolutionary errors. This has required a purge in which, lamentably, the just may find themselves paying for the sins of others . . ." There followed anxious weeks of waiting, with a relentless fear that kept him far from Martínez de Ballesteros or any others who might make unseemly remarks on recent events in the presence of third parties. Abbot Marchena's whereabouts were unknown, and some said he had been guillotined. A Great Fear was poisoning the nights on the coast. Myriad eyes peered out into the streets from the cracked shutters of houses in shadows. Just before dawn, Esteban would leave his hotel on foot, taking to the nearby villages despite the falling rain, drinking rotgut in whatever inn he found, or in the seamstress shops where they sold bulk needles, a cowbell, a patch, buttons by the dozen, jars of marmalade packed in shavings—attempting in this way to overcome his apprehensions. He would return after nightfall, frightened of encountering an unknown visitor or a summons to report on some "matter of concern to him" at the Château-Vieux of Bay-onne, now transformed into a barracks and gendarmerie. So weary he was of that hermetic, silent country, now suffused with danger, that whatever parts of it might be thought beautiful repelled him: the walnuts and holm oaks, the homes of the lesser nobility, the flight of the white-tailed kites, the cemeteries full of strange crosses carved with solar runes . . . When a guard entered bearing a document, his trembling fingers couldn't tear the envelope. He had to break the seal with his teeth, which still obeyed his will. The handwriting was familiar to him. Giving precise instructions to hurry to Rochefort, Victor Hugues offered him a post as scribe in the armada soon to depart for the Île de Aix. Possessor of a document that would serve as a safe conduct, Esteban should depart Saint-Jean-de-Luz with a regiment of Basque huntsmen assigned to join the expedition—a hazardous expedition, committed to facing whatever challenges might arise, as they'd had no news from the French possessions in the Antilles and were uncertain whether the English had occupied them. Their destination, in theory, was the island of Guadeloupe, and if they were unable to disembark, they would sail on to Saint-Domingue . . . Victor embraced the young man coldly after their long separation. He was a bit thinner now, but his sculpted face reflected a vigor that had grown with his authority. Surrounded by officers, he was busy with the toil of the last preparations, studying maps and dictating letters in a room filled with weapons, surgeon's utensils, drums, and furled flags. "We'll talk later," he said, turning his back to read a dispatch. "Go speak to the quartermaster." Then he corrected himself, changing from *tu* to *vous*, though the former was generally embraced as a sign of revolutionary spirit. "Wait for my orders," he added, and Esteban realized Victor had imposed on himself the first commandment of a Leader of Men: not to have any friends.

XV.

That's tough.

GOYA

In Year II, on Floréal 4, without tumult or blasts from the
bugle, their small squadron departed: two frigates, the *Pique*
and the *Thétis*, the barque *L'Espérance*, and five regiments of
troops, among them one artillery company, two companies of
infantry, and the Battalion of the Huntsmen of the Pyrenees,
which Esteban had accompanied to Rochefort. Behind them
stood Île d'Aix with its turreted fortress and a convict ship, *Les
Deux Associés*, where more than seven hundred prisoners were
writhing in the hold, weary, sick, and mangy, pestilential, with
suppurating wounds, unable even to lie down as they waited for
deportation to Cayenne. The ships had set sail under a bad sign.
The latest news from Paris did nothing to rouse the enthusiasm
of Chrétien or Victor Hugues: the islands of Tobago and Santa
Lucia had fallen into English hands; in Martinique, Rocham-
beau had been forced to surrender. Guadeloupe was subject to
continual attacks that were exhausting the military government's resources. Besides, everyone knew the colonists in the
French Antilles were a band of monarchist bastards; they had
openly opposed the Republic since the King and Queen's execution, and were favoring the enemy's designs in the hopes of a
decisive occupation by the British. The squadron set forth, slipping past the English blockade on the coast in a swift departure
from Europe. Their orders were clear: lighting lamps after sun-
set was forbidden, and soldiers were to retire early to their hammocks. They lived in constant distress, arms ever at the ready,
awaiting the probable confrontation. But the weather favored
their undertaking, lowering obliging fogs over a placid sea. The
ships were packed with firearms and provisions, crates, barrels,
bundles, and sheaves, and the men had to share the scant free
space on deck with horses that ate hay from boats used as
troughs. The bleating of the sheep rose at all hours from the
hold; and radishes and vegetables destined for the officers'

tables grew in boxes of soil piled up on platforms. Esteban hadn't managed to speak with Victor Hugues after their departure, and had passed the time in the company of two typesetters traveling with the armada—Loeuillet, *père et fils*—with a small press for publishing bulletins and proclamations . . . As the ships drifted away from the continent, the Revolution behind them grew simpler in the men's minds; far from the vociferous huddles in the street, the high-flown rhetoric, the oratorical clashes, the Event was reduced to its outlines and disburdened of its contradictions. Danton's recent condemnation and death shrank to a mere misfortune in the course of developments that seemed to each individual from afar as though cut to the measure of his longings. Naturally, it wasn't easy all at once to recognize the infamy of tribunes who just yesterday had been beloved as idols, acclaimed as debaters, as leaders of men. But once the storm was over, something would arise that accommodated everyone: for the Basque, en route with his scapular, the future would be more tolerant of religion; for him who ached for his Lodge, it would be less hostile to the Masons; more egalitarian, communitarian, sensed the man dreaming of a final reckoning with hidden powers that would put an end to all privileges. But first, their task as Frenchmen was to wage war against the English, and away from the citizens' taverns and gossip mills, their old misgivings dissolved. Just one nagging doubt continued to torment Esteban: when he thought of Marchena—who had to fall, given his collusion with the Girondins—it pained him that so many foreigners, threatened with death in their home countries for their love of liberty, should face suppression for the crime of believing too readily in the Revolution's power to spread. There was too much trust in the confidences and accusations of persons of little standing. Even Robespierre, addressing the Society of Friends of Liberty and Equality, had condemned ill-considered denunciations as plots dreamed up by adversaries of the Republic to discredit its finest men. Esteban had left at the right time, he thought, being himself among those who had fallen into disgrace. And yet he yearned to work in a Higher Dimension, to take part in

Something Great, as ardently as when Brissot had sent him to
the Pyrenees, telling him he was laying the foundation for Great
Events—Great Events that halted, in the end, at the foot of the
Pyrenees, where Death, faithful to his medieval temper, remained governed by theological allegories from the Flemish
paintings Phillip II had hung in El Escorial . . . In those hours,
Esteban would have liked to approach Victor Hugues to share
with him his doubts. But the Commissar rarely revealed himself. And when he did, it was unexpectedly, to impose discipline
by surprise. One night, showing up on the orlop deck, he caught
four soldiers playing cards by the light of a candle shoved into
a cone of rag paper. He marched them across the deck, the tip
of his saber pointed at their buttocks, and made them throw
their cards into the sea. "The next time," he said, "you will be
the Kings in this game." He slipped under the hammocks of
men asleep to see if the fabric betrayed the outlines of a pilfered
bottle. "Lend me your rifle," he would tell a guard, as though
anxious to fire at a fin emerging in outline over the sea. Then,
abandoning his target, he would look the weapon over, inevitably finding it dingy and badly oiled. "You're a swine!" he would
shout, throwing it to the floor. The next day, the artillery would
shimmer as though freshly retrieved from the armory. At times,
at night, he would climb up to the crow's nest, wedging his
boots in the rope ladder, swaying in the void when he lost his
footing. Then he would stand there next to the lookout, ostentatious, magnificent, his figure less visible than guessed at in the
shadows, like an albatross presiding over the whole of the ship,
stretching out its wings. "Theatrics," Esteban thought. But theatrics that gripped him as they did every other spectator, giving
him a sense of the dimension of the man who took on such a
role.

A concerted blast from the bugles, blown full-throated along
the ship, told the soldiers one morning that the danger was behind them. The navigator upturned his hourglass, putting
away the pistols that had weighed down his maps before then.
Hailing the start of an ordinary journey with a swig of brandy,
the men turned to their habitual labors with a jubilation that

broke with the tension, the distress, the furrowed brows of recent days. The men sang as they tossed spadefuls of horse apples into the sea and the beasts sank their heads in the
trough-boats. The men sang as they polished their arms. Singing, the butchers filed their knives to slaughter the rams later
that day. Iron and grindstone, brush and saw, currycomb and
shimmering flank all sang; the anvil under the awning sang to
the rhythm of bellows and hammers. The last mists of Europe
bled away under a sun still veiled, very white, but warm, which
gleamed on all ends of the ship, on uniform buckles, the gold
of braid, the patent leather, the bayonets, the saddle trees
brought out into the light. The artillery was unpacked, not yet
with haste to load it, but only to slide the ramrod down the
bore and polish up the brass. In the aftercastle, the Huntsmen
of the Pyrenees Battalion's band was practicing one of Gossec's
marches, with a trio joining in for amusement and blowing a
Basque fife; and the playing of the latter so outshone the rustic,
poorly tuned rendition of the sheet music that the troops took
to mocking the performance. Each person was absorbed in his
doings, looking hopeful at the horizon, singing, laughing with
a cheer that rose from the orlops to the crows' nests, when Victor Hugues appeared in his commissar's uniform, grandiose,
face beaming, though not for that reason more approachable
than otherwise. He crossed the deck, stopping to watch the repairs to the carriage of a canon and the doings of a carpenter
further on; he clapped a horse on the neck, flicked a drum-
head, asked after the health of an artilleryman with his arm in
a sling . . . Esteban noticed the men fell suddenly silent when
they saw him. The Commissar inspired fear. With slow steps,
he climbed the stairs that led to the prow. On the waist, barrels
were stacked side by side beneath a broad cloth kept in place
by ropes on the gunwales. Victor gave instructions to an official, who immediately ordered the barrels taken elsewhere.
Then a canoe with a pennant was lowered into the sea: the
Commissar, on that first day of bonanza and peace, went to
lunch aboard the *Thétis* with Captain De Leyssegues, head of
the armada. Chrétien, seasick since their departure, remained closed up in his cabin. When the plumed hat of Hugues

disappeared behind *L'Espérance*, which was navigating now between two frigates, jubilation reigned again onboard the *Pique*. The officers, freed from their worries, shared the troops' good cheer, singing, and jeering at the band, which, with no more Basque aires or virtuoso blowing on the fife, couldn't even manage a decent "Marseillaise." "We've never practiced together before," the director shouted back to the catcallers, by way of an excuse. But the men laughing at him would have laughed at anything: the urgent thing was to laugh, even more now that the drummers of the *Thétis* were saluting the Commissar of the National Convention when he was somewhere else, off in the distance. The Plenipotentiary was feared. Perhaps he enjoyed being feared.

XVI.

Three more days passed. Each time the navigator flipped the hourglass, the sun seemed fuller and the sea smelled more of sea, speaking to Esteban now in its manifold effluvia. One night, to relieve the heat swelling in the orlop and holds, he stepped out on deck to contemplate the immensity of the first entirely clear sky he had witnessed during the crossing. A hand rested on his shoulder. Behind him was Victor, without his topcoat, smiling as he had used to before: "We could use a woman around here. Don't you think?" And the young man, as if moved by yearning, by thirst, recalled those places the two of them had been to in Paris, where so many complaisant and attractive ladies could be found. Naturally, he hadn't forgotten Rosamunda, the German from the Palais Royal; Zaïre with her Voltairean name; Dorina with her dresses of pink muslin, or the mezzanine where the successive and subtle arts of Angelica, Adela, Zéphyr, Zoe, Esther, and Zilia could be had for two Louis d'or. Each of them embodied distinct female types and played—in strict observance of a drama magnificently suited to the character of her beauty—the frightened demoiselle, the libertine bourgeoise, the down-at-heel ballerina, the Venus from the isle of Mauritius—that was Esther—or the drunken

Bacchanalian—that was Zilia. After having been object of each Archetype's astute solicitude, the visitor was thrown at last into the firm lap of Aglaé of the buoyant breasts pointing to a chin like that of an ancient queen, who stood at the top of a progressive scale of superbly consummated seductions. At another time, Esteban would have laughed at the somewhat silly reminiscence. But he remained uneasy, incapable of communicating— Victor hadn't looked in on him since their encounter in Rochefort—and his repertoire of monosyllables soon faltered in the face of that unexpected garrulousness. "You sound like a Haitian," Victor said. "There, they answer everything with an *oh! oh!* and you never know what any of them are thinking. Let's go to my cabin." The first thing one saw there, between the nails where Hugues hung his hat and tailcoat, was a large portrait of the Incorruptible, with a lamp like a votive burning at the foot of it. The Commissar set a bottle of brandy on the table and filled two glasses. "Salut!" Then he looked at Esteban with slight scorn. In a voice of perfunctory courtesy, he apologized for not calling on him since their departure from the Île d'Aix: he had worries, obligations, duties, and so on, and then again, their situation was hardly auspicious. True, they had evaded the English blockade. But there was no telling what the armada would have to face when they arrived. Their chief objective was to assert the Republic's authority in France's American colonies and suppress separatist sentiment with every means at their disposal, reconquering, if necessary, whatever territories might presently be lost. Long silences pierced his monologue, punctuated at times by that half-grunted, half-grumbled *Oui!* that Esteban knew very well. He praised the high tone of civility he had noted in the young man's letter—it was that tone that had convinced him to take him on: "Anyone unfaithful to the Jacobins would be unfaithful to the Republic and to the cause of Freedom," he said. Still, an irritable look crossed Esteban's face. It wasn't the words as such, but the fact that Collot d'Herbois had first uttered them, and had done so on repeated occasions; that old braggart, increasingly a slave to drink, struck him as the man least suited to dictate the moral precepts of revolution. Unable to swallow his objections, he exposed them at length. "You may be right," Victor said. "Collot drinks too much, but he's a good patriot." Fired by the two glasses of brandy, Esteban pointed to the portrait of the Incorruptible. "How can this giant place his trust in a drunk? Collot's very speeches stink of wine." The Revolution had forged sublime men, it was true; but it had also given wings to a multitude of failures and grousers, exploiters of the Terror who, as a sign of their lofty civic spirit, had bound the Constitution in human skin. Those weren't just rumors. He had seen those horrible books with their covers of tawny, porous leather—resembling withered petals, rag paper, chamois, or lizard hide. They had disgusted him, and his hands refused to touch them. "Lamentable, indeed," said Victor, his expression going cold. "But we can't keep an eye on everything." Esteban accepted his obligation to make a profession of faith that left no doubt as to his revolutionary conviction. But he was exasperated at certain of the citizens' rituals; at the unjustified promotions; at the satisfaction of superior men with many others who were mediocre. The most idiotic drama could have its hour on the stage, so long as a Phrygian cap appeared in the end; *The Misanthrope* was appended with a citizens' epilogue, and Agrippina dubbed a *citoyenne* in the new version of *Brittanicus* at the Comédie Française; classical tragedies were censored while the state subsidized a theater offering the inept spectacle of Pope Pius VI feuding with scepter blows and tiara against Catherine II and a King of Spain who fell in the skirmish, losing his enormous cardboard nose. For some time now, contempt for the intelligentsia had been encouraged. More than one committee had heard the barbarous cry: "Trust no one who has written a book." Carrier had famously shut down all the literary circles of Nantes. That fool Henriot had gone so far as to demand the Bibliothèque Nationale be burned to the ground, and the Public Health Committee was sending illustrious surgeons, eminent chemists, scholars, poets, and astronomers to the guillotine . . . Esteban stopped, seeing that Victor was becoming impatient. "Another skeptic," he said, finally. "This must be how they speak in Koblenz. Have you, by chance, asked yourself why the literary clubs in Nantes were shuttered?" He slammed his fist on the table. "We are changing the face of the globe and all you people worry about is the poor quality of the offerings at the theater. We are transforming human life itself, and you gripe because a few men of letters are unable to gather anymore to read their idylls or whatever shit they find worth their while. Those men would happily spare the life of a traitor, an enemy of the people, so long as he'd written a few pretty verses!" On the deck, they could hear men dragging wood. Now that paths were clear between the bundles, the carpenters were taking boards to the prow, followed by sailors bearing large, oblong crates. One of them, when opened, caught the light of the moon in a steely triangle, and the sight of it shocked Esteban. The men, outlined in silhouettes against the sea, seemed to be engaged in a mysterious, sanguinary rite, with the bascule, the braces laid out on the deck taking shape horizontally according to the dictates of a paper consulted in silence, by lamplight. They were giving form to a projection, the descriptive geometry of a vertical reality; a false perspective, a two-dimensional simile for that which would soon possess height, width, and abominable depth. Ceremoniously, the night blackened men persevered in the labor of assemblage, removing beams, runners, hinges from crates that looked like coffins—coffins too long for human beings, but the proper width to accommodate their flanks, with a yoke or lunette destined to close a circle above the average human body as measured from shoulder to shoulder. Hammers struck in sinister rhythm with the immense disquiet of the sea, where clumps of gulfweed had already begun to appear . . . "This, *too*, has come with us then," exclaimed Esteban. "Naturally," replied Victor, turning back to his cabin. "*This*, and the printing press, are the most important cargo we have, apart from the cannons." "*La letra con sangre entra*," said Esteban. "Don't pester me with your Spanish proverbs," the other replied, refilling their glasses. He looked at his interlocutor with deliberate resolve, reached for a calfskin portfolio, and opened it slowly, taking a sheaf of sealed papers that he threw down on the table. "Yes, we've brought the machine with us. But you know what else I'm bringing the men of the new world?" He paused and added, stressing every word:

"The Decree of 16 Pluviôse of Year II, *which declares slavery abolished*. From now on, all men living in our colonies shall be French citizens endowed with equal rights, without prejudice to race." He peeked out the door of his cabin to observe the carpenters' work, then continued talking, sure of being listened to. "For the first time, a squadron is advancing on America without raising the cross—the same cross Columbus's fleet had painted on its sails. The cross was a symbol of the Slavery to be imposed on the men of the New World in the name of a Redeemer who died—the chaplains would say—to save men, solace the poor, and confound the rich. We," and turning back brusquely he pointed at the decree, "without cross, without redeemer, without God, are coming in ships without chaplains aboard to vanquish privilege and guarantee equality. Ogé's brother shall have his revenge." Esteban lowered his head, ashamed of the objections he had uttered before, maladroitly, to alleviate his intolerable doubts. He laid his hand on the Decree, felt the several seals swelling the paper: "Still and all," he said, "I'd prefer if we could accomplish our mission without making use of the guillotine." "That depends on the people," Victor said. "On them as well as us. Don't think I trust all of our fellow passengers. We have to see how more than one of them behaves on land." "Are you saying that because of me?" Esteban asked. "Because of you, because of others. My work forces me to trust in no one. Some argue too much. Some yearn too much. Some are still hiding their scapularies. Some say life was better in a whorehouse under the ancien régime. There are soldiers too friendly with one another, with dreams of turning on the commissars once they've drawn their sabers. I know everything said, thought, done onboard these godforsaken ships. Mind your words. Whatever you say, I shall soon know of it." "Do you suspect me?" Esteban asked with a sour smile. "I suspect everyone," Victor said. "Why don't you try out the machine tonight on me then?" "I'd have to rush the carpenters. Too much bother for such a pointless lesson." Victor began to remove his shirt. "Go to bed." He gave Esteban his hand cordially, clapping it tight, as he used to do. When he looked at him, the young man was surprised by the resemblance between

his face and that of the Incorruptible in the painting in his
cabin, how evidently Victor imitated the other man's stare, his
expression, at once courteous and implacable, his way of holding his head. Glimpsing that weakness, that wish to resemble
physically the person he admired above all, assuaged Esteban in
a way, like a minor victory. Invested with power, his ambitions
indulged, the man who had once disguised himself as Lycurgus and Themistocles at their home in Havana was now trying
to mimic another, mindful of his superiority. For the first
time, Victor Hugues's dominance was humbled—perhaps
unconsciously—before a Greater Dimension.

XVII.

The Machine was still cloaked on the prow, reduced to one
horizontal and one vertical plane, bare like the outlines of a
theorem, when the squadron entered the warm waters that
hinted at the presence of land, seconded by the appearance of
tree trunks dragged away by currents, the bamboo roots, the
mangrove branches, the leaves of coconut palms that floated on
the clear green here, there over the sandy bottoms. Again, it
was possible they might run into British ships, and unsure of
events in Guadeloupe since the last reports they'd received on
embarking, all were in a state of expectancy only heightened
with every day of uneventful sailing. If they couldn't anchor in
Guadeloupe, the ships would be forced to travel on to Saint-
Domingue. But the English might have taken possession of
Saint-Domingue, too. In that case, Chrétien and Victor Hugues
would take whatever route they could to reach the coast of the
United States and seek refuge in the friendly nation. Aghast, almost disgusted at what he saw—when he looked at it coldly—
as his own intolerable selfishness, Esteban still could not help
but feel a stirring in his heart when it was said the squadron
might dock in Baltimore or New York. That would mean the
end of an already absurdly drawn-out adventure: no longer useful to the French armada, he would ask for his freedom—or
would take it, which amounted to the same thing—returning

full of history and histories to a place where they would listen in awe to the pilgrim back from Sacred Lands. With a paucity of action, but an abundance of experience, his first foray into the Great Wheel of the World would prove to have been his initiation for future exploits. For now, he had to do something that would give meaning to his existence. He wanted to write; to reach, through the medium of writing and its attendant disciplines, whatever conclusions might be drawn from all he had seen. He could not say what his work would consist in. Something important, at any rate; something the era demanded. Something that might greatly displease Victor Hugues—and the thought of this brought him pleasure. Perhaps a new Theory of the State. Perhaps a revision of *The Spirit of the Laws.* Perhaps a study of the mistakes of the Revolution. "Just what an émigré swine would write," he told himself, abandoning the project before he'd begun. In those past few years, Esteban had witnessed a critical disposition growing inside him— unwelcome, at times, as it deprived him of the pleasure of those sudden enthusiasms everyone else shared in—that refused to submit to general opinion. No sooner was the Revolution presented to him as sublime, devoid of defects or failings, than it became, in his eyes, questionable and perverse. Yet, against a monarchist, he would have marshaled the same arguments in its defense that maddened him coming from the mouth of a Collot d'Herbois. He detested the boundless demagoguery of *Le Père Duchesne* no less than the émigrés' apocalyptic harangues. He was a cleric among the anticlericals, an anticlerical among clerics; a monarchist when it was said every king—a James of Scotland, a Henry IV, a Charles of Sweden—was a degenerate, an anti-monarchist when he heard the praises sung of the Spanish Bourbons. "I am a skeptic," he admitted, remembering what Victor had said to him a few days before. "But I am skeptical of myself, and that is worse." When the Loeuillets, who had gradually loosened their tongues, informed him of the terror the Public Accuser had unleashed in Rochefort, he thought of Victor with a blend of spite and unease, of indulgence and envy. Spite, at being shut out from his domain; unease at his ruthlessness in the tribunal; almost feminine indulgence in gratitude at any sign of friendship he might ever deign to show him; envy at his possession of a Decree that would confer a historical dimension on that baker's son, born among ovens and kneading troughs. Esteban passed days in inward dialogue with the absent Victor, advising him, asking for explanations, raising his voice, mentally preparing himself for an argument that might never take place and which would, if it ever did, modify the character of those discourses as he imagined them, adding sentimentality and even tears where as yet whispered reproaches, accusations, bold questions, and threats of rupture were voiced . . . In those days of uncertain expectation, Victor would go early to the *Thétis* in the canoe flying its flag to exchange impressions with De Leyssegues. Both leaned over maps showing the reefs and shallows where the squadron was navigating. Esteban tried to place himself in his path when he was coming or going, feigning absorption in some task or other when he passed by. But Victor never spoke a word to him when his captains and assistants were in tow. That plumed gathering, in gleaming braid, constituted a world he was barred from. Watching Victor depart, Esteban would gaze fascinated and incensed at his mighty back pressed against the sweat-soaked fabric of his tailcoats; the back of a man who knew the most intimate secrets of his home, who had penetrated his destiny like a hand of fate, taking him down ever more uncertain paths. "Don't embrace frozen statues," the young man told himself, quoting Epictetus with wounded ire, considering the distance that separated him now from his companion of other days. He had seen that frozen statue carousing with women of experience—women selected in light of their experience—on countless escapades during their early days in Paris, when they sought nothing more than the pursuit of pleasure. That unclothed Victor Hugues, preening and flexing before his lovers of an evening, prey to wine and coarse humor, retained a freshness of character invisible now in the furrowed brows of the Glittering Man, proud of his Republican insignia, who reigned today over the fate of the armada, usurping the functions of admiral with an aplomb that alarmed even De Leyssegues. "Your Uniform's gone to your head," Esteban thought. "Beware the

intoxication of the Uniform; it is the worst intoxication of all."
At dawn one day, two gannets lighted on the boom of the
Pique. The breeze smelled of pasture, of molasses, of firewood.
The squadron, sailing slowly, sounding the depths, was approaching the feared reefs of La Désirade. Since midnight, all of
the men had been on alert, and now, gathered on the gunwales,
they looked at the island with its sullen profile, which appeared
at dawn like an enormous shadow stretching from the sea to a
very low mass of clouds that lay motionless over the terrain.
The water then, at the beginning of June, was so still that the
arcing of the flying fish was audible from a distance; so clear
that the paths of the needlefish were visible below the surface.
The ships stopped on an abrupt coast without a trace of homes
or planted fields. A canoe with several sailors left the *Thétis* and
rowed full speed toward the island. Captain De Leyssegues and
Generals Cartier and Rouger soon boarded the *Pique* to wait for
news with Chrétien and Victor Hugues . . . After two hours, at
the peak of expectation, the canoe reappeared. "What, then?"
the Commissar shouted to the sailors when he thought they
were within earshot. "The English are in Guadeloupe and
Santa Lucia," one shouted, raising a black Sabbath of curses on
the decks of the ships. "They took the islands just as we were
leaving France." Bitterness followed tension. The uncertainty of
prior days returned: now would come another hazardous departure across seas populated by enemy ships, toward an island
of Saint-Domingue most likely occupied by forces aided by rich
colonialists, monarchists who had gone to the English side
along with their hordes of negroes. They would avoid the English danger only to try their strength against the Spanish one,
with a hundred detours taking their squadron near the Baha-
mas at the worst time of year—and Esteban recalled some
verses from *The Tempest* that spoke of the hurricanes of the
Bermudas. Defeatism overtook the men. Since nothing could
be done in Guadeloupe, it was best to depart as soon as possible. Some were frustrated by the stubbornness of Victor Hugues, who made each of the messengers repeat over and over
the story of their brief forays onto land. There was no doubting.
They'd heard the tale from different sources: a black fisherman,

a farmhand, the waiter from a rundown tavern, and last, the guard at a small fort. All had glimpsed the ships of the squadron, but, seeing them from a distance, they confused them with the vessels under the command of Admiral Jarvis that were meant to depart, or had departed already, or were departing just then from Pointe-à-Pitre en route to Saint Kitts, an island hedged by reefs that was dangerous in the extreme: "I don't believe we should wait any longer," Cartier said. "If they find us here, they'll do us in." Rouger shared his opinion. But Victor refused to cede. Soon their voices rose violently. The chiefs and commissars argued with a grand racket of sabers, braids, sashes, and rosettes, invoking Themistocles and Leonidas with as many foul words as a Frenchman in Year II could level. Victor Hugues silenced his fellows with a cutting phrase: "In a Republic, soldiers don't argue: they obey. They sent us to Guadeloupe, and to Guadeloupe we will go." The others bowed their heads, as though cowed by a lion-tamer's whip. The Commissar gave the order to depart, without delay, toward Les Salines in Grande Terre. Soon Marie-Galante came into view in a blur of opalescent mists, and then all Hell broke loose. As the racket of rolling gun carriages, the creak of cables and pulleys, shouts, preparations, harried formations drowned out the whinnies of the horses smelling nearby land and fresh pasture, Victor Hugues had the typesetters bring him several hundred documents printed in bold letters during the crossing, reproducing the text of the Decree of 16 Pluviôse, which proclaimed the abolition of slavery and granted equal rights to all the inhabitants of the island without prejudice to race or status. Then he crossed the waist with a firm step, approaching the guillotine, and tore away the tarred cloth covering it, so that it shone for the first time, blade bare and well honed, beneath the light of the sun. Immobile, stony, flaunting the emblems of his Authority, right hand resting on the Machine's stanchions, Victor Hugues had transformed suddenly into Allegory. Alongside Liberty, the first guillotine had arrived in the New World.

XVIII.

Ravages of War
GOYA

Chrétien and Victor Hugues departed in one of the first boats—perhaps to show the army that, when the hour of action struck, they were no less daring than the soldiers themselves. When the troops reached land, they heard a few disparate shots, followed by a brief exchange of gunfire that faded into the distance. Night fell, and silence overtook the ships, where navy troops remained behind with the two companies of the Huntsmen of the Pyrenees under the command of Captain De Leyssegues. And three days passed without incident, nothing heard, nothing learned. To still his anguish, Esteban fished in the company of the typesetters, who for the moment were unable to exercise their profession. With most of the army gone, space was so abundant on the ships that the decks resembled theater stages after the end of a grand spectacle. Abandoned bundles, empty crates, and loose robes hung about. A man could walk at ease, nap in the shadows of the sails, have his bowl of soup wherever it pleased him, pick at his fleas in the open air, play cards with his eyes ever drawn to the horizon, imagining, between antes, the apparition of an enemy supply ship's sails far away. It might have seemed a pleasant respite in the Windward Islands, had the absence of news not soured so many spirits. There was no point in scrutinizing the landscape of the coast. There, nothing changed. A child pulled clams from the sand; dogs tussled, chest-deep in water; a family of negroes passed, enormous bundles on their heads, as though their wanderings were never to end . . . Some assumed the worst when, on the morning of the fourth day, a mail boat came level with the *Thétis* with orders to guide the fleet to Pointe-à-Pitre. But the Army of the Republic was victorious. After a skirmish upon disembarking, the French advanced cautiously without encountering the expected resistance. Victor Hugues attributed the retreat of the English troops to the terror of the monarchist colonists whose filthy white flags they knocked aside with their Republican ones. The crews of the merchant ships were more spirited. Taken by surprise in the port, they had organized a resistance at Fort Fleur d'Épée with sixteen pieces of artillery. Just last night, Cartier and Rouger attacked their redoubt, catching unawares the nine hundred men defending it, and overtook it by saber and bayonet without firing a shot. Chrétien, excessively gallant in his desire to set an example, had fallen facing off against the enemy. The English, demoralized by their loss, were entrenched now in Basse-Terre behind the Salt River—a minuscule stretch of water thick with mangroves, which, despite its slenderness, divided Guadeloupe into two different territories. Victor Hugues had been in Pointe-à-Pitre since midnight installing his government. Eighty-seven merchant ships had left the port since the French took power. The warehouses were bursting with merchandise. The squadron was urgently needed ... They prepared to depart as the transport canoes were returned to their bays. An immense, heartfelt, almost visceral joy moved the men from the lookouts to the holds, and they climbed, ran, pushed the cannons, raised the sails, unfurled, furled, heaped. Victory, that was fine. But better still, there would be wines and fresh hams studded with cloves of garlic, lots of wine, and ox with new carrots, all that very night; much wine, and the finest of rums, and the kind of coffee that leaves a stain in the cup, women even, maybe, red-skinned, copper-skinned, pale, dark—some with high heels under the lace fringe of their petticoats; others who smelled of frangipane, of orange blossom perfume, of vetiver, and most of all, of female. And with chants and shouts and hurrahs for the Republic, raised on the jetties and echoed back from the ships, the squadron steered into the town port on that day of Prairal of Year II, with the guillotine erect on the prow of the *Pique*, so polished it looked new, unveiled for all to see, that they should come to know it well. Victor and De Leyssegues embraced. And they went together to the former building of the Sénéchal—where the Commissar proceeded to install his offices and chambers—to bow before the body of Chrétien, laid out in his ribbons and rosettes over a black mound flowering with red carnations, white spikenards, and blue plumbago. Esteban was dispatched to the Grain Exchange for foreign commerce. Today he would begin his employment, composing a Registry of Confiscated Property to tally the goods of the many ships the enemy had abandoned. Posters were hung all round proclaiming the abolition of slavery. The patriots jailed by the *White Lords* were set free. A dense, jubilant multitude wandered through the streets cheering the recent arrivals. Another cause for celebration was the discovery that General Dundas, British Governor of Guadeloupe, had died in Basse-Terre the night before the French disembarked. This was propitious for the Army of the Republic. But the debauchery the sailors had promised themselves that evening was long in coming: soon after midday, Captain De Leyssegues ordered them to start work on fortifications and defenses in the port, sinking old ships in the silt to block access and arranging cannons along the docks, their muzzles facing the sea . . . Four days later, their luck changed. A battalion on Morne Saint-Jean, beyond the Salt River, began systematically bombarding Pointe-à-Pitre. Admiral Jarvis, landing his army in Le Gosier, laid siege to the city. Terror overtook the population. Projectiles fell from the sky, hammering wantonly, collapsing roofs, piercing floors, sending tiles flying in deluges of red clay, rebounding off the masonry, the pavement of the streets, the corner posts, before rolling with thunderous clamor toward whatever could be toppled—a column, a balustrade, a man stunned by the speed of everything bearing down on him. A scent of quicklime, dry and ashy, enveloped the city in an atmosphere of demolition, parching throats, burning eyes. A cannonball, crashing into a quarry stone wall, rose up over the wooden houses, hurled itself down a set of stairs, struck a cabinet full of bottles, a vitrine of fine china, a cellar, where its trajectory ended in a chaos of shattered staves atop the destroyed body of a woman in labor. Loosened by the impact, a bell had fallen with a clangor of bronze so tremendous that its sound reached the enemy cannoneers. It was the sorriest of refuges against ordnance of iron, that domain of blinds, partitions, dainty balconies, slats, wooden grilles, trellises, and battens—all made to take

advantage of the softest breath of breeze. Each shot was a mallet blow against a wicker cage, leaving corpses under the walnut table where a family had sought refuge. Soon more horrors
came to light: a battalion with ovens posted on Morne Savon
was peppering the town with red-hot shells. Everything still
standing began to burn. After the quicklime came the fire. The
first fire wasn't tamed before another started, further off, in the
cloth shop, at the sawmill, at the rum cellar which, when
touched by the blaze, sent forth a slow stream of blue flames
that followed the footways down the surrounding slopes. Many
of the humbler houses had roofs of leaves and braided fibers,
and a single heated projectile sufficed to destroy an entire block
of them. The lack of water meant they had to fight the flames
with axes, sawdust, and machetes. Added to the destruction descending from the sky was another waged conscientiously by
the children, women, and the old. A black, dense smoke from
the basements, where old and filthy things burn, cast sudden
midday shadows across the tortured city. Though intolerable,
impossible to bear for even an hour, it stretched on through day
and night, in a perpetual racket of ruin mingling with the cry,
the crackling of fire and the thundering on the ground of things
that roll, strike, collide, thrusting like battering rams. Disaster
was in the air, and after each apparent climax, some bit of news
came that made matters worse. Three offensives against the
murderous battalions had come to nought. Haggard from insomnia and fatigue, and ill-suited to the climate, General Cartier died. General Rouger, struck by a projectile, was agonizing
in a room of the building making do as a field hospital. Stealthy
Dominican friars had re-emerged from their hideouts and stood
tall at the beds of the ill with a potion or tisane in hand. At the
time, no one paid attention to their habits, accepting the care
and solace they offered, which was soon followed by an unveiling of Crucifixes and Holy Oils. Religious contraband slithered
in where gangrene and wounds were most abundant, and many
clamored for last rites, throwing their insignia to the ground,
when they sensed the proximity of death . . . Thirst was now
added to the numberless torments. Dead bodies had fallen into
the reservoirs, and the poisoned water couldn't be drunk. The

soldiers boiled sea water to make salty coffee that they would sweeten with huge quantities of sugar and alcohol. The water carriers who supplied the population with barrels borne on boats or carts couldn't reach the local streams under enemy fire. Rats teemed in the streets, scuttled through the rubble, invading everything, and, if that weren't pestilence enough, gray scorpions climbed out of the old wood, aiming their barbs at whatever they could sting. Several ships in the port were reduced to drifting piles of charred planks. The *Thétis*, struck by a possibly mortal wound, keeled in a panorama of broken masts, of shattered hulls, their ribs like bones. On the twentieth day of the siege, Miserere Colic made its appearance. Within hours, people were exhausted, their life draining from their intestines. A Christian burial being impossible, the bodies were interred wherever they could be, at the foot of a tree, in a pit, by the side of the latrines. Falling on the Old Cemetery, the cannonballs had unearthed bones, hurling them over the sunken tombstones and uprooted crosses. Victor Hugues, with his best troops and his last remaining generals, was entrenched at the Morne du Gouvernement, a hill overlooking the city, with the walls of a stone church protecting its perimeter . . . Numb, stupefied, incapable of thought in the midst of the cataclysm that had lasted nearly four weeks, Esteban passed the time lying in a sort of lair, a horizontal pit that he'd dug between sugar sacks in the storehouse in the port where the bombardment had surprised him while he was taking inventory. The Loeuillets, father and son, had followed his example, and were sheltering in front of him in a roomier hollow in the sacks, where they had preserved some of the parts from their printing press—in particular, the box of types, which was impossible to replace in these lands. Thirst didn't afflict them, as there were several butts of wine stored there, and for refreshment, from fear, or simply to have a drink, they drained pitcher after pitcher of that turbid liquid, which grew sourer by the day and left a purple crust on their lips. In those moments of misery, Loeuillet the elder, son of a Camisard, brought out the family Bible he'd kept hidden in a box of paper. When the bullets struck close by, and his drinking had stoked his courage, he would shout, from the depths of his hovel, a few verses from Revelations. And nothing accorded better with reality than those words John the Theologian had uttered in prophetic delirium: "The first angel sounded, and there followed hail and fire mingled with blood, and they were cast upon the earth: and the third part of trees was burnt up, and all green grass was burnt up." "Our many impieties," the typographer moaned, "have brought the End Times upon us." And just then, he heard in Jarvis's artillery the exemplary ire of the Old Great Gods.

XIX.

One morning, the gunfire died down. The tension eased; the animals rested their ears; the prone remained there lying prone, undisturbed by further shocks. Waves lapped in the port, and when a boy throwing a rock shattered the last intact window, people were frightened by the noise's strange clarity. Survivors emerged from their pits, their caves, their pigsties, covered in soot, in grime, in excrement, filthy bandages dangling a palm's length from their wounds. The cause of the portent was soon revealed: two nights before, Victor Hugues, warned that the English were decapitating his vanguard and were on the verge of entering the city, had made a desperate, fevered descent from the Morne du Gouvernement, repelling the enemy repeatedly and at last giving them chase, until they crossed back over the Salt River and retreated to their trenches in the fields of Berville in Basse-Terre. In this part of the country, the French were victors . . . A convoy of water sellers appeared at midday, and a multitude in rags fell on it bearing marmites, buckets, troughs, basins. The families threw themselves on the ground to drink, pushed past the muzzles and snouts of their beasts, sinking their heads in the vessels, fighting, licking, vomiting what they had drunk too quickly—stealing pitchers from each other in a tumult that had to be broken up with blows from the rifle butts. Thirst slaked, they set to clearing the main roads, dragging corpses up from the rubble. Now and then, an enemy projectile still fell, toppling a passerby, tearing down a grating, splintering an altarpiece. But no one cared about such trifles, after what they'd suffered for four terrible weeks. It came out that General Aubert, the last of the expedition's military chiefs, was on his deathbed with yellow fever. Victor Hugues was the sole remaining lord of the Grande-Terre. Calling the Loeuillets to his office, with its shattered windows and half-burnt curtains hanging like festoons of misery, he dictated, to their astonishment, a proclamation of a state of siege and the formation, by forced conscription, of a militia of two thousand men of color fit to bear arms. Any inhabitant who spread false rumors, who proved himself an adversary of Liberty, or who tried to pass over to Basse-Terre would be summarily executed, and good patriots were encouraged to betray their confidants. Promotions were granted by decree: Captain Pelardy became Division General and Commander in Chief of the Armed Forces, and Commander Boudet was made Brigadier General, tasked with instructing and disciplining the local troops . . . Esteban admired the energy the Commissar had shown since the day they had disembarked in Les Salines. He was a powerful commander, and incomparably lucky. The successive deaths of Chrétien, Cartier, Rouger, and Aubert were uniquely propitious for him, as now, the only men who might in some way have been capable of opposing him were gone. Tensions between the military command and civil authority were nullified de facto. Victor Hugues, who had argued bitterly at times with the expedition's generals—prone to flaunting their braid, their plumes, and their seniority—relied from that day forward on two fanatically devoted underlings who knew, moreover, that it was up to him whether the Convention would confirm their promotions . . . That night, wine coursed like water through the town, and the soldiers who had energy enough found relief from their prolonged estrangement from women. At a banquet of officers Esteban attended with the Loeuillets, father and son, the Commissar was jovial, witty, eloquent. Mulatta waitresses brought glasses of rum punch on trays, and didn't anger when they felt a hand grab them around the waist or pinch them under their skirts. Between toasts, Victor Hugues announced that the Morne du Gouvernement would henceforth be known as the Morne de la Victoire, and that the Place Sartines, so beautifully open onto the port, would now be called Place de la Victoire. As for Pointe-à-Pitre, its new name was Port de la Liberté. ("They'll go on calling it Pointe-à-Pitre," Esteban thought, "just as Chauvin-Dragon never stopped being Saint-Jean de Luz.") At dessert time—some early hour of the morning—the young man heard calls for the maidservants to sing nostalgic verses by the Marquis de Bouillé, a cousin of Lafayette who had been the governor of Guadeloupe in his youth. Summoned home to France twenty-four years ago, he composed a lament in the island's local dialect that still echoed in everyone's memory:

> *Adieu, oh shawls and madras robes,*
> *Adieu oh jewels and gold adored,*
> *My darling's left to cross the globe*
> *And—lo—is gone forevermore.*

> *Bonjour, Monsieur le Gouverneur,*
> *I come to you on bended knee:*
> *Use your powers to secure*
> *My darling's safe return to me.*

> *Madame, I fear the hour is past*
> *To bring your darling back to land*
> *The sails are swelling on the masts*
> *And on the deck he stands.*

Drunk from the hearty helpings of punch, Esteban rose from his seat, inspired, calling for a toast to the *doudou* with the dulcet voice, but pleading the terms *Monsieur* and *Madame* be stricken from the song—as they clashed with its democratic spirit—and replaced with *Citoyen Gouvernour* and *Citoyenne*. Victor Hugues lowered his brows and stared down the young man, silencing the applause that had greeted that profoundly republican sentiment. By now, everyone was singing in chorus *I've Lost It All and I Don't Care,* a new song by François Giroust that resonated splendidly with the feeling of recent victory:

Times were I had my table laid,
With fine capons and fattened hens,
And bread I'll never see again,
And bread I'll never see again.

Since the last days of the war
I've eaten crumbs and nothing more
And still, proud-hearted, I dare to roar
To George of England, tyrant, coward,
The shame is yours, the honor ours,
The shame is yours, the honor ours.

At dawn, everyone was asleep in armchairs and on benches, surrounded by half-empty glasses, trays of fruit, and leftover meat, while the Commissar washed before the open windows of his chambers, chatting with the barber, who already was stropping his razors . . . Soon, the reveilles sounded. Around eight, amid a hailstorm of hammers, masts, banderoles, garlands, and allegories rose up in the *ci-devant* Place Sartines, where the Huntsmen of the Pyrenees in their grand uniforms were playing raucous revolutionary airs with a bold racket of cornets and Turkish drums. Carpenters were building a stage for the authorities to preside over a public ceremony. Their homes abandoned and in ruins, the populace invaded the square, drawn by the oddity of a concert at the break of day. Esteban walked to the Grain Exchange, where he had a bed, to relieve his migraine with vinegar compresses and have a few teaspoons of rhubarb syrup to restore his liver, and he lazed for a while awaiting that which—as he knew from living in revolutionary Paris—always was long in coming. At ten, when he returned to the square, it was filled with an ebullient, picturesque multitude oblivious to its recent sufferings. The civil and military leaders were already on the dais, with Victor Hugues, Generals Pelardy and Boudet, and Captain De Leyssegues at the head. The people squeezed in around their new leaders, seeing them for the first time in their solemn vestments. Only the wing beats of doves in a nearby courtyard punctured the silence. After gazing around slowly, taking in the scene, the Commissar of the Convention began to speak. He congratulated the slaves of yesterday for passing over to the condition of free citizens. He praised the entirety of the people's commitment during the fateful days of the bombardment, paying homage to the victims and ending that first verbal sally with an emotional elegy in memory of Chrétien, Cartier, Rouger, and Aubert—the last of whom had expired in the Military Hospital building only half an hour ago—waving a wrathful hand as if to say that death had slain the very best among them. Then he said a few words about Christopher Columbus, who had found that island, on his third journey to America, peopled by happy, simple creatures devoted to that wholesome way of living that constituted human beings' state of nature, and had named it after the ship he was sailing in. But alas, there had arrived alongside the Discoverer Christian priests, agents of fanaticism and of an ignorance that had weighed on the world like a curse ever since Saint Paul spread the false teachings of a Jewish prophet, son of a Roman legionnaire named Pantera—Joseph of the manger was a mere legend, one the philosophers had dispelled. He lifted his arm toward the Morne du Gouvernement, announcing that the church there would be razed, to expunge all traces of idolatry, and the priests, whom he'd heard were still hiding out in the regions of Le Moule and Sainte-Anne, would be forced to say an oath to the Constitution. Esteban, attentive to the expressions of a mulatta whose three-button madras dress kept shouting to him, *There's room for you in here* in that sartorial language instantly grasped by every inhabitant of the island, was too carried away by the contemplation of puckering lips, fingers toying with bracelets, shoulders forming hollows over a softly shadowed spine, to follow a speech that, at that moment, had christened the Place Sartines with the name Place de la Victoire. Victor's voice, metallic and clear, reached him in bursts, and his emphatic tone made shimmer, now and again, a crucial phrase, a notion of Liberty, a quotation from Latin or Greek. There was eloquence there, and there was nerve. And yet, in the end, the Word failed to harmonize with the spirit of the people, who had gone there as one attends a feast, and were jesting and rubbing against each other, the men against the women, and didn't always bother to follow a language that differed greatly—with that southern accent, which Victor flaunted like a family crest—from the savory local patois. The Commissar was now finishing, leveling accusations against the French West India Company and the *White Lords* of Guadeloupe, and he announced that the struggle was far from over: they would still have to annihilate the English in Basse-Terre, and soon the final offensive would begin, bringing peace to a land freed forever now from slavery's yoke. His speech had been clear, well delivered, without excesses of rhetoric; and the public was applauding a finale crowned by a quotation from Tacitus when De Leyssegues noticed a foreign vessel forcing its way into the harbor, drifting toward the nearest moorings. But there was no reason to worry over one miserable boat: it was an old sloop, so decrepit, chipped, and filthy, with sails made of badly sewn sacks, that it gave the impression of a ghost ship from a tale of stranded sailors. The sloop docked, and the crowd grew unquiet: men strode toward the Commissar's tribune with shapeless hands and ears, toothless, hobbling, skin silvery with scaly welts. They were lepers from La Désirade there to swear an oath of fidelity to the Revolution. With well-timed aplomb, Victor Hugues treated them as ill citizens, handing them a tricolor ribbon and promising to go soon to their island to learn their needs and remedy their miseries. After this unexpected incident, the people's regard for him grew further, and several times they called him back to the stage with shouting and applause. When he was done, he retired to his office, his military chiefs in tow. At intervals, the odd cannonball badly fired by enemy artillery still crossed the resplendent sky, landing harmlessly in the waters of the bay. In the city reigned a stench of carrion. But at nightfall, the lemon trees blossomed. And after so many Tenebrae, that was an Epiphany of trees.

XX.

Strange devotion.

GOYA

Despite announcing an imminent offensive in Basse-Terre, Victor Hugues was hesitant to commence. Perhaps their paucity of arms troubled him; he feared the colored militia was undertrained, and was waiting, with evident impatience, for reinforcements he'd requested from France at the beginning of the siege of Pointe-à-Pitre. For weeks, enemy fire tore sporadically through the town. But after what they'd suffered, the people bore these lesser attacks with something like relief, shrugging their shoulders, uttering a curse, or lifting a hand in an obscene gesture. The guillotine, assembled and oiled, had remained prudently locked away, waiting for Monsieur Anse, former executioner of the Rochefort Tribunal—a mulatto of fine manners, educated in Paris, and a charming violinist, his pockets always stuffed with candies for the children—to set in motion that trusty mechanism invented by a piano maker. The Commissar knew the price France had paid in occupied neighboring lands for its excessively zealous use of the Machine. He would not have Guadeloupe turned to a little Belgium. For that matter, he had no cause for complaint from the inhabitants, whose tumultuous history had accustomed them to making peace with the master of the hour. He found solace in the great manumitted masses, jubilant at their status as new citizens, though this occasioned an early difficulty for the government: convinced they now needed obey no owners, the former slaves were loath to go work in the fields. Weeds overtook the arable lands, and no punishment was enough for those who alleged patriotic pretexts for refusing to bend their backs to clear stray twigs and infinite nettles from the soil packed into the tilled furrows beneath a sun that fed all species equally, oblivious to the preferences of man . . . Now the *Bayonnaise* appeared, bringing arms, provisions, and infantrymen—but far fewer in number than what the military leaders had requested. The Convention was short on men, and unable to sacrifice whole contingents to defend a remote colony. Esteban, surprised by a summons to Victor Hugues's office to retrieve a set of proofs, found the Commissar absorbed in reading of what he had most anxiously awaited apart from the official dispatches: the press from Paris, which occasionally mentioned his name. Leafing through the papers the other had already set aside, Esteban was appalled to learn of the Festival of the Supreme Being, and even more disconcertingly of the condemnation of atheism as an immoral and, thus, aristocratic and counterrevolutionary posture. All at once, atheists had been deemed enemies of the Republic. The French People recognized the existence of the Supreme Being and the Immortality of the Soul. The Incorruptible had said that even if the existence of God, of the soul, was nothing more than a dream, still, these were the highest conceptions of the human spirit. Godless men were now called "desolate monsters . . ." Esteban laughed so effusively that Victor, looking out over the top of his paper, furrowed his brow and asked: "What's the joke?" "It was hardly worth ordering the chapel on the Morne du Gouvernement razed only to find this out now," said Esteban, who had rediscovered, in the forgoing days, the good humor of his race in this place whose luscious fruits, maritime scents, and trees brought back to him his personality from before. "To my mind, everything is in order," Victor said, not responding directly. "A man like Him cannot be mistaken. If he felt this was necessary, then I consider it well." "And they're even praising his actions in the tone of Te Deums, Lauds, the Magnificat," Esteban said. "As suits his stature," Victor said. "I must say, I fail to see the difference between Jehovah, the Great Architect, and the Supreme Being," said Esteban. And he reminded the Commissar of his impiety of old, his sarcastic barbs about the Masons and their "Solomonic masquerades." Victor didn't listen: "There was too much Judaism in the Lodges. And as for the Catholics and their God, whom the friars marshaled for the evils of inquisition and tyranny, that's irrelevant to the realization that an eternal, boundless Superior Being does exist, deserving of rational and dignified reverence of a kind whose exercise is commendable among free men. Let

us invoke not the God of Torquemada, but the God of the philosophers." Esteban was taken aback at the slavishness of a
mind dynamic and energetic, but utterly subservient to politics,
fleeing the critical examination of matters of fact, looking away
from the most flagrant contradictions; faithful to the point of
fanaticism—for this could indeed be called fanaticism—to the
dictates of the man who had conferred on him his powers.
"And what if they open the churches back up tomorrow, and
the bishops are no longer thought 'mitred bipeds' and the saints
and virgins are paraded through the streets of Paris?" the young
man asked. "That would mean there was a compelling reason
for it." "But you . . . do you believe in God?" Esteban
shouted, thinking he'd cornered him. "That is a personal
question that in no way affects my revolutionary obedience,"
Victor responded. "For you, the Revolution is infallible." "The
Revolution . . ." Victor said slowly, looking toward the port,
where workers tried to righten the capsized hull of the *Thétis*,
"the Revolution has given a purpose to my existence. I have
been granted a role in the great enterprise of the era. In carrying
it out, I shall try to rise to my highest stature." He paused, and
that made more sonorous the shouts of the sailors tugging a
row of ropes in time with the shanties. "Will you institute the
Cult of the Supreme Being here, then?" asked Esteban. For him,
this notion of restoring God to the throne seemed the height of
recantation. "No," the Commissar responded, after a brief hesitation. "They haven't even demolished the church on the
Morne du Gouvernement. Now would be too soon. We must
take things slower. If I were to suddenly speak of the Supreme
Being, the people here would be toting icons of Him nailed to a
cross, with a crown of thorns and a wound in his side, and that
would get us nowhere. We are not in the same latitudes as the
Champ de Mars." Esteban felt the malicious satisfaction of
hearing from the lips of Victor Hugues words Martínez de Ballesteros might well have uttered. And yet, *over there*, many
Spaniards had been hounded and guillotined for objecting that
methods dictated in Paris were ill suited to countries where certain traditions ran deep: "It would be a mistake to go to Spain
preaching atheism," they had counseled. In the cathedral in

Zaragoza, the lovely breasts of Mademoiselle Aubry in the guise of the Goddess Reason could not be flaunted as they had been in Notre-Dame, before the church was put on sale, even if no one saw fit to acquire for their own use a building so gothic, so monumental and inhospitable . . . "Contradictions and more contradictions," murmured Esteban, "the Revolution I dreamed of was nothing like this . . ." "Who told you to believe in things that weren't?" Victor asked. "Anyway, this is all idle blather. The English are still in Basse-Terre. That is all we should be worried about." And he added in a cutting tone: "Revolution is to be *waged*, not debated." "When I think," Esteban said, "how the altar on the Morne du Gouvernement could have been saved if only the dispatch from Paris had arrived sooner! If a stronger wind had blown over the Atlantic, God could have stayed in his house! Who knows what is being waged here, and by whom!" "Get to work!" Victor said, planting a heavy hand between his shoulders and pushing him toward the door, which closed so loudly the mulatta singer, busy polishing the handrail on the staircase, asked sarcastically: *"Monsieur Victor faché?"* Esteban crossed the dining room, followed by the twitter of the serving girls mocking him.

The Loeuillets' printing press worked frantically producing pamphlets destined for the French laborers on the neutral islands, promising them official positions and property if they recognized the advantages of revolutionary government. This strengthened the armed contingents, though weeks passed before they gathered the resolve needed to cross the Salt River. The situation remained unchanged until late September, when the Commissar was informed that yellow fever was wreaking havoc on the British side, and General Grey, fearful of the cyclones that lashed the Windward Islands at that time of the year, had taken much of his squadron to Fort Royal in Martinique, whose port offered greater protection from hurricanes. They debated how best to take advantage of the situation, deciding in the end that the French army should be divided into three columns under the command of De Leyssegues, Pelardy, and Boudet. They would try their luck with a landing at three different points in Basse-Terre. They confiscated canoes, boats, dinghies, even the Indians' kayaks, and one night, they attacked. Two days later, the French were the lords of Lamentin and Petit-Bourg. On the morning of October 6, they laid siege to the entrenched positions at Berville . . . These were expectant hours in Pointe-à-Pitre. Some said that the siege would be long, because the English had had time enough to strengthen their positions. Others felt General Graham was demoralized by the resolve of the revolutionary government in Grande-Terre, where people scoffed at the volleys of cannon he fired with fury at the city from the heights of Morne Savon . . . Esteban met frequently then with Monsieur Anse, the guillotine's custodian and operator, who was assembling a Cabinet of Curiosities, gathering gorgonians, bits of mineral, embalmed sunfish, roots with animal shapes, and luminous conches. They liked to take their rest on the splendid inlet of Le Gosier, with its island glimmering like a chalcedony heart. Monsieur Anse would bury a couple of bottles of wine in the sand to cool them down. Taking an old violin from its case and turning his back to the sea, he would play one of Philidor's poignant pastorals, embellishing it with variations of his own. He was a good companion on excursions, capable of wonder at a chunk of sulfur, a butterfly of Egyptian outline, or any unknown flower that appeared in their path. At midday on October 6, Monsieur Anse received an order to load the guillotine onto a cart and to depart for Berville forthwith. The town square was theirs. Victor Hugues, before ordering an attack, had given General Graham four days to surrender. And when the Commissar set foot on the field full of trenches, strewn with rubbish abandoned in the stampede, he found there twelve hundred English soldiers who didn't speak English: in his retreat, Graham had abandoned them on shore, taking with him only twenty-two monarchist settlers who were particularly close to him. Shocked at such perfidy from a man who had been their leader, the French who had fought under the British flag were sorted into pitiful groups before they'd even had time to remove their uniforms. "Some things just can't be done," Monsieur Anse said when departing, with an ambiguous gesture toward the carriage where the Machine lay hidden under sackcloth, to protect it from the rain the wind would soon bring in, which was falling already on Marie-Galante, changing the island's color from bright green to leaden gray, its contours blurred by a scintillating cloud . . . "Some things just can't be done," Monsieur Anse repeated the next morning, soaked and shivery on his return, trying and failing to warm his body with rum from the inns. Slightly drunk, he told Esteban the guillotine couldn't be used for mass executions. His work took time, proceeded according to its own rhythms, and it was hard to say how the Commissar, who was well acquainted with the Machine, had thought the eight hundred sixty-five men sentenced to death might pass one by one beneath its blade. Anse had done everything humanly possible to speed up the operation. But at midnight, only thirty of the disloyal prisoners had received their due punishment. "Enough!" the Commissar had shouted. And the rest were shot in groups of ten, of twenty, while the carriage dodged depressions in the road on its return to Pointe-à-Pitre. Victor Hugues had shown mercy to the few Englishmen captured in Berville, disarming them and letting them return to their defeated armada. To a young British captain reluctant to depart, he said: "I am bound by duty to be here. But you . . . who orders you to contemplate the French blood I am forced to spill . . . ?" The era of the White Lords was over in Guadeloupe. This was said, with a great roll of the snare drums, in the Place de la Victoire. "Some things just can't be done," Monsieur Anse repeated, pained at his poor performance on his first day with the Machine: "Eight hundred sixty-five there were. A colossal task." Esteban listened to the tale and listened to it again, as if the man were speaking of a volcanic eruption in some faraway territory. Berville was, for him, just a name. And moreover, eight hundred sixty-five faces were too many to imagine a single one of them.

XXI.

A few dens of resistance remained in Basse-Terre. But the men Graham had betrayed lost their valor no sooner than they'd got hold of a sloop that would carry them to a neighboring island. With the fall of Fort Saint-Charles, the campaign was said to be at an end. La Désirade and Marie-Galante—whose governor, a former deputy in the Assembly who had passed over to the English side, choosing suicide over armed resistance—were now in French hands. Victor Hugues was the lord of Guadeloupe, and announced to all that they would work together in peace. And looking for a symbolic gesture to give weight to his words, he planted trees that would one day give shade on the Place de la Victoire. Soon came the event they had all been waiting for, patiently but with anxious curiosity: the guillotine set to work in public. The day of its unveiling, for use upon the persons of two monarchist chaplains found on a farm with a cache of rifles and munitions, the whole city poured into the agora, where a large stage with a stairway up the side was built in the Parisian style over four posts of cedar. Republican manners having made their way into the colony, mestizos arrived dressed in short blue jackets and trousers with red stripes, while the mulattas wore new madras dresses in the colors of the victors. Never had such a raucous multitude been seen, merry in fabrics dyed indigo and strawberry that seemed to flutter in time with the flags on that clear sunny morning. The Commissar's serving girls peeped through the windows, shouting and laughing—and laughed still more when an officer's trembling hand climbed the backs of their knees. Many children had mounted the roofs of the buildings to see better. Fried food gave off smoke, pitchers overflowed with juice and *garapiña*, and light rum, drunk early, lifted the spirits high. And yet, when Monsieur Anse stood on the heights of the scaffold in his finest ceremonial garb—grave in his occupation, cleanly shaven by the barber—a profound silence took over. Pointe-à-Pitre was not Cap Français, where an excellent theater had existed for some time now, fed with novelties by traveling

companies headed to New Orleans. Here there was no such
thing, no one had ever seen an open stage, and through it, just
then, the people were discovering the essence of Tragedy. Fate
was there among them, blade at the ready, prompt and inexo-
rable, stalking those who, with wicked inspiration, had turned
their arms against the City. And the spirit of the Chorus came
to life in every spectator, with strophes and antistrophes
sounding and resounding over the scaffold. A Messenger appeared, the Guards opened a pathway, and the cart made its
way into the vast pageantry of the Public Square, bearing two
condemned men, hands tied, with a single rosary joining their
bound wrists. The solemn rolling of the drums was heard; the
bascule was checked and bore a corpulent man's weight without buckling; and the blade fell in the midst of a clamor of anticipation. Minutes later, the first two executions were carried
out . . . But the multitude remained there, while still-flowing
blood dripped through the cracks in the stage, temporarily surprised, perhaps, that the dreadful spectacle had been so brief.
Soon, to elude the horror that held them in a kind of stupefaction, many turned merry, hoping to lengthen the day, which
already had the character of a festive reprieve. They had to call
attention to their newly donned clothes, to do something to affirm life in the face of Death. And since figure dances put the
garments on display best, throwing up the sunflowers of the
carmagnole skirts, some lined up for contra dances, stepping
forward and back, changing partners, bowing, and gripping
each other's waists, ignoring the self-declared masters of ceremony who tried in vain to maintain order among the rows and
groups. With time, all that revelry, all that yearning to dance
and frolic and laugh and clamor, brought them together in an
enormous wheel, which broke again into groups that took
turns around the guillotine, filed off into the neighboring
streets, came and went, invading backyards and gardens, until
nightfall. That day was the beginning of the Great Terror on
the island. The Machine now labored continually in the Place
de la Victoire, the rhythm of its slicing ever swifter. And in a
place where everyone knew everyone on sight or from some
dealings—and this man held a grudge against that one, and

so-and-so could not fail to remember when so-and-so had humiliated him—there was always curiosity to see who was being executed, and the guillotine became the center of town life. The people of the Market moved slowly to that comely square in the port, with its windows and niches, its corner posts and sunny stalls, hawking their buns and their peppers, their soursops and puff pastries, their annonas and fresh porgies at all hours while there rolled the heads of those only yesterday respected and adored. An auspicious setting for the conduct of business, the plaza transformed into a moveable exchange for rubbish and abandoned objects, where a grille, a mechanical bird, or the oddments of a set of china were sold to the highest bidder. A harness might be traded for a metal pot; playing cards for firewood; elegant watches for Margarita pearls. In just a day, greengrocer and peddler were raised to the rank of wholesaler, dealers in mixed—extremely mixed—goods: cookware, emblazoned gravy boats, real silver, chess pieces, tapestries, and miniatures. The scaffold was the mainstay of a bank, of an auction house that never closed. The haggling, disputes, and negotiations no longer stopped for the executions. The guillotine was an aspect of their everyday reality. There, between the parsley and oregano, tiny decorative guillotines were offered for sale, and many customers took one home with them. The children honed their intellect designing machines to behead cats. A beautiful mulatta, a favorite of one of De Leyssegues's lieutenants, offered his guests liqueurs in wooden bottles of human shape that lay on a bascule and were uncorked—naturally, droll human faces had been painted on the stoppers—by the action of a toy blade brought down by a minute mechanical executioner. Many novelties and diversions arrived in those days to interrupt the island's tranquil, pastoral life; nonetheless, some did notice that the Terror was descending the social staircase and starting to reap at the level of the ground. Informed that many negroes in the commune of Les Abysses had embraced their status as free men and were refusing to labor in the expropriated fields, Victor Hugues ordered the unruliest among them taken prisoner and condemned to the guillotine. With some perplexity, Esteban noted that, despite the Commissar's words of praise for the sublime Decree of 16 Pluviôse of Year II, he failed to show much sympathy for the negroes: "They're lucky we even recognize them as French citizens," he often said bitterly. He retained certain racial prejudices from his long stay in Saint-Domingue, where the colonists had been harsh in their treatment of the slaves—who had the reputation of layabouts, idiots, shirkers, and thieves, *propres-à-rien*, among the men who worked them from sunup to sundown. The Republic's soldiers, notwithstanding their weakness for dark flesh of the female sort, lost no opportunity to club and lash the negro men under the flimsiest of pretexts, even while admitting that there were magnificent shooters among them, like that stout leper by the name of Vulcain. Brothers in war, the blacks and whites were divided in peace. Soon, Victor Hugues introduced forced labor. Any negro accused of sloth or disobedience, of insubordination or rebellion, was condemned to death. This was a lesson the entire island had to learn, and so the guillotine was taken from the Place de la Victoire and began to wander, to travel, to roam: at dawn on Monday, it stood in Le Moule; on Tuesday it was at work in Le Gosier, where someone was convicted of idling; on Wednesday it chastened six monarchists hiding in the old Parish Church of Sainte-Anne. It was carted from village to village, paraded past the taverns. The executioner and his men accepted drinks and gratuities to bring the blade down over the empty air, so all could witness its workings. The band of drummers who drowned out the shouts of the condemned in Pointe-à-Pitre had been unable to accompany them; in their place, a large bass drum was loaded onto the wagon, and its pounding brought a festive sort of joy to the executions. The peasants, curious to see how powerful the machine was, laid the trunks of banana trees on the bascule—with its sheaf of damp and porous ducts, nothing better resembles a human neck than a banana tree's trunk—to watch them being severed. To settle a bet, six sugarcanes were bundled beneath the blade, and even that didn't stop it. When all this was over, the illustrious visitors continued on their way, smoking and singing to the beating of the bass drum, their red Phrygian caps turned chestnut brown by sweat. On their return, the bascule was so laden with fruits it seemed to be borne by a Car of Plenty.

Early in Year III, Victor Hugues found himself raised to the summit of glory. Pleased with the notices they'd received, the Convention ratified the promotions of his officers, approved his nominations and decrees, congratulated him in panegyric prose and announced a consignment of reinforcements: soldiers, arms, and munitions. But the Commissar no longer needed them: through forced conscription, he'd created an army of ten thousand adequately trained men. Fortifications were being built on all the vulnerable points of the coast. Confiscated goods filled the chests, and the warehouses were bursting with all the necessities. On a journey to the island's other side, Victor Hugues—remembering he had been there many years before—was taken with the beauty of the town of Basse-Terre, with its rumor of flowing water, its public fountains that cooled delightfully the avenues lined with tamarinds. It was nobler, more distinguished than Pointe-à-Pitre, with cobblestone streets, a shady esplanade, large stone houses that evoked certain corners of Rochefort, Nantes, La Rochelle. The Commissar would happily have moved his home to the calm and welcoming parish of Saint-François; but the port, well suited to receipt of cattle from the neighboring islands—cattle thrown overboard on arrival and left to swim ashore—could scarcely harbor his fleet. At the end his tour as victorious leader, he was acclaimed by the lepers of La Désirade, the *little whites* of Marie-Galante, even the Indians on that Caribbean island, whose chief communicated their request that they be permitted to enjoy the benefits of French citizenship. Aware that these men were magnificent seamen and knew everything about the archipelago, which they traveled through in swift boats long before the ships of the Great Admiral of Isabella and Ferdinand had arrived in those parts, he passed around rosettes and promised them everything they asked for. Victor Hugues was kinder to the Caribs than to the negroes: he valued their pride, their aggression, their haughty assertion that *the Caribs alone are true men*—and his esteem only grew now that they'd hung tricolor cockades from the cords of their loincloths. In Marie-Galante, the Commissar asked to visit the beach where those frustrated lords of the Antilles had impaled the French bucca-neers who had made an attempt on their women years before. The skeletons, bones, skulls were still there on stakes planted next to the sea: transfixed by wood like an insect pierced with a naturalist's pin, within days the corpses had attracted so many vultures that the coast, seen from a distance, seemed obscured beneath boiling lava . . . The Commissar did not for-get, among such copious acclaim, that the English were still marauding in nearby waters in the hopes of imposing a block-ade. Victor liked to pass his evenings shut away with De Leys-segues, who now sported the insignia of rear admiral, tracing out a naval strategy that would encompass the entire Carib-bean. The project was kept secret, and they were in the midst of their machinations when Esteban entered the Commissar's office one day and found him unkempt and sweating, his face tense with rage. He was walking around a long table, stopping behind the officials, who had abandoned their work and were fighting over the pages of the recently delivered newspapers. "Have you heard?" the young man shouted, pointing with a trembling hand at an article relating the incredible events that had taken place in Paris on the ninth of Thermidor. "The bas-tards!" Victor shouted. "They've struck down our finest men." The ruthlessness of the affair left Esteban speechless. And the distance made these impressions doubly dramatic. Like a man carrying in his mind the image of an object long contemplated, keeping it present even when the object itself has disappeared, they had spoken, in that room, with reference to immediate and future reality, of a man who had ceased to exist several months before. While they had argued, in this very place, over the Cult of the Supreme Being, its founder had already un-leashed at the scaffold's foot the terrible cry provoked when the executioner tore the bandage from his broken jaw. There was no limit to Victor Hugues's indignation, and the implications were such that the mind refused to lay boundaries to conjec-ture. Not only had the giant fallen whose portrait hung there showing him at the height of his glory, standing as an example to all; not only had the Commissar lost a man who'd put faith in him, with grants of power and authority; still worse, he would have to wait for weeks, maybe months, before knowing the direction things had taken in France. Likely, the forces of reaction would seek merciless revenge. Perhaps a new government would step forth and destroy all that the earlier one had wrought. In Guadeloupe, there would be new Plenipotentiaries with gruff faces and contrary expressions, obedient to inscrutable orders. Victor Hugues's report to the Convention on the massacre of Berville might now be used against him. Perhaps he had already been relieved of his duties, or put on trial in absentia, and his career, his life might already be over. He read and reread the list of those fallen on 9 Thermidor, as to decipher therein the keys to his fate. Some of those present insinuated meekly that they might now enter a period of leniency, of indulgence, with religion reestablished. "Or the monarchy might be restored," thought Esteban, and the idea brought him at once a sense of relief, of peace regained after so many storms, and of revulsion, of contempt for the Throne. If men had gone to such lengths, if so many had prophesied, suffered, acclaimed, fallen in the fires and triumphal arches of a vast apocalyptic dream, then at least Time should not turn back. The tarnished gold of royalty was too paltry a payment for blood spilled. There was still hope for justice; one fairer, perhaps, than that justice that so quickly ceased to be so when words—all that talk was one of the evils of the age—meandered into abstraction. Hope for a Liberty less proclaimed than enjoyed; for an Equality brought about rather than frittered away in talk; for a Fraternity that eschewed denunciations and was manifest in the restoration of real tribunals, manned once more by juries. Victor went on pacing through the room, calmer now, hands behind his back. At last he came to rest before the Incorruptible's portrait. "Here, at any rate, all shall continue as before," he finally said. "I take no notice of this news. I do not accept it. And Jacobin morals remain the only sort I acknowledge. No one shall move me from here. And if the Revolution is lost in France, may it continue in the Americas. The time has come for us to turn to the Mainland." And addressing Esteban: "You are immediately to translate into Spanish the Declaration of the Rights of Man and the Citizen and the text of the Constitution." "The Constitution of '91 or '93?" the young man asked. "The one of '93—the only one I recognize. From this island shall proceed the ideas that will shake Spanish America to the core. If we have partisans and allies in Spain, then we shall have them on the Continent as well. Perhaps even more, because dissatisfaction is more abundant in the colonies than in the metropole."

XXII.

When the old Camisard Loeuillet was told he would have to print texts in Spanish, he realized with horror he had brought no ñ in his cases of type. "Who would ever think of disguising that sound in its own letter?" he asked, furious with himself. "Can you imagine the noble, even majestic word swan spelled *ciñe* rather than *cygne*?" That no one had advised him that this character might prove necessary only showed the disorganization of these men who intended to govern the world. "It never crossed their mind that they use the tilde in Spanish!" he shouted. "Band of fools!" Eventually he chose to replace the tildes with circumflex accents trimmed from other letters, greatly complicating the work of typesetting. But soon they had printed a Declaration of the Rights of Man and the Citizen in Spanish, handing in their edition to the Commissar's offices, where the atmosphere was thick with disconcertment and grief. The wind of Thermidor blew over many consciences. Criticisms some had kept to themselves were aired now in secret meetings that kept all outsiders at bay. When Esteban gave Loeuillet his Spanish version of the Constitution of '93, the typographer railed against the cynical contrivances of propaganda that vaunted its ideals to create the illusion of realities that were the very thing these ideals had failed to achieve—in a land where, moreover, the finest intentions had produced the most atrocious consequences. Should the Americans now put into practice those same principles the Terror had transgressed almost to the letter, violating them once more in turn in response to the political demands of the moment? "No one here says a word about starvation or barges," said the Camisard, alluding to the vessels sitting in every French port on the Atlantic bursting with their cargo of aggrieved prisoners—like the notorious *Bonhomme Richard*, named sardonically after Benjamin Franklin's famous almanac. "Let's get back to printing," Esteban would tell him. For now they had a task to get through each day, and the young man performed it conscientiously, finding solace, a relief in his ruminations, in his attempts to translate as best he could; he grew meticulous, almost a purist, in his search for the exact term, the truest synonym, the right punctuation, and bemoaned that the backward Spanish of the day failed to accommodate the concise and modern turns of phrase of the French. He found a kind of aesthetic pleasure in translating well, however indifferent the content of the phrases in question. For whole days, he polished his version of Billaud-Varenne's report concerning "The Theory of Democratic Government, and the Need of Inspiring Love for the Civic Virtues Through Public Festivals and Moral Institutions," even if the turgid prose of a man who ceaselessly evoked the names Tarquin, Cato, and Cataline struck him as no less passé, no less false, no less irrelevant to the present era than the lyrics of the Masonic anthems he had been taught to intone years ago in the Lodge of United Foreigners. The Loeuillets, father and son, sought his help in the arduous work of typesetting texts in a language unknown to them, asking for explanations of accents and spelling or where a word should break at the end of a line. The old Camisard worried over the pages' appearance with the care of a good artisan, bemoaning the absence of a colophon or an allegorical vignette to bring a piece of writing to a beautiful close. Neither the editor-translator nor the typographers had any particular faith in the words their labor would multiply and diffuse. But if a man must work, he must do so properly, neither running roughshod over the language nor disparaging the material it was written on.

They proceeded with the impression of a *carmagnole améri-caine*, a variant of an older version written down in Bayonne and destined to the peoples of the New World:

Verse: *I am one of the shirtless*
                   I'll dance wherever I'm found
                   And in place of guitars
                   The cannons will resound,
                   The cannons will resound,
                   The cannons will resound.

Chorus: *Let the shirtless dance*
                   And let us hear the songs of the poor
                   Let the shirtless dance
                   And long live the cannons' roar.

Verse: *If anyone should ask me*
                   Why my chest is bare,
                   Well, the king he taxed me
                   Till I've got nothing left to wear,
                   Till I've got nothing left to wear,
                   Till I've got nothing left to wear.

Chorus: *Let the shirtless dance . . .*

Verse: *All the kings across the world*
                   Are tyrants fit to curse,
                   But of all the kings across the world
                   Charles must be worst,
                   Charles must be worst,
                   Charles must be worst.

Chorus: *Let the shirtless dance . . .*

In the later verses, the anonymous author, apprised of what was happening in the Americas, gave the Governors, Magistrates, and Mayors their just due, along with the Trial Judges and Superintendents and Administrators in league with the

Crown. Nor could the versifier be unaware of the Cult of the Supreme Being when he wrote further on: *God protects our creed, / Our hand is guided by the Lord / The King with his misdeeds / Shall feel his righteous sword.* It concluded: *Long live love for the Fatherland!/ And long live liberty! / May the despots perish / And with them the tyranny of kings!* That was precisely how the Spanish conspirators in Bayonne had always spoken. Esteban had only vague news of them. He was certain that Guzmán, Marat's friend, had been guillotined. It was hinted, but without certainty, that Abbot Marchena might have escaped the massacre of the Girondins. As for the good Martínez de Ballesteros, he'd have found another reason to live—to survive—lending his services to a Revolution unconnected to the one that had fired his early enthusiasms. In those times, an acquired haste, a persistent impulse, led many to continue striving for a world very different from the one they'd previously hoped to forge, bitter, disappointed, but, like the Loeuillets, incapable of flagging in their faithful execution of their prescribed duties. They offered no more opinions: to live, that was what mattered—to have a task that permitted one to return to the peace of work day after day. They lived for the day, envisioning the reward of a late afternoon drink, a swim in cool water, the breeze brought by nightfall, the flowering of orange blossoms, the girl who might come, even today, and pamper them. In the midst of events so grave they overwhelmed the powers of the average man to grasp, to measure, to assess, there was wonder to be found in observing the transformations of mimetic insects, the nuptial maneuvering of a beetle, a sudden multiplication of butterflies. Never before had Esteban taken such an interest in the minute—quivering tadpoles in a barrel of water, the maturation of a mushroom, ants that gnawed at the leaves of a lemon tree until they resembled bobbin lace—as in those days invested with the eternal and momentous. One day, a handsome mulatta in luminous bracelets and pressed skirts, her swishing petticoats smelling of vetiver, entered his bedroom with the empty pretext of borrowing a pen and ink. A half-hour after their bodies had mingled in delicious complication, the woman, not wearing even a single scrap of fabric, had introduced herself with a graceful bow: Mademoiselle Athalie Bajazet, *coiffeuse pour dames*. "What a marvelous country!" the young man exclaimed, forgetting his worries. Since then Mademoiselle Athalie Bajazet had slept with him every night. "Whenever she takes off her skirt, she presents me with two tragedies by Racine . . ." Esteban told the Loeuillets amid laughter . . . Called by his accountant's duties—needing to take an inventory of certain shipments in the island's ports—the young man went occasionally to Basse-Terre, driving his horse down uneven roads where the vegetation was particularly lush due to the many streams and torrents that drained over the eternally mist-capped *mornes*. On these journeys, he discovered a vegetation like that of his home country, which his illness had prevented his getting to know well back there, and which he now took in fully, redressing a lacuna from his youth. He sniffed lustily at the mellow fragrance of the annonas, the gray acidity of the tamarinds, the fleshy gentleness of so many fruits with red and yellow pulp, which harbored, in their recondite folds, sumptuous seeds with tortoiseshell textures, the color of polished ebony or mahogany. He sank his face in the cool white of the soursops; he scratched the amaranth violet of the star apple, the glassy swan shot hidden in the depths of its flesh. One day, while his unsaddled horse was kicking its four hooves and lurching through the waters of a stream, Esteban ventured to climb a tree. And having prevailed in the initiation rite he perceived in the struggle to reach its branches, he ascended to the crown along an increasingly dense staircase of thin limbs, footholds arrayed grandly with leaves, a green hive, a sumptuous gable seen from the inside for the first time. A strange, profound, inexplicable exaltation brought Esteban joy as he straddled a fork at the peak of that quivering edifice of wood and verdure. Climbing a tree was a private mission he would perhaps never undertake again. Whoever embraced the high breasts of a tree realized a sort of nuptial, deflowering a veiled world never seen by other men. All at once, the gaze takes in every beauty and imperfection of the Tree. Two tender branches open like the thighs of a woman, hiding a handful of green moss in their juncture;

round wounds are revealed, left behind by the shearing off of
dry progeny; the splendid ogees open high, strange bifurca-
tions that have driven sap to a favored stretch, leaving others
emaciated and suited like tinder to the flames. Reaching his
lookout, Esteban grasped the arcane relationship between
Mast, Plow, Tree, and Cross. He recalled the text of Saint Hip-
polytus: "This wood belongs to me. I eat of it, it sustains me; I
shelter in its roots, I lie on its branches; I give myself to its
breath as I give myself to the wind. This is my narrow path;
this is my narrowed road; Jacob's ladder, and at the top, my
Lord." The great signs of the Tau, of the Cross of Saint An-
drew, the Brazen Serpent, the Anchor, and the Ladder, were
implicit in every Tree, with Creation foretelling Construction,
giving proportions for the Builder of future Arks. The shadows
of evening found Esteban swaying in the heights of the trunk,
caught in a somnolent luxury he might have prolonged indefinitely. Then he noticed novel silhouettes, certain vegetal beings
from below: papayas with udders hanging from their necks
seemed to come to life and march off into the lush distances of
La Soufrière; the ceiba, *mother of all trees*, as the black wise-
men called it, turning to an obelisk, a rostral column, monument and elevation over the fading light. A dead mango tree
transformed into a coil of serpents poised to bite; or a live one,
swelling with sap that oozed down its bark and the mottled
skin of its fruits, burst into flower, suddenly glowing yellow.
Enthralled, Esteban observed the life of these creatures as he
might have the evolution of a zoological being. First appeared
germinating fruits that looked like green glass beads, their
sour juice tasting of frozen almonds. Then that hanging organism would take on form and contour, stretching out to cast a
shadow like a witch's crescent chin. Color came into its face. It
passed from moss green to saffron yellow and ripened in ce-
ramic splendor—sometimes Cretan, sometimes Mediterranean, but always Antillean—before the first black circles of
decrepitude ate into its flesh reeking of tannin and iodine. And
one night, coming loose and falling with a dull thud amid the
grass damp with dew, the fruit made its impending death
known, with freckles that spread and sunk until they erupted

in wounds and the flies nestled inside them. Like the corpse of a prelate in an exemplary danse macabre, the fallen matter shed its skin and entrails, leaving nothing but a streaked, colorless seed, enveloped in the tatters of its shroud. But here, in this world without winter deaths or resurrections on Flowery Easter, the cycle of life began again posthaste: in weeks arose, from the seed in repose, like a tiny Asiatic tree, a sprout of pinkish leaves, soft like human skin, which hands dared not to touch . . . At times, a storm surprised Esteban in his travels through the brush. In his aural recollections, the young man would compare the differences between the rains of the Tropics and the monotonous drizzle of the Old World. Here, a potent and vast noise, its tempo majestic, drawn out like the prelude of a symphony, announced the downpour's advance from afar as the mangy vultures, flying low in ever tighter circles, finally abandoned the landscape. A coaxing scent of wet forest, earth overrun by humus and sap, expanded out toward the universal scent, swelling the ruffs of the birds and making horses prick up their ears—infusing Esteban with a rare sensation of physical yearning, an ill-formed desire to press against a flesh that shared his longings. Dry flicks in the highest branches accompanied the rapid shadows cutting across the light. A frigid joy descended, drawing singular resonances from all matter—striking clear notes on the vines and banana trees, on the tuning fork of membranes, percussing when it struck the larger leaves. The water broke up high in the crowns of the palm trees, which scattered it like cathedral gutters until it resonated, grave and drumming, over the lower fronds. Drops ricocheted off the patches of tender green before falling on foliage so dense that when it reached the level of the eddoes, tense as the skin of a tambourine, the various levels of vegetal matter had divided, fragmented, atomized it a thousand times, and then, as it touched the soil, it made the Bermuda grass and esparto rejoice in a hail of voices. The wind imposed its rhythms on the immeasurable symphony, which soon transformed stream beds into flash floods, stridently dislodging pebbles that collapsed in an avalanche. Tumultuous descents hollowed out the bottoms of the streambeds, dragging stones from higher up, the dead trunks of trees, barbs, roots wound with tassels and tatters that lodged in the silt like stranded ships. And then the sky grew calm, the clouds dispersed, twilight settled in, and Esteban continued on his way, his horse wet and vigorous, under a dew of trees, their voices each distinct, amid a vast Magnificat of scents . . . When Esteban returned to Pointe-à-Pitre from such journeys, he felt that the era was foreign to him, that he was a stranger in a bloody, remote world where everything seemed outlandish. The churches remained closed there, while in France, they might well have reopened. The blacks had been declared free citizens, but those who hadn't been conscripted as soldiers or sailors bent their backs from sunup to sundown beneath the lashes of their overseers, same as before, except that now there loomed over them the merciless azimuth of the guillotine. Newborn children were named Cincinnatus, Leonidas, or Lycurgus, and taught to recite a Revolutionary Catechism that no longer coincided with reality—and in the recently founded Jacobin Club, they spoke of the Incorruptible as if he were still alive. Fattened flies swarmed over the sticky boards of the scaffold, and Victor Hugues and his officers were getting all too used to taking long naps under tulle mosquito nets with mulatta mistresses watching over their repose and cooling them with fans of palm.

XXIII.

Esteban suffered from Victor Hugues's growing isolation with an almost feminine tenderness. He watched as the Commissar played his part with implacable rigor, spurring on the tribunals, giving the guillotine no rest, bellowing yesterday's rhetoric, dictating, editing, legislating, judging, always in the middle of everything; but whoever knew him well could see that the motive for his immoderate activity was a recondite desire for self-abnegation. He knew many of his most obedient subordinates dreamed of seeing the arrival of a sealed letter decreeing his dismissal in the elegant hand of some faithful amanuensis. Esteban would have liked to be by him, to accompany him, to soothe him in those moments. But the Commissar grew more elusive, shutting himself away to read until dawn, or else riding at evening to the cove of Le Gosier in a coach occasionally shared with De Leyssegues. Dressed in nothing but linen breeches, he would row to the uninhabited island, not returning until the nocturnal swarms of insects emerged from the mangrove swamps on the coast. He reread the works of classical orators, wishing, perhaps, to make a show of his elegance, should he be forced to speak in his own defense. He gave orders hastily and often with contradictions, was prone to unpredictable accesses of rage, and would suddenly sack his allies or ratify a death sentence all had assumed would be commuted. One inauspicious morning, he ordered the remains of General Dundas, former British governor of the island, disinterred and scattered in the public thoroughfare. For hours, the dogs fought over the best pieces of carrion, dragging from one street to another the putrid human residue still clinging to the ceremonial uniform in which the enemy leader had been buried. Esteban wished he could placate that man's perturbed soul, alarmed by the first unexpected sail that flickered on the horizon, his solitude only growing in concert with his historical dimension. Harsh and hard, determined like few others, endowed with military genius, Hugues's success on the island outstripped in many ways the other achievements of the Revolution. And yet, a faraway turn of the political tides had taken place, with White Terror following Red, unleashing unknown forces that would likely bring to the colony people incapable of governing it. And moreover, it transpired that Victor Hugues's protector, Dalbarade, whom Robespierre had defended tooth and nail when they'd accused him of friendship with Danton, had passed over to the Thermidorian side. Disgusted by these events, reacting to tidings and rumors that poured in by the day, the Commissar accelerated the first stages of undertaking he had spent months preparing with Rear Admiral De Leyssegues. "To Hell with them all!" he shouted one day, thinking of those in Paris who held his fate in their hands. "By the time they show up with their papers, I'll be powerful enough to wipe my ass with them and shove them in their face."

One morning, there was unusual commotion in the port. A number of light ships—sloops, above all—were being hauled onto land and put in dry dock. Carpenters, caulkers, and tar brushers set to work on the larger vessels; men labored in raucous concert with brushes, saws, and hammers, and gunners loaded light cannons into rowboats and carried them onboard. Looking out a window of the old Grain Exchange, Esteban saw more men engaged in the minor task of changing the names of the ships. The *Calypso* became the *Tyrannicide*; *La Sémillante* was renamed *La Carmagnole*; *L'Hirondelle* was transformed into *La Marie-Tapage*; *Le Lutin* into *Le Vengeur*. And painted in bright characters over seasoned timbers that had served the King so well, *La Tintamarre*, *La Cruelle*, *Ça-ira*, *La Sansjupe*, *L'Athènienne*, *Le Poignard*, *La Guillotine*, *L'Ami du Peuple*, *Le Terroriste*, and *La Bande Joyeuse* were born. *La Thétis*, cured of the wounds received during the bombardment of Pointe-à-Pitre, was now dubbed *L'Incorruptible*, surely at the behest of a Victor Hugues well aware that the epithet's uncertain gender might shield him from a charge of sedition. Esteban was asking himself the cause of that commotion when Mademoiselle Athalie Bajazet informed him that he was urgently required in the Leader's office. The glasses of punch one of his maids cleared away made it plain that the Commissar had been drinking, but he still possessed that self-assurance in gesture and thought which liquor often redoubled in him rather than diminished. "Are you committed to staying here?" Victor said with a smile. Caught off guard by the question, Esteban leaned against a wall, running a trembling hand through his hair. Before now, leaving Guadeloupe had been so evidently impossible that the thought of it had never crossed his mind. He asked again: "Are you committed to staying in Pointe-à-Pitre?" A ship appeared, sent by providence, in Esteban's imagination, luminous, sails orange from the glow of a regal setting sun, navigating to some safe harbor. Perhaps a threatening letter, or the force of his inner anguish, had convinced the Commissar to abandon his post, traveling on to some Dutch port that would offer free passage to wherever he wished to go. The Robespierrists were fleeing in droves now, and it was known that many intended to reach New York, where there were French printers willing to publish memoirs and affidavits. In the colony, too, more than one man dreamed of New York. Esteban spoke frankly: as for him, he no longer saw what use he could be on the island, which would soon be under the control of Persons Unknown. The reaction would surely eliminate the present government in its entirety. (He looked over at the trunks and baggage already gathered in the office; porters brought more in, and Victor motioned for them to be placed in the corner.) Esteban wasn't even French, and for that reason, they would treat him as they treated those foreigners from factions faithful to the enemy. He might share the same fate as Guzmán and Marchena. If offered a way to leave, he would take it without hesitation . . . Victor's face grew exceptionally hard during the confession. By the time Esteban noticed, it was too late: "Poor idiot!" he shouted. "So you think the Thermidorian scum has beaten me, that they'll push me aside, crush me? You too take secret pleasure in the thought of two guards bursting in and dragging me off to Paris? That mulatta you're so fond of, she did well to tell me how you waste your time talking defeatist tripe with that old cur Loeuillet! I had to pay the whore a pretty penny to squeal! You want to leave before this is over, then? Well . . . It shall never be over! You hear me . . . ? It shall never be over!" "Rubbish!" Esteban shouted, frustrated that he had spoken openly with a man who had set him a trap, making the woman who shared his bed spy on him. Victor turned peremptory: "This very day, you are to take your books, your writing utensils, your arms and baggage, and board *L'Ami du Peuple*. This will give you respite from what you hypocritically refer to—don't think I don't know—as my *inevitable cruelties*. I am not cruel. I do what I must. That is something very different." His tone softened as if he were talking distractedly with one of his lieutenants and, looking at the trees on the Place de la Victoire, new leaves already sprouting over their firm trunks, he told Esteban British pressure was still bearing down on the island; an enemy fleet was gathering in Barbados, and they would have to stay ahead of the developments. In the Caribbean, the only naval strategy that had produced real results was marque and reprisal—classic, grand, incomparable—with light mobile ships that could hide in shallow inlets and maneuver through the coral reefs that had hindered the heavy Spanish galleons before and would now hinder the English ships with their loads of heavy armaments in turn. The Corsair Fleet of the French Republic would operate in small squadrons with complete autonomy in a zone delimited by the Mainland, including all English and Spanish possessions in the Antilles without prejudice to latitude. The Dutch would be left undisturbed. Naturally, a ship or two might fall into enemy hands, bringing joy to traitors of the Revolution. ("And these exist, yes they do," said Victor, patting a thick bundle of confidential reports, denunciations written on rag paper then recopied in an anonymous hand, with subtlety, without spelling errors, on fine filigreed sheets.) There had been no end to the indulgence shown to those deserters who had known to tear off their Phrygian caps at just the right time. They presented themselves to journalists as victims of an intolerable regime, especially if they were French. They rambled on about their disappointments and sufferings beneath a tyranny worse than any ever known, and they were given means to return home and ruefully retell their misadventures on the summits of impossible utopias. Esteban was aghast to find himself accused of harboring such intentions. "If you think I would ever lend myself to such treachery . . . why would you put me on one of your ships?" Victor stuck his nose in Esteban's face, as though mimicking a fight between marionettes. "Because you are an excellent scribe and we need one for each fleet to compose the Letter of Marque and Reprisal and take inventory quickly, before some rascal can sink his nails into the Republic's rightful possessions." Taking a pen and a ruler, the Commissar traced out six columns on a broad sheet of paper: "Come here," he said, "and don't look so glum. You will compose the Record of Confiscations in the following way: First column: *Total seizures*; Second column: *Earnings from sales and auctions* (assuming there are any); Third column: *Five percent for any invalids onboard*; Fourth column: *Fifteen centimes for the invalids' treasurer*; Fifth column: *Owed to the corsair captains*; Sixth column: *Legal expenses related to the shipment of liquidations* (in case, for whatever reason, they must be sent to another squadron). Is this clear?" Just then, Victor Hugues looked like a canny provincial shopkeeper, busy with his end-of-the-year accounting. Even his way of holding his pen had something in it of the former merchant and bread baker in Port-au-Prince.

CHAPTER THREE

XXIV.

They take what they can.
GOYA

In a vast eruption of salvos, tricolored flags, and revolutionary music, the little squadrons departed from the port of Pointe-à-Pitre. After lying a last time with Mademoiselle Athalie Bajazet, biting her breasts with a savagery that owed much to his rancor, Esteban slapped the buttocks of the informer, the tattler, till they bruised—her body was too beautiful for him to bring himself to strike her elsewhere. The woman was left moaning, regretful, and perhaps in love for the first time. She had helped him dress, calling him *mon doux seigneur* and now, onboard the barque, which had already passed the Îlet à Cochons, the young man looked back at the distant city with a delightful feeling of relief. The squadron—two small ships and the larger one he was assigned to—struck him, in all honesty, as feeble resistance for the stout English luggers or their narrow-beamed, agile cutters. But he preferred this to remaining in the increasingly demonic world of a Victor Hugues determined to grow to fit the hypostatic prominence assigned him by the American press, which already referred to him as "the Robespierre of the Islands . . ." Esteban took a deep breath, as if to empty his lungs of mephitic inhalations. He was going to sea, past the sea, into the immense Ocean of odysseys and anabases. The further they were from the coast, the greater the depths of blue the sea displayed, and he passed into a life governed by its rhythms. Onboard was a maritime bureaucracy, with each person devoted to his duties—the steward up to his nose in the storeroom, the carpenter tinkering with the oarlocks of a canoe, one man slathering tar, another setting clocks, while the cook hurried to be sure the fresh hake was on the officers' table at six and the immense tureen of leek, cabbage, and sweet potato soup was poured into bowls on the trestle tables before the twilight glow went dim. That afternoon, normal existence seemed to envelop them, the long day's events unpunctuated by the dreadful scansion of the guillotine—as though they'd emerged from frenzied temporality and entered the immutable and eternal. They would live without newspapers from Paris, without readings of pleas and allegations, without refractory shouting, instead looking at the sun, discoursing with the firmament, questioning the almucantar and the North Star . . . No sooner had *L'Ami du Peuple* set out on the open sea than a whale calf, spitting water with the elegance of a fountain, rose up and sank again suddenly, wary of being rammed by one of the sloops. And above the almost violaceous water of the afternoon, the enormous fish's silhouette in a water made darker by its shadow was for Esteban the immediate metaphor of an animal from centuries before that had strayed through foreign latitudes, perhaps, for some four or five hundred years . . . The squadron—the *Décade* and the *Tintamarre*, as well as the barque—saw no other ships for several days, as though it had set forth on a pleasure jaunt rather than a bellicose assignment. It laid anchor in some inlet, the sails went slack, and the seamen left for the shore, some for firewood, some for clams—so abundant you could find them half a palm's length beneath the sand—and they idled there lying among the grape vines and bathing in the coves. The clarity, the transparency, the coolness of the water in the early morning hours gave rise to a physical exaltation in Esteban that resembled lucid drunkenness. Frolicking wherever he stepped, he soon learned to swim, and could never bring himself to return to land when it was time to do so; he felt so happy, so enveloped and saturated with light, that at times, on terra firma, his gait was dazed and hesitant like a drunkard's. When this happened, he said he was "water-addled," and would offer his nude body to the sunrise, belly in the sand or face-up, legs opened, arms outspread, with such delight in his expression that he seemed a beatific mystic blessed with an Ineffable Vision. Stirred by the new energies that suffused him with such life, he spent hours exploring the cliffs, climbing, leaping, splashing around—marveled by all he discovered at the foot of the rocks. There were forests of madrepore, the speckled and harmonious apples of cowries, the cathedral-like suppleness of sea snails which, with their teeth and spines, could not be seen as other than gothic inventions; the rocaille frizz of tentacles, the Pythagorean spirals of shells—which deceptively, beneath a poor semblance of plaster, concealed the luminosity of a palace draped in gold. There was the sea urchin stilled its purple darts, the timid oyster closed, the starfish shrank before the human's step, while the sponges, clinging to a submerged crag, swayed in the wavering reflections. In that prodigious Island Sea, even the Ocean's pebbles had style and charm; some were so perfectly round, they seemed to have been polished by the hands of a gem cutter; others had abstract, dancing forms, yearning, levitating, slender, arrowlike, prey to an impulse birthed by matter itself. The transparent stone with alabaster radiance, and the stone of purple marble, and the granite covered with glimmers that shifted under the water, and the humble stone stippled with sea urchins—Esteban dug their algae-flavored flesh from their tiny, blackish-green shells with the spine from a cactus. Prodigious cactuses stood guard on the flanks of those nameless Hesperides where the ships arrived amid their exploits; tall candelabras, panoplies of green helmets, green pheasants' tails, green sabers, green blotches, hostile melons, vile quinces, spikes lingering in treacherous taut skins—a world not to be trusted, poised to wound, but torn open in the birthing of red or yellow flowers offered to man as a gift with the thorny prickly pear and nopal, whose flesh could be had at the cost of tearing through still more agonizing bristles. Foil to that armed vegetation, coated in nails, which kept him from climbing the crests layered with ripe soursops, there lay below in that Cambrian world forests of corals with textures of flesh, lace, or wool, infinite and always diverse, their flaming trees transmuted, auriferous; trees of Alchemy, of grimoires and hermetic treatises; nettles of untouchable soils, flamiferous ivies, woven in counterpoints and rhythms so ambiguous as to abolish all demarcation between inert and throbbing, vegetal and animal. In the coral forest lingered, amid a growing economy of zoological forms, the first baroque movements of Creation, its early luxuries and squanderings: hidden treasures man might never see without mimicking the fish he had once been before the womb gave him form, and he would yearn for gills and a tail to penetrate those extravagant landscapes he might choose as his eviternal home. Esteban saw in the coral forests a tangible image, an intimate yet ungraspable figuration of Paradise Lost, where the trees, still badly named, with the clumsy and quavering tongue of a Man-Child, were endowed with the apparent immortality of this luxurious flora—this monstrance, this burning bush—for which the sole sign of autumn or springtime was a variation in tone or a soft migration of shadows . . . From one surprise to the next, Esteban discovered the multiplicity of beaches where the Sea, three centuries after the Discovery of America, deposited the first shards of polished glass; glass invented in Europe, unknown in America, from bottles, flasks, cylinders, shapes foreign to the New Continent; green glass with opacities and bubbles; fine glass destined for nascent cathedrals, hagiographies now erased by the waters; glass fallen from boats, salvaged from shipwrecks, thrown on the Ocean's shores like a mysterious novelty, rising now to the earth, polished by waves with the skill of a jeweler or goldsmith bringing light to its tarnished facets. There were black beaches of pulverized slate and marble, where the sun shed trickles of sparks; yellow beaches of variable slopes, where every wave traced out an arabesque in an endless smoothing out and redrawing; white beaches, so white, so splendorously white that in places the sand was a kind of impasto over the vast cemetery of shells shattered, whirled, battered, ground away—reduced to a powder so fine that they slipped through the hand like a fluid impossible to grasp. It was marvelous, amid the multiplicity of Oceanids, to see the ubiquity of Life, roiling, sprouting, creeping over withered rocks as over trunks of driftwood, in a perennial confusion of plant and animal; of things adrift, stranded, hurled onto the shore, and things moved by their own impulse. Here were reefs that forged themselves and grew, aging rock, an immersed crag devoted for centuries to the task of sculpting itself in a world of fish-plants, fungus-medusas, fleshy stars, wandering plants, ferns that took on saffron, indigo, or purple tints at certain hours. On the submerged wood of the mangroves, a white dusting of flour appeared. And the flour made sheetlets of parchment, and the parchment swelled and hardened, transforming to scales clinging with their feet to a stalk, until, one fine morning, an oyster in its dressing of gray shell was visible against the wood. And the boatmen brought in these oysters on branches, hacking away a limb with a machete: a shrub of shellfish, branch and root, a handful of leaves, shells, and salt crystals, offered to human hunger like the strangest, most inexplicable of delicacies. No symbol better expressed the Idea of the Sea than the amphibious females of ancient myths, whose softest flesh offered itself to men's hands in the pink hollows of the conches, the sound of which had echoed for centuries when the oarsmen of the Archipelago pressed their lips to the shell, to tear from it the coarse sonority of the sea storm, the roar of the Neptunian bull, the solar beast, blowing over the immensity of the Sun's vast domains . . . Transported to the symbiotic universe, sunken to the neck in wells whose waters were endlessly frothed by collapsing ribbons of waves broken, lacerated, shattered by the bite of the living rock of dog's tooth calcite, Esteban marveled at how language on these islands had resorted to agglutination, verbal amalgam, metaphor to translate the formal ambiguity of matter that partook of several essences. There were trees called *acacia-bracelets*, *pineapple-cowries*, *wood-ribs*, *ten-brooms*, *clover-cousins*, *pine-nut jugs*, *philter-clouds*, and *iguana-sticks*, and many marine creatures were given names that fixed an image contrary to reason, yielding up a fantastical zoology of dogfish, ox-fish, tiger-fish, snorers, blowers, flyers, red-tails, stripers—some tattooed, some with mouths on their back or jaws on their abdomen—lions, white-bellies, broadswords, and kingfish; one was known to devour men's testicles, another was herbivorous; the morays of the sandbars were mottled in red, and one was venomous when it had eaten the fruit of the manchineel; then again, there was the old lady fish, the captain fish with its sparkling throat of golden shells, the woman-fish—the mysterious and elusive manatee, glimpsed at the mouths of rivers, where salt and sweet water mingled, with feminine appearance, mermaid breasts, frolicking nuptially in waterlogged plains. But nothing was comparable in joy, in eurythmia, in grace of impulse, to the play of dolphins, slung from the water in twos, in threes, in twenties, their disparate forms beneath a wave emphasizing its arabesque. In twos, in threes, in twenties, the dolphins turned in unison, integrated into the essence of the wave, living its movements in consonant pauses, leaps, and dives as though they bore it over their bodies, impressing upon it time and measure, pattern and sequence. Loss and diffusion followed, a search for new adventures, but with time, a meeting with a ship would once more draw up from the sea these dancers that seemed only to know how to turn in pirouettes and tritonades that gave visual testimony to the myths that surrounded them . . .

Now and then, a great silence was flung across the waters and the Event would occur—enormous, laggard, unwonted, a fish from other epochs would appear, its face placed strangely at one extreme of its mass, sealed in the eternal fear of its own languor; its skin like a hull in disrepair, crusted in vegetation and parasites; its spine rising long with a whipping of oars. With the solemnity of a galleon hauled up from the deep, of a patriarch from the abyss, of Leviathan dragged into the light, it cast foam across the seas in perhaps its second surfacing since the arrival of the astrolabe to these parts. The monster opened its pachydermic eyes, and, seeing a derelict sardine fisher's dinghy row close by, it sank again, anguished and fearful, down to the solitude of its undercurrents, to wait another century before rising again to this world replete with perils. The Event past, the sea returned to its doings. Across the sand where the hippocamps lodged, the empty sea urchins, their spines worn away, dried out into apples of such geometric elegance they might be etched into one of Dürer's Melancholies; the altar lamps of the parrot-fish lit up, while the angelfish and devilfish, the roosterfish and the Saint Peter's fish submitted to the sacrament of the Great Theater of Universal Devoration, where all were eaten by all,

consubstantial, forever imbricated in the unicity of the fluid . . .
The islands were narrow in places, and Esteban, to forget his
era, would walk alone to their other end, where he felt himself
lord of all creation; the seashells and their music of the foreshore
were his; his the turtles with their topaz armor hiding eggs in
holes they would fill back in and sweep flat with scaly feet; his
the splendors of the blue stones twinkling on virgin sand of flint
never trod by human soles. His too were the gannets, scarcely
wary of man because they scarcely knew him, flying haughtily
in the lap of the waves, cheeks and gullet stuffed with mussels,
then rising impulsively and diving straight down, beak driven by
the weight of their bodies, wings retracted to hasten their descent. The bird lifted its head in triumphal boast, the bolus of its
prey passed into its neck, then came a joyous shaking of abundant feathers, a testimony of pleasure, a thanksgiving, before it
rose in low and undulating flight, gliding parallel to the movement of the sea as the dolphin swam vertiginously below. Lying
nude on sand so soft that the smallest insect left tracks as it
crossed it, Esteban, alone in the world, looked at the clouds, luminous, immobile, so slow to change their forms that at times,
not even an entire day sufficed to efface a triumphal arch or the
head of a prophet. Pure serenity, without place or epoch. Te
deum . . . At other times, chin resting on the cool leaves of a
grapevine, he would lose himself in contemplation of a snail—
just one—arrect like a monument obscuring the horizon at the
height of his brow. The snail was the Mediator of the evanescent, the fleeting, lawless immoderation of the fluid and the land
of crystallizations, structures, and alternations, where everything was graspable and subject to ponderation. From the Sea
subject to the cycles of the moon, fickle, open or furious, bundled or unwoven, eternally elusive to modules, theorems, or
equations, rose those dazzling carapaces, symbols in cyphers and
proportions of the very thing the Mother lacked. Fixed linear
evolution, legislated volutes, conic architectures of marvelous
precision, equilibria of volumes, tangible arabesques that intu-
ited every baroque flourish that would ever come. Contemplating a snail—a single one—Esteban thought of the Spiral's
presence across millennia, gazed upon in fishing villages not yet

capable of grasping or even perceiving its reality. He dwelled on the pulp of the sea urchin, the helix of the razor clam, the striations of the scallop, symbol of Saint James, awed by that Science of Forms so long ago revealed to a humanity that still lacked eyes to contemplate it. How much is there around me already defined, inscribed, present, that I still have yet to grasp? What sign, what message, what admonition lies in the fringes of chicory, the alphabet of mosses, the geometry of the rose apple? To look at a snail. Just one. Te deum.

XXV.

Despite his fright when they were first called to action and he'd sought shelter in the furthest corners of the ship—his vital importance as scribe allowed him to do so—Esteban soon realized that the profession of corsair as Captain Barthélemy, leader of the squadron, understood it, was, in the main, hardly abundant in adventure. When they came across a large and well-armed supply ship, they would pass without raising the colors of the Republic. If the prey was vulnerable, they would hem it in with the light boats while the barque fired a cannonball as a warning. The enemy flag would lower without resistance, in a sign of submission. They would grapple the other ship, the French leaping to the opposite deck, and take an inventory of the cargo. If it was trifles, they would seize the valuables— including the money and personal effects of the frightened crew—returning to *L'Ami du Peuple* with their booty. The humiliated captain would be escorted to his vessel, where he would go on his way or return to his port of call to report the misadventure. If there was significant valuable freight, they were instructed to seize it, ship and all—especially if the ship was worthy—and take it with its crew to Pointe-à-Pitre. But this hadn't happened yet for Barthélemy's squadron, whose books Esteban kept with bureaucratic rigor. More sloops and Bermuda boats with their three-cornered sails than proper merchants' vessels plied those seas, and rarely was their cargo of interest. Certainly, they hadn't left Guadeloupe to look for sugar, coffee, or rum, which they had more than enough of there. And yet, even in the worst maintained and most miserable looking craft, the French always found something they could lay hands on: a new anchor, weapons, gunpowder, tools, a recent map with useful directions for circumnavigating the Mainland. Then there was all one discovered ferreting around in trunks and dark corners. One man might find two good shirts and a pair of nankeen trousers; another an enamel snuff box, or the bejeweled chalice of a priest from Cartagena, which he would threaten to throw in the sea if the man didn't *make with the whole Mass get-up*, the cross and monstrance, which might be made of gold. This chapter of private rapine necessarily escaped Esteban's accounting, and Barthélemy pretended to know nothing of it to avoid quarrels with his people, realizing that nowadays, in a fight with the Republican navy, the captain was fated to lose, particularly one like him, who had served in the King's armada. And so there appeared on the deck of *L'Ami du Peuple* an exchange for barter and sale, with items displayed on crates or hanging from ropes. The sailors from the *Décade* or the *Tintamarre* would pay visits after laying anchor in a cove to go cut firewood, and they too would bring whatever they wished to trade. Amid the garments, caps, belts, and kerchiefs, the most singular objects appeared: tortoiseshell reliquaries; cabaret dresses from Havana with lace like sea foam on their flounces; nutshells housing a wedding feast of fleas in Mexican dress; mounted fish with tongues of carmine satin; jaunty demons of wrought iron; boxes of shells, rock sugar birds, tres guitars from Cuba or Venezuela; aphrodisiac potions of yawweed or the famous guaco of Saint-Domingue; and any trophy vaguely associated with the idea of woman: hoop earrings, glass bead necklaces, petticoats, breechcloths, locks of hair tied with ribbons, nude drawings, licentious prints, and even a doll of a sheepherder girl that concealed, beneath her skirts, silky and well apportioned pudenda so perfectly executed despite their tiny proportions that the sight of them was a marvel. The owner of the figurine asked an exorbitant price, and those who couldn't pay denounced him as a cutpurse; Barthélemy, fearing a quarrel, had the barque's supercargo purchase it, thinking it

would make a fine gift for Victor Hugues—who had, since 9
Thermidor, taken unconcealed pleasure in the reading of pruri-
ent books, perhaps to make it known that Paris and its politics
no longer interested him . . . The crew was pleased one day to
find, after giving chase to a Portuguese vessel, that the *An-
dorinha* was loaded to the brim with so much wine—reds, *vin-
hos verdes*, Madeira—that the hold smelled of a cellar. Esteban
hurried to take a hasty inventory of the barrels before the
thirsty mariners could get to them; already they had gotten
hold of more than a few casks, dispatching their contents in
long gulps. Alone in the shadowy cellar of the hold, away from
disputants and greedy hands, the scribe served himself in a
wide mahogany bowl, and the flavor of his draft mingled with
the perfume of cool, dense wood, which had a fleshy feel when
it touched his lips. In France, Esteban had learned to enjoy the
great ancestral juice that flowed from the nipples of its vines
and had nourished that stormy and sovereign Mediterranean
civilization—carried on now in the Mediterranean of the Caribbean, where the Confusion of Traits initiated many millennia ago would go on in this region of the Peoples of the Sea.
Here the descendants of the Lost Tribes came to meet, at the
end of a long dispersion, mingling accents and headdresses,
pledged to novel mongrelisms, mixed and intermixed, stripped
bare and recolored, brightened then darkened again in a leap
backward, an endless proliferation of new profiles, proportions, and inflections; reached in turn by wine, from Phoenician
ships, from the storehouses of Gades, from the amphoras of
Markos Sestios, handed down, with the vihuela and the tejo-
leta, to the caravels of the Discoverers to arrive at these shores
ripe for the transcendental encounter between Olive and Maize.
Sniffing his damp bowl, Esteban recalled now, with emotion,
the aged casks, patriarchal, of the company in Havana—so distant, so estranged from his current itineraries—where the isochronous dripping of certain taps had the same sound he heard
here. Suddenly, the absurdity of his present was so palpable—
he was standing before a Theater of the Absurd—that he leaned
into the bulkhead, stupefied, eyes frozen, as though overwhelmed by the vision of his own figure upon a stage. In these

recent days at sea, physical life, the vagaries of navigation, had made him forget himself, in a way, in thrall to the animal satisfaction of his own growing vigor and strength. But now he found himself before a seaside vineyard unknown to him the day before, wondering what he was doing in such a place. He was searching for a path that was denied him, waiting for an opportunity that would not arise. Bourgeois by birth, a Corsair Scribe by profession—even saying this aloud was absurd. Nominally free, he was a prisoner de facto, whose situation tied him to a race of men combatted the world over. Nothing so resembled a nightmare as that place where he observed himself, sleeping but awake, judge and advocate, protagonist and spectator, surrounded by islands resembling the one island he couldn't reach, and perhaps wouldn't for the remainder of his life, barred from smelling the aromas of childhood, from finding in houses, in trees, particular casts of light (oh blurs of a certain orange, those doors of blue, those pomegranates edging over a wall!), from the frame of his adolescence, bereft forever of what was his, what had belonged to him since childhood and youth. One afternoon the Knocker at the Front Door of his Dwelling had echoed, and a diabolical operation was set in motion, upturning three lives that had previously been one, with games that would rouse Lycurgus and Mucius Scaevola from their tombs, before traveling to a city with its bloody tribunes, an island, several islands, a whole sea where the will of One Man, posthumous Executor of a Silenced Will, loomed over every single life. Since Victor Hugues had appeared—the first thing they noticed was that he carried a green umbrella—the I pondered on that stage of barrels and casks had belonged to itself no more: its existence, its becoming, were ruled over by the Will of another . . . It was better to drink and throw a fog over that unwanted lucidity, so maddening in those moments that it tempted one to shout. Esteban placed the bowl under one of the spouts and filled it to the brim. Above him, the men chanted verses from *The Three Gunners of Auvergne*.

The next day, he disembarked on a deserted, wooded coast, where the navigator of *L'Ami du Peuple*—a Caribbean and

black half-breed born in Marie-Galante, whose familiarity
with the Antilles was thorough beyond question—knew where
to find wild pigs to make *boucan*, a fit accompaniment for the
wines, which they would put to cool in the mouth of a stream.
The hunt was soon organized, and when the beasts were
brought back, their snouts wearing the same scowl as when
they were cornered, the men handed them off to the cooks.
They took scaling knives to their bristles and black hairs and
stretched their bodies over grilles piled high with glowing coals,
their backs to the heat, their bellies turned toward the sky, the
cavity held open by thin wooden rods. Soon, a fine rain of
lemon juice poured over their flesh, and bitter orange, salt, pepper, oregano, and garlic. A bed of green guava leaves scattered
over the embers raised a white, quivering smoke—aspersion
from above, aspersion from below—and the scent of green enveloped the skin toasted tortoiseshell brown, which split in long
fissures with an occasional dry crackle, releasing fat that
dripped down, raising flickers from the pit's depths, so that
even the soil smelled of scorched pork. When the pigs were
nearly done, their open bellies were stuffed with quail, squab,
moorhens, and other freshly plucked birds. Then the rods that
held them open were removed, and the ribs closed on the fowl,
an elastic oven that accommodated their forms, the flavor of
those sparse dark meats permeating the fat pallor in what Esteban called the *Boucan* of *Boucans*—the song of songs. Wine
flowed into gourds in time with the gluttony—with barrels
shattered by drunken hatchet blows; barrels hurled down gravel
hills, staves flying when they struck a sharp rock; barrels broken by men rolling them back and forth in mock combat; barrels caved in, riddled with bullets, stamped on by a dismal
flamenco dancer, a part-Spanish Ganymede who served as scul-
lion on the *Décade*, and had made his way on board as a friend
of Liberty—so profusely that the crew fell asleep gorged and
moribund, at the foot of grape trees or on the sand, which conserved the heat of the sun . . . Stretching laboriously at dawn,
Esteban saw many of the sailors walking toward the shore,
gazing at the ships, which now were five, counting the *An-
dorinha*. The recent arrival, with its half-broken figurehead, its

quarterdeck filthy and chipping, was so old, so outmoded, that it seemed emerged from another century, the ship of men who still believed the Atlantic opened onto the Mare Tenebrosum. Soon a caique took off from the battered vessel and was rowed to the beach by a group of nearly naked negroes who paddled to the rhythm of a savage river shanty. The man who seemed to be their chief jumped onto land, genuflecting in what might be seen as a gesture of friendship, calling out to one of the black cooks in a dialect that the latter—born, perhaps, in the regions of Calabar—seemed somewhat to understand. At the end of a dialogue punctuated with much waving of the hands, the interpreter told them the old ship was a Spanish slave vessel. The mutineering slaves had thrown the crew overboard and were now seeking the protection of the French. Word had spread across the coasts of Africa that the Republic had abolished slavery in the American colonies, where the negro lived as a free citizen. Captain Barthélemy shook the chief's hand, then passed him a tricolor ribbon, which his fellows received with jubilant shouts and passed from man to man. The boat returned and brought back more and more negroes, and others, the impatient ones, even swam to shore to hear the news. Unable to restrain themselves, they leaped at what was left of the boucan, gnawing bones, devouring discarded offal, sucking at the cold fat, frantic after weeks of starvation. "Poor men," Barthélemy said with misty eyes. "This alone will cleanse many of our wrongs . . ." Esteban, feeling generous, filled his cup with wine, offering it to those who just yesterday were slaves, and they kissed his hand in reply. In the meanwhile, the supercargo of *L'Ami du Peuple*, who had gone to take an inventory of the ship, came back with the news that there were women, many, still onboard, hiding in the orlop, trembling with misery and fright, with no idea of what was happening on land. Barthélemy prudently gave the order that they stay where they were. A canoe took them meat, biscuit, bananas, and a bit of wine, and the crew did as they had the night before, setting off in search of more swine. To-morrow they would return to Pointe-à-Pitre with the Portuguese ship, the miscellaneous merchandise they'd pilfered, the shipment of wines, and the negroes, who would be useful filling

the ranks of the colored men's militias, ever in need of hands for
the arduous fortifications intended to safeguard Victor Hugues's domains . . . In late afternoon, they resumed the feast
from the day before, but now their spirits were much changed.
When the wine rose to their heads, the men grew vexed about
the women, whose griddles could be seen burning against the
lights of the setting sun and whose laughter was audible from
the shore. Details were sought from the sailors who had been
onboard the slave ship. Some of the women were very young,
they reported, some strapping, some comely—the slavers didn't
traffic in old women, as they were impossible to sell. Heated by
drink, they delved into fine points: *Y'en a avec fesses comme
ça* . . . *Y'en a qui sont à poil* . . . *Y'en a une, surtout* . . . Suddenly ten, twenty, thirty men ran for their boats and rowed toward the old ship, ignoring the shouts of Barthélemy, who tried
to detain them. The negroes stopped eating and gestured frantically as they stood. The first negresses arrived in the midst of
truculent greed, crying, begging, frightened, but seeming to
submit to the men who dragged them to the nearby underbrush.
No one listened to the officers, even when they unsheathed their
sabers. In the midst of the tumult, more negresses arrived, then
more, and chased by the seamen, they ran across the beach. Believing they were assisting Barthélemy, who was shouting futile
curses, threats, and orders, the negroes grabbed stakes and
threw themselves on the whites. There was a bitter struggle,
with bodies rolling in the sand, stomped, kicked; bodies raised
in midair and hurled onto the gravel; people falling into the sea,
tangled, wrestling, one trying to drown the other, heads shoved
underwater. Finally, the negroes were cornered in a rock hollow, and chains and clamps were brought from their ship to
manacle them. Disgusted, Barthélemy returned to *L'Ami du
Peuple*, leaving his men to their violence and orgies. Esteban,
sure to take a damp cloth to lie down on—he knew what the
sand could do—led one of the slave girls to a kind of cradle of
dry lichen he had discovered among the boulders. Very young,
very docile, preferring this brutality to worse ones, the girl un-
wound the torn cloth that covered her. Her adolescent breasts,
the nipples broadly colored ochre; her thighs, fleshy and hard,

able to squeeze, to stand, to bring her knees to the level of her breasts, yielded their tension and suppleness to the young man. A concert of muted laughter echoed across the island, exclamations, murmurs, and at times a vague roaring above it, like the cry of an ill beast hidden in some nearby lair. Now and then came the noise of a quarrel—two men arguing over one woman, perhaps. Again, Esteban found that scent, those textures, the rhythms and panting of the One who had revealed to him, in a house in El Arsenal in Havana, the paroxysms of his own flesh. Only one thing mattered that night: Sex. In its rites, Sex multiplied into a collective liturgy, wild, oblivious to all authority or law . . . Dawn broke amid a symphony of reveilles, and Barthélemy, determined to impose his authority, ordered the crews to return to their ships immediately. Whoever remained on the island would be left behind. There were renewed disputes with sailors who wanted to hold onto their negresses, considering them legitimate spoils and their personal property. The Squadron's Captain eased their minds with a formal agreement to release the women only upon their arrival at Pointe-à-Pitre. Manumission would take place there and not before, in accordance with the legal procedures of nomination and registration that would transform the slaves to French citizens. The negro men and women returned to their ship and the squadron set a course for their return. But no sooner had they raised their sails than Esteban, whose sense of direction had grown sharper in recent days—and who had, moreover, acquired a rudimentary knowledge of navigation—seemed to notice that the route the ships were taking was not one that would lead them to Guadeloupe. Barthélemy furrowed his brow when the scribe spoke. "Keep it to yourself," he said. "You know damned well I can't keep the promise I've made to these bandits. Just think of the precedent it would set. The Commissar wouldn't stand for it. We've set course for a Dutch island, and we'll sell the shipment of negroes there." Esteban looked at him stupefied and invoked the Decree of the Abolition of Slavery. The Captain removed from his effects a sheet of instructions written in Victor Hugues's hand: *France, by virtue of its democratic principles, cannot engage in the slave trade. But the captains of corsair ships are authorized, if they deem it convenient or necessary, to sell in Dutch ports those slaves they may acquire from the English, the Spanish, or other enemies of the Republic.* "But this is vile!" Esteban exclaimed. "We've abolished the trade but we can sell slaves to other nations?" "I'm simply following what's written," Barthélemy replied dryly. And sensing the obligation to appeal to a jurisprudence now abolished: "We are living in a world that's lost its mind. Before the Revolution, a slave ship used to ply these waters that belonged to a *philosophe* owner, a friend of Jean-Jacques Rousseau. And you know what that ship was called? *The Social Contract.*"

XXVI.

Within months, revolutionary privateering had become a fantastically prosperous business. Ever more audacious in their raids, fired by their successes and profits, anxious for bigger prey, the captains from Pointe-à-Pitre journeyed farther—to the Continent, Barbados, or the Virgin Islands—unafraid to be seen in the vicinity of islands where they might well encounter a formidable squadron. As the days passed, they perfected their techniques. Drawing on older corsair traditions, the sailors chose to navigate in regiments composed of small vessels—sloops, cutters, lithe schooners—which were easy to maneuver and to hide, quick to flee, tough in battle, rather than manning large, slow-moving provision ships—easy targets for enemy artillery, especially for the British, who disdained the French method of dismasting and whose gunners preferred aiming for the wooden hulls when the waves made the bores of the cannons sink. Withal, the port of Pointe-à-Pitre was full of new ships and the storehouses no longer had room for so much merchandise, for such an abundance of things, and so sheds were built by the mangrove swamps on the edge of the city to receive the shipments that came back each day. Victor Hugues had gotten a bit fat, though he was no less active since his body had begun stretching the fabric of his tailcoat. Despite what many expected, the Directory, faraway and busy with its own affairs, confirmed the Commissar in his post, recognizing that his efforts at salvaging and defending the colony had been a success. In that part of the globe, the commander had come to embody a kind of unipersonal government, autonomous and independent, thus realizing to an astonishing degree his unconfessable aspiration to make himself one with the Incorruptible. He had wanted to *be* Robespierre, and he *was* a Robespierre in *his* way. Like Robespierre in other days, who had spoken of *his* government, *his* army, *his* squadron, Victor Hugues spoke now of *his* government, *his* army, *his* squadron. His erstwhile arrogance restored, the Plenipotentiary conceded himself, at the hour of chess and card games, the role of One and Only Perpetuator of the Revolution. He boasted of no longer reading the newspapers from Paris, which "stank of dastardliness." Esteban saw that Victor Hugues, grown smug about the prosperity of the island and the money he kept sending back to France, was recovering that spirit of the affluent merchant who grins as he weighs his riches. When his ships returned with fine merchandise, the Commissar was there to see them unloaded, examining bundles, barrels, utensils, and armaments with an expert eye. He had opened a general store through intermediaries in the vicinity of Place de la Victoire, and maintained a monopoly on certain items available there at prices arbitrarily set. Late in the day, Victor inevitably passed through the shop to examine the books in the shadows of his office redolent of vanilla, its arched doors in their fine iron fittings opening onto two corner streets. Even the guillotine had adopted bourgeois manners, working nonchalantly, one day on and one day off, and Monsieur Anse left the work to his assistants, devoting his own time to completing the Collections in his Cabinet of Curiosities, rich in coleoptera and lepidoptera ennobled with impressive Latin names. Everything cost dearly, but there was always money to pay in that world of closed economy where prices rose continually, and currency returned to the same pockets again and again, debased, its metal diminished by rasping and filing readily apparent to the touch . . . During a stay in Pointe-à-Pitre, Esteban—so bronzed, he looked like a mulatto—was pleased to hear word, however late, of the peace treaty between Spain and France, which he imagined would reestablish communications with the Continent, Puerto Rico, and Havana. Great was his disappointment on being informed that Victor Hugues would not acknowledge the Basil accord. Determined to keep preying on Spanish vessels, he deemed them *suspected of trafficking in English contraband of war* and authorized his captains to *requisition* them and to use their own judgment as to the meaning of this term, *contraband of war.* Esteban would have to go on exercising his profession in Barthélemy's squadron, watching slip his chance at abandoning a world that life at sea, timeless and governed by the Law of the Wind alone, had made increasingly strange to him. As the months passed, he resigned himself to living for the day—and the days were never counted—taking solace in the little pleasures he might encounter in a good day of work or a bountiful catch of fish. He had grown fond of some of his fellow travelers: Barthélemy, who held onto his officer's manners from the ancien régime, and looked scrupulously after his garments even in moments of deepest crisis; the surgeon, Noël, working eternally away at a tedious treatise on the vampires of Prague, the women of Loudun possessed by demons, and the spastics of the Cemetery of San Medardo; the butcher Achille, a black man from the island of Tobago, who played astonishing sonatas on pots and basins of various sizes; citizen Gilbert, a master caulker, who recited long stretches of classical tragedies in a southern accent so strong that the verses, stuffed with extra syllables, never followed the alexandrine meters, with *Brutus* transformed to *Brutusse* or *Epaminondas* to *Epaminondasse.* For the rest, the world of the Antilles fascinated the young man, with its perpetual sunflower of lights at play over forms diverse, prodigiously diverse within the unity of a common clime and vegetation. He loved mountainous Dominique, with its profound verdures and its villages with names like Bataille and Massacre in memory of horrifying events badly told by history. He came to know the clouds of Nevis, which lay so motionless upon its hills that the Great Admiral, on seeing them, had taken them for impossible glaciers. He dreamed of someday climbing the pointed peak of Santa Lucía, which rose from the sea in a mass that from a distance resembled a lighthouse built by unknown engineers to await the ships that would one day bring the Tree of the Cross upon their masts. Soft and embracing when overtaken from the South, the islands of this endless archipelago turned abrupt, uneven, eroded by high waves that broke into foam where their shores defied the North Wind. A whole mythology of shipwrecks, sunken treasures, unmarked graves, deceitful lights that glowed on stormy nights, predestined births—of Madame de Maintenon, of the Sephardi miracle worker, of the Amazon who became Queen of Constantinople—was linked to these lands whose names Esteban repeated to himself softly, relishing the euphony of the words: Tortola, Santa Ursula, Virgen Gorda, Anegada, Granaditas, Jersualén Caída . . . There were mornings when the sea awoke so still and silent that the isochronous creaking of the ropes—the short ones high pitched, the long ones lower—combined to produce, from stem to stern, anacruses and up- and downbeats, appoggiaturas and plucked notes with the harsh fermata of a harp of tense hawsers suddenly strummed by a trade wind. On today's journey, the soft winds had suddenly picked up speed, pushing the waves higher and thicker. The clear green sea had become ivy green, opaque, ever rising, turning now from ink green to smoke green. The seasoned sailors sniffed at the gusts, realizing they smelled different, amid black shadows that bore down on them and brusque moments of reprieve, and then came warm rains with drops so heavy they seemed composed of mercury. On the edges of twilight stood the walking column of a cyclone, and the ships passed from swell to swell, as if gliding over the tops of palm trees, scattered through the night, their beacons lost. They tumbled over the unpredictable roiling of the water, which rose willfully, struck them headlong and from the side, throwing volleys to the keel, and no rapid righting of the helm could keep the water from sweeping the deck when the boat turned away from the onslaught. Barthélemy ordered jacklines strung to ease movement: "There's no way out," he said as a classic October storm kicked up, and he warned them the worst would come after midnight, he was sure of it. The

thought that he would have to endure the storm alarmed Esteban, who shut himself up in his cabin and tried to sleep. But he
couldn't, feeling that his viscera were shifting no sooner than
he'd laid his body down. The ship was perforating a colossal
roar that spanned the horizons, forcing creaks from each
board, each rib. While the men struggled on deck above, the
barque lurched unbearably onward, rising, rising, falling, keel-
ing, heaving, penetrating deeper into the hurricane's heart.
Esteban had abandoned all attempts at composure, and pressed
into his bunk, queasy, suffused with terror, waiting for the
water to start pouring in through the portholes, filling the hold,
forcing the doors . . . Then, a bit before daybreak, the sky's bellowing seemed to abate, and the buffets to become less frequent. On deck, the seamen had gathered in a chorus, chanting
a full-throated hymn to Our Lady of Perpetual Help, intercessor between men at sea and divine fury. Opportunely resorting
to ancient French tradition, they called on the Mother of the
Redeemer in her misery to placate the waves and calm the
wind. Their voices, which had sung so many crude verses in
counterpoint, pleaded for mercy now in the language of the liturgy from Her Who Conceived Without Sin. Esteban crossed
himself and stepped onto the bridge. The danger was past:
alone, without knowing the fate of the other ships—lost perhaps, perhaps sunken—*L'Ami du Peuple* steered toward a gulf
teeming with islands.

Teeming with islands, but with the peculiarity that they were
all very small, sketches almost, ideas of islands to come,
massed the way studies, drafts, the hollow appendages of statues are massed in the workshop of a sculptor. None of these
islands resembled the others and none was made of the same
material. Some were of a sort of white marble, perfectly sterile,
monolithic, and smooth, like a Roman bust submerged in
water to the shoulders; others were mounds of schist scored
with parallel fissures, with the multiple claws of two or three
very ancient trees, withered antlers, clinging to their crests—or
just one sometimes, like an enormous kelp, trunk white from
the salt air. Some were so hollowed by the work of waves that

they seemed to float without any apparent anchor; others were blemished by thistles or were collapsing in on themselves. Caverns opened in their flanks, and on their ceilings, giant cactuses hung upside down, red or yellow flowers elongated in festoons, like strange, theatrical chandeliers that gave sanctuary to the enigmas of rare, geometric, isolated forms mounted on plinths—a cylinder, pyramid, polyhedron—like occult objects of veneration, a stone of Mecca, a Pythagorean emblem, the materialization of some abstract form of worship. As the barque breached that strange world the navigator had never set eyes on and could not place after the previous night's storm threw them horribly off course, Esteban expressed his astonishment at the *things* there were to see, inventing names for them: that must be Angel Island, with those Byzantine outspread wings painted like a fresco on the cliffside; here was the Gorgon Island, with its crown of green serpents, there the Shattered Sphere, the Anvil Incarnate, and the Soft Island, with its mounds of guano and gannet excrement that made it appear a bright bulk lacking in consistency, dragged along by the current. They went past the Votive Stairway and the Face-That-Seemed-to-Be-Looking; the Galleon-Stranded-at-the-Citadel plumed with sea foam left by waves that tore through its narrow vestibules and turned to enormous feathers when they broke high on a steep outcrop. They passed Brow Rock and the Horse's Skull—with fearsome shadows in the eyes and nostrils—and the Ragged Islands: there were rocks so poor there, so old, so humble they brought to mind beggar ladies covered in rags, while other stones, younger by many millennia, were bright, shimmering ivory. They passed the Temple-Cave, devoted to the Triangle of Diorite, the Condemned Island, fractured by the roots of marine ficus that wove their arms between the stones like cordage, swelling from year to year before provoking a final catastrophe. Esteban marveled at this Gulf of Prodigies, a kind of forestage of the Antilles—a schema reuniting in miniature all that would be seen in the Archipelago on a larger scale. Here, too, volcanoes drove up through the waves, but fifty seagulls sufficed to cover them in snow. Here, too, they passed the Fat Virgin Islands and ones so thin that ten Venus fans grown side by side would suffice to gauge their breadth . . . After hours of slow navigation, constantly checking the plumb line, the barque found itself at a gray beach lined with posts where long nets were stretched out to dry. A fishing village was there—seven houses of thatched roofs with shared lean-tos to shelter the boats—dominated by a gravelly lookout where a watchman with a surly face awaited the appearance of a school of fish, with his shell at arm's reach, ready to blow the summons. In the distance, on the crown of an embankment, a merloned castle was visible, somber and cyclopean, rising up over a wall of violaceous rocks. "The Araya salt mines," the navigator told Barthélemy, who gave the order to veer off and avoid going near that mighty fortress, work of the Antonellis, military architects of Phillip II—the guardhouse of the Spanish treasury for centuries. Dodging sandbanks, the ship set off at full sail from what they now knew to be the Gulf of Santa Fe.

XXVII.

Months passed in the same tasks, the same labors. Barthélemy, preferring the certainty of success and practicable undertakings, unconcerned with styling himself the scourge of the seas, had an enviable instinct for finding the richest and worst-defended prey. Once they'd had a nasty encounter with a Danish craft from Altona whose crew defended itself with brio, refusing to strike their flag and ramming the ships that came in their path; but for the rest, life with the squadron was peaceful and prosperous, and the scribe, who lacked the makings of a hero and was much inclined to reading, was told often to run and hide in the hold, as a prank, when unknown fishing boats were sighted. But *L'Ami du Peuple*, continuously at sea, returning one day only to depart the next—its captain, roused by the sight of so many colleagues so quickly enriched, had been seduced by the demon of lucre—was showing signs of exhaustion. The first sign of bad weather was enough to turn the ship effeminate, plaintive, feeble, and dejected. Its every board creaked.

Abscesses of paint blistered on the masts and beams. The railings looked filthy and battered. Repairs were needed, and Esteban was sent back to a Guadeloupe whose transformations he had seen little of in his brief stops in recent times. Pointe-à-Pitre was now the richest city in America. Even in Mexico, the land of legend, with its vast spinning mills, its silver- and goldsmiths, and its mines in Taxco, such prosperity was inconceivable. Gold shimmered in the sun here in an endless stream of *louis tournois*, single and quadruple, British guineas, Portuguese *moëdas* stamped with the faces of John V, Queen Maria, and Peter III. Silver they had in six-livre coins, Philippine and Mexican piastres, and eight or more sorts of vellon, notched, punched, and filed to suit their owners. Vertigo gripped the small shopkeepers of before, who now owned their own corsair ships, some thanks to their initiative, others with partnerships or joint-stock companies. The old India Companies, with their arks and chests, were born again on this remote edge of the Caribbean, where the Revolution was bringing joy to multitudes. A list of 580 vessels of all type and provenance—boarded, sacked, dragged into port by the fleets—now thickened the Registry of Confiscated Property. Few cared anymore what might be happening in France in those days. Guadeloupe could manage on its own. On the mainland, the Spanish were well-disposed to, even envious of the colony, whose propaganda reached them through their Dutch possessions. It was an exhilarating sight when the ships returned from a profitable exploit and the adventurers emerged from the belly of the ships bearing their glittering goods through the streets. Holding up samples of calico, of orange and green muslin, Masulipatnam silks, turbans from Madras, Manila shawls, and every precious fabric they could wave in the women's eyes, they dressed in miraculous garments that soon became the local fashion, barefooted—or in stockings but forgoing shoes—beneath sunflower dress coats with braided trimming, shirts lined with fur and ribbons at the collar, and their crowning glory—absolutely mandatory, by now this was a question of amour propre—the extravagance of a felt hat, brim half turned down, with feathers dyed in the colors of the Republic. Vulcain, the negro, hid his leprosy beneath such regalia that he seemed an emperor borne in triumph. Joseph Murphy, the Englishman, standing on stilts, pounded cymbals at the height of the balconies. Leaving their ships behind, escorted by the hurrahs of the multitude, they went one and all to the Morne-à-Cail neighborhood, where an invalid companion had opened a café: *Au rendez-vous des Sans-Culottes*, with a cage of toucans and mockingbirds by the counter and walls covered in allegorical caricatures and obscene drawings traced out in charcoal. The revelry, once sparked, would last for two or three days in a haze of brandy and women, while the ship owners stayed behind to watch their goods unloaded, placing their merchandise on tables lined up beside the ships for examination. Esteban was surprised to find Victor Hugues in the café in Morne-à-Cail one afternoon, surrounded by captains who were speaking of grave matters, for once. "Sit down, my boy, and order something . . ." the Agent of the Directory said. Though he had been in that post for some time, his tone— of a man trying too hard to get assent—indicated he was not yet universally accepted. Repeating numbers and details, citing fragments from more or less official reports, he accused the North Americans of selling arms and ships to the English with the aim of expelling France from her American colonies, despite all France had done for them: "The mere word American," he shouted, repeating what had been written in a recent proclamation, "inspires feelings of contempt and horror among our likes. After deceiving the world with their Quaker dumb show, the Americans have turned reactionary, enemies of every ideal of liberty. The United States is committed heart and soul to its haughty nationalism and opposed to anything that might call its dominion into question. The same men who fought for their independence now refuse to others the very thing that made them great. We must remind that perfidious people that without us—without the blood we shed, the money we spent to give them their independence—George Washington would have been hanged as a traitor." The Agent crowed that he had written the Directory, pressing them to declare war on the United States. But their responses had revealed a lamentable ignorance of reality, recommending prudence first, then anxiously calling for order. The blame lay—Victor said—with career soldiers like Pelardy, whom he'd tossed out of the colony after violent disputes. They meddled in what didn't concern them and were now in Paris conspiring against him. He referred to his successful initiatives, the purge of the Island, the prosperity now reigning. "For my part, I remain hostile to the United States. The interest of France demands it," he concluded, with an aggressive insistence that revealed his intent to muffle all objections beforehand. For Esteban, it was evident that Victor, who up to now had exercised absolute authority, was sensing the presence around him of others spurred on by their own achievements and wealth. Antoine Fuët, a mariner from Narbonne whom Victor had assigned a splendid ship with American-style rigging and mahogany gunwales sheathed in copper, had become a legend, acclaimed by the masses, since firing on a Portuguese ship with cannons loaded with gold coins for lack of other ammunition. The surgeons of the *Sans-Pareil* had struggled over the dead and wounded, salvaging the currency lodged in their bodies and entrails at the point of a scalpel. This same Antoine Fuët—nicknamed Captain Moëda—had the audacity to forbid the Agent, who was a civil authority and not a soldier, from entering a club the powerful captains had opened in a church and jokingly called the Palais Royal. Its gardens and dependencies covered an entire city block. And Esteban was astonished to hear of the rebirth of Masonry, which was thriving among the French corsairs. Their Lodge was in the Palais Royal, where the Jachin and Boaz pillars were erected once more. Through the fleeting recourse of the Supreme Being, they had returned to the Great Architect—the acacia and the mallet of Hiram Abiff. Captains Laffite, Pierre Gros, Mathieu Goy, Christophe Chollet, the renegade Joseph Murphy, Pegleg Langlois, and even a mestizo named Petréas the Mulatto served as masters and knights, devotees of a tradition revived thanks to the zeal of the brothers Modeste and Antoine Fuët. Far from the fire of the short-bored rifles of corsairs commandeering a ship, fine ritual swords clashed in rites of initiation, held by hands that had once dug into the flesh of corpses to pull out coins black with coagulated blood . . . "All this confusion," thought Esteban, "is because they are yearning for the Cross. No one can live as a bullfighter or corsair without a Temple to turn to, a place to thank Someone that one is still alive. Soon enough we'll see ex-votos to the Virgin of Perpetual Help." And inwardly, he was pleased to see that hidden forces had begun to eat away at Victor Hugues's power. Active in him was a kind of inverse affection that makes one wish for the humiliation or fall of one admired when he has become too prideful or arrogant. Esteban looked toward the guillotine, always erect upon its stage. Aghast at himself, he succumbed to the temptation of thinking that the Machine, now less active than before, sometimes remaining in its sheath for weeks, was sitting in wait for the Plenipotentiary. Precedents weren't wanting. "I'm a swine," he said softly. "If I were a Christian, I would confess."

Days later, there was a great uproar around the port, that is to say, in the entire city. Captain Christophe Chollet, whom no one had heard from for months, was returning with his people amid thundering salvoes, bringing nine ships captured in a naval battle in the waters of Barbados. They flew Spanish, English, North American flags, and one of the last to arrive was holding the rarest of cargo: an opera company, with musicians, sheet music, and set pieces. The troupe belonged to Monsieur Faucompré, a splendid tenor who had for years taken Grétry's *Richard Coeur-de-Lion* from Cap Français to Havana and New Orleans as part of a repertoire which also included *Zémire et Azor*, *La Serva Padrona*, *La Belle Arsène*, and other magnificent productions, complemented at times with subtle stage machinery, magic mirrors, and storm scenes. His mission of taking lyrical art to Caracas and other cities in the Americas where lesser companies, being cheap to transport, had begun to bring in great profits, had ended in Pointe-à-Pitre, a city without a theater. But when Monsieur Faucompré, a businessman as well as an artist, heard of the colony's new-found wealth, he was pleased to have landed there, after the fright of being boarded, when he'd astutely assisted his patriots, giving helpful instructions from the shelter of a hatchway. His company was French, he was among Frenchmen now, and the singer, who had known how to fire up royalists in the colonies with the aria "Oh, Richard! Oh, mon Roi!," had readily yielded to the revolutionary sentiment of the times, belting out "Le Réveil du Peuple" from the quarterdeck of the admiral's ship to the crew's delight, with fermatas that made—as the supercargo confirmed—the glasses in the officers' mess quiver. Faucompré came accompanied by Madame Villeneuve, whose talent was versatile enough, when needed, to play the innocent shepherdess, the mother of the Gracchi, or an ill-fated queen, and the chatty blonde Demoiselles Montmousset and Jeandevert, who had thoroughly mastered the lighter style of Paisiello and Cimarosa. The ships taken in gallant combat were forgotten when the company disembarked, with its women in showy, sophisticated gowns of a style still unknown in Guadeloupe, where few had seen floppy hats, Greek sandals, or those nearly transparent tunics, the waistline just below the breasts, that flattered the body by following its contours. Out came trunks stuffed with suits as lavish as they were sweaty, columns and thrones borne on men's shoulders, a clavichord taken for concerts to the governor's house on a mule-drawn cart no less carefully than if they were transporting the Ark of the Covenant. The Theater had arrived to a theaterless city, and opportune preparations were made . . . The platform for the guillotine being well suited for a stage, the Machine was moved to a courtyard nearby, abandoned to the hens, who slept high on its uprights. The boards were washed and brushed till no traces of blood remained, and the players stretched a canvas between the trees to start rehearsals of a work favored above all the others in their repertoire for its universal fame and for certain of its verses that proclaimed the revolutionary spirit: *The Village Soothsayer*, by Jean-Jacques Rousseau. Monsieur Faucompré had brought along few musicians, and attempts were made to swell their ranks with the Basque Huntsmen's band and instruments. But seeing the latter's gallant determination to execute their parts five beats behind the others, the conductor of the Company chose to relinquish their services, leaving the accompaniment to a pianist, a small wind section, and the violins, which were indispensable and which Monsieur Anse had gone to the trouble of tuning. One night, there was a gala in the Place de la Victoire, an evening gala where all the newly (extremely) rich of the colony turned out. Once the lower classes had filled the spaces adjacent to those reserved for their superiors, the plebes being cordoned off with velvet ropes with tricolor ribbons, the captains stepped forth in abundant braid, insignia, ribbons, and rosettes, arm in arm with their bejeweled, braceleted, bespangled *doudous*, whose precious and not so precious stones, Mexican silver, and Marguerite pearls shone wherever they could be placed to favorable display. Esteban attended with a Mademoiselle Athalie Bajazet sparkling and transfigured, glowing with sequins, nude under a Greek tunic of the latest fashion. In the front row, Victor Hugues and his functionaries, in the midst of devoted and solicitous women, had themselves passed trays of punch and wine without turning their heads to those in the back: the mothers of the lucky concubines, obese, big-bottomed, their hefty udders unworthy of display, in outmoded dresses laboriously let out, adjusted, patched, to accommodate their overflowing humanity. Esteban saw Victor furrow his brow when Antoine Fuët's arrival was greeted with an ovation, but just then, the Overture sounded, and Madame Villeneuve attacked Colette's aria, silencing the clapping hands:

> Lost is all my peace of mind
> Since Colin proved unkind.
> Alas! He's gone forever . . .

The Soothsayer appeared with his exaggerated Strasbourg accent, and the play went on to elicit a delight in its audience that the guillotine's novel action had provoked not long before. The public, quick to catch any passing allusion, applauded all the verses that alluded to revolution, which the character Colin, interpreted by Monsieur Faucompré, underscored with winks at the Agent of the Directory and the officers and captains with their consorts.

> My charming mistress I'll see again,
> Goodbye to my riches, comforts, domaines . . .

> What great lords did every hour
> For my Phoebe fondly sigh!
> Yet in spite of their power
> They are less happy than I.

There were shouts of enthusiasm when the Finale came, and they repeated it five times before the public's insatiable demands:

> They boast of noise and splendor in town
> But more heartfelt enjoyments our festivals crown:
> While dance and song
> Our bliss prolong
> And beauty warms
> With artless charms
> What music e'er can with our pipes compare?

The festivities ended with revolutionary hymns roared by Monsieur Faucompré in a sans-culotte attire, then a grand soiree was held in the Palace of Government, with a toasting of wines from great estates. Victor Hugues, unmindful of the insistent Madame Villeneuve, whose mature beauty recalled the sumptuous Ledas of the Flemish masters, was immersed in intimate dialogue with a Martinican mestiza, Marie-Anne-Angelique Jacquin, whom he'd seemed strangely attached to since, hemmed in by intrigues, he'd come perhaps to crave that human warmth which as a Sovereign he wished to disdain. That night, the friendless man showed himself friendly to all. When he passed behind Esteban, he gave him a fatherly clap on the shoulder. Just before dawn, he retired to his rooms, while Modeste Fuët and Commissar Lebas—a man in the Agent's confidence held by some, perhaps without reason, to be a spy of the Directory—left for the outskirts of the city with the two pretty ladies, Montmousset and Jeandevert. The young scribe, well in his cups, returned on dark streets to his hotel, amused at how Mademoiselle Athalie Bajazet, taking off her antique-style sandals, pulled her tunic halfway up her thigh to step over the puddles left behind by the previous day's rain. The thought of splashing mud on her clothing continued to worry her, and finally she pulled her dress over her head, leaving it slung around her shoulders and neck. "It's a hot night," she said as an excuse, swatting the mosquitoes that swarmed around her buttocks. Behind them rang out the last hammer blows of men striking the set of the opera.

XXVIII.

On July 7, 1798—there were events for which the Republican calendar was unsuitable—the United States declared war on France in American waters. The news resounded like a thunderclap through all the ministries of Europe. But for a long while, the prosperous, voluptuous, sanguinary island of Our Lady of Guadeloupe knew nothing of the news, which had to cross the Atlantic twice to reach her. People went about their business, complaining daily of summer, which had been particularly torrid that year. An epidemic carried off the occasional livestock; there was a lunar eclipse; the Battalion of Basque Huntsmen's band gave public concerts; and there were fires in the fields of esparto desiccated by the sun. Victor Hugues knew the spiteful General Pelardy was doing everything in his power to discredit him in the Directory's eyes, but after surviving so many tribulations, he felt there was no one who could replace him. "So long as I can send the gentlemen their ration of gold," he liked to say, "they will leave me in peace." In the wateringholes of Pointe-à-Pitre, people said his personal fortune had grown to more than a million pounds. There was talk of a possible marriage between him and Marie-Anne-Angelique Jacquin. In that moment, propelled by a growing appetite for riches, he formed an agency responsible for the administration of émigré property, public finances, the arming of the corsairs, and the monopoly on customs dues. Great was the furor this initiative unleashed, affecting many his government had favored up to then. So much talk there was of its arbitrariness in the streets and in the plazas that the guillotine was brought out again for a brief new period of terror intended to serve as a timely warning. The wealthy, the privileged, the prevaricating functionaries, those profiting from estates abandoned by their landlords, all had to swallow their protests. Behemoth was become merchant, ringed in by measures, weights, and scales, at all hours counting the takings his warehouses engulfed. When word came of the United States' declaration of war, the same men who had sacked American ships blamed Victor Hugues for what they saw now as a disaster, with catastrophic consequences for the colony. As the news had been a long time in coming, the island, already surrounded by enemy ships, might well be attacked today, this very afternoon, or maybe tomorrow. There was talk of a powerful squadron coming from Boston, of troops disembarking in Basse-Terre, of an impending blockade . . . This unease and agitation dominated the public mood on the afternoon when the carriage Victor Hugues used for his jaunts through the city's outskirts stopped at the Loeuillet printing shop, where Esteban was correcting a set of proofs. "Put that aside," the Agent shouted through a window, "and come with me to Le Gosier." On the way, they spoke of trivial events. When they reached the cove, the Agent told him to climb into a boat and, removing his coat, he rowed them to an islet. On the beach he stretched languidly, uncorked a bottle of English cider, and began to speak in measured tones: "They're turning me out. There's no other way of saying it: they're turning me out. The gentlemen of the Directory wish for me to travel to Paris and give an account of my administration. Not just that: they're sending over one of their minions from the army, General Desfourneaux, to be my substitute, while that bastard Pelardy will be making his triumphal return as Commander of the Armed Forces." He lay back on the sand, looking at the sky, which was starting to cloud over. "I'm supposed to hand over power now. But I still have people on my side." "Will you declare war on France?" asked Esteban. After what had happened with the United States, he felt there was nothing Victor wasn't capable of. "France, no. Its despicable government . . . perhaps." In the long silence that followed, the young man wondered why the Agent, so little inclined to sharing confidences, had chosen him to relieve himself of the burden of news still unknown to all—catastrophic news for a man who had known no grave adversity throughout his career. Victor spoke again: "There's no reason for you to stay in Guadeloupe. I'll give you a safe conduct to Cayenne. From there you can travel on to Paramaribo. There are Spanish and North American ships there. You'll manage." Esteban suppressed his jubilation, afraid he was falling into a trap, as he had before. But now everything became clear. Defeated, Victor told him he had been sending medicine, money, and provisions to several deportees in Sinnamary and Kourou. Esteban knew many of the great heroes of the Revolution were imprisoned in Guiana, but how things truly stood was never clear, since more than once, he'd heard men referred to as *deportees* and later seen their signatures on articles published in the Paris press. He was ignorant of the fate of Collot d'Herbois in American domains. He'd been told Billaud-Varenne was somewhere near Cayenne, raising parrots. "I've just found out the swine from the Directory have forbidden all shipments to Billaud from France. They want him to die poor and starving," Victor said. "Wasn't Billaud one of the men who betrayed the Incorruptible?" Esteban asked. Victor rolled up his sleeves to scratch at the rash reddening his forearms. "This is no time to reproach a great revolutionary. Billaud made his mistakes: the mistakes of a patriot. I will not stand by while they starve him like a dog." For now, however, he'd best avoid being seen as the protector of a former member of the Committee of Public Safety. What he wished for from Esteban, in exchange for his liberty, was that he embark the next day on the *Vénus de Médicis*, a schooner leaving for Cayenne with a cargo of flour and wine, to deposit a large sum of money in the hands of his disgraced friend. "Watch out for Jeannet, the local Agent of the Directory. He has a sick envy for me. He tries to imitate me in everything he does, but he's a sorry caricature. A cretin. I nearly declared war on him." Esteban noticed that Victor, whose complexion had always been healthy, had an unpleasant yellow shade to his skin, and his belly swelled immoderately under his badly buttoned shirt. "Well, *petiot*," he said with unwonted affection, "I will jail this Desfourneaux on his arrival. And then we'll see what happens. For you, the great adventure is over. You will go home now, back to your family and their warehouse. It's a good firm: take care of it. I can't imagine what you must think of me. That I'm a monster, perhaps. But don't forget: there are moments in history that are not made for gentle men." He grabbed a bit of sand and let it spill from one hand into the other as if they were the twin bulbs of an hourglass. "The Revolution is crumbling. I've nothing to hold onto. I believe in nothing." Night was falling. They crossed the cove once more, returned to their coach, and departed for the government offices. Victor gathered a few parcels and envelopes sealed with wax. "This is the safe conduct, with money for you. This is for Billaud. This letter is for Sofía. Bon voyage, mon émigré." In a sentimental transport, Esteban embraced the Agent: "Why did you ever get involved in politics?" he asked, remembering the days when his friend had yet to lose his freedom to the exercise of a power that had become a kind of tragic vassalage. "Perhaps because I was born a baker," Victor said. "If the negroes hadn't burned my bakery that night, the United States Congress might never have met to declare war on France. *If Cleopatra's nose* . . . who was it who said that . . . ?" Once outside, walking to his lodgings, Esteban had the sense of living in a future forged by proximity to great changes. He was strangely disengaged from his surroundings. Everything known and common became foreign to his life. He stopped at the Corsairs' Lodge, knowing he was looking at it for the last time. He entered a tavern to take leave of his own presence there, alone, with a glass of brandy spiced with lemon and nutmeg. The bar, the barrels, the bellow of the mulatta waitresses, all of them were things of the past. The ties were broken. Again those tropics that had absorbed him for so long had turned strange, exotic. In the Place de la Victoire, Monsieur Anse's assistants were busy dismantling the guillotine. On the island, the Machine had seen its vile labors through to the end. The gleaming, steel-blue triangle, raised high in its guides by the Plenipotentiary, lay once more in its casket. They took away the Narrow Door through which so many had passed, going from light to the night of no return. The Instrument, the only one of its kind to reach America, like a secular appendage of Liberty, would grow moldy now amid castoff iron stored in some warehouse. The night before he gambled it all, Victor Hugues was secreting away the artifact he had seen, along with the printing press and armaments, as an absolute necessity, favoring a form of dying—for himself, perhaps—in which man, in the supreme attitude of pride, could contemplate himself in death.

CHAPTER FOUR

XXIX.

The beds of death.

GOYA

When Esteban, weary from walking from Porte de Rémire to Place des Armes and from the Rue du Port to Porte de Rémire, sat on a bollard on a street corner, discouraged by all he had seen, he had the feeling of plunging into the madhouse in *The Rake's Progress*. Everything in this city-island of Cayenne struck him as unreal, unhinged, out of place. It was true, what he had been told onboard the *Vénus de Médicis*. The nuns of Saint-Paul-de-Chartres, who oversaw the hospital, walked through the streets in habits as though none of the events in France had ever occurred, ministering to revolutionaries who depended on their assistance. The grenadiers were all Alsatians with thick accents—who knew why—so ill-adapted to the climate that hives and boils covered their faces the whole year long. Several negroes, of the kind now called freemen, stood exposed, ankles fettered to an iron bar, in punishment for some act of idleness. There was a leper colony on the island of Le Malingre, but many of the dying strolled about at leisure, exhibiting their horrifying bodies in the hope of getting alms. The colored men's militia was ragged; the people in general were, so to speak, oily; all the whites of any standing had an ill-humored appearance. Accustomed to the handsome attire of the people of Guadeloupe, Esteban could not but be shocked by the shamelessness of the negroes strolling about naked to the waist—a sight hardly pleasing to the eye in the case of the old women, whose cheeks were bursting with wads of tobacco. There was a novel presence there: the Indian with sylvan traits, who came to the city in a canoe to offer guavas, medicinal guaco, orchids, or herbs for infusion. Some brought their women to whore them out in the moats of the Fortress, in the shadows of the Munitions Depot, or behind the cloister of Saint-Saveur. Some had their faces tattooed, some slathered in strange inks. Most peculiar of all was the way, even as the sun burned Esteban's eyes and its light lent notes of exoticism to the setting, that busy world of picturesque images remained sad and smothered, everything diluted in aquatint shadows. A Tree of Liberty, planted in front of the ugly and poorly maintained building that served as the House of Government, had dried up from lack of water. The colony's officials had founded a Political Club in a large house with many galleries, but they were too enervated even to reiterate the speeches of yesterday, and the place had turned into a drinking den, with men cutting cards amid swarming flies at the foot of the Incorruptible's portrait, which no one bothered to take down, despite pleas from the Agent of the Directory, because the frame had been nailed to the wall at each corner. The wealthy, those with administrative sinecures, knew no greater distraction than to drink and gorge at interminable feasts that started at midday and stretched on into the night. The bluster, the sunflowers of skirts, the new fashions that gladdened the streets of Pointe-à-Pitre were nowhere to be found. The men dressed in threadbare suits left over from the ancien régime, and the sweat soaked through the thick cloth of their tailcoats, leaving damp blotches on their backs and armpits. Their women's skirts and finery resembled the costumes of the villagers in an opera chorus in Paris. There was not a single handsome residence, a lively tavern, a place to be. Everything was uniform and mediocre. Where a Botanical Garden seemed to have been, there was nothing but a stinking scrubland, a rubbish dump, a public latrine frequented by mangy dogs. Turning inland, one was faced with vegetation dense and hostile, more impenetrable than the walls of a prison. Esteban felt a kind of vertigo when he thought how the jungle that began there extended relentlessly, without clearings, to the banks of the Orinoco and the Amazon, to the Venezuela of the Spaniards, to Lake Parime, to remotest Peru. What had been pleasing in Guadeloupe's Tropics turned aggressive, impenetrable, convoluted, and hard, with immense trees that devoured each other, fettered by climbing vines, gnawed through by parasites. For the wanderer come from lands with beautiful names like Le Lamentin, Le Moule, or Pigeon, the words Maroni, Oyapock, Approuague had a disagreeable, biting sound evocative of marshlands, pitiless floods, implacable proliferation . . . Esteban went with the officers from the *Vénus de Médicis* to pay his respects to Jeannet, giving him a letter from Victor Hugues that he read with almost ostentatious reluctance. The Agent of the Directory in Guiana—impossible, with that face, to believe he was Danton's cousin—was a repulsive sight: his skin had a greenish tint from some disorder of the liver, and he'd lost his left arm, which they'd had to amputate after he was bitten by a boar. Esteban learned Billaud-Varenne had been sent to Sinnamary with the mass of deportees from France—many now imprisoned in Kourou or Counanama—who were forbidden entry to the city. Jeannet told him they had arable land in abundance and all they needed to serve in the most dignified conditions the sentences the various revolutionary governments had imposed on them. "Do you have many refractory priests there?" Esteban asked. "We have all sorts," the Agent replied with studied indifference, "deputies, émigrés, journalists, magistrates, scholars, poets, French and Belgian churchmen." Esteban felt it indiscreet to inquire as to the exact destinations of certain parties. The Captain of the *Vénus de Médicis* had advised him to send the moneys meant for Billaud-Varenne through intermediaries. Hoping to find some, he had taken lodgings in the inn of a certain Hauguard, the finest in Cayenne, where the wine was good and the food acceptable. "The guillotine has never been used here," Hauguard told him, while the negresses Angesse and Scholastique, after clearing their plates, retrieved a bottle of tafia. "But our lot may be worse. It's better to perish by a single cut than to die by installments." And he explained to Esteban what Jeannet had meant by the *arable lands* the deportees were allegedly blessed with. If life was miserable in Sinnamary, where Jeannet had been exiled, there was at least a sugar mill and a few more or less prosperous estates in the region. By contrast, the mere names of Kourou, Counanama, Iracoubo were synonymous with slow death. Restricted to arbitrarily designated zones, not authorized to leave, the deportees were clustered in groups of nine or ten in filthy shacks, the sick with the healthy, as in the hold of a ship, on fallow soils unsuited to cultivation of any sort, hungry and impoverished—deprived of even the most basic medicines, unless some surgeon sent by the Agent of the Directory on an official inspection brought them a bottle of brandy as a crude panacea. "The dry guillotine, they call it," Hauguard said. "A sorry state of affairs," Esteban replied. "But more than a few of Lyon's executioners, public accusers, and assassins wound up here; people who arranged the bodies of the judged in obscene postures at the foot of the guillotine." "The righteous mingle with the sinners," said Hauguard, whipping his fan to ward off the flies. Esteban was about to ask about Billaud when an old ragged man in a cloud of brandy fumes approached the table, yelling that any calamity that befell the French was more than deserved. "Leave the gentleman in peace," the innkeeper said, but showing some indulgence toward the corpulent old man, whose profile, despite his penury, did not lack a certain majesty. "Time was we were like biblical patriarchs, surrounded by peasants and cattle, lords of farms and haylofts," the intruder said in a strange, heavy, slightly sputtering accent Esteban had never heard before. "Our lands were Prée-des-Bourques, Pont-des-Bouts, Fort-Royal, and many more the likes of which you won't find elsewhere in the world, because our piety, our great piety, brought God's favor upon them." He crossed himself slowly, with a gesture so forgotten in those days, it struck Esteban as the height of originality: "We were the Acadians of Nova Scotia, faithful subjects of the King of France, and for forty years we resisted putting our signatures to the accursed documents compelling us to recognize as our sovereign Fat Anne Stuart and a certain King George, both of whom the Archfiend will use to kindle the fireplaces of his mansions. And for that reason, we fell victim to the Great Upheaval. English soldiers came one day and threw us out of our homes, took our horses and cattle, emptied our coffers, and deported us to a man to Boston, or worse, to South Carolina or Virginia, where they treated us worse than the niggers. And despite our misery and the protestants' malice and

the hatefulness of those who stood by watching us walk through
the streets like beggars, we went on singing the praises of our
Masters: him who reigns in Heaven and him, from father to
son, who reigns on earth. A hundred times they offered to restore our lands, our granaries, in exchange for loyalty to the
British Crown; but Acadia would never be what it had been
when the Lord Most High gave his blessings to our fields, and
sir, a hundred times we refused. We were decimated, we'd
scraped ourselves with Job's potsherd and lain among ashes,
then the French armadas came to our rescue. And we arrived to
our county's remote domains, sir, certain of salvation. But they
scattered us across poor lands and wouldn't listen to our pleas.
And we said: 'It's not the good King's fault, he may not even
know of our tribulations, and he can't imagine what Acadia
meant to our fathers.' Some, like me, were brought here to Guiana where the soil speaks an unknown tongue. Men of fir and
maple, of holm oak and birch, we're made to live here, where
all that blooms and buds is malignant, monstrous; where the
tilling of a day is undone at night by the Devil's work. The
Devil shows his presence here in the impossibility of establishing order. The straight turns crooked, what must be crooked
turns straight. The sun, which was the life and joy of our Acadia after the spring thaw, is a curse here on the banks of the
Maroni. There it multiplied the grain, here it's a scourge that
smothers and rots it. Still and all, I had one thing left, my pride,
for I had never flagged in my loyalty to the King of France. I
was among Frenchmen, and at least they viewed me with respect, because I'd belonged once to a people free like none
other, and yet had chosen ruination, exile, and death before dis-
loyalty. Ours, sir, were the lands of the Prée-des-Bourques, of
the Pont-des-Bouts, of the Grand Prée. One day, Frenchmen
like you," the drunk said, pounding the knuckles of his clenched
fist on the table, "dared to decapitate our King, producing the
Second Great Upheaval, and stripped away our honor and our
dignity. I was suddenly a *suspect*, an enemy of God-knows-
what, hostile to God-knows-what—I, who suffered more than
sixty years because I refused not to be a Frenchman; I, who lost
my inheritance, who watched my wife die from the ravages of

childbirth in the hold of a prison ship, all because I refused to forswear my fatherland and faith . . . the only true Frenchmen left in the world, sir, are the Acadians. The rest have turned to anarchists, defying of God and all others, and they dream of mixing with the Laplanders, Moors, and Tartars." He reached for an old bottle of tafia and stumbled off, pouring a long draft down his gullet and flopping down on some sacks of flour where he fell asleep on his stomach, grumbling about trees that wouldn't grow in this soil . . . "They were great Frenchmen indeed," Hauguard said. "The problem is they're still alive in an age that is no longer theirs. They're like people from another world." How ludicrous, Esteban thought, that these Acadians in Guiana, convinced of the unalterable grandeur of a regime embodied in pomp and allegories, in portraits and symbols, should live alongside others who had grown intimately aware of the weaknesses of this regime and had devoted their lives to destroying it—Martyrs at a Remove who would never understand the Martyrs in the Thick of It. Those who had never seen a Throne imagined it as monumental and unblemished. Those who had laid eyes on it knew its chinks, and where the gold had rubbed through. "What must the angels think of God?" Esteban said, in a question that must have struck Hauguard as the height of incoherence. "That he's a solemn idiot," the other man responded, laughing, "though you know, at the end of his life, Collot d'Herbois did nothing but plea for His intercession." Esteban was now told of the squalid last days of the executioner of Lyon. When he arrived at Cayenne, he was lodged with Billaud in the nuns' hospice, occupying, in a cruel coincidence, a cell called the Saint-Louis Room—he, who had pleaded for the condemnation *sans sursis* of the last of the Louises. From the beginning, he had taken relentlessly to the bottle, scratching out, in the taverns, disjointed fragments of the True History of the Revolution. On drunken nights, he would bemoan his ill fortune, his solitude in this Hell, grimacing and raving like an aged actor of the stage, and exasperating the austere Billaud: "You're not in the theater," he would shout. "Do like me, hold onto your dignity at least, in the certainty that you did your duty." The whip of the Thermidor reaction, arriving late to the colony, had driven the negroes to turn against the former members of the Committee of Public Safety, who couldn't step outside without jeers and insults coming their way. "If we had to do it over," Billaud would hiss between his teeth, "I wouldn't grant liberty to men who don't know what it's worth; I would abrogate the Decree of 16 Pluviôse, Year II." ("How proud Victor was that he brought it to America," thought Esteban.) Jeannet removed Collot from the city, exiling him to Kourou. There, Père Gérard turned to alcohol, wandering the streets in a torn coat, his pockets full of filthy papers, haranguing people, lying down in the ditches to sleep, starting trouble in bars when they refused to give him credit. One night, perhaps thinking it was brandy, he drank an entire bottle of medicine. Poisoned half to death, he was dispatched by a field doctor to Cayenne. But the negroes charged with transporting him left him on the roadside, calling him a murderer of God and of men. Afflicted with heatstroke, he eventually found himself in the Hospice of the Sisters of Saint-Paul-de-Chartres, where he was laid for a second time in the Saint-Louis Room. He shouted for the Lord and the Virgin, begging forgiveness for his faults. Such was the racket that an Alsatian guard, outraged by his late penitence, reminded him of how, just a month before, Collot had induced him to curse the sacred name of the Mother of God, and called the legend of Saint Odile a tall tale invented to bamboozle the common man. Collot pleaded for a confessor, soon, as soon as possible, sobbing and shaking, moaning that his entrails were in flames, that the fever was devouring him, that he would not be saved. In the end, he rolled on the floor, and perished vomiting blood. Jeannet got word of his death while he was playing billiards with a group of officials: "Bury him. He deserves no more honor than a dog," he said, not loosening his grip on the cue, which he'd lined up for a cannon shot. But on the day of the funeral, a festive clatter of drums filled the city. The negroes, well informed that something in France had changed, had recently gotten the idea of celebrating the Carnival of the Epiphany, forgotten during the years of official atheism. In the morning, they dressed as Kings and Queens of Africa, as devils, sorcerers, generals, and buffoons, filing into the streets with gourds, rattles, and whatever could be pounded or shaken in honor of Melchior, Caspar, and Balthasar. The gravediggers, feet tapping impatiently in time to the distant music, dug a squalid pit as quickly as they could, shoving in the casket with its cracking boards and badly nailed lid. At midday, while the people were dancing all round, several pigs appeared, gray, hairless, with big ears; rooting in the tomb, they found tasty flesh beneath the wood, which the weight of the soil had splintered. The sordid, avid beasts rooted and shoved, unearthing the body. One of them carried off a hand, which crackled like acorns between its teeth. Others ravaged the face, the neck, the flanks. The vultures, already posted on the cemetery walls, waited to finish off what was left. And so ended the tale of Jean-Marie Collot d'Herbois beneath Guiana's sun. "A fitting death for such a bastard," said the old man, who had heard the tale to its end, sitting on a flour sack and scratching at his mange.

·XXX·

A couple of days sufficed for Esteban to realize Victor Hugues had been too optimistic when he told him the journey from Cayenne to Paramaribo would be easy. Jeannet, envious of Guadeloupe's prosperity, now had corsairs of his own: rapacious little skippers, none as skilled or admirable as Antoine Fuët, they threw themselves at any solitary or strayed vessel they came across, justifying the term *The Brigands' War* the Americans used to describe the French naval campaign in the Caribbean. For his own enrichment, Jeannet sold in Suriname, at whatever price, all that these people brought him. The safe conducts needed to enter Dutch territory he reserved for men of his confidence, those who took part in his enterprises. He excused his sternness as needed to avoid the flight of deportees—months earlier, some had escaped thanks to the assistance of the regime's enemies. Anyway, in Cayenne, they didn't take kindly to new faces. Every stranger was seen in advance as a potential spy of the Directory. If Esteban failed to attract attention, it was because he was assumed to be another crew member of the *Vénus de Médicis*, which was still anchored, waiting for cargo, in the port. But soon its departure date would come, with the inevitable return to Pointe-à-Pitre, where civil war might already have broken out, or where the inquisition of the White Terror might well be underway. Just the thought of it occasioned a feeling of inner devastation in the young man. His pulse pounded dully, and a sinking in the middle of his chest took away his breath. A previously unknown fear took hold of him, dwelling inside like an affliction. He couldn't sleep a whole night through. Soon after he lay down, he would awaken with the impression that everything was bearing down on him: the walls were closing in, the ceiling lowering, the air he breathed was turning thinner; the house was a cell, the island a prison, the sea and forest were walls of immeasurable thickness. The lights of dawn brought him a certain relief. He would get up bravely, thinking today something would happen, some unforeseen event would open a path for him. But as the day slipped past without incident, despair would creep in, leaving him drained and dispirited by nightfall. He would collapse onto his bed, so motionless—petrified, incapable of the least gesture, as if oppressed by the weight of his own body—that the negress Angesse, fearing him afflicted with intermittent fever, would pour spoonfuls of quinine syrup down his throat to revive him. Then, in dread of solitude, he would walk down to the dining room at the inn, where he would beg for company from Hauguard, some jovial drinker, the Acadian with the Biblical recollections, anyone, just to lose himself in talk. On one of these nights, he learned the Directory had dismissed Jeannet in favor of a new Agent, Burnet, who was said to hold Billaud-Varenne in great esteem. The officials in the colony received this news with fright. Fearing the inmates of Sinnamary would denounce their neglect and sufferings, they sent medicines and victuals to those personalities who held sway there, whose complaints might reach the ears of the new governor. Strange as it was, the last of the Jacobins, persecuted in France, were now raising their heads in America, inexplicably favored with powers and official posts. There was suddenly vigorous traffic between Cayenne, Kourou, and Sinnamary, and Esteban thought the time ripe to get rid of the letters and parcels he'd been entrusted with by Victor Hugues. He could just as easily have destroyed the contents of those bundles sewn in canvas, or kept for himself the money sealed in envelopes with wax. If he did so, he'd need no longer worry about compromising materials should the police come calling, as they did often in those days, or being called to account for his questionable mission, though now, when the fortunes of the Maximum Deportee were changing, it was not so questionable as before. Esteban felt an enduring distaste for Billaud-Varenne. But he was also well acquainted with the revolution's methods, and this turned him superstitious. He believed that bluster about one's health or luck could bring about illness or perdition. Fate, he felt, was hardest on all who trusted too naively in their good fortune. And he believed, moreover, that a task left incomplete, or in certain cases even the failure to aid the unfortunate, could produce a paralysis of favorable energies or currents, rendering one guilty of selfishness or torpor before some Unknown Force that judged one's actions. And since he hadn't found a way, not even an implausible one, of traveling to Paramaribo, he hoped circumstances might change in his favor if he punctiliously fulfilled the task Victor Hugues had assigned him. With no one else to confide in, he opened up to Hauguard, a man used to dealing with people of all stripes, who lived between his hearth and his negresses without losing sleep over politics. The latter told him that the general contempt directed at Collot d'Herbois had turned him to a drunk, a pathetic, histrionic whiner, a coward even, toward the end; but, far from cowing him, the hatred Billaud sensed from all corners stoked his pride, to the astonishment of those whom his indirect or forgotten orders had consigned to the rigors of deportation. In the midst of so many men crestfallen and penitent, the Implacable One of yesterday refused to back down in the slightest; alone, gruff, but entirely of a piece, he declared that if History turned back and he were faced once more with the contingencies he'd lived through, he would act exactly as he had before. It was true that he raised parrots and cockatoos, but only to allow himself the sarcastic quip that his birds, like his people, repeated everything they

were told . . . Esteban would have preferred to avoid traveling
to Sinnamary, leaving his consignment to some trusted acquaintance of the innkeeper. Hauguard advised him, to his
great surprise, to speak to the Mother Superior of the Sisters of
Saint-Paul-de-Chartres, whom Billaud-Varenne had held in
high regard, referring to her as *most esteemed sister* since she
had cared for him during a grave illness he contracted not long
after arriving to the colony . . . The next day, the young man
was led to a narrow room in the Hospice where he stopped, astonished, before a large crucifix hanging over a window open
to the sea. Between four whitewashed walls, with two stools as
the lone furnishings, one covered in cowhide and the other in
braided horsehair—flesh of the Ox and of the Ass—the dialogue between Ocean and Symbol took on a sustained and perennial pathos situated beyond all contingency and place. All
that might be said of Man and his World, all that Light, Procre-
ation, and Shadow could accommodate, was spoken—spoken
forever—in the projections from a bare geometry of black
wood that entered the fluid and Unique immensity of the universal placenta, with a Body Interposed in an ecstasy of agony
and rebirth . . . So much time had passed since Esteban had
been in the presence of the Christ that he had the impression of
committing a deeply fraudulent act when he looked at him now
up close, as though reuniting with an old friend clandestinely
returned to a common fatherland from which they had both
been exiled. That personage had been witness and confidant of
his childhood; was present at the head of every bed in his paternal home, faraway, where the return of the Absentee was
awaited. And then, there was the memory of so much they both
knew. No words were needed to invoke the flight to Egypt and
the storied night in the stable with the kings and pastors (*I remember now the music box with the shepherdess, brought to
my bedroom on an Epiphany especially painful as a result of
my ailment*), or the merchants selling trinkets at the gates to the
temple or the fishermen of the lake (*with their beards and rags,
they looked to me almost exactly like the men who hawked
fresh squids in the city where I was born*), or storms placated
and green branches on a certain Sunday (*Sofía brought me the*

*royal palm fronds the Clarists had given her, spry and bitter,
and for days they remained there, still damp, woven into the
bars of my bed*), or the great trial, the sentence, and the driving
of the nails. "How long would I have held out?" Esteban had
asked himself since he was a child, thinking that a nail punctur-
ing the center of the hand must not hurt too much. And he had
tried, a hundred times, jabbing himself with a pencil, a knitting
needle, the spout of an oil can, pushing and sinking it, and
hadn't particularly suffered. His feet being thicker, the torture
would certainly be more painful. Quite possibly, crucifixion
was not the worst of the torments man had invented. But the
Cross was an Anchor and a Tree, and the Son of God had to
suffer his agony upon that form, which symbolized at the same
time Earth and Water—wood and sea, whose eternal dialogue
had entranced Esteban that morning in the narrow room in the
Hospice. Drawn from his timeless reflections by the blast of a
cornet in the heights of the fortress, he thought suddenly that
the weakness of the Revolution, which had deafened the world
with shouts of a new *Dies Irae*, lay in its lack of valid gods. The
Supreme Being was a god without history. He had not produced
a Moses of such grandeur that he could hear the words of the
Burning Bush, building an alliance between the Eternal and his
chosen tribes. The Supreme Being had not been made flesh and
had not dwelled among us. Sanctity was lacking in the ceremonies celebrated in his honor; continuity of purpose was lacking,
that resistance to the contingent and immediate that had endured across centuries, in the Stoned Man of Jerusalem and the
Forty Martyrs of Sebaste; the Archer Sebastian, the Pastor Ire-
naeus, the doctors Augustin, Anselm, and Thomas, the modern
Philip of Jesus, martyr of the Philippines, honored with Mexican shrines adorned with Chinese Christs made of sugarcane
fiber, their texture so fleshlike that, when the hand grazed it, it
recoiled from the illusion of a throbbing still alive in the wound
that the Lance—the only Lance so reddened—had opened in
their side . . . Freed of the yearning for prayer, because he was
a man without faith, Esteban savored the company of the Crucified, feeling returned to a familiar clime. This God belonged
to him by heritage and right; he could reject Him, but He

formed part of the patrimony of those of his race. "Good day,"
he said to him jovially, in a muffled voice. "Good day" came
the response from behind him, in the gentle voice of the Mother
Superior. Esteban informed her without preambles of the object
of his visit. "Go to Sinnamary as our emissary," the nun said,
"and look for Abbot Brottier, you can leave your dispatches
with him. He is the only true friend Monsieur Billaud-Varenne
has in the colony." "It's true," Esteban thought, "strange things
happen in these parts."

XXXI.

The deportations had transformed Sinnamary into a strange
place, with something unreal and fantastical lurking in the sordid reality of its poverty and purulence. Nestled in vegetation
dating back to the world's origins, it was like an Ancient State
ravaged by the plague, overrun with funerals, whose men, in
the manner of Hogarth, were engaged in an endless caricature
of their professions and duties. The Priests, with their prohib-
ited books brought once more into the light, celebrated Mass
now in the Cathedral of the Forest: collective home of the Indians, its clearings like a kind of Gothic nave, with sloping
joists holding up a high ceiling of palm fronds. The Deputies,
divided, argumentative, schismatic, invoked History, citing
classical texts, reigning over the Agora of a tavern's back patio,
surrounded by corrals where the pigs nudged their snouts between bars when the discussions became too heated. The Army
was represented by the implausible Pichegru—Pichegru was
someone Esteban couldn't quite place in his reflections on the
Guianese characters—who gave orders to an army of ghosts,
oblivious to the Ocean that separated him from his soldiers. And in their midst, taciturn, detested like one of the At-
rides, was the Tyrant of other days, whom no one directed a
word to. He was deaf, absent, indifferent to the contempt his
presence aroused. Children would stop in their tracks before
the ex-President of the Jacobins, ex-President of the Convention, ex-Member of the Committee of Public Safety: the man

who had approved massacres in Lyon, in Nantes, in Arras, signer of the Praedial Laws, advisor to Fouquier-Tinville, who sought without hesitation the deaths of Saint-Juste, Couthon, and even Robespierre, after pushing Danton toward the scaffold—none of which mattered especially to the negroes of Cayenne alongside the matricide they perceived in the decapitation of the Queen, who had been, in their imagination, Queen of Europe itself in all its grandeur. Strange as it was, that entire chronicle of tragedy, lived out on the vastest stage of the world, conferred a chilling majesty on Billaud-Varenne—a power of fascination that even those who hated him most were not immune to. While some, presumably his friends, made a great show of keeping their distance from him, others appeared on his doorstep with the most curious of pretexts: a shabby Breton priest, a former Girondin, a landlord ruined when the slaves were freed, or a shrewd abbot with an encyclopedist's spirit, like this Brottier, whose door Esteban was knocking at now, after a tedious journey in a schooner along a low coast dense with marshlands and mangroves. The man who opened up to receive him was a Swiss farmer with a white wine drinker's glowing nose. His name was Sieger, and he, too, was waiting for the Abbot: "He's out tending to the dying," he said. "That swine Jeannet has finally deigned to send them medicine, garbanzos, and anise, now that the deportees are dropping off at a rate of ten to twelve a day. By the time Burnel arrives, this will be nothing more than an enormous graveyard, like Iracubo already." Esteban learned that Billaud was so confident of the new Agent of the Directory's protection that he had stepped into an important role in the colony, redacting—in expectation of a formal appointment—a program of administrative reforms. Frowning, imperturbable, this Orestes walked at evening through the fringes of Sinnamary in scrupulous dress, marking a singular contrast with the growing carelessness of the other deportees, whose months of suffering could be counted at first sight by the shabbiness and filth of their garments. Recent arrivals shielded themselves behind a dignity their Uniforms enlarged in that world of beings huddled and nude. Surrounded by beggars and the defeated, a Magistrate raised his head, swearing he would soon be in Paris vexing and punishing his enemies; a disgraced General showed off his medals and braid, speaking of *his* officials, *his* infantry, *his* cannons. Forever deposed, the Representative of the People went on seeing himself as such; the vengeful Author, whose family presumed him dead, penned satires and vengeful songs. To a man they composed Memoirs, Apologies, Histories of the Revolution, countless Theories of the State, reading their pages in huddles in the shadows of a carob tree or a clump of bamboo. This exhibition, in the midst of the tropical undergrowth, of pride, animus, spite, was a new Danse Macabre, with those who flaunted their Rank and Distinctions already succumbing to hunger, illness, and death. One put his trust in some well-placed party's friendship; another in his lawyer's tenacity; a last one in an imminent appeal of his *case*. But back in their huts, they saw their feet devoured by insects that burrowed under their toenails, and every morning, their bodies emerged from sleep with new wounds, abscesses, and scabies. At first, it was always the same: a new batch would come in with a bit of energy still left, and would join in Rousseauian communities, doling out tasks, imposing schedules and discipline—citing the *Georgics*, to instill themselves with valor. They repaired the huts left free by the death of their previous tenants; some went out for firewood and water while the rest felled trees, tilled the soil, and sowed. They hunted and fished while waiting for the first harvest to come. And since the Magistrate could not soil his only tailcoat or the General besmirch his uniform, they donned crude canvas suits and serge smocks, which were stained with resin and sap that resisted soap and bleach. Soon they all looked like farmhands from Le Nain, with thick beards and eyes that sank ever deeper into their faces. Diligent, assiduous, Death was already at work where they labored, weeding, lending a hand with the hoe, pushing the seeds down in their furrows. One man felt feverish; another vomited green bile; a third, with a swollen stomach, began to retch. In the meanwhile, the jungle plants invaded the cleared land, and the newly sown crops were ravaged by a hundred species of vermin. They were already gaunt beggars by the time they managed to tear something from the soil; then the rains broke out, so thick and relentless that people woke in the morning to find the water in their homes risen to midcalf. The rivers flooded their banks, the pastures couldn't absorb another drop. It was then that the negroes chose to cast spells on the would-be settlers, whom they saw as intruders, banished arbitrarily to lands they considered their own. Upon rising, the Magistrate, the General, the Representative of the People, discovered menaces as frightful as they were inscrutable: a cow skull with horns painted red; gourds filled with tiny bones, grains of corn, and iron filings; stones in the shape of faces, with embedded shells resembling eyes and teeth. Pebbles were wrapped in bloody cloths; black hens hung head-down from doorjambs; locks of human hair were hammered soundlessly to doors with nails of uncertain provenance in a place where every nail was precious. An atmosphere of malice enveloped the deportees, beneath black clouds weighing down on their roofs. To soothe themselves, some thought of the witches of Brittany or the dragon of Poitou, but peaceful sleep eluded them as they were surrounded, watched over, visited by nocturnal officiants who left no trace and affirmed their presence with mysterious signs. Eaten through by an invisible moth, the uniform of the General, the tailcoat of the Magistrate, the Tribune's last decent shirt, were picked up one fine day and found to be mere rags, unless a rattlesnake hidden in the underbrush had already made short work of their owners, shooting forth like a spring with a powerful flick of its tail. In mere months, the Magistrate, the conceited General, the former Tribune, the Representative of the People, the refractory Priest, the Public Accuser, the loose-lipped-Policeman, the Man-of-expired-influence, the Shyster, the Backsliding Monarchist, and the Babouvist determined to abolish private property had turned into lamentable creatures in rags, dragging themselves to a tomb of cold, damp earth, with a stone whose cross and epitaph would be washed away with the coming rains. Worse still, vile colonial officials circled the devastated fields, extortionists who would seize a wedding band, a pendant, a medallion with a family's coat of arms—belongings defended to the point of collapse as a last justification for living—in exchange for posting a letter, the promise of sending for a surgeon, of getting hold of some tincture, a bottle of rum, or a bit of food.

Night was falling when Sieger, bored of waiting, told Esteban that they should visit the Detested One's home, where Abbot Brottier was likely to be found. Up to now, Esteban had shown no interest in seeing the notorious deportee in person; but the news that he would soon hold some authority in Cayenne convinced him to accept the Swiss's proposal. With a blend of curiosity and fear, he entered the crumbling house, which was, despite everything, extraordinarily clean, where Billaud, with eyes that reflected his months of tedium, was sitting in an armchair ruined by woodworms, reading old newspapers.

XXXII.

Fierce monster.

GOYA

There was something of the dignity of a dethroned king in the slightly distant deference with which the Terrible One of days gone by received his dispatch from Victor Hugues. He seemed little interested in knowing the contents of the bundles or the lacquered envelopes, offering Esteban a seat at his table and a bed—which he shyly called *Lacedaemonian*—to pass the night. He asked them if they'd had news in Guadeloupe that had not yet arrived to *the world's pigsty*, by which he meant Cayenne. Hearing Victor Hugues had been called to Paris to give an account of his government, he stood in a fit of rage and shouted: "Now this . . . ! Now this . . . ! Those cretins aim to destroy those who saved the island from falling into the English colonizers' hands! Now they'll lose Guadeloupe, in the hopes that perfidious Albion will overtake Guiana." ("His language hasn't changed much," Esteban thought, recalling he had translated a famous discourse of Billaud's in which he railed against "perfidious Albion" and its attempts to master the seas "spanning the oceans with floating fortresses.") But just then, Abbot Brottier arrived, upset by something he'd seen: to bury the day's dead faster, the soldiers from the negro barracks in Sinnamary were digging appallingly shallow pits— stamping on the bellies of the corpses to force them into holes hardly big enough for a sheep. In some places, they didn't even bother to carry the bodies, instead dragging them by the feet to the burial grounds. "And they've left five to bury later, wrapped in their hammocks, already stinking, they said they were tired of hauling all that carrion around. Tonight the living and dead will stay together in the homes of Sinnamary." (Esteban could not but think of another paragraph in that same speech of Billaud's, uttered four years before: *Death is a call to equality, which a free people should sanctify by a public act that constantly reminds them of this appeal. A Funeral Rite is a consoling homage that erases even the horrible handprint of death: it is nature's final farewell.*) "And to think we freed those people!" Billaud said, returning to an idea that had obsessed him since his arrival in Cayenne. "We needn't persist in depicting the Decree of 16 Pluviôse as a noble error of revolutionary humanitarianism," Brottier observed ironically, in the relaxed tone of a man at liberty to argue with the Terrible One. "When Sonthonax thought the Spanish were going to overtake the colony in Saint-Domingue, he announced the negroes were free, at his own risk and on his own account. That was a year before you all were weeping with enthusiasm at the Convention, declaring equality among the inhabitants of the overseas French possessions had finally come. In Haiti, they did it to get rid of the Spanish; in Guadeloupe, to be sure they could throw out the English; here, to bring to bay the landowners and Acadians, who would just as well have sided with the British and the Dutch to keep Pointe-à-Pitre's guillotine out of Cayenne. It was colonial politics, nothing more!" "And the results were miserable!" said Sieger, who had lost his laborers as a result of the Decree of 16 Pluviôse. "Sonthonax has fled to Cuba. And now the negroes in Haiti want their independence." "As they do here," Brottier said, recalling that two liberationist conspiracies in the Guianas had been dismantled, and attributing, perhaps fancifully, the initiative for the second to

Collot d'Herbois. (Esteban failed to stifle a giggle, inexplicable to the rest, at the thought of Collot trying to found a Black Koblenz in these parts.) "I still recall," Sieger said, "that ridiculous proclamation Jeannet posted to the walls of Cayenne, when he announced the Great Event." And, softening his tone: "*No more are there masters or slaves . . . The citizens formerly called Maroons may return to be again with their brothers, who shall grant them the safety, protection, and joy that are the fruit of the rights of man. Those who were slaves may deal as equals with their former masters on those labors to be finished or begun.*" And, lowering his voice: "All the French Revolution did in the Americas is give legal sanction to a Great Emancipation that began in the sixteenth century. There were countless occasions when the negroes didn't bother waiting for you to declare them free." And with a knowledge of the American chronicles unusual for a Frenchman (but just then, Esteban remembered he was Swiss), the farmer gave an inventory of uprisings of blacks that had taken place on the Continent with fearsome continuity. The cycle had opened in Venezuela with a thundering of drums, when the Negro Miguel, rising up with the miners of Buría, founded a kingdom on lands so white and dazzling they seemed formed of ground crystal. Organ pipes didn't blow there, but shafts of bamboo pounded rhythmically against the ground in an act of consecration when a Congo or Yoruba Bishop, unknown in Rome but still furnished with mitre and crosier, placed a royal crown upon the temples of the Negress Guiomar, wife of the first African monarch in the Americas—and Guiomar was in no way Miguel's inferior. Already then, the drums were pounding in Cañada de los Negros in Mexico, and along the coast of Veracruz, where Viceroy Martín Enríquez, to set an example for the Maroons, had ordered the castration of all fugitives "without any other proof of wrongdoing or excesses . . ." And if those attempts had been fleeting, the Quilombo dos Palmares, founded in the depths of the Brazilian jungle by the high chief Ganga Zumba, had endured for sixty-five years. Against its frail fortifications of wood and fiber, more than twenty Dutch and Portuguese military campaigns had foundered, their artillery useless against the wiles of the Numidian guerrillas, who even mimicked animals to instill panic in the white men's souls. Zumbi, nephew of King Zumba, invulnerable to bullets, served as Marshal to an Army that walked over the roof of the forest, falling over the enemy armies like ripe fruit . . . Forty years were yet to pass in the War of Palmares when in Jamaica, the runaways took to the mountains, forming a free State that lasted nearly a century. The British Crown had to approach the highlanders and deal with them as one government with another, promising their leader, a hunchback named Old Cudjoe, the manumission of his people and the cession of fifteen hundred acres of land. Ten years later, the drums thundered in Haiti: in the Cape region, Mackandal the Mahommedan, a man with a missing arm, said to possess lycanthropic powers, undertook a Revolution by Poison, strewing mysterious venoms in homes and pastures that slew man and beast alike. And no sooner had the Mandinga been burned in the public square than Holland had to gather an army of European mercenaries in the forests of Suriname to combat the formidable runaway forces of three popular chiefs, Zan-Zan, Boston, and Arabay, who threatened to destroy the colony. Four exhausting campaigns failed to fully extirpate a secret world fluent in the tongue of wood, pelts, and fibers, that vanished into villages hidden in impenetrable forests, reverting to the adoration of ancestral gods. Only seven years ago, the Order of the Whites had seemed restored on the Continent when Bouckman, another black Mahommedan, rebelled in the Bois Caïman of Saint-Domingue, burning houses and devastating fields. It was just three years ago that the negroes of Jamaica had mutinied again to avenge the sentence of two thieves tortured in Trelawny Town. They'd had to mobilize the troops of Fort Royal and send packs of Cuban hunting dogs to Montego Bay to stifle the uprising. Even now, in the Revolt of the Tailors, the coloreds of Bahía were banging the drumheads, demanding, to the beat of the macumba, the privileges of Equality and Fraternity, the thuds of their Djukas now echoing in tune with the French Revolution. "It is perfectly evident," Sieger concluded, "that the renowned Pluviôse Decree brought nothing new to this

Continent, save perhaps one more reason to carry on with a Great Emancipation that had always been here." "Think what a wonder it is," Brottier said after a silence, "that the negroes in Haiti repudiated the guillotine. Sonthonax managed to raise it just a single time. The negroes came out en masse to watch it decapitate a man. Once they saw how it worked, they threw themselves on it enraged and broke it to pieces." The Abbot had fired the arrow, certain of striking where it hurt. "Was there a great need for severity to reestablish order in Guadeloupe?" asked Billaud, who must have had a clearer sense of where matters stood there. "At the beginning especially," Esteban said, "when the guillotine was in the Place de la Victoire." "A harsh reality, clement neither with women nor with men," Sieger added in an ambiguous tone. "I don't recall a woman ever being guillotined there, though," Esteban said, realizing immediately how inopportune his observation was. The Abbot, impatient to take the conversation elsewhere, lost himself in commonplaces. "Only the whites submit women to the most extreme rigors of the law. The negroes wreak havoc, rape, disembowel, but they would never execute a woman in cold blood. I, for one, know of no example of their doing so." "For them, a woman is a womb," Esteban said. "For us, a woman is a head," replied Sieger. "Having a womb between your legs is mere destiny. Having a head on your shoulders is a responsibility." Billaud shrugged, to suggest that the Swiss's conclusion had failed to impress him. "Let us turn back to our clocks," he said, a slight smile crossing his otherwise immobile face, so aloof that it was never clear if he was following the conversation or ruminating on other matters. The Swiss returned to his record of desertions: "What I know for certain is Bartolomé de las Casas was one of the greatest criminals in history. He created, nearly three centuries ago, a problem of such a scale that it dwarfs even the magnitude of the Revolution. For our grandchildren, the horrors of Sinnamary, of Kourou, of Cananama, of Iracubo, will seem no more than the insignificant vagaries of human suffering, but the problem of the negro will still stand. We give legal status to the fugitives in Saint-Domingue, and right away they throw us off the island. Next they'll claim the right to live in full equality with the whites." "They'll never achieve it," Billaud shouted. "And why not?" Brottier asked. "Because we are *different*. I'm quite weary of philanthropic dreams, Monsieur L'Abbé. A Numidian has a long way to go before he becomes a Roman. Nor is a Garamantian an Athenian. And this Euxine Sea they've exiled us to is no Mediterranean . . ." At this moment appeared Brigitte, Billaud's serving girl, whose comings and goings to and from the kitchen and the disordered hovel that served as a dining room had caught Esteban's eye, her fine features being rare in a woman without a drop of white or Indian blood. She couldn't be more than thirteen, but her small body was already shapely, its round forms stretching the coarse cloth of her dress. In a soft, respectful voice, she announced that dinner—a teeming pot of rotten yams, bananas, and salt meat—was served. Billaud went for a bottle of wine, an extraordinary luxury he had enjoyed for just three days, and the four of them sat facing each other, while Esteban struggled to grasp the extraordinary chain of circumstances that had occasioned this strange friendship between the Detested One, an Abbot whose deportation he may well have ordered, and a Calvinist farmer who'd lost everything as a result of ideas the master of the house incarnated. They began to speak of politics. It was said that Hoche had died of poisoning. That the Bonaparte's popularity was growing by the day. That revealing letters had been found among the Incorruptible's papers, exposing his plans to go abroad, where he had property in good hands, when the events of Thermidor had struck him down. For some time, Esteban had grown tired of this eternal prying into the affairs of today's upstarts or yesterday's lords. Every conversation turned on the same subjects. He missed the possibility of peaceful dialogue about the City of God, the life of beavers, or the marvels of electricity. Overwhelmed by a powerful urge to sleep, he excused himself early, before eight o' clock had struck, reluctant to continue sitting there nodding and assenting, and asked permission to lie down on the straw mattress Billaud had offered him. He took a book someone had left on a stool, *The Italian, or the Confessional of the Black Penitents*, a novel by Ann

Radcliffe. He felt alluded to personally in a phrase he came on by chance: *Alas, I have no longer a home, a circle to smile welcomes upon me. I have no longer even one friend to support, to rescue me! I—a miserable wanderer on a distant shore . . . !*

He woke not long after midnight. In the adjoining room, Billaud-Varenne was writing by candlelight, shirtless on account of the heat. Now and again he would kill with a potent swipe the insects that landed on his shoulders or the nape of his neck. Young Brigitte, nude, was stretched out next to him on a pallet, fanning her breasts and thighs with an old issue of *La décade philosophique.*

XXXIII.

That October—an October of cyclones, of violent nocturnal rains, unbearable heat in the morning, and sudden midday storms that did nothing but swell the damp air with vapors smelling of mud, brick, wet ash—was, for Esteban, a moment of unceasing moral crisis. The death of Abbot Brottier, brought down during a brief stay in Cayenne by a plague from Sinnamary, affected him deeply. The young man had hoped the influence of that bustling, affable churchman might help him find his way to Suriname. Now, with no one to confide in, Esteban was left a prisoner, with an entire city, an entire country, for a cell. And that country's forests were so dense that the only door out of them was the sea, and that door had been locked with enormous keys of paper, and those were the very worst kind. Those days saw a universal proliferation of papers, stamped, sealed, signed, and countersigned all over, exhausting all possible synonyms of *permission, safe conduct, passport,* and whatever words might signify authorization to move between countries, between territories—at times even between cities. The collectors of taxes, tariffs, and imposts, of duties and fees such as he had encountered in the past, were a mere picturesque foretaste of the entourage of officials and policemen now diligently working wherever one turned—some fearing

Revolution, others Counterrevolution—to constrain man's liberty as it related to the primeval, fertile, creative possibility of moving across the planet he was fated to inhabit. Esteban lost his composure, kicking and shouting with fury, when he saw how a human being could be stripped of his ancestral nomadism and made to submit his sovereign will to move to a piece of *paper.* "Clearly," he thought, "I was not born to be one of those we presently describe with the term *good citizen* . . ." For that month, Cayenne was all confusion, racket, and disorder. Jeannet, furious at his destitution, rallied the negro militias against the Alsatian troops, who were demanding months of back pay. Then, dismayed at the turn events were taking, he predicted an imminent blockade by American forces, with starvation as a possible consequence; in alarm, the people lined up outside the grocers' doors. "With that, he finally sold off the merchandise he had in store before anyone else could get to it," said Hauguard, a seasoned observer of colonial swindles . . . And at the beginning of November, tensions were eased with Burnel's arrival aboard the frigate *L'insurgente,* which was greeted from the fort with volleys of cannon fire. Immediately upon moving into the House of Government, the new Agent of the Directory—unmindful of the people convening in his chambers to *inform* him of endless matters—sent for Billaud-Varenne in Sinnamary, hugging and embracing him affectedly to the horror of those who had thought the Terrible One of earlier days long forgotten. In Cayenne it was said the two men had been shut in an office together for three days, and had their wine and cheese brought to them between meals while they remained there discussing problems of local politics. Perhaps they had also considered the situation of the deportees, as several of the sick men from Kourou were taken unexpectedly to Sinnamary. "A bit late for that now," Hauguard hissed between his teeth. "In the best months, mortality in Kourou, Conanama, and Iracubo is thirty percent. I know of a group of fifty-eight people the *Bayonnaise* took there a year ago, and only two of them are still alive. One of the latest to die was a scholar, Havelange, rector of the University of Louvain." The innkeeper was right: exile had outdone itself in those fields of death, replete with black vultures, skeletons, and tombs. Four great rivers of Guiana had lent their Indian names to vast cemeteries of whites—many of whom perished for their abiding devotion to a faith the white man had failed for three centuries to instill in the Indians . . . The Swiss Sieger, who had come to the city with the object of discreetly purchasing an estate for Billaud-Varenne, revealed something to Esteban, to the latter's surprise, that made plain how far a certain Jacobin spirit, *cordelier* and *enragé*, was reasserting itself in the government of Cayenne: Burnel, who secretly had the Directory's support, intended to dispatch secret agents to Suriname in order to provoke a general uprising among slaves in the name of the Decree of 16 Pluviôse, in order thereafter to annex the colony—a crime beyond compare, particularly when one considered that for now, Holland was the only true ally France had in those parts. That night, Esteban invited the Swiss to his room to share with him the finest wines at the inn with the maids Angesse and Scholastique. Neither of the ladies needed much cajoling to take off their blouses and skirts once Hauguard, whose guests' predilections didn't scandalize him in the least, left for bed. When the revelry was over, Esteban opened himself to Sieger, begging him to use his influence to get him a passport for Suriname. "I could be useful there as a propagandist or agitator," he said with a knowing expression. "You're wise to try and get out of here," the other man told him. "This country's no longer of interest to anyone but speculators, friends of the government. Either you're a politician or you're a lackey. You were good to Billaud. We'll try to get you the paper you need." A week later, the *Diomède* disembarked under the new name *L'Italie Conquise*, sailing to the neighboring colony to try and sell there, this time for Burnel's benefit, merchandise seized by Jeannet's corsair captains.

When Esteban found himself on the streets of Paramaribo after anguished waiting in the depressive and sordid atmosphere of Cayenne—a world whose history was nothing but a succession of rapine, epidemics, slaughters, exiles, and collective agony—he had the feeling of arriving to a town painted and garlanded

for a grand party, a town with a little of the kermesse about it
and a great deal of the tropical paradise. Abundance prevailed,
as though a still life had been emptied across the avenues lined
with orange, tamarind, and lemon trees, with beaming houses
of handsome wood—some of them three, four stories high—
with gauze curtains in their open windows. Inside them stood
large armoires filled with the fruits of prosperity and tulle mosquito nets over swaying hammocks with elegant frill trim.
Again Esteban saw the girandoles and chandeliers, the mirrors
with their depths as of water, the windscreens, the windows of
his childhood. Barrels rolled over the loading docks; geese
squawked in the courtyards; in the garrisons, fifes blew, and
from the heights of Fort Zeelandia, a guard marked the passage
of the hours on a sundial, striking a bell with the circular gesture of a quintain. In the grocers', beside the butchers' stalls
where turtle meat lay on display next to garlic-studded pork,
stood once more the marvels—Esteban had nearly forgotten
them—of bottles of porter, thick Westphalian hams, smoked
eel and mullet, pickled anchovies with capers and bay leaf, and
manly Durham mustard. Ships with gilded prows and lighted
beacons plied the rivers, with negro oarsmen in white loincloths
paddling under awnings or canopies of bright silk or Genoese
velvet. So refined was this overseas Holland that the mahogany
floors were scrubbed each day with bitter oranges, and their
juice, absorbed by the wood, gave off a delicious spiced perfume. The Catholic church, the protestant and Lutheran houses
of worship, the Portuguese synagogue, the German synagogue,
resonant with their handbells, organs, chants, hymns, and
psalmodies on the Sabbath and on and feast days, on Christmas and on Yom Kippur, on Passover and on Holy Saturday,
with texts and liturgies, gilded candles, fires, sumptuous Han-
nukah menorahs, rose up before Esteban's eyes as symbols of a
tolerance that man, in certain parts of the world, had struggled
to achieve and defend, not buckling before religious or political
inquisitions . . . While *L'Italie Conquise* proceeded to unload
and sell its merchandise, the young man frolicked on the banks
of the Suriname River, which was like the city's public baths,
watching the frequent arrival of ships from North America,

among them a svelte sailboat called the *Arrow*. Without daring to hope his time in Paramaribo might coincide with the appearance of Captain Dexter's ship—after six years, it had surely changed crews—Esteban felt he was in the final stage of his adventure. He would remain in Paramaribo, when the French vessel departed, as a commercial agent for the government of Cayenne, assigned with distributing, wherever its effect would be greatest, several hundred printed copies of the Decree of 16 Pluviôse, translated into Dutch and accompanied by calls to sedition. Esteban had already chosen the place he would throw out the papers, tied tight to large stones, so they would disappear forever in the bottom of the river. When that was done, he would wait for a Yankee ship to arrive, one that would, before returning to Baltimore or Boston, make a stop in Santiago de Cuba or Havana. While he waited, he would try to bed down with one of those bountiful and pliant blonde Dutchwomen, almost golden in the lace that hugged their bodies as they emerged from the windows after dinner to inhale the night air. Some sang, accompanying the lauds; others took their weaving from door to door on surprise visits. Their tapestries offered striking views—a street in Delft, a distinguished city hall facade reconstructed from memory, or a colored confusion of coats of arms and tulips. Esteban had heard foreigners were treated with special favor by these ladies, who knew their husbands kept dark-skinned lovers on the country estates where all too often they stayed the night: *Nigra sum, sed formosa, filiae Jerusalem. Nolite me considerare quod fusca sum quia decoloravit me sol.* This festering conflict, moreover, affected all sides. Many white men, once they'd overcome their initial scruples, developed a taste for warm, dark flesh so strong that they seemed to be spellbound. Legends ran wild about infusions, drugs, mysterious waters secretly administered to pale-skinned lovers to tie them down, hold onto them, alienate them from their will until they'd grown insensible of women of their race. It pleased the Masters to play the Bull or Swan or the Shower of Gold, supplementing their sacred seed with gifts of bangles, kerchiefs, calico skirts, and floral essences brought from Paris. The white man, whose strayings in the lesser territories were looked upon with indulgence, lost none of his prestige when he approached a negress. And were he to end up with a brood of quadroons or octaroons or griffes or sacatrases, their profusion brought him renown as a Fecund Patriarch. The white female, on the other hand, on the very rare occasions that she dared approach a man of the wrong color, was seen as an abomination. There was no worse role, from Natchez County to the shores of Mar del Plata, than that of the colonial Desdemona . . . *L'Italie Conquise* was gone, and with the arrival of the *Amazon*, a cargo ship from Baltimore on its way home from the Plate River, Esteban's stay in Paramaribo came to an end. He had enjoyed, in the interim, the favors of a mature lady, a reader of what she took to be contemporary novels, like Richardson's *Clarissa* and *Pamela*. Her flesh was cool, aromatic, always softened with rice powders prodigiously employed, and she treated him to Portuguese wines while her husband slept on the *Egmont* estate for motives not difficult to guess at . . . Two hours before taking his bags aboard the *Amazon*, Esteban met with Greuber, the chief surgeon at the hospital, to assure himself of the harmlessness of a small swelling bothering him under his left arm. The good doctor rubbed a salve into the irritated spot and saw him off from a room where nine negroes, under the custody of armed guards, were apathetically smoking acrid fermented tobacco that stank of vinegar from clay pipes, the bits gnawed away almost to the bowl. To his horror, he was told that the Suriname Court of Justice had convicted these slaves of flight and sedition and ordered the amputation of their left legs. The sentence was to be executed cleanly, in accordance with scientific techniques, avoiding those archaic procedures of more barbarous eras that caused excessive suffering or endangered the lives of the condemned, and so the nine slaves were brought to the finest surgeon in Paramaribo, who would carry out, saw in hand, the Tribunal's judgment. "They also amputate the arm," Doctor Greuber said, "of those slaves that lift a hand against their master." And turning toward those waiting, the surgeon shouted: "Send the first one in!" When he saw a tall negro of defiant mien and powerful muscles stand in silence, Esteban, on the verge of fainting, ran to the nearest tavern and shouted for a brandy, for anything, to dampen his dread. And he looked toward the outer wall of the hospital, unable to tear his eyes from a closed window, haunted by what was taking place behind it. "We are the worst beasts of all creation," he repeated to himself with fury, enraged with himself, and if he'd had the means, he would have burned the building to the ground . . . Standing onboard the *Amazon*, which was headed downriver in the middle current of the Suriname, Esteban hurled several bundles into a fishing canoe rowed by several black men. "Read this," he shouted to them. "And if you don't know how, find someone to read it to you." They contained the Dutch versions of the Decree of 16 Pluviôse. He was glad now he hadn't thrown them in the water, as he was about to do days before.

XXXIV.

. . . They found themselves facing the Dragon's Mouths, on an immensely starry night, in the same place the Great Admiral of Ferdinand and Isabella saw sweet water struggling with salt as it had since the Creation of the World. "The sweet water pushed against the other so it could not enter, and the salt against the sweet so that it could not leave." Today as yesterday, great logs from the inland, torn away by the August swells, pounded by the river rocks, floated toward the sea, fleeing the sweet water and dispersing through the immense salt sea. Esteban watched them floating toward Trinidad, Tobago, or the Grenadines, sketched out in black over quivering phosphorescences, like the long, long ships that had penetrated these same domains not so many centuries ago in search of the Promised Land. In that Stone Age—still so present to many—the Empire to the North had fascinated all who gathered at night around the bonfires. And yet they knew almost nothing of it. Fishermen heard tales from the mouths of other fishermen, who themselves had heard from other fishermen further to the north, and these had heard what they knew from others further away still. Objects had traveled, though, through barter and the innumerable landings of ships. They existed, enigmatic and solemn, of inscrutable manufacture. They were tiny stones—what did the size of them matter?—that spoke through their forms; stones that stared, defied, laughed, or stiffened into strange grimaces, from a land of immense esplanades, bathing virgins, unimaginable buildings. With time, all that talk of the Empire to the North made the men feel entitled to it. Words had created things, and these were handed down through the generations, making of those *things* a kind of collective patrimony. The distant world was then a Land-in-Waiting, and the Chosen People must go there when the stars gave the signal to depart. In expectation, the human mass grew by the day, joining the anthill of peoples at the mouth of the Endless River, the Mother-River, hundreds of days south of the Dragon's Mouths. Tribes had come from their mountain ranges, abandoning the villages they'd inhabited since time immemorial. Others deserted the right bank, and those from the heart of the jungle emerged from the undergrowth in thin groups under the new moon, with the awed eyes of people who had walked long months through green shadows, following tributaries, avoiding the boglands . . . And still, the wait stretched on. So vast was the undertaking, so long the road to be traveled, that the chiefs could not take a decision. Children and grandchildren grew old, and still they were there, teeming, lethargic, their talk always the same, contemplating Objects which grew in prestige with the delay. And one night, never forgotten, a flaming shape crossed the sky with a loud whistle, over the path the men had determined long ago would lead them to the Empire to the North. And the horde began to march in hundreds of groups of warriors, penetrating foreign lands. The men of the other peoples were exterminated without remorse, their women preserved for the multiplying of the conquerors. In this way were created languages: the language of women, of cooking and birth, and the language of men, of war, the knowledge of which was held to be a sovereign privilege . . . The march lasted more than a century, through jungles, plains, passes, until the invaders found themselves standing before the sea. They had heard the inhabitants of the villages, learning of the Southerners' pitiless advance, had gone to the islands that lay far, but not so far, over the horizon. New Objects like those they'd encountered before hinted that the Island Path might be best for reaching the Empire to the North. And as it wasn't time that mattered, but only the fixed idea of one day arriving to the Land-in-Waiting, the men stopped and learned there the arts of navigation. The broken canoes abandoned on the beaches served as models for the boats the invaders fashioned from hollowed tree trunks. Then, having to ford long distances, they made them larger and more slender, grander in scale, with high pointed prows and room for sixty men. And one day, the great-great grandchildren of those who had begun the overland migration began the maritime migration in turn, setting forth in fleets of ships to discover the islands. They crossed the straits easily, bested the currents, leaped from land to land and slew the inhabitants—tame farmers and fishermen, oblivious to the arts of war. The mariners advanced across the island, ever bolder and more adept, used now to guiding themselves by the position of the stars. As they traced out their route, the towers, the esplanades, the buildings of the Empire to the North rose before their eyes. They felt its nearness in the islands that grew and were increasingly mountainous and prosperous. In three islands, in two, even in one—they counted by islands—they would at last reach the Land-in-Waiting. The vanguard had already touched shore in the largest country of all—perhaps it was the final stage. The marvels to come were no longer to be the preserve of the invaders' grandchildren. No, these eyes of mine shall see them. The rhythm of the sea songs and the oars quickened at the very thought, and they plunged through the sea in succession, driven onward by impatient hands.

But there, on the horizon, strange shapes appeared, unfamiliar, with perforated flanks and tall trees holding cloths that trembled or swelled and flaunted unknown signs. The invaders met other invaders, unforeseen, unforeseeable, arrived from who knew where, come to annihilate a dream of centuries. The Great Migration had been futile: the Empire to the North would pass into the hands of the Unenvisioned. In spite, in visceral ire, the Caribs threw themselves on the enormous ships, their audacity shocking the men who defended them. They climbed onboard, attacking in raw desperation, which the new arrivals couldn't understand. In this struggle without compromise, two irreconcilable historical moments collided, pitting the Man of Totems against the Man of Theology. Because, suddenly, the disputed Archipelago had become a Theological Archipelago. The islands shed their identities, drawn into a Sacramental Act of the Great Theater of the World. The first island seen by the invader from a continent unimaginable to those from here was given the name San Salvador, the Christ, and a first cross of wood branches was planted on its shore. The second had been consecrated to the Sacred Mother, and called Santa María de la Concepción. The Antilles transformed into a stained-glass window, immense and pierced with lights, the Donors were present in the shorelines of Ferdinand and Isabella; Thomas the Apostle, John the Baptist, Saint Lucy, Saint Martin, Our Lady of Guadalupe and the supreme beings of the Trinity were each given their territory; the towns of Navidad, Santiago, and Santo Domingo were born against the blue curtain of a sky spangled white by the labyrinth of the Eleven Thousand Virgins, numberless like the stars of the *Campus Stellae*. Spanning millennia, this Mediterranean was made heir to its double, receiving, with wheat and Latin, Wine and the Vulgate, the Imposition of Christian Signs. The Caribs, a race thwarted and wounded to the death in the triumphal moment of their centuries-long quest, would never reach the Mayan Empire. Of their failed Great Migration, which may have begun on the left bank of the Amazon River when *the others'* chronicles were recording a thirteenth century that was no such thing for any but themselves, nothing remained on the shores and beaches but the Carib petroglyphs—artifacts of an epic never to be written—their creatures drawn, engraved in stone, beneath a haughty solar emblem . . . Esteban was in the Dragon's Mouths, on a still starry dawn, where the Great Admiral watched the sweet water struggle with the salt, as it had since the days of the Creation of the World. "The sweet water pushed against the other so it could not enter, and the salt against the sweet so that it could not leave." But that sweet water, so swift-flowing, could come only from the Infinite Land or else—and this was far more credible for men who still believed in the monsters cataloged by

Isidore of Seville—from Paradise on Earth. Many a time the cartographers had moved that Paradise on Earth, nurtured by springs fed by the great rivers, now to Africa, now to Asia. And when the Admiral drank of the water his ship was rowing through, he found it "ever fresher and tastier," and supposed that the river that carried it to the sea must flow from the foot of the Tree of Life. Stunned by such a thought, he began to doubt the classical texts: "I do not find, nor have I ever found, a scripture in Latin or Greek that states the location in this world of Paradise on Earth, and I have not seen it on any map." And as Venerable Bede and Saint Ambrose and Duns Scotus situated Paradise in the Orient, and the men from Europe believed they had reached that Orient navigating with and not against the Sun, they were dazzled to learn the truth: that the Spanish Isle called Santo Domingo was Tarsis, was Cathay, was Ophir, and was Ophar, and was Cipango—islands and territories mentioned by the ancients, a part now of the *closed* universe encompassed by Spain, just as the Peninsula had been absorbed in the Reconquista. Then came the *late years* Seneca had announced, "in which the ocean shall relax the bonds of things, and a great land shall be discovered; and a new seaman, like him who guided Jason, shall discover a new world; Tiphys shall unveil new worlds, and Thule shall no longer be the utmost extremity of the earth." The Discovery took on a theological dimension. The journey to the Gulf of Pearls of the Land of Grace was written in glowing letters in the Book of Prophecies of Isaiah. Joachim of Fiore's prediction was affirmed that Spain would give rise to one who would rebuild the House of Mount Zion. The world had the shape of a woman's breast, and the Tree of Life grew from its nipple. And its inexhaustible spring, which could slake the thirst of every living thing, was seen now to feed not only the Ganges, the Tigris, and the Euphrates, but also the Orinoco, which carried Great Trunks and emptied them into the sea; and at its headlands, found at last after an interminable wait—able to be reached, tamed, known in all its splendor—lay Paradise on Earth. In these Dragon's Mouths, of water pierced by the birthing Sun, the Admiral shouted exultantly, seeing the centenary combat between salt water and sweet: "And now ought the King, Queen, Princes, and all their dominions, as well as the whole of Christendom, give thanks to our Savior Jesus Christ who has granted us such a victory and great success. Let processions be ordered, let solemn festivals be celebrated, let the temples be filled with boughs and flowers. Let Christ rejoice upon earth as he does in Heaven, to witness the coming salvation of so many people, heretofore given over to perdition." These lands' abundant gold would end the abject servitude man had suffered in the scarcity of Europe. The Prophets' visions, the predictions of the ancients, the theologians' inspirations were affirmed. The perennial Combat of the Waters before them revealed that they were finally arrived, after an agonizing wait of centuries, to the Promised Land . . . Esteban was in the same Dragon's Mouths that had devoured so many expeditions sailing from salt water into sweet in search of a Promised Land shifting and evanescent—so shifting and evanescent that in the end, it retreated forever behind the cold mirror of the lakes of Patagonia. He thought, leaning against the gunwales of the *Amazon*, facing a broken, wooded coast unchanged since it was looked upon by the Great Admiral of Ferdinand and Isabella, of the tenacity of the myth of the Promised Land. The myth's character changed with the color of the centuries, reacting to ever new appetites, but its essence was always the same: there was, there had to be, there must be in the present—in whatever present was at hand—a Better World. The Caribs had imagined this Better World in their way, as the Great Admiral of Ferdinand and Isabella had likewise imagined it in these roiling Dragon's Mouths, stirred, exhilarated by the taste of water flowing in from afar. The Portuguese had dreamed of the admirable kingdom of Prester John, just as the children of the Castilian plain would someday dream of the Jauja Valley after their dinner of a crust of bread with oil and garlic. The Encyclopedists had found a Better World in the society of the Ancient Incas; the United States had seemed a Better World when its ambassadors arrived in Europe without wigs, wearing buckled shoes, their way of speaking plain and clear, imparting blessings in the name of Freedom. And Esteban had journeyed to a Better World not so long ago, dazzled by the great Pillar of Fire he saw towering over the Orient. And he had abandoned it and was returning now with overwhelming weariness, seeking vain solace in the memory of pleasant adventures. As the days passed onboard, his life came to seem a long nightmare—a nightmare with fires, persecutions, and chastisements, prefigured by Cazotte with his camels vomiting spaniels; by the endless augurs of the End Times brought together in this century, which totalized, in its extension, the action of several centuries. Colors, sounds, and words persecuted him, producing in him a profound disturbance like those that occur in certain regions of the heart, when anguish is made palpable in skipped beats and asymmetries in vital rhythms in the aftermath of an infirmity that might well have been fatal. All he'd left behind him evoked blackness and tumult, drums and death rattles, shouts and slashing, brought together in his mind under the idea of the earthquake, collective convulsions, ritual furor . . . "I am back from life among barbarians," Esteban told Sofía when she opened for him, with a solemn creak of the hinges, the heavy door of his family home, still standing on the corner with its singular adornment of soaring grillwork painted white.

CHAPTER FIVE

With or without reason.

GOYA

XXXV.

"You!" Sofía exclaimed when she saw that grown man, his frame broader now, with hard, uncared-for hands, burnt by the sun, carrying his scant possessions like a sailor in a canvas bag slung over his shoulder. "You!" And she kissed him passionately on his poorly shaved cheeks, on his forehead, on his neck. "You!" Esteban said, amazed, shocked to see the woman he was now embracing, a woman in full, so firm, so consummate, so different from the narrow-hipped girl whose image he had carried in his mind—the girl who had been too much of a mother to be a cousin, too much of a girl to be a woman: an unsexed playmate, solace in his crises, that was the Sofía of before. He looked around now, rediscovering everything, but with the dogged feeling of being a foreigner. He, who had so dreamed of the moment of return, didn't feel the expected emotion. Everything he once knew so well seemed strange to him, and he was incapable of reestablishing intimacy with all that surrounded him. Here he saw the harp of other days, at the foot of the tapestry with the cockatoos, unicorns, and greyhounds; there the great beveled lamps and the Venetian mirror, with its flowers of mist; there, the library, its tomes neatly arranged. Sofía followed him to the dining room with its heavy furnishings and varnished still lifes of pheasants and hares lying among fruits. He passed the kitchens to the neighboring bedroom that had been his since his childhood. "Wait, I'll go for the key," Sofía said. (Esteban recalled that in these old homes of Spanish families it was a custom to lock forever the bedrooms of the dead.) When the door opened, he saw a dusty concatenation of puppets and scientific paraphernalia, scattered over the floor, the chairs, the iron cot that had been the bed of his torments for so long. The faded Montgolfier balloon still hung from its cord; the little theater stage was still here with its decor of a Mediterranean port, good for playacting *The Impostures of Scapin*. There, surrounding the monkey orchestra, lay the broken Leyden jars, barometers, and communicating vessels of before. That reencounter with childhood—or with a childhood prolonged through adolescence, which was the same thing—broke Esteban, and he began to sob. He cried a long time, head sunken in Sofía's lap, the same way he had turned to her in grief in his days as an infirm, ill-suited to living. Forgotten ties were reestablished. They began to talk of certain objects. They returned to the salon through the vestibule adorned with paintings. There were the harlequins livening up carnivals and pilgrimages to Cythera; the still lifes of pots, fruit bowls, two apples, a piece of bread, a wild leek, by some imitator of Chardin, glowed timeless and beautiful beside the monumental canvas of the deserted square, the *airless* technique of which—with its lack of atmospheric densities—owed much to the style of Jean Antoine Caron. Hogarth's fantastical figures were still in their place, and past them the *Decapitation of Saint Denis*, the colors of which, far from fading amid the glow of the Tropics, seemed to have taken on an extraordinary brilliance. "We recently had them restored and varnished," Sofía said. "I can tell," said Esteban. "The blood here looks fresh." As they walked on, he saw new oils where scenes of reaping and harvests had hung before, done in a cold style with stolid brushwork, depicting edifying scenes from Ancient History, Tarquinades and Lycurgeries of the same sort that had so dismayed Esteban during his final years in France. "You have these things here, too?" he asked. "This is the art that people like now," Sofía replied. "There's something more than color here: these works contain ideas; they offer models to live by; they make you think." Esteban stopped, deeply shaken, before the *Explosion in a Cathedral* by an anonymous Neapolitan master. It seemed to prefigure so many events he had witnessed, and he felt staggered by the endless interpretations this prophetic canvas invited—anti-plastic, estranged from all known pictorial subjects, brought into their home by an obscure coincidence. If the cathedral was, according to doctrines he had learned long ago, the representation—ark and tabernacle—of his own being, an explosion had occurred within it, however deferred and gradual, shattering altars, symbols, and objects of veneration. If the cathedral was the Age, then a formidable explosion had collapsed its supporting walls, burying beneath an avalanche of rubble the very men who may have built the infernal machine. If the cathedral was the Church, then there was, Esteban noticed, a row of robust columns still intact while just past it, another crumbled and collapsed—and this was an augur of resistance, endurance, and renewal after an epoch of devastation and stars foretelling doom. "You always did like to stare at that painting," Sofía said, "and I always found it disagreeable and, frankly, absurd!" "Ours is a disagreeable and absurd age," Esteban responded. Then, remembering suddenly he had another cousin, he asked after Carlos. "He went out early with my husband to the fields," Sofía said. "They'll be back later." And the expression of stupor, of aggrieved astonishment, on Esteban's face left her at a loss. Taking a light and unworried tone, uncharacteristically verbose, she told him how, a year ago, she had married the man who was now Carlos's associate in the business—and she pointed toward the door set deep in the wall that led to the courtyard where the two palms stood like columns that had wandered away from the house. Carlos had sacked Don Cosme after the end of the anti-Masonic delirium—which remained, in the end, a series of idle threats—and soon began searching for a partner possessed of the experience and knowledge of commerce he lacked, one who would bring these to the company in exchange for a significant percentage of their revenues. And he met at the Lodge a man both talented and well versed in economic matters. "The Lodge?" Esteban asked. "Let me continue," Sofía said, devoting a panegyric to the man who had restructured the company not long after joining, and had made the most of the country's present affluence, tripling, quadrupling the warehouse's profits. "You're rich now!" she shouted to Esteban, cheeks bright with enthusiasm. "Well and truly rich! And you, we, have Jorge to thank for it. We've been married for a year. His grandparents were Irish. He's related to the O'Farrils." Esteban found repulsive Sofía's invocation of one of the most notable and powerful families on the island. "You must be throwing lots of parties now?" he asked, contemptuous. "Don't be a fool! Nothing's changed. Jorge is no different from us. You'll get along well with him." She told him how content she was, what good fortune it was to make a man happy, how safe, how tranquil a woman felt when she had a companion. And, she added, as if seeking forgiveness for her betrayal: "You and Carlos are men. You will start a home of your own one day. Don't look at me like that. I'm telling you, everything is just as it was before." But he regarded her with enormous sorrow. Never could he have expected to hear this rigmarole of bourgeois commonplaces coming from Sofía's lips: *to make a man happy, how tranquil a woman feels when she has a companion in life.* He was horrified at the thought that a second brain, situated in her womb, was uttering its own ideas through Sofía's mouth—Sofía, whose name defined its bearer as possessor of a *cheerful wisdom*, a gay science. In Esteban's imagination, Sofía's name had always appeared beneath the shadows of the great cupola of Byzantium; wound in branches of the Tree of Life, surrounded by Archons, inseparable from the great mystery of the Woman Intact. And now, physical contentment, borne, perhaps, of still concealed jubilation at an incipient pregnancy—announced by the cessation of an outflow of blood that had poured from deep springs since the time of puberty—had sufficed to make a good wife of the Older Sister, the Young Mother, the clean feminine entelechy of before, a woman consequent and measured, mind centered on her Sheltered Womb and on the future comfort of its Fruits, proud to have a husband related to an oligarchy that owed its riches to the centuries-long exploitation of gigantic gangs of negroes. If Esteban had felt strange—a foreigner—on entering *his* house once more, stranger still—more foreign still—did he feel before that woman, that queen, that mistress of a house where everything, for his tastes, was too orderly, too clean, too safe from blows and injury. "Everything here smells of the Irish," Esteban said to himself, asking permission (yes, *permission*) to take a bath, and Sofía accompanied him, as was their custom, and stayed talking to him until he had nothing left to remove but his breeches. "All this secrecy over a thing I've seen who knows how many times," she said, laughing, and tossed him a bar of Castilian soap over the screen. They lunched alone, after Esteban, taking a turn through the kitchen and pantry, had embraced Rosaura and Remigio, boisterous and jovial, just as he had left them: she in fine form, he in that indeterminate middle age of the negro destined to endure a full hundred years of life in the kingdoms of this world. They spoke little, or they spoke of trifles, looking at each other a great deal, with so many things to say that none managed to take shape. Esteban alluded vaguely to the places he had been, never lingering over details. When the climate of intimacy dissipated by his long absence was finally restored, and he began to talk in earnest, he would need hours, days, to take a verbal inventory of his experiences in those convulsive and frenzied years. They seemed short to him, the years, now that they lay behind him. And yet, they had aged certain things tremendously: certain books, above all. Encountering Abbé Raynal on the library shelves made him want to laugh. Baron d'Holbach, Marmontel with his comic-opera Incas, Voltaire with his tragedies that had seemed so subversive, so contemporary, just ten years before, all struck him as remote, out of time—as outmoded as a fourteenth-century Pharmacopeia. But nothing for him was so anachronistic, so splintered, fissured, diminished by events, as *The Social Contract*. He opened their copy, its pages full of admiring interjections, glosses, notes, traced out in his own handwriting—his handwriting from before. "Remember?" Sofía said, leaning her head on his shoulder. "I didn't understand it back then. Now I understand it well." The two of them ascended to the upstairs rooms. Esteban stopped at that symbol of shared intimacy with an unknown party, the broad and yet all-too narrow *marriage bed*, each of its nightstands laden with different sorts of books, with cordovan house shoes laid next to Sofía's slippers. Again, he felt himself a foreigner. When she offered him the neighboring room—*it used to be Jorge's study, but he never used it*—Esteban instead returned to his room from before; piling the scientific contraptions, music boxes, and puppets in a corner, he hung his hammock from the two rings embedded in the walls—the same ones that once held the sheet twisted like a noose where he would rest his head during his asthma attacks. Sofía then asked him about Victor Hugues. "Don't speak to me of Victor Hugues," the man said, looking into his sailor's sacks. "I have a letter from him for you. He turned into a monster on us." And tucking a few coins in his pocket, he went outside. He was eager to breathe the air of a city that had struck him as very changed when he disembarked. After a brief walk, he found himself standing before the Cathedral with its sober entablatures of maritime stone—already rich in antique tones before the stone carvers had touched it— crowned by subdued baroque flourishes. That church, amid palaces with balconies and grilles, showed an evolution in the tastes of those who reigned over the architectural fate of the city. He walked until dusk, straying through the Calle de los Oficios, the Calle del Inquisidor, the Calle de Mercaderes, crossing from the Plaza del Cristo to the Church of the Holy Spirit, from the renovated Alameda de Paula to the Plaza de Armas, and beneath its arcades, congregating at dusk, he saw the aimless transients engaged in fevered conversation. Dimwits gathered at the windows of a house to hear the novel sounds of a pianoforte brought recently from Europe. Barbers strummed guitars in the doorways of their shops. In a courtyard could be seen the deceptive spectacle of a talking head. Whoring themselves for the benefit of some very Catholic, very honorable lady—a practice common in the city—two succulent slaves solicited him as he passed. Esteban touched his coins, felt the weight of them in his hands, and accompanied both into the shadows of a dodgy inn . . . It was night when he returned home. Carlos hurried to embrace him. He was little changed: a bit more mature, a bit more self-important—perhaps a little bit fatter. "We businessmen lead a sedentary life . . ." he said, laughing. Then Sofía brought out her husband: a thin man who could have passed for twenty-five despite his thirty-three years, his face was handsome, with fine and noble features, his mouth sensual if slightly imperious. Apprehensive of encountering a small-minded, garrulous, and superficial merchant's apprentice, Esteban was impressed by this character, even as he observed in his carriage, attitudes, and dress the sort of affected, condescending seriousness, cool deference, and slight melancholy which—along with a preference for dark garments, broad, loose collars, and ostentatiously unkempt hair—was a trait of the young men who, for the past few years, had been educated in Germany or—as in the present case—in England. "Don't tell me he isn't handsome," Sofía ventured, looking at her husband with tender admiration . . . The lady of the house had set out that night a great abundance of candelabra and silver for the first dinner since the family was reunited. "I see you've slain the fatted calf," Esteban said on seeing the finest fowl garnished with the most elaborate sauces on a series of platters, reminding him of dinners the three adolescents had treated themselves to in that dining room long before, dreaming of being in the Palace of Potsdam, the baths of Carlsbad, or some rococo palace on the outskirts of an imaginary Vienna. Sofía said such galantines, such croutons, such truffled stuffing and sherry sauces were suited to one who, after living in Europe, must have a deeply refined palate, trained in the ponderation of the exquisite. But looking back, Esteban was forced to confess—he had never thought about it before—that his initial astonishment at the pyrotechnics of a cuisine dense with aromas, nuances, subtleties of fat, alloys of herbs, the phantom aftertaste of essences, had been brief. Perhaps because he'd had to content himself for months on the peppers, bacalao, and pilpil of the Basques, Esteban had grown used to the cooking of hunters and seamen, and preferred the flavor of honest ingredients to what he called, with a marked contempt for sauces, *sludgy* fare. He sang the praises of the batata, perfumed and clean when cooked under ash; of green plantains glazed with oil; of hearts of palm; thick stalks of asparagus, long and pliant like trees; of boucans of roasted turtle and grilled wild boar; of sea urchin and mangrove oysters; of fresh gazpacho with soldiers' bread; and of baby crabs whose fried carapaces broke apart between your teeth, seasoned with the sea salt of their own flesh. Above all, he recalled sardines caught in nets, thrown still alive on the coals of a camp stove at the end of a midnight catch, devoured on deck with raw onions and black bread, and between bites, drafts from a wineskin full of thick, rustic red. "I tortured myself all afternoon studying cookbooks to listen to this," Sofía said, laughing . . . Coffee was served in the grand salon, where Esteban missed the disorder of former days. The grandchild of the Irish and Consort of the Lady of the House had evidently imposed certain standards of formality in the mansion. Sofía, moreover, was exceedingly attentive to his inclinations, going, coming, bringing matches for his pipe, sitting on a little footstool next to his armchair. There was a feeling in the husband's silence, in Carlos's smiling expectancy, in Sofía's undue restlessness—now she had gone off again to get a cushion—that all were waiting for Esteban to begin, like a voyager of old, the saga of his adventures. For them, situated at an enormous remove from events, he was like a Sir John Mandeville of the Revolution. But the words rose only with difficulty to his mouth, when he thought of how the first ones would bring forth so many more until dawn surprised him there, still sitting on that same divan, still talking. "Tell about Victor Hugues," Carlos said at last. Seeing that tonight, Ulysses would not be freed from narrating his Odyssey, Esteban told Sofía: "Bring me a bottle of your cheapest wine, and chill another one for afterward, because this story will be a long one."

XXXVI.

There's no use in shouting.

GOYA

He began his tale in a cheerful tone, recalling his misadventures when crossing from Port-au-Prince to France in a ship packed with refugees who wound up being Masons almost to a man, members of a club of Philadelphians influential in Saint-Domingue. It was a picturesque sight, all those philanthropists, friends of the Chinese, the Persians, the Algonquins, swearing

the most dreadful reprisals would come once the negro rebellion was crushed and they were free to settle accounts with the
ungrateful servants who had hurried to set fire to their haciendas. Esteban told them sardonically of his Huronades in Paris,
his dreams and hopes, his errancies and experiences, along
with the story of the citizen determined to build a colossal monument on the French border covered in daunting, hostile
symbols—with a bronze giant whose face alone inspired
terror—so that the Tyrants, upon seeing it, would retreat with
their frightened armies; or another about a man who, when the
nation was in danger, had wasted the assembly's time caviling
about how *Citoyenne*, the title given to women, was objection-
able, as it failed to make clear whether the women in question
were married or not; he told them how the *Misanthrope* had
been given a revolutionary finale, with Alceste returning suddenly reconciled to the human race; he mocked the enormous
success in France after his departure of a novel that had reached
him in Guadeloupe—*Émile*, in which a village boy is taken to
Versailles and learns to his astonishment that even the Dauphin
went pee pee . . . He tried to preserve his good cheer, but slowly
the events, the spectacles remade in words, were bathed in
darker and darker shadows. The red of the ribbons turned a
dark fleshy carmine. The Day of the Trees of Liberty gave way
to the Day of the Scaffolds. At an imprecise, indeterminate, but
tremendous moment, an exchange of souls had taken place;
whoever was meek the night before woke up fearsome; whoever
had limited himself to rhetoric now put his signature to death
sentences. A Great Vertigo arrived—a vertigo all the more
incomprehensible when one considered where it had originated:
in the very place where civilization had achieved supreme equi-
librium; in the land of serene architecture, tame nature, incomparable artisanry, where the very language seemed made to
the measure of classical verse. No people could be more alien to
the tableau of the gallows than the French. Their Inquisition
had been clement when compared with the Spanish. Their Bartholomew's Day Massacre was a trifle beside the slaughter of
protestants demanded by King Phillip. Reminiscing, Esteban imagined Billaud-Varenne, absurd against a backdrop of

majestic columns, in the midst of gardens with discreet vegetation, surrounded by statues by Houdon, in the exotic, grisly posture of an Aztec priest raising high his obsidian knife. No doubt, the Revolution had responded to an obscure millenary impulse, and had occasioned the most ambitious undertaking humanity had ever known. But Esteban was shocked at the cost of it: "Too soon we forget the dead." The dead of Paris, of Lyon, of Nantes, of Arras (and he went on naming cities, like Orange, whose tremendous torments had newly come to light); the dead in prison ships on the Atlantic, on the fields of Cayenne, in so many other places, not to forget the dead who would never be counted—those abducted, dismissed from their posts, disappeared—to whom must be added the walking corpses, the men whose lives had been shattered, frustrated in their callings, their labors cut short, forever dragging out a lamentable existence when they lacked the necessary resolve for suicide. He praised the ill-fated Babouvists, to his mind the last pure revolutionaries, faithful to the purest ideal of equality, tragic contemporaries of those in the colonies who still preached Fraternity and Liberty, ideals that for most were no more than political ruses to conserve their old lands or acquire new ones. The Jehovah of Old, whose churches and cathedrals were opening again in places formerly consigned to atheism, had emerged from the ordeal victorious. His adorers could say now that what had happened had been nothing more than a manifestation of His Rage against all those philosophes who, in this century that was now in its last weeks, had dared to tug his beard, calling Moses an imposter, Saint Paul a fool—even insinuating, as Victor Hugues had done in a speech that owed much to the Baron d'Holbach, that the true father of Jesus had been a Roman legionnaire. The narrator concluded bitterly, draining his last glass of wine: "This time, the Revolution has failed. Perhaps the next one will succeed. But, to get to me when it breaks out, they'll have to look under every last stone. We must be wary of fine words: of the Better Worlds that words create. There is no more Promised Land than what man can find inside himself." When he said this, Esteban thought of Ogé, who had so often quoted a phrase from his master, Martínez de

Pasqually: *The human being can only be illuminated through the development of the divine faculties made dormant in him by the preponderance of matter* . . . The lights of dawn appeared in the windowpanes and mirrors of the salon. The first matins sounded on that Sunday, when the north winds began to lash the morning. The bells familiar from childhood mingled with the vulgar tocsin of the new cathedral. The night had ended, as in their happy days of disorder, with singular haste. And now, with no need to sleep soon, wrapped in blankets they had brought down throughout the night to bundle up in their armchairs, the four of them remained in silence, seeming absorbed in private reflections. "Well, *we* are not in agreement," Sofía said abruptly, with a bittersweet little voice that foretold her readiness to argue. Esteban was obliged to ask her whom she meant by *we*. "The three of us," Sofía responded, waving her hand in a circle, casting him out of the family domain. And, as though speaking to herself, she embarked on a monologue, and by their faces, it was apparent that Carlos and Jorge were in agreement with her. No one could live, she said, without a political ideal; the destiny of the race could not be fulfilled in one attempt; grave errors had been committed, surely, but those errors would serve as a useful lesson for the future; she understood Esteban had passed through certain painful experiences— and she commiserated with him deeply on that account—but he had perhaps been victim of exaggerated idealism; the excesses of the Revolution were deplorable, she admitted, but the highest human endeavors had only been achieved thanks to pain and sacrifice. In a word: nothing great was ever done on earth without bloodshed. "Saint-Just said that before you did," Esteban exclaimed. "Because Saint-Just was young. Like us. It astonishes me, when I think of Saint-Just, how tightly he clung to his pupil's desk." She knew everything her cousin had told her—about politics, of course—and perhaps *better than he*, for he had only managed to gain a partial and limited view of the events, a view altered at times by proximity to minor inconsistencies, inevitable moments of naivety that in no way minimized the grandeur of that superhuman undertaking. "You mean that descending into Hell has served me for nothing?"

Esteban shouted. All she intended to say was that from a distance, one had a more objective, less impassioned impression of
events. She did deplore the destroyed monasteries, so beautiful,
the lovely churches that had been burned, the mutilated statues,
the shattered stained glass. But if the happiness of mankind required it, half the gothic could vanish from the face of the
earth. The word *happiness* infuriated Esteban: "Careful! It's
the beatific believers like you, the gullible ones, devourers of
humanistic writings, the Calvinists of the Idea, who raise the
guillotines." "If only we had one here, the sooner the better,
right in the Plaza de Armas of this ignorant, putrescent town,"
Sofía replied. Gladly she would watch fall the heads of all those
inept functionaries, the exploiters of slaves, the smug and sordid rich, the wearers of gold braid who swarmed across the island, keeping Knowledge at bay, banished to the ends of the
earth, reduced to an allegory for a tobacco box by the sorriest
and most immoral government in contemporary history. "Here
more than a few would have to go to the guillotine," Carlos as-
sented. "A good number indeed," Jorge adjudged. "I might have
expected anything," Esteban said, "but to find myself in a Jacobin club here." Jacobins—not exactly, they told him. But in any
case, people who *knew* (hearing again this word Sofía had used
threw Esteban into a rage), people who were determined *to do
something*. To act with certainty in a changing world, to be
aware of the age and have an object in life, that was what mattered. In recent years, Carlos had devoted himself to the creation of a small Androgynous Lodge—androgynous because
there were too few right-thinking men to dispense with intelligent and eminent women—to the end of diffusing the philosophical writings the Revolution had produced, and with them
some of its grounding texts: The Declaration of the Rights
of Men, the French Constitution, important speeches, civic cat-
echisms, etc. They brought him several broadsides and opuscules
that betrayed—by their outmoded typefaces, the coarseness of
the composition—their origins in the clandestine presses in
New Granada or Havana, or perhaps the River Plate or Puebla
de los Ángeles. Esteban was well acquainted with that prose. So
much so that, by the personal touch in certain turns of phrase,

the cleverness of certain transpositions, the presence of an adjective whose equivalent in Castilian he had struggled long to find, he could identify his own translations, undertaken in Pointe-à-Pitre at the direction of Victor Hugues to be printed at the Loeuillets' shop. And now these texts were returning to him, reproduced by presses on the Continent . . . "*Vous m'emmerdez!*" he shouted, knocking over armchairs as he left. Crossing the courtyard, he saw a key in the lock of the door leading to the warehouse. He was curious to see that place which, in a certain way, belonged to him now. It was a Sunday and the workers were away. The scent of salt meat, of germinating potatoes, of onions, so unpleasant to him in days past, gathered in his nostrils like a rich and vivifying humus. This was the scent of shipyards, of grain exchanges, of well-stocked cellars. Hearty reds dripped from the taps; the rinds of the Manchego cheeses were going green; the lard stained the clay of its big-bellied tubs. Now there reigned an order here unknown in former days. Everything was layered, hung, placed in rows as best served it: the hams and the strands of garlic hanging from cedar beams above, the grain sacks lined up like low walls, the barrels of anchovies and pickles down below. Further on, beneath the new roof that now spanned the patio, there were locked cabinets exhibiting an assortment of the merchandise that had expanded the business's scope: salt cellars, reliquaries, and candle snuffers of Mexican silver; fine English porcelain; graceful chinoiserie imported from Acapulco; mechanical toys, Swiss watches, wines and cordials from the former estates of the Conde de Aranda. Esteban went to the offices, where books, inkwells, penknives, trays, rulers, and balances stood in their appointed places, waiting for those who would use them the following day. Seeing two particularly imposing desks placed in the handsomest quarters, the young man imagined a third, perhaps destined for him, along a mahogany-paneled wall that featured an oil portrait of his father, the Founder—brow eternally furrowed, exuding honor, severity, the enterprising spirit. And he saw himself, on splendid mornings in the future, seated there among samples of rice and garbanzos, noting down, appraising, arguing with a late payer or some provincial retailer, while the sun shimmered outside on the waters of the bay and a clipper passed on its way to New York or Cape Horn. He knew *that* would never interest him enough to devote the best years of his life to it. Now that he'd been saved from Hell, he could not place himself—feel like himself—in this reality, in this normalcy regained. He went to his room. Sofía, sitting surrounded by the puppets and scientific instruments, was waiting for him with great sorrow reflected on her face, not yet able to go to bed. "You resent us," she said, "because we have faith in something." "Faith in something that changes its face by the day will bring you great and terrible disappointments," Esteban said. "You know what you hate. That is all. And knowing it, you place your trust, your hope, in anything that is not it." Sofía kissed him, as she used to do when he was a child, and tucked him into his hammock. "We can all think what we like, and we'll go back to what we were before," she said as she left. Esteban, alone now, realized that was impossible. Some epochs are made for decimating the flock, confounding languages, dispersing the tribes.

XXXVII.

The days passed, but Esteban could not resign himself to starting work in the storehouse. "Tomorrow," he would say by way of excuse to those who had asked nothing of him. And when tomorrow came, he would spend it wandering through the city, or would cross the bay to the village of Regla by boat. There, the bar tops were laid with sugarcane liquor, harsh sangrias, and roasted suckling pigs that reminded him of the boucans of before. In a niche in the bay, docked close like beggars huddled on a winter night, the sail boats with their luster of green, abandoned for having grown old and rickety, shook in the tame waves that climbed their corroded gunwales, covered in barnacles and violet algae. Somewhere still stood the ruined barracks where the Jesuits expelled from the Kingdoms of Spain were confined for months after arriving via Portobelo from remote convents in the Andes. Hawkers of prayer books,

ex-votos, occult objects—magnets, bits of jet, iron, and coral—
sold their goods in the open. Every Christian church had its
counterpart in a temple for runaway slaves consecrated to
Obatalá, Oshun, or Yemayá. These stood behind the sacristy,
and the parish priests couldn't protest, because the free blacks
reverenced the old gods of Africa using figures indistinguish-
able from those placed on the altars of the Catholic houses of
worship. At times, on his way back, Esteban would enter in the
Theater of the Coliseum, where a Spanish company brought to
life, to the tune of *tonadillas*, a world of *majos* and *chisperos*,
evoking a Madrid made inaccessible by war . . . Around Christ-
mastime, Jorge's family invited Sofía, Carlos, and Esteban to
spend the Christmas holidays on one of the most prosperous and flourishing estates on the island. Too busy at year's
end with buying and selling to leave the warehouse, Carlos and
Jorge decided Sofía should depart earlier with Esteban, and
they would follow eight days later, once their dealings in the
city were done. The idea didn't displease Esteban, who always
had the sense that Sofía's husband pushed him away from her;
moreover, he no longer felt the same camaraderie as before with
Carlos, who was too attached to the firm, and at night set off
for the Masonic Lodge or was so weary from the workday that
all he could do was doze off in some armchair in the salon after
dinner, pretending to listen to the others' discussions . . . "Now
is when I meet you again," Esteban said to Sofía when he found
himself alone with her in the intimacy of the carriage driving to
Artemisa. Sitting as though cradled beneath the oilskin roof,
they were jolted side to side by bad roads. They ate in road-
houses and inns, reveled in ordering the most rustic or rare
dishes—potato stew with dark broth or grilled squabs—and
Sofía, who avoided wine at family dinners, treated herself to
fine-looking bottles, nothing like the usual strong waters and
bitter reds. Her face would light up, her temples sweat, and she
laughed with the laugh of former days—less ladylike, less
housewife-like, as though freed from a tolerated but active cen-
sure. Along the way, she begged Esteban to speak of Victor Hugues. He asked Sofía about the letter he had brought her.

"Nothing," she said. "I expected more. You know him: jokes that lose their charm when written down. Little more than sorrow, really. He claims he has no friends." "His punishment is his solitude," Esteban said. "He believed it necessary to renounce friendship for the sake of greatness. Not even Robespierre went that far." "He was always driven to ask too much of himself," she responded. "And when he aimed to rise above his station, he showed his lack of mettle. He hoped to be a tragic hero, but he remained a bit player. Even the stages he stood on were execrable. Rochefort, Guadeloupe . . . The service stairs of the Revolution!" "He's an inferior sort of man. He revealed that in many ways." Esteban searched in his memory for anything that could diminish Victor's haughty bearing: an inept phrase overheard one day; a trivial expression; a trifling adventure; a show of weakness—like that famous day he'd fallen silent, smiling scornfully, when Antoine Fuët threatened to have him lashed if he appeared uninvited at the Corsairs' Lodge. Then there was his worship of Robespierre, insistent to the point of parody . . . Esteban's accusations against his friend of yesterday mounted, and his erstwhile love for him made these weaknesses all the less admissible: "I'd like to speak well of him, but I can't. There is too much that soils his memory." Sofía listened, assenting in her way, with little grunts that could be taken as manifestations of surprise, of shock, of alarm at some cruelty, some mistake, some meanness or abuse of power: "Let's leave Victor be. He was a monster borne of a great revolution." "A monster who made his money and married rich, when all was said and done," Esteban observed, "unless they've jailed him in Paris for embezzlement. Or perhaps for sedition. And we have yet to consider what the magistracy of the new Terror may have done." "Let's leave Victor be." But after two leagues of road, they turned to Victor Hugues again, energetically condemning him in commonplace terms: "He's vulgar . . ." "I don't know how we could ever find him so interesting . . ." "A philistine: his speeches are mere citations of the most recent book he's read . . ." "A mercenary . . ." "That's all he ever was, a mercenary . . ." "He charmed us because he came from

elsewhere and had traveled . . ." "Brave, there's no doubt of
that . . ." "And audacious . . ." "Fanatical from the first, but
that may have been a cover for his ambition . . ." "A political
animal . . ." "Men like that discredit a revolution . . ."

Surrounded by palm trees and coffee plants, the home of Jorge's
parents was a sort of Roman palace, with high Doric columns
framing verandas adorned with porcelain plates, antique
vases, mosaics from Talavera, and flowerpots abounding with
begonias. The salons, the archways of the main courtyard, the
dining rooms could have easily accommodated a hundred people. At all hours, fires burned in the hearths, and they spent
their days nibbling on inexhaustible delicacies, breakfasting,
lunching, and snacking, with a cup of chocolate or a glass of
sherry eternally at hand. It was marvelous to contemplate, amid
the pomegranate trees, bougainvillea, and vegetation wound in
creeping vines, the statues of white marble that adorned the
gardens. Pomona and Diana the Huntress watched over a natural reservoir, tapestried in ferns and eddoes, in the opening of a
stream. Long avenues shadowed by almond trees, locusts, and
royal palms grew dim in the distant verdure, where the mystery
of an Italian pergola of climbing roses revealed itself, or a tiny
Greek temple raised to shelter a mythical goddess, or a labyrinth of box shrubs, pleasant to ramble through when the shadows of twilight stretched forth. The masters of the house, ever
attentive to the comfort of their guests, kept generally to themselves. The old principles of Spanish colonial hospitality left all
free to do as they pleased, and while some took to the roads on
horseback, others went hunting or walking, and the rest dispersed, one with a chessboard, one with a book, across the
vastness of the parks. A bell hanging in a high tower set the
rhythms of daily life, calling to dinners or gatherings whoever
wished to attend. After the long evening meal that ended in the
chill of ten o' clock, strands of lamps were lit along the esplanade behind the house, and a concert would begin, with thirty
negro musicians and a German conductor, a former violinist
with the orchestra in Mannheim. Beneath a starry sky—so
starry it appeared saturated—they heard the grave overture to

a symphony by Haydn, or the instruments vaulted into a gay allegro by Stamitz or Cannabich. At times, with the participation of those invitees who could sing, they put on a Telemann operetta or Pergolesi's *The Maid Turned Mistress*. And so time passed, in those last days of a Century of Light that seemed, because of all that had occurred, to have drawn on for more than three hundred years. "How wonderful life is," Sofía said. "And yet, behind those trees lies *something* intolerable." She pointed toward the row of tall cypresses rising like greenish black obelisks over the surrounding vegetation, which hid another world of shacks where the slaves would sometimes bang their drums, evoking a remote hailstorm. "I feel the same as you," Esteban replied. "But we are not strong enough to change things. Even with a grant of Plenary Powers, others failed in the attempt . . ." On the evening of December 24, while some rushed to ready things for Christmas, making certain that the turkeys were roasted gold in the ovens and the perfume of the sauces had grown pungent, Esteban and Sofía walked to the edge of the estate, to the monumental gateway, to wait for Carlos and Jorge, who would not be long in coming. They took shelter from a sudden storm in one of the pergolas, which glowed with newly bloomed poinsettias. The rain lifted aromas from the ground, distilling essences from the leaves that had fallen on the roads. "For, lo, the winter is past, the rain is over and gone; The flowers appear on the earth; the time of the singing of birds is come," murmured Esteban, citing a biblical text he recalled from his readings as an adolescent. Then the epiphany occurred. He felt rescued, restored to himself, by a euphoric revelation: now you understand Everything. You know what it was that was ripening within you all those years. You look at her face and understand the one thing you ought to have understood, you who were so ardent in the pursuit of truths that surpassed your understanding. It was her, the first woman you knew, the mother you embraced in place of the one you never met. She is the woman who revealed to you the lavish tenderness of Woman watching over your sleepless nights, pitying your sufferings and calming you with caresses at dawn. She is the sister who knew the successive forms of your body as only an impossible lover who grew up alongside you could. Esteban laid his head on a shoulder seemingly made of his own flesh and burst into sobs so deep, so rending, that Sofía, bewildered, took him in her arms, kissed his forehead, his cheeks, drew him toward her. His anxious, thirsty lips looked greedily for hers. Pushing his face with her hands, she wriggled away quickly and stood up in front of him, watching his reactions like a person observing the movements of an enemy. Esteban looked at her, wounded and inert, but with such ardor in his eyes that the woman, feeling looked upon as a woman, took another step back. Now he spoke to her, spoke to her of what he had just grasped, what he had discovered in himself. In a voice nothing like the voice of before, he uttered a series of unprecedented, unacceptable words, which, far from moving her, had about them the hollow resonance of commonplaces. Uncertain what to do, what to say, she was ashamed, almost, at having to suffer through that monologue of fevered confessions that mentioned trivial deceptions in the bedroom, unfulfilled cravings, the obscure hopes that had brought the visitor back from arid lands to the place of his departure. "Enough!" shouted Sofía, rage painted across her face. A different woman, perhaps, might find some interest in listening to this. But in her intransigence, it all sounded false, counterfeit. And as the other spoke faster, she kept shouting *Enough!* raising the diapason to conclusive, decisive, unimpeachable intonations. A silence rife with anguish followed. Their bodies both throbbed from within, as though they had emerged from some trying endeavor. "You've ruined everything; you've destroyed everything," she said. And now Sofía broke into tears, running off beneath the rain. Night fell over his prone body. Nothing would be as it was before. What had burst from him in that moment of crisis would erect an unbreachable wall of distrust, reticent silences, harsh looks, and he would be incapable of bearing it. Better to leave, he thought, abandon the family, but he knew he lacked the energy to do so. The times were so hazardous that the traveler setting forth could expect the worst, as in the days of the Middle Ages. And Esteban knew well the tedium the word *adventure* could conceal . . . The rain stopped. Lights and costumes filled the hedges. Pastors arrived, millers with flour-dusted faces, negroes who weren't negroes, old ladies played by twelve-year-olds, people bearded and with cardboard crowns, shaking rattles, cowbells, tambourines, and castanets. In chorus, the little girls sang:

> Here comes the dowager
> With alms for the poor.
> She tells us be grateful
> When we ask for more.

> Oh green of the grapevines,
> Oh flowers adored,
> God bless Mother Mary
> And Jesus our Lord.

Behind the pots of bougainvillea, the house shimmered with candelabras, lamps, and Venetian chandeliers. They would all wait together till midnight, surrounded by trays of punch. Twelve bell strokes from the belfry, and each would swallow the ritual twelve grapes. Then there would be the interminable supper, prolonged in table talk, with hazelnuts and almonds cracked in nutcrackers. Tonight, the negro orchestra would present new waltzes, after getting their roles the night before and practicing them since early morning. Esteban yearned to flee the festivities, the children harassing him, the servants calling him by name, entreating him to play some game or drink the wines and liquors that had raised such laughter in the lighted doorways. He heard the mincing trot of horses. Riding in the box seat of the mud-spattered carriage, Remigio appeared at the end of the avenue. But the carriage itself was empty. Stopping to speak with Esteban, Remigio informed him that Jorge had lost consciousness and was lying in bed, victim of an epidemic now laying waste to the city—the epidemic thought responsible for innumerable deaths on the battlefields of Europe. Its foul miasmas had arrived on the Russian ships that had recently docked, bearing incomparable merchandise they traded for the tropical fruits so beloved of the rich gentlemen of Saint Petersburg.

XXXVIII.

The house stank of sickness. Even from the doorway, the scent of mustard and linseed in the distant kitchens could be felt in the throat. Tisanes and poultices, potions and oil of camphor, came and went down the hallways and over the stairs, with trays loaded with waters of mallow and lily to cool the skin of a man who, in the grips of a tenacious fever, rambled deliriously now and then. After a rushed, despondent journey home, with scarcely a word exchanged between them, Sofía and Esteban had found Jorge in grave condition. His was not an isolated case. Half the city had been laid low by an epidemic whose consequences were often fatal. When he saw his wife, the sick man looked at her with debilitated eyes, grabbing her hands as if to find in them salvation. The doors to his room were closed off from breezes, and the atmosphere was suffocating and dense, smelling of pharmaceutical vapors, alcohol, and wax; the candles stayed lit because Jorge was oppressed by the intimation that if he fell asleep in the dark, he would never reawaken. Sofía bundled him, lulled him to sleep, put a vinegar compress on his burning forehead, and went to the warehouse so Carlos could tell her in detail what treatment the doctors recommended; but they knew little about how to combat the previously unknown disease . . . And they entered the New Century amid insomnia and vigils, days of waiting and days of despair—in which, as though called to by mysterious voices, cassocks appeared in the tiled hallways, offering to bring miraculous icons and relics. The furnishings of the upper floor were covered in prescriptions and medicine bottles and half-burned wicks for cupping. Wounded but serene, Sofía remained at her husband's bedstead, unmindful of the oft-repeated warning that the illness was highly contagious. Rubbing herself with aromatic lotions and keeping a clove in her mouth, she otherwise did nothing to protect herself, and attended to the ailing man with a solicitude and gentleness that reminded Esteban of his adolescence, when asthma had tormented him. Now Sofía's solicitude—perhaps an unconscious glimmer of the maternal sentiment—took another man as its object, and the sight of it grew increasingly painful for Esteban, who longed more than ever for the days of a Paradise Lost—as lost now as it was neglected when he might have recognized the rarity of his fortune but had instead— because it was the stuff of habit—looked upon it as his right. Night after night Sofía stayed awake in her armchair, eventually drowsing, but so softly that Jorge's least sigh would wake her. At times she left the room with an expression of extraordinary grief: "He's raving," she'd say, bursting into tears. But her fortitude would return when she saw his faculties restored, how he clung to life with unexpected energy, protesting with vitality at the jabbing pains in his ribs, proclaiming that death would not defeat him. In his fleeting moments of reprieve, he worked on projects for the future: No, a man couldn't waste the best years of his youth trapped between the walls of a company. Humanity wasn't born for that. No sooner than his convalescence was over, the two of them would travel overseas; they'd take the trips they'd always spoken of. They'd go to Spain; they'd go to Italy; he would recover his strength in the temperate climes of Sicily. They would leave forever this insalubrious island, where the people were prone to epidemics like those that ravaged Europe centuries before. Learning of these plans, Esteban felt a stinging anguish at the thought that they were practicable, and that he might well find himself bereft of the lone justification for his present existence, which lacked all ambition, ideals, or inclinations. The extent of his disappointment was clear to him when he had to receive those visitors come at all hours to see the sick man. No one interested him. He remained aloof from all conversations. Particularly when the visitors were novice philanthropists from the Androgynous Lodge his family had founded and he had obstinately refused to set foot in since returning to Havana. The *ideas* he had left behind reached him once more in a setting where everything seemed contrived to gainsay them. Those who just yesterday had purchased more negroes to work the soil of their haciendas took pity now on the fate of the slaves. Those who nurtured corruption in the shadows, who profited by it, now condemned the corruption of the colonial government. Those who would happily have wrangled for a title from the Hand of the King began now to speak of independence. Common now among the prosperous here was that same cast of mind that had led so many aristocrats in Europe to build their own gallows. Forty years after the fact, they were reading the books that had sparked a revolution, and were discredited by that same revolution when it turned down unforeseen paths . . . After three weeks, there was reason for hope for the afflicted. Not that he had improved. But he seemed as though frozen in a vulnerable state at the far end of suffering which for others would have terminated soon in death. The doctors, now more knowledgeable after observing numerous cases, had chosen to apply a treatment similar to that used to combat pneumonia. The mood was hopeful. Then, one afternoon, the knocker thudded against the front door. Esteban and Sofía, peeking over the courtyard railing to see who was calling so noisily, saw Captain Caleb Dexter in his blue frock coat and ceremonial gloves. Unaware that there was a sick man in the house, he had come without notice, as he had before, when the *Arrow* was moored in the Havana port. Esteban hugged with joy this man whose presence made him relive happy moments from his past. They told the American of Jorge's state, and after much lamenting, he resolved to fetch a fomentation from his ship whose efficacy had been proven among his men. Sofía tried to dissuade him: Jorge's skin was so fiery from the poultices that even the mildest ones he could hardly bear. But Caleb Dexter, certain of the value of his remedy, set off, and returned at the hour when the lamps were being lit, bringing unguents and pomades that smelled of corrosives. They laid down a new tablecloth, and the appearance of a stately and voluminous English tureen announced the first hopeful dinner that had taken place beneath their roof for weeks. Jorge was asleep, watched over by a Clarist nun Sofía had called for from the convent. "He'll survive," Carlos said. "My heart tells me he's out of danger." "May God hear you," said Sofía, using an unwonted expression that from her lips had the character of a propitiatory spell, and Esteban wondered whether the God she was invoking was the biblical Jehovah, the God of Voltaire, or the

Great Architect of the Masons—such was the Confusion of Gods adored in the recently ended Century of Light. Inevitably, Esteban was called upon to retell his travels through the Caribbean: but this time he did it with pleasure and good humor, since the sailor knew the settings of his great adventure. "By the by, the war between France and the United States won't last much longer," Caleb Dexter said. "The peace negotiations have already begun." As for Guadeloupe, perpetual disorder had reigned there since Victor Hugues, unwilling to hand his government to Pelardy and Desfourneaux, had finally been deported by force. Military uprisings were the order of the day, and the erstwhile White Lords had risen from their ashes and were waging war against the New White Lords and reclaiming their former privileges. In the French colonies, there was a general tendency to turn back to the practices of the ancien régime, especially since Victor Hugues had taken up his new post as Agent of the Directory in Cayenne. "You hadn't heard?" the mariner said, seeing his companions' stupefaction. For them, Victor Hugues was a man defeated, his career shattered, perhaps a prisoner, perhaps already condemned to death. And now they discovered he had won his battle in Paris and had returned to the Americas a victor, with a new bicorne hat on his head and invested with new powers. When word of it spread—the Yankee said—the wind of terror blew through Guiana. People hurried to the streets, shouting that unspeakable tragedy was in the offing. The deportees in Sinnamary, Kourou, Iracubo, and Conanama, no longer hoping to survive the plagues, prayed, shouted, praised the honor of the Most High, begging to be freed from further sufferings. The collective panic was like the prelude to the coming of the Antichrist. Posters were glued all over Cayenne to make it known that times were different, that the events of Guadeloupe would not be repeated here, and that the new Agent, animated by a generous and just spirit, would do all he could to bring happiness to the colony. (*Sic*, Esteban said, recognizing the rhetoric of old.) And the tragicomic part of it was that in a show of benevolence, Victor Hugues had arrived in Cayenne with a band standing brazenly on the prow of the ship—in the same place the guillotine had stood when he

came to Guadeloupe as a chilling admonition to the populace.
They played clanging marches by Gossec, modish tunes from
Paris, rustic contra dances for fife and clarinet, just where, six
years earlier, the sinister swish of the falling blade had been
heard as Monsieur Anse raised and lowered it in the guides.
Victor Hugues had come alone, leaving his wife back in
France—or perhaps he hadn't even married: Caleb Dexter
didn't know that for sure, he'd gotten his news in Paramaribo,
where the people were apprehensive that the Agent of France
was so near. To the astonishment of all, the Agent had proved
magnanimous, visiting the deportees, improving their miserable lives a bit, promising many could soon return to their home-
lands. "The wolf has donned sheep's clothing," Esteban said.
"A mere political instrument adjusting to the mandates of the
day," Carlos said. "An extraordinary character, despite everything," Sofía said. Caleb Dexter retired early, as his ship would
set sail a bit before dawn: they would talk again in a month,
when he would stop in Havana on his way south. They would
then celebrate—with very fine bottles—the sick man's recovery.
Esteban accompanied him to the docks, driving the carriage . . .
On returning, he found Carlos at the front door to the house.
"Go get a doctor," he said. "Jorge's suffocating. I'm afraid he
won't make it through the night."

XXXIX.

The sick man continued to struggle. It beggared belief that this
pallid, fragile creature, looking like the last of his line, could
possess such reserves of vitality. Choking almost continuously,
consumed by fever, he yet had the strength to shout in his de-
liria that he refused to die. Esteban had seen an Indian, a negro
die several times: for them things happened quite differently.
They lay prostrate without protesting, like wounded beasts,
growing alien to their surroundings, wanting more and more to
be left in peace, as if resigned in advance to eventual defeat.
Jorge, on the other hand, twitched, pleaded, moaned, unable to
accept what was evident to the rest. To such a degree had

civilization dispossessed man of all composure before his death, despite the many arguments forged across the centuries to elucidate it and accept it with tranquility. Even now, when death was inexorably near and the clock was ticking down, one had to try and convince oneself that death wasn't an end, but a journey, that beyond it lay another life one would enter with certain guarantees vouchsafed on this side of the barrier. Jorge himself solicited the presence of a priest, who took as a final confession what was nothing more than a babble of disjointed phrases. Seeing the doctors had given up, Rosaura persuaded Sofía to let her bring a very old black shaman to the house. "What's it matter?" the young woman said. "Ogé too had respect for shamans . . ." The medicine man proceeded to *purify* the room with aromatic waters, threw shells on the floor, noting whether they fell faceup or facedown, then brought plants from an herb vendor whose stall lay near the marketplace. Whatever he had done, they had to admit he'd known how to calm the sick man's gasps, reanimating a heart that showed, at times, an agonizing weakness . . . But little more could be hoped for. The mechanisms of Jorge's body were failing, one by one. The negro's concoctions gave only a passing relief. The Corpse-bearer and the Gravedigger lurked around the house at all hours. Esteban was unsurprised when he saw Carlos's tailor arrive with mourning clothes. Sofía had ordered her own from her seamstress, in such abundance that they filled several baskets placed willy-nilly in a room in the back where the young woman had dressed and undressed since the beginning of her husband's illness. Perhaps from respect for some private superstition, she refused to look inside them. Esteban understood: by having them send her these black dresses, she had carried out a rite of conjuration. Taking them out would mean accepting what she didn't wish to accept. Everyone had to feign belief that black cloth would not need reappear under the roof of that house. And yet three days later, after his heart inevitably gave out, the black cloth made its entrance through the front door just past four in the afternoon; the black of nuns' habits, the black of cassocks, the black suits of friends, customers, fellow Masons, acquaintances, and employees; the black of the Mortuary, of grave mound and shovels; the black of black persons, distant relatives from four generations back, ancillary kin like forgotten shadows who emerged from their faraway neighborhoods to form plaintive choruses beneath the arcades in the courtyard. In their ruthlessly compartmentalized society, the Vigil was the one ceremony that broke the barriers of class and race, allowing the barber who had once razored the cheeks of the deceased to rub elbows beside the coffin with the Captain General of the Colony, the Rector of the College of Physicians, the Count of Pozos Dulces, or the rich estate owner, recently granted the title of Marqués by Royal Proclamation. Overwhelmed by the hundreds of unknown faces—Havana's traders and industrialists to a man had come that night to the house of tall timbers—Sofía, haggard from her vigils, hardened by that inner pain exempt from the need to show itself in plaints and tears, played the role of widow with a dignity and grace that even Esteban admired. Pallid, dejected, dizzy, perhaps, from the perfume of so many flowers, whose mingled odors transformed to a waxy stench amid the fetor of the tapers and altar candles and the medicinal vapors of mustard and camphor still lingering between the walls, Sofía retained in the detachment of mourning a beauty untouched by her imperfections. Her forehead was perhaps too willful, her brows too thick, her eyes too reluctant to commit, her arms too long, her legs too weak to sustain the architecture of her hips. But she exuded, even beneath the onerous demands of the moment, a glow of pure femininity that emerged from her inner depths, and as he glimpsed it, Esteban grasped the secret springs of her allure. He walked out to the courtyard to escape the hum of prayers that filled the salon where the body was laid out. He went to his room, where the marionettes offered a bizarre counterpoint to the present, resembling a drawing by Callot. He collapsed into his hammock, unable to free his mind of the stubborn realization that tomorrow there would be one man fewer in the house. Those imagined travels that had so troubled him days before were now the mere memories of words. A year of toilsome mourning would begin, with Masses said in memory of the deceased and mandatory visits to the cemetery. He had a year before him to convince the others of the need to change their lives. It would be easy to revisit that subject that had fed their conversations since adolescence. Carlos, obsessed with the business, might only accompany them for two or three months. He would arrange to meet with Sofía somewhere in Europe, and he thought of Spain, a country now less threatened than before by the wars in France that had leaped past the Mediterranean and landed, preposterously, in Egypt. It was a matter of not rushing, of not falling prey to the impulses of a moment, of drawing on the inexhaustible resources of hypocrisy. Of lying when it was useful to do so. Of playing, but deliberately, the role of Tartuffe . . . He returned to the sullen vigil, shaking hands and accepting consoling embraces from the people who kept filing through the front door and filling the galleries. He looked at the coffin. The man that lay there was an intruder. An intruder who would be taken away tomorrow, on others' shoulders, and Esteban had been freed from the intimate crime of longing for his physical elimination—as the philosophes of the Century Before had called the execution of a scoundrel. Mourning would close the house, reduce the family circle to its proper proportions, recreate the atmosphere of earlier days. Perhaps the old disorder would return, as if time had traveled backward. After the long night of the vigil; after the funeral with its orations, its crossbearers, offerings, vestments, tapers, crepe and flowers, obituary and requiem, and who had come in pomp, and who had wept, and who had said that we were nothing . . . After the end of mourning, the duty of shaking a hundred sweaty hands under a sun that tormented the eyes with its reflections on the marble headstones, a natural bond would return with all they'd left behind . . . When the drear of the funeral obligations was done, they sat once more around the big table in the dining room, Carlos, Esteban, and Sofía—on a Sunday—before a dinner ordered from a nearby hotel. Remigio, who hadn't been able to go to the market because he was at the cemetery, brought trays covered in cloth, bearing almond-crusted seabream, marzipan, squab *à la crapaudine*, truffled this and confited that, which Esteban had ordered personally, saying whatever they didn't have should be found, irrespective of the cost. "What a coincidence!" Sofía said. "I seem to remember we ate almost the same thing after . . ." (and her voice trailed off, because they never spoke of their father in the house). "The very same," Esteban said. "In hotels the food varies little." And he noticed his cousin had placed her elbows on the table, and the slovenly manners of earlier years seemed to have returned. She sampled bits of everything in no particular order, looking at the tablecloth, playing mechanically with the glassware. She went to bed early, exhausted by the nights of vigil. There was no reason to expose herself to contagion now that Jorge was gone. She had her narrow spinster's bed removed from a bedroom they used for storage and placed in the room where the baskets with her mourning clothes still waited, unopened. "Poor Sofía!" Carlos said when the two men were alone. "To be left a widow at her age!" "She'll marry again soon," said Esteban, fingering a gray seed on a golden thread that had been his personal talisman in his sailing days, to keep storms at bay and ward off disaster . . . In the days that followed, to make himself useful in some way, he went regularly to the storehouse, taking Jorge's office—pretending the business now interested him a great deal. Daily contact with merchants in the square and people from the provinces kept him abreast of surprising events. Mute apprehension was spreading across the island. The rich landowners lived in constant distress, believing a conjuration of negroes was determined to repeat here what the negroes of Saint-Domingue had done there. Rumors circulated about the existence of an invisible, nameless mulatto chief, who roved the fields and provoked the crews at the sugar mills. Too many pockets hid the writings of the *damned French*. Anonymous placards, plastered by mysterious hands on the city walls at night, hailed the Revolution in the name of *freedom of conscience*, and announced the imminent erection of the guillotine in the public squares. Any act of violence committed by a negro—even a drunk or a madman—was attributed to subversive intent. At the same time, the ships brought news of political agitation in Venezuela and New Granada. All over, the winds of conspiracy blew. It was said that the barracks were on alert and that new cannons had arrived from Spain to reinforce the battalions of the

Castillo del Príncipe . . . "Hogwash!" Carlos said when the news reached him, taking the conversation prudently back into the terrain of business. "In this overgrown hamlet, people have nothing else to talk about."

XL.

Bitter presence.

GOYA

One night when Carlos and Sofía were absent from home, attending some ceremony at the Androgynous Lodge, Esteban, with a slight cold, moved to the salon, placing a large glass of punch nearby, to read an old collection of predictions and prophecies published a half century before by Torres Villarroel, the Great Piscator of Salamanca. It shocked him to find that this man who boasted of being a Doctor of Chrysopoeia, Magic, Natural Philosophy, and Transmutation—all this to sell his almanacs—had foreseen, in terms of chilling accuracy, the fall of the Throne of France:

> *When you count to one thousand*
> *With three hundred doubled*
> *And fifty times two,*
> *With nine more tens,*
> *Then you will see,*
> *Miserable France, calamity*
> *Awaits you,*
> *With your King and Prince,*
> *And your greatest glory*
> *Shall see its final end.*

He then turned to Villarroel's biography, very amusing for the picaresque adventures and winding roads the poet passed through. He was a guide for blind hermits, a student and bull-fighter, a barber surgeon, a dancer, a watchman and a mathematician, a soldier in Porto and a professor, before ending his days serenely in a monk's habit. He reached the mysterious episode of the phantom knockers that disturbed the peace of a mansion in Madrid, tearing paintings from the walls, when he noticed that the early evening storm had turned to a heavy rain whipped by harsh winds. He resumed his reading, paying no attention to an upstairs window that sounded to have been left open; and it amused him to hear its shutter clacking just as he reached those pages that told of horrors and apparitions. But the noise soon grew irritating, and Esteban went upstairs. The open window was in the room where Sofía slept. It had been foolish not to close it before, as the rain had poured straight through it, soaking the floor as if thrown from buckets and soaking the bedroom carpet. Next to the armoire, a puddle was forming over uneven floorboards. And in it lay the still-unopened wicker baskets full of mourning clothes, avidly soaking up water. Esteban set them on a table. But they were so wet, he thought it best to remove the garments inside them. He opened the first, expecting to stick his hand into the darkness of black cloth, but instead found a fiesta of bright fabrics, satin and silk, with showy adornments of a kind he had never seen in Sofía's wardrobe. He lifted the lid of the next one and saw a costly display of flounces, Valenciennes lace, fine fringes, blouses, and extremely delicate intimate wear. Stupefied, feeling guilty for violating a secret, Esteban closed the baskets, leaving them there on the table. He took down several blankets to dry the floor. As he did so, he couldn't take his eyes off the wicker baskets, which had arrived at the house with their contents while Jorge was sweating out his final fever in the adjoining room. At the vigil, his cousin had worn her mourning clothes, it was true. But they amounted to no more than three dresses, which she donned one after the other, and even then, it seemed strange that Sofía should choose to wear something so humble and lackluster—Esteban had supposed her to be guided by a will to mortification. But this sentiment he'd imagined before was impossible to reconcile with that other will, seen only now, to have made for her garments as costly, unseemly, and useless as those he had just discovered. There were dresses there meant for drawing the eyes of crowds at balls and

theaters; leggings by the dozen; embroidered sandals; sumptuous gowns destined for urbane ostentation, but also for the
deepest intimacy. He lifted the top of the one basket that was
still unopened. Inside it were more normal, more understated
dresses, unceremonial, meant for wearing out, with robes of
fine texture—bright and merry—and garish details. But the
enigma was the same: nothing he had found there was black,
and nothing spoke of mourning or any expression of grief.
Sofía knew how quickly women's fashions changed, in those
times particularly. In the city, which was thriving economically
once again, the women kept up with what was worn in Europe. It was unthinkable that Sofía would buy so sumptuous
an array of clothing, knowing that when her year of mourning
was over—and when the burden of half-mourning still lay
ahead of her—her garments would be out of style . . . Esteban
was tormenting himself with questions, resorting to the most
excruciating suppositions—imagining his cousin led a double
life, unsuspected even by her brother—when he heard the carriage entering the gate. Sofía appeared on the threshold of
the bedroom, where she stopped, looking surprised. Esteban,
wringing a blanket over a pail, told her what had happened.
"Your clothes must be soaked," he said, pointing at the baskets.
"I'll take them out. Leave me alone," she said, accompanying
him to the door. After she had told him goodnight, she locked
the door behind her.

The next day, Esteban was in the storehouse, unable to concen-
trate on his tasks, when a tumult broke out in the street. Windows slammed shut as shouts proclaimed that the negroes had
risen up as they had in Haiti. The peddlers carried off their
chests, going home in a wild retreat, some with carts full of
toys, some with sacks full of religious paraphernalia. In the
doorways, old women talked of death and rape in the midst of
voices shouting to be heard over the commotion of a carriage
overturned after taking the corner too quickly. Choruses
formed here and there and conveyed the most contradictory notices: that two regiments had been sent to the city walls to repel
the advance of a column of slaves; that the coloreds had tried to

blow up the gunpowder depot; that French agitators had come from Baltimore by boat and were causing havoc in the city; that fires had broken out in the Arsenal neighborhood. Soon it came to light that the uproar was down to a dust-up between trouble-makers and American sailors who, after enjoying all the women, liquor, and cards that the famous dive bar La Lola had to offer, had tried to leave without paying, beating the dealer, kicking the barmaid, and breaking the furnishings and mirrors. A battle erupted when a gathering of Congo negroes got in-volved, stopping on their way to the Church of Paula, torches raised, preparing to render homage to a patron saint. At the end of a clash with clubs and machetes, made worse when the watchmen hurried in, several of the wounded were left lying on the ground. An hour later, order was restored in that always unruly quarter. But the Governor, intending to use the moment to put an end to other conflicts, issued a proclamation an-nouncing measures against anyone suspected of spreading subversive ideas, pasting up placards—this was a frequent occurrence—advocating for the abolition of slavery, or making remarks injurious to the Spanish Crown . . . "They're still play-ing at Revolution," said Esteban at home that evening. "Better to play at something than at nothing," Sofía replied abrasively. "At least I have no secrets to hide," Esteban said, staring her down. She shrugged, turning her back to him, her expression hard and willful. During dinner she remained silent, dodging all interrogating looks—not with the shame of one caught act-ing unsuitably, but with the haughty manner of a woman re-solved to keep her reasons to herself. That night, while Esteban and Carlos played a desultory game of chess to checkmate, Sofía hid her face behind an enormous tome of star charts. "The *Arrow* arrived this afternoon," Carlos said, moving his bishop toward Esteban's last remaining knight. "Tomorrow we'll have the Yankee over for lunch." "I'm glad you remem-bered," Sofía said from the distance of her constellations. "We'll put another setting on the table."

Esteban arrived home the next day at supper time expecting to find all the lamps lit. But when he entered the salon, he saw that something strange was happening. Dexter, nervous, was pacing from one wall to the other, offering strange explanations to a weeping, dejected Carlos, whose incipient obesity had something parodical about it as he writhed in grief: "There's nothing I can do," the North American shouted, opening his arms wide. "She's a widow and has reached the age of majority. I must treat her as a passenger like any other. I've spoken to her. She won't listen to reason. Even if she was my daughter, there's nothing I could do." He strayed off into details: She had bought her passage from Miralla & Co., paying in cash. Her papers, facilitated by a brother Mason, showed all the requisite stamps. She was traveling to Barbados, where she would abandon the *Arrow* to embark on a Dutch ship to Cayenne. "To Cayenne," Carlos said, stupefied. "To Cayenne, you say! Not Madrid, not London, not Naples!" And noticing Esteban's presence, he spoke to him as if he knew something: "It's as if she's lost her mind. She says she's tired of this house, tired of the city. And she's going abroad like this, without warning, without saying goodbye. She's been on the ship for two hours now, with her luggage and everything." He had gone to try and dissuade her: "It's like talking to a wall. I can't just drag her here. She's determined to leave." He turned back to Dexter: "You, as captain, have the right to refuse a passenger. Don't tell me you don't." The other, irritated at a resolve that called into question his probity, raised his voice: "No moral or legal reason compels me. Let her do as she wishes. No one will stop her from going to Cayenne. If she doesn't this time, she will soon. And if you lock the doors, she'll crawl out the window." "Why?" the others barked threateningly. The captain swiped them away with a firm palm. "Get it into your heads for once that *she* knows perfectly well why she wants to go to Cayenne." And, index finger raised in warning like a preacher, he cited a Biblical proverb: "Weak seem the words of the heedless, but they invade even the secrets of the womb." That phrase, its tone darkened by the final word, had the effect of a stimulus for Esteban. Grasping the seaman by the lapels of his frock coat, he asked for clear, firm explanations without circumlocutions. Dexter uttered a cold phrase that made everything clear: "While you and Ogé were out trawling for whores on the docks of Santiago, she stayed onboard with *the other one*. My sailors told me everything. It was a scandal. I found *it* so repugnant that I moved back the hour of our departure . . ." Now there was nothing more for Esteban to ask. Everything had come together. This explained that shipment of luxurious clothing soon after she'd heard that Someone had risen again, omnipotent in a nearby part of America. He understood the hidden intention of a thousand questions in the past: in exchange for a few denigrating adjectives about *the other one*, she'd managed to find out every relevant detail of his life, his achievements, his errors. Hypocritically, she called him a monster, an abomination, a political beast, to learn more and more, in snippets, in bits, in steps, about the yearnings, the doings, the peculiarities of the fallen and rehabilitated Plenipotentiary. That buried will had gone on working tenaciously in silence until it erupted in appetites not even stanched by the presence of a man in his death throes. In this there was something of the sordid promiscuity of mortuary flowers or funeral tapers, with wretched thoughts all too evident in the purchase of intimate garments made to adjust to the contours of her naked body. Sofía revealed herself to Esteban all at once as the ignoble, inadmissible larva of a woman devoted, acquiescent, luxuriant beneath the weight of a man who had known the pliancy of her uncorrupted flesh. Remembering the disgust she'd felt one night at that world of whores who were no more than ancillary protagonists—*disinterested*, perhaps—of human coupling, Esteban struggled to reconcile the two personalities inhabiting that same figure: the one, blushing with indignation and ire at an act that her religious education endued with filthiness, and the other which, not long later, had succumbed to desire, yielding to the play of deception and complicity. "It's your fault for marrying her off to a cretin," Esteban shouted, looking for someone to blame for what he took as a monstrous defection. "That never was a good marriage," Dexter said, standing before a mirror to smooth the lapels the other man had wrinkled. "When husband and wife have an understanding in the bedroom, you can tell, even when they argue. What they had was a comedy. *Something* was missing. Just one look at his hands, and you knew: they were the hands of a Catholic nun, with soft little fingers that didn't know how to grab hold of anything." And Esteban remembered the excessive care Sofía showed in exercising at all times and places—even at the edge of the tomb—the functions of the good wife, with a submission, a solicitude, an opportuneness ill-suited to her independent and disordered cast of mind. It almost pleased him that she hadn't entered as a virgin into that cheap wedding which for him was the most unpardonable capitulation to the customs of a detestable society. But thinking this evoked for him that Sovereign Presence that continued to weigh upon their house from so far away. Seeing the inertia of Carlos, who remained baffled and lachrymose, he rose and said, "I will bring her back, one way or another." "You'll get nothing from it but a scandal," Dexter said. "She has a right to leave." "Go," Carlos said. "Make one last effort . . ." Esteban slammed the door and departed for the port. When he had reached the wharf where the *Arrow* was moored, the scent of recently caught fish made him gasp: he walked between hillocks of porgies, combers, sardines, whose scales glimmered by the light of firebrands. A fisherman sank his hand beneath a jute cloth and pulled out a handful of squid, throwing it on the scale. Sofía was standing high on the prow, still in her mourning clothes, dark, elongated, as though impervious to the stench of scaling, ink, and blood rising up toward her. There was in her something of the impassibility of a mythological heroine contemplating the offerings brought to her dwelling by some People of the Sea. Esteban's fury was placated upon seeing that immobile woman who watched his approach impassively, her eyes disarming in their fixity. All at once, he was afraid. He felt helpless at the thought of hearing certain words which, in her mouth, would acquire a deafening eloquence. He didn't dare climb up to face her. He contemplated her in silence. "Come," he finally said. She turned toward the port, leaning on the gunwale. On the other shore glimmered the lights of neighborhoods never visited; further on lay the confusion of lights of the vast baroque candelabra that was the city with its red, green, orange windows, bright amid colonnades. To the left was the

dark passage that led to the shadowy sea: the sea of exploits, of
hazardous navigations, of wars and skirmishes that had forever
stained red this Middle Sea with its thousand islands. She was
traveling toward him who had made her aware of herself and
who, in a letter brought her by that weepy child standing there
below, had spoken to her of his solitude in the midst of triumph. Where he was, there was still much to be done; a man of
his stature could not but commence great enterprises; projects
in which all found their true measure. "Come back," the voice
repeated below. "You think you're stronger than you are." To
go home would be to doubt that force; to consummate a second
defeat. She had known too well nights of frozen flesh, of the
pretense of an absent jubilation. "Come back." In the distance,
the old mansion, which clung to her body like a shell; beyond it
lay the dawn, the lights of immensity, past the proclamations
and bells. Here, the parish church, the alms box, the tedious
transit of a life lived in the eversame; there, an epic world inhabited by Titans. "Come back," the voice repeated. Sofía
stepped away from the gunwale, hiding in the shadows on deck.
The other went on talking, his voice louder now. But the din of
the fishermen muffled that monologue ascending in gusts of
words that spoke of a house built by all that would now be left
in ruins. "As if a comity of brothers and sister sufficed to make
a home," she thought. Esteban, leaning against the ship's keel,
continued unheeded. That enormous wooden body, smelling of
salt, of algae, of marine vegetation, was soft to him, almost
feminine, with the smooth submissiveness of its damp flanks.
Above, a figurehead on the prow, with the face of a woman,
white plaster eyes surrounded by a thick blue line, stood in for
the other woman who would depart at dawn, immensely
wealthy, returned to desiring, freed of the black that diminished her beauty and enchained her bliss. She would leave the
family circle to profane its secrets, telling them to another who
perhaps was already waiting for her. Esteban felt miserable,
denuded—denuded with a nudity too familiar to her to perceive
it as such—when he saw that his will to violence had diminished into feeble imploration. Above, Sofía waited for the sails
to stretch and the wind to swell them. She would advance

toward that foreign seed, the furrow within her open; would be cup and ark, like the woman in Genesis who, joining hands with a man, was forced to leave her parents' home . . . People were staring at him, listening in, laughing at what they thought they understood. He walked away from the ship and found Captain Dexter between the baskets of fish: "Is everything settled?" the seaman asked. "Completely settled," Esteban responded. "Safe travels to all."

XLI.

Now he was standing on a corner near the docks, wavering, ashamed at his defeat. He muttered phrases that he should have said before but that had failed to emerge from his lips. The ship was there close, surrounded by bollards, its silhouette malevolent in the night. The mermaid on the prow, her split tail clinging to the rails, emerged from the shadows when a lamp threw light across her face, which resembled a death mask, as if she'd been taken from a tomb. Esteban felt the welling of unuttered words that arranged themselves in speeches, reprimands, warnings, reproaches, violence that skirted insult and insults that ended with abominable words beyond which language is exhausted. If she stood firm through this verbal ambush—and her character suggested she could—Esteban would be left as defenseless as before. Now ill intentions reared their head. It was eight. Captain Dexter's ship would depart at five in the morning. There were nine hours left; enough time to do something, perhaps. Esteban overlaid his spite, his resentment, with a theory of duty: it was his *obligation* to prevent Sofía from traveling to Cayenne. He must not shy before the most radical measures to prevent her moral suicide. Going there, for her, would be tantamount to a descent into Hell. Sofía had reached the age of majority. But Carlos had legal recourse to prevent her going. He could allege mental alienation. There had already been a case, months before, of a young widow with an illustrious name who had tried to run off to Spain with one of those actors who sang popular ditties in the Coliseum. The authorities were always well-disposed when the honor of honorable families was at stake. Colonial society took a dim view of fits of passion and was always ready to call the bailiff when a lovers' quarrel or rebellious woman disturbed the peace. The Church, too, got involved in such matters, standing in the way of the guilty . . . Esteban, prepared to go to any length to bring this intolerable situation to a close, arrived home panting, sweaty from so much running, and burst in on a group of men of gruff, policemanlike appearance who had invaded the house and were busy opening wardrobes, inspecting cabinets and desks, walking back and forth between the stables and the upper floors. The detectives passed papers among themselves, making certain the texts Sofía had kept under her bed were indeed *The Declaration of the Rights of Man and the Citizen* and the French Constitution. Rosaura approached Esteban and told him, "Go. Señor Carlos escaped over the roof." He crept back into the alcove soundlessly, with measured steps, and returned outside. But two men were already posted at the front door. "You're under arrest," they told him, ordering him to a corner of the salon where they could keep an eye on him.

They had him wait for several hours before they interrogated him. They walked past him repeatedly, as though unaware of his presence, looking to see if there was anything hidden behind the paintings or under the rug. They sank iron bars into the soft soil of the flower beds to feel for boxes buried under the couch grass. Another took books from the shelves, staring at the covers and weighing them in his hand, before throwing to the floor the odd volume of Voltaire, Rousseau, Bouffon, and generally anything printed in French prose—verse being less worthy of preoccupation. Finally, at three in the morning, the search was deemed concluded. There was more than enough evidence that their home was a den of conniving Freemasons, spreaders of Revolutionary writings, enemies of the Crown who intended to seed anarchy and godlessness in the Overseas Domains. "Where is the lady?" they asked, being told by their informers she was one of the wickedest conspirators of all. Rosaura and Remigio replied that they had no idea. That she had left early. That she was rarely away from home, but that today, she was gone despite the late hour. Someone recommended they register the ships in the port to avert an attempt at escape. "You'll be wasting your time," Esteban said, speaking up from the corner. "My cousin Sofía has never had anything to do with all this. You've been badly informed. I put those papers in her bedroom this very afternoon without her knowing." "Does your cousin often sleep away from home?" "That is a private matter of hers." The investigators exchanged an ironic glance: "Husband dead in his hole, wife out on the stroll," one said, laughing boorishly. And again they spoke of going to the ships. They instructed Esteban to write a few lines on paper. Their request struck him as strange, but the detainee scribbled down a few verses of Saint John of the Cross he had read in recent days, and which remained very present in his mind: *Oh thou, given over to this loving love candescent . . .* "The handwriting is the same," one of the interrogators said, brandishing a copy of *The Social Contract* in the margins of which Esteban had noted down antimonarchical ideas years before. Attention turned entirely to him: "We know you returned recently from a long voyage." "That is true." "Where were you then?" "In Madrid." "That's a lie," one of them said. "In his cousin's desk, we found two letters postmarked in Paris, which expressed, by the by, great enthusiasm for revolution." "That could be," Esteban said. "But afterward I went to Madrid." "Let me talk to him," one said, opening a path. "I'm no Galician nor Catalan." And he began to ask him about streets, fairgrounds, churches, and other sites in the capital, none of which Esteban was acquainted with. "You've never been in Madrid in your life," he concluded. "Possibly," Esteban said. And then another stepped forward. "How did you make your living in France, seeing that the war with Spain meant your family couldn't send you money?" "I was paid for translations." "Translations of what?" "Various things." The clock struck four. Again there was talk of Sofía's inexplicable absence and the need to go to the ships . . . "This is idiocy," Esteban shouted, striking his fist against the table: "You think you can search a house in Havana and put an end to the idea of Liberty in the world! It's too late! No one can stop

what's already begun!" The veins swelled in his neck as he repeated what he'd already said, adding this time Fraternity and
Equality, forcing the scribe's pen to race across the page. "Very
interesting. Very interesting. Now we're starting to understand
each other," said the interrogators. And their Chief cornered
Esteban, pelting him with questions: "Are you a Mason?" "I
am." "Do you deny Jesus Christ and the sanctity of our Religion?" "My God is the God of the philosophes." "Do you
share, and have you publicized, the ideas of the French Revolution?" "In full awareness of what that means." "Where were
the proclamations we found here printed?" "I am not a snitch."
"Who translated them into Spanish?" "I did." "And these
American carmagnoles?" "Those, too." "When?" At that an
officer who had remained upstairs, obstinately determined to
find more, appeared before them. "The lady of the house had
quite a collection of fans," he said, opening one, which featured
a scene of the storming of the Bastille. "And that's not all. She
has all sorts of jewel boxes and pincushions in the most suspect
colors." Esteban, seeing those tricolor trifles, thought tenderly
of the adolescent enthusiasms that had driven a person as strong
as Sofía to horde these trinkets that for years could be found
anywhere in the world. "One way or another, we'll have to get
our hands on the bitch," said the Chief. And again, they talked
of going to the docks. Esteban then admitted everything, at
length and in detail: he returned to the arrival of Victor Hugues
in Havana, to draw out and add color to the tale that the scribe
was passing to paper in flowery calligraphy. He spoke of his
personal contacts with Brissot and Dalbarade; his propaganda
work in the Basque Country; his friendship with those blackguards, the traitors Marchena and Martínez de Ballesteros; the
departure for Guadeloupe; the Loeuillets' printing press; the
Cayenne episode, where he had worked hand in hand with
Billaud-Varenne, the sworn enemy of the French Kingdom . . .
"Note it down, scribe, note it down," the Chief said, stunned at
these revelations. "Billaud . . . is that spelled with a *y*?" the
scribe asked. "With a double *l*," Esteban replied, launching into
a digression on French Grammar. "The repetition of the *l* is due
to . . ." "We're not going to get lost in debates about a

consonant or two," the Chief shouted, crossing his arms with frustration. "How did you return to Havana?" "For a Freemason, all doors are open," Esteban replied, spinning a yarn that made him out to be a notorious conspirator. But his words turned farcical as the hands of the clock approached five. His interrogators couldn't grasp why, instead of defending himself, he had volunteered a confession so replete with misdeeds that it could mean his death by garrote vil. Now, with nothing left to tell, Esteban repeated vulgar jokes about the Bourbon Messalina, the Prince of Peace cuckolding His Majesty, the rockets that would soon explode in King Charles' backside. "He's a fanatic," the officers said. "A fanatic or a madman. America is teeming with Robespierres like this one. If we're not careful, they'll start cutting off heads left and right around here." Esteban talked on, indicting himself for actions he'd never been part of, boasting of personally distributing revolutionary documents in Venezuela and New Granada. "Write it down, scribe, write it down. There'd better not be a single drop left in your inkpot," the Chief said, his questions at their end . . . It was five-thirty. Esteban asked to be accompanied to the roof, where he had left an object of some personal significance in an antique vase on the balustrade. Eager to discover further evidence, several investigators followed him. But the vase contained nothing apart from a nest of wasps that tried to sting them. Ignoring their insults, Esteban looked toward the port: the *Arrow* had departed, the place where the ship had moored was empty. He returned to the salon. "May the good scribe note down the following," he said. "I declare before God, my Lord and master, that everything I have said is a lie. You will find not a single proof that I did any of the things I said, other than that I was in Paris. No witnesses or documents will demonstrate otherwise. I said all that I said to aid a fugitive. I did this because it mattered to me to do it." "You'll save yourself from the garotte, perhaps," the Chief said. "But nothing will keep you out of prison in Ceuta. We've sent people to the quarries in Africa for less." "As if I cared now about my fate!" Esteban responded. He stopped before the *Explosion in a Cathedral*, where splinters of wood, thrown up by a conflagration, were suspended in a nightmare atmosphere: "Even the stones I will go to break now were already present in this picture." Grabbing a stool, he hurled it against the painting, tearing the canvas, which fell loudly to the floor. "Take me away, damn it," Esteban said, so exhausted, so needful of sleep, that all he cared for was to rest, even if he had to do so in prison.

CHAPTER SIX

XLII.

The waves came from the South, calm and balanced, weaving and unweaving the lace of their slender foam, which resembled, over the waters, the nervure of dark marble. The greens of the coast were behind her, and they were sailing now in waters of a blue so deep they seemed made of molten, though hibernal and vitreous, matter, shaken by distant throbbing. Not a creature appeared in that entire sea that gathered over buried mountains and abysses like the First Sea of Creation, before murex and argonaut. Only the Caribbean, despite the swarming creatures within it, ever had that look of an abandoned ocean. As though called to mysterious duties, the fishes fled the surface, medusas sank, the gulfweed disappeared, and what remained before the eye was conveyed in infinite values: the eternally postponed boundary of the horizon; space, and beyond space, stars present in a sky the mere mention of which evoked the entire crushing majesty that word had once held for those who first uttered it—the earliest of all words, perhaps, save those that had only begun to describe pain, fear, or hunger. Here, on a barren sea, the sky took on an enormous weight, with those constellations seen since time immemorial, which human beings persisted in dividing and consecrating across the centuries, projecting myths on the unattainable, bending the locations of the stars to the contours of the figures that peopled the imaginations of those perpetual inventors of fables. There was a sort of infantile intrepidness in their crowding of the firmament with Bears, Dogs, Bulls, and Lions, thought Sofía, leaning on the railings of the *Arrow*, facing the night. That was a way of simplifying eternity; of sealing it in precious books of prints like the volume of star charts in the family library, the plates of which seemed to detail terrible combats between centaurs and scorpions, eagles and dragons. In naming the constellations, man returned to the primordial language of his ancestors so faithfully that when the people of Christ appeared, there was no place in a sky overrun with pagans. The stars had been given to Andromeda and Perseus, to Hercules and Cassiopeia. Their entitlements, passed down through bloodlines, were not transferable to the simple fishermen of the Lake Tiberias, nor did the fishermen have need of stars to guide their boats to the place where Someone, soon to spill his blood, would forge a religion heedless of stars . . . When the Pleiades paled and the light emerged, mottled helmets advanced toward the ship by the thousand, casting shadows over long red festoons that etched phantasmal medieval warriors beneath the water, the silhouettes of Lombard princes clad in chainmail—like chainmail were the filaments dragged across their path, running shoulder to hip, neck to knee, ear to thigh on the bodies, pierced by splinters of light, of those creatures Captain Dexter referred to as *men-of-war*. The submerged army opened to let the vessel through, closing rank afterward in their silent march from the unknown, which would proceed for days until their heads burst beneath the sun and their festoons were eaten away to nothing . . . At midmorning, they entered a new country: that of the Gorgons, open like the wings of birds, at the edge of a water whitened by their migration. And then little thimbles appeared in dun swarms, opening or closing in hungry contractions, followed by a band of vagrant snails, clinging to a raft of hardened foam . . . A sudden storm transfigured the sea, turning it glaucous and opaque. A saline scent rose from the water percussed by rain, drops of which the timbers of the deck absorbed. The sails' canvas sounded of slate beneath hail, and every fiber of the taut lines creaked. The thunder traveled from West to East, pounded like a patient drummer over the ship, then marched off with the clouds, leaving the midafternoon sea bathed in a strange, auroral light, as calm and iridescent as a lake on a plateau. The prow of the *Arrow* ploughed the still surface, leaving foamy arabesques in its wake that divulged, for a few hours, the passage of a ship. At twilight, the wakes grew pale over depths replete with night, tracing paths and crossings over the newly deserted water—a map so deserted that those who looked upon it felt they were the lone navigators of their era. And until the morning, they remained in the Land of Phosphorescences, with light coming from below, open in fans, in trickles of brilliance, drawing shapes like anchors and grape bunches, anemones or heads of hair—or fistfuls of coins, or altar candles, or remote windows of stained glass, submerged cathedrals, pierced by the cold rays of abysmal suns . . . Years before, Sofía had leaned on the same gunwale, sucking in the breeze from the nose of the same prow—but this time, she was undisturbed by adolescent heartache. Her decision had matured her, and she was traveling toward something that could not be other than she imagined it. For two days, all she had left behind weighed heavily on her spirit. On the third day, she woke with an exultant sense of liberty. Her bonds were broken. She had escaped the quotidian and was penetrating a timeless present. Soon the great task, awaited for years, would begin in its chosen dimension. Again, she knew the joy of standing at the departure point, on the threshold of herself, just as once before she had climbed into this ship and begun a new stage of her existence. She rediscovered the acrid odors of pitch, jerk meat, flour, and bran, familiar from days whose evocation was enough to abolish time past. She closed her eyes at Captain Dexter's table, acquainted again with the flavor of smoked oysters, English ciders, rhubarb pie, and medlars from Pensacola, reliving the sensations of her first voyage at sea. But their path was different this time. Despite Toussaint Louverture's enthusiasm for establishing trade relationships with the United States, the North American merchants doubted the negro leader's solvency, and left that risky market to the gunrunners, whose merchandise was always paid for in cash, even when the people had no flour to knead their daily bread. Departing the coast of Jamaica, they sailed for several days in the emptiest part of the Sea of Antilles, destined for the Port of La Guaira, where the last of Guadeloupe's corsairs appeared on occasional evenings, in sailboats christened the *Napoléon*, the *Campo Formio*, or the *Conquest of Egypt*. One morning they feared a skirmish, seeing a small ship rowing toward the *Arrow* with undue haste. But the disquiet of a moment soon turned to delight when they discovered it was the fabled *Friar's Sloop*, sent by a French missionary of loose morals who had for many years dedicated himself to trafficking contraband in the Caribbean territories. Otherwise, they saw nothing but schooners filled with salt meat plying the route from Havana to New Barcelona and back, leaving behind when they passed the ineradicable stench of smoked flesh. To still her impatience to arrive, Sofía tried to lose herself in the English books in Dexter's library next to the Acacia, the Pillars, and the Tabernacle of his Masonic apron, which he stored in the same vitrine as before. But the climate of *The Nights* was no less foreign to her mood than was the oppressive atmosphere of *The Castle of Otranto*. After a few pages, she closed them, not very sure what she had read, prey to every reflection that entered into her pores, imploring her senses rather than her imagination . . . One morning she saw a violaceous bulge on the imprecise verdures misting the horizon: "The Saddle of Caracas," Dexter said. "We are some thirty miles from the mainland." And the crew bustled in anticipation of a port of call: those not working just then freshened up, cut their hair, cleaned their nails, washed their hands. On deck appeared razors, combs, soap, clothes to be darned, perfumes to be splashed on faces. One man mended a torn shirt; another patched a ragged shoe; further off, a third gazed at his toasted face in a woman's mirror. All were moved by a disquiet due not simply to their pleasure at seeing a happy journey through to its end: beyond that, at the foot of the hill stretching upward against the chain of mountains bordering the shore, was Woman—unknown, almost abstract, a Woman without a face, but already implicit in the Port itself. The sails of the ship swelled over the tumescent masts, signaling to her figure, towering solicitously over the roofs in the cove, that the men were on their way. Seeing those sails from the coast, the women in the houses in the port came and went, drawing up buckets from the wells, shaving, perfuming, splashing, and dressing chaotically. No words were needed for this dialogue across a sea already dotted with fishing boats. The *Arrow* veered parallel to the mountains that descended from the clouds to the water, sloping so drastically that not a single cultivated field was visible on their flanks. Now and then, a sheer face sank to reveal a hidden beach hugged in shadows between rock walls with vegetation so dark and dense that it seemed to harbor unused tatters of night within it. A wondrous damp scent from the still groggy Continent emerged from these bays where the sea's progeny was cast ashore, thrown up by a final lashing of the waves. Then the mountains receded, but whatever lay behind them remained invisible, and there remained a narrow fringe of soil with roads and dwellings amid forests of hairy coconut palms, grape vines, and almond trees. They rounded a promontory that seemed carved from a block of quartz, and the port of La Guaira appeared, open to the ocean like a colossal amphitheater with terraced roofs for stands . . . Sofía would have liked to see Caracas, but the road was long and arduous, and the *Arrow*'s stay would be brief. She let the seamen on leave disembark—they knew where they were expected—then traveled to shore in a canoe with Dexter, who had routine formalities to take care of. "Don't think you're obliged to look after me," she told him, seeing he shared in his men's eagerness. And she took off walking toward steep streets that skirted a dry stream, marveling at the dainty plazas with statues between houses with wooden railings and shuttered doors that reminded her of Santiago de Cuba. Sitting on a stone bench, she watched the pack animals advance up the mountain paths in the shadows of mesquites, which thinned on the misty summits, past a castle crowned by merlons, like many that defended the Spanish ports in the New World—so similar each to each that they seemed the work of a single architect. A peddler from the Canary Islands, dead set on selling her satin ribbons, told her, "Until recently, some Masons come over from Madrid were imprisoned there. For something called the Saint Blaise Day Conspiracy. They tried to take the Revolution to Spain. And Miss, you won't believe this, they kept on with their conniving right there in that very prison . . ." It was happening, then, and she hadn't been wrong to sense that the Event was imminent. Now she was even more impatient to reach her journey's end, and was afraid of arriving late, when the man destined to perform the Great Work would already have set forth, parting the verdure of the jungles like the Hebrews parting the waters of the Red Sea. What Esteban had told her so many times was true: in light of the Thermidorean reaction, Victor—with his American Carmagnoles, with his Constitution translated into Spanish—was bringing to the American mainland the lights that had gone dead in the Old World. To grasp this, she needed only look at the Wind Rose: from Guadeloupe, the squall had blown to the Guianas and from there to Venezuela, whence it would pass to the far edge of the Continent, to the baroque palaces of the Kingdom of Peru. It was there that the Jesuits had first raised their voices—Sofía was acquainted with the writings of Vizcardo y Guzmán—demanding an independence for this world conceivable only in revolutionary terms. Everything became clear: Victor's presence in Cayenne was the beginning of something that would take shape in armies of horsemen crossing plains, ships sailing storied rivers, high mountains being scaled. An epic was being born, and what had failed in dying Europe would be carried to completion in these lands. Those who may defame her in her family home would learn that her longings were not, like those imposed on normal women, to be measured by dress patterns and diapers. Scandal, they might say, unaware that the scandal would be far vaster than they thought. This time she would play *Attack*, shooting generals, bishops, magistrates, and viceroys.

The *Arrow* set sail two days later, navigating along Margarita Island to pass between the British protectorates of Granada and Tobago and on toward Barbados. And at the end of a tranquil journey, Sofía found herself in Bridgetown, discovering a different world from the one she had known previously in the Caribbean. The atmosphere she breathed in that Dutch city was different, the architecture different from the Spanish, the ships different, framed with broad timbers from Scarborough, Saint George's, or Port of Spain. Newly minted coins with gracious names, the Pineapple Penny and the Neptune Penny, circulated there. She felt transported to a city on the Old Continent when she noticed a Masonic Street and a Synagogue Street. She lodged in a clean inn owned by a sweating mulatta that Captain Dexter had recommended. At the end of a goodbye lunch in which the overjoyed Sofía tried everything, not disdaining the bottles of porter, the Madeira, and the French wines on offer, the two of them took a drive through the outskirts. For hours, they rolled over the roads of the tame Antilles with their softly undulating fields—here nothing was big, nothing prodigious, nothing menacing—that were cultivated right down to the seashore. The sugarcane here resembled green wheat, the grass was neat, even the palms no longer had the air of trees from the tropics. There were silent mansions, hidden in the brush, their columns like those of Greek temples soaring up to pediments obscured by moss or ivy; their windows opened onto the pomp of salons, the varnish on the portraits hung there gleaming under bright lights; there were homes covered with tiles, so small that when a child peeked out the window, he hid the large family gathered for dinner in a room where a chess table would have been an obstacle; there were ruins shaggy with creepers, where ghosts met to moan on windy nights—the whole island, the coachman said, was overrun with them; and there were, beside the sea, nearly mingled with the beaches, eternally deserted cemeteries in the shadows of cypresses, their gray stone tombs—modest when one thought of the ornamented mausoleums of Spanish cemeteries—telling of a Eudolphus and Elvira died in a shipwreck who must have been heroes of a romantic idyll. Sofía remembered *La nouvelle Héloise*. The Captain thought rather of *The Nights*. And though it was far, and the horses were tired, and the need to find replacement mounts meant they would not return till late into the night, Sofía, whose entreaties struck the North American as overdone, had the coachman take them to the rocky bastion of St. John. Behind its church was a gravestone, and surprisingly, the epitaph referred to the death on that island of a person whose name was heavy with the crushing presence of centuries: HERE LYETH YE BODY / OF FERDINANDO PALEOLOGUS / DESCENDED FROM YE IMPERIAL LYNE / OF YE LAST CHRISTIAN EMPERORS OF GREECE / CHURCHWARDEN OF THIS PARISH / 1655-1656 . . . Somewhat maudlin after draining a bottle of wine on the way, Caleb Dexter respectfully removed his hat. As the lights of dusk reddened the waves breaking in dense foam against the craggy monoliths of Bathsheba, Sofía laid bougainvillea cut from the presbytery garden on his grave. During his first visit to her home in Havana, Victor Hugues had talked a long time of the tomb of this unsung grandson of a man fallen during Byzantium's last stand, who preferred dying to profanation by those Ottomans who overthrew the Ecumenical Patriarch. Now they had found it, in the designated place. Above the gray stone marked with the cross of Constantine, a hand followed now the itinerary of another hand from the faraway past, which also had sought the hollow letters with its fingertips . . . To interrupt this unforeseen ceremony, which had gone on too long, Caleb Dexter observed: "And to think the last legitimate proprietor of the Hagia Sophia ended his days on this island. . . ." "It's getting late," the coachman said. "Yes, let's go back," Sofía replied. It was strange to her to hear her name in the captain's idiotic reflection, a coincidence too extraordinary not to be taken as a revelation, a message, a premonition. A prodigious destiny awaited her. Since the day the bearer of that Will pounded the door knockers of her house, a future had been gestated for her. Those words hadn't appeared by chance. A mysterious power shaped them in the mouth of an unwitting oracle. *Sophia.*

XLIII.

Told the rocks of Grand Connétable would be visible a little after dawn, Sofía emerged at daybreak on the deck of the *Batavian Republic*—an old Dutch merchant ship with a new name that traveled all year between the Continent, the Jungle, and deforested Barbados bringing mahogany for the carpenters of Bridgetown and timbers to adorn the houses of Oistins, famous for their gallery porches in the Norman style. For weeks, she had waited in her hotel in the port for the hour of departure, tormented by impatience, weary of walking through the tiny city's streets, hearing with dismay of the peace treaty between France and the United States; had word reached her sooner, she could have arrived more quickly, traveling from Havana in one

of the North American vessels that had already renewed trade
with Cayenne. But she forgot all of this facing the crags and is-
lets that presaged their arrival, graced in the morning by whorls
of gannets and gulls. Now they sighted the islands of La Mère
and Les Deux Filles, which Esteban had once described to her.
In the meantime, the vegetation and settlements on the coast
grew brighter and more bustling. Everything seemed sumptuous, fascinating, extraordinary to Sofía just then. The world's
greens seemed to welcome her in a single landscape. The military authorities were perplexed, when they came onboard, that
a single woman from a city as alluring as Havana would wish
to stay in Cayenne. But when Sofía spoke the name Victor Hugues, it sufficed to turn suspicion to deference. Night had fallen
when she made her way into the city with sleepy streets, arriving at Hauguard's inn, where she wisely concealed her relation
to Esteban, sensing his departure for Paramaribo was an escape
of some kind . . . The next morning, she sent a message announcing her arrival to the former Agent of the Directory, now
the Agent of the Consulate. In early evening, she was handed a
brief message scribbled on official paper: *Welcome. Tomorrow
I will come by coach to see you. V.* Sofía was waiting for an
impatient summons, and instead there came to her those cold
words that plunged her into a night of confusion. A dog barked
in a nearby pen, enraged by a passing drunk who walked down
the street scratching his mange, shouting frightening prophecies
about the scattering of the just, the punishment of regicides,
and the appearance of all before the Lord's Throne in a Final
Judgment that would be held—but why?—in a valley in Nova
Scotia. When the voice faded in the distance and the guard dog
returned to sleep, invisible insects set to work in every wall in
the building, drilling, scratching, eating away at the wood. A
tree shed seeds as heavy as lead over several upturned troughs.
In front of the inn, two Indians argued, their voices like something from a chronicle of adventures. Nothing was soothing for
a person consumed in lucubrating conjectures. For that reason,
when the coach arrived the next morning, Sofía stepped inside
it exhausted, with swollen eyes. She had believed they would
drive her with her trunks and suitcases to the House of

Government, but instead the horses stopped at a quay where a
canoe with slender railings waited, with cushions, awnings,
and canvas wind screen. She was informed she would be taken
to a hacienda a few hours away by boat. None of this was what
she had envisioned, but she found flattering the courtesies extended her by the crew. The boat was captained by a young official named De Sainte-Affrique, who described the progress
that had occurred in the colony since the arrival of Victor Hugues. Agriculture was flourishing, the shops were full, and
peace and prosperity were in the air. The deportees had mostly
returned to France, but there remained behind in Iracubo, as a
testament to their sufferings, a vast cemetery with the grave-
stones of famed revolutionaries . . . In midafternoon, the canoe
turned onto a river bordered by marshland; on its waters the
leaves of a kind of water lily floated, with purple flowers that
rose over the surface of the water. Soon they reached the dock
of a large, Alsatian-style house standing on a hill amid lemon
and orange trees. Attended by a swarm of solicitous negresses,
Sofía installed herself in an apartment on the second floor, its
walls adorned with delicate old prints that evoked events from
the ancien régime: the Siege of Namur, the Coronation of the
Bust of Voltaire, and the ill-fated Calas family, interspersed
with pleasant seascapes of Toulon, Rochefort, the Island of
Aix, and Saint-Malo. While the chirping maids placed her
things in the wardrobes, Sofía peeked out the windows that
opened onto the fields: a garden with abundant rosebushes
soon gave way to orchards and sugarcane fields bounded by a
dour wall of sylvatic vegetation. Mahogany trees with tall silvery trunks cast shadows on the paths edged with Balsam of
Peru, nutmeg, and yellow pepper trees.

Hours of anxious waiting passed, then at last, a rowboat edged
in toward the dock. In the evening shadows already darkening
the avenue, in a dazzle of gold braid and finery, a suit of military cut emerged, crowned and, as it were, exalted by an extravagant plumed hat. Sofía, stepping forth from the vestibule,
failed to notice in her haste a drove of black pigs just past the
door rooting gleefully in the flower beds, digging up tulips and

rolling with jubilant grunts in the recently watered soil. Seeing the door open, the animals stormed the house, their muddy bodies grazing Sofía's skirts, and she waved her arms and shouted for them to stop. Victor ran home in a rage: "How dare they let them out! This is beyond the pale!" Making his way to the salon, he smacked his saber against the pigs filing through the rooms and climbing the stairs, and his servants and several negroes came from the rear of the house to help. Eventually, the beasts were sent away howling, dragged by their ears, lifted up, kicked out. The doors to the kitchen and the other rooms were closed. "Have you seen yourself?" Victor asked Sofía when the porcine commotion had died down, pointing at her mud-stained dress. "Go change while I have them clean up in here." Seeing herself in her bedroom mirror, Sofía felt so miserable she began to cry, seeing the sad reality of this Great Encounter she had dreamed of during her crossing. The dress she'd had made for the occasion fell from her body, covered in mud, ripped, stinking like a pigsty. She threw her shoes into a dark corner and tore off her leggings in a rage. Her body reeked of the drove, of mud and filth. She sent for pails of water, however grotesque it felt to bathe just then. There was something ridiculous in having to splash around in that basin, knowing they must hear her below. Throwing on whatever lay close to hand, she limped down to the salon, unconcerned with her appearance, despairing like an actress who has botched her grand entrance. Victor had her sit beside him and squeezed her hands. He had traded his splendid suit for the loose garb of the prosperous yeoman: white breeches, broad-collared shirt buttoned low, and a calico jacket: "You must forgive me," he said. "But this is how I always walk around here. A man needs a rest from all those ribbons and rosettes." He asked about Esteban. He knew he had departed Paramaribo and assumed he had made it to Havana. And as if wishing her to know how he'd lived since the end of his administration in Guadeloupe, he told the story of his rebellion against Desfourneaux and Pelardy, which left him a defenseless prisoner, forced onto a departing ship. In Paris, his vigorous arguments had pulverized Pelardy's accusations. Consul Bonaparte then selected him to take over the government of Cayenne . . . He spoke at length, with the glibness of earlier days, as if to unburden himself of a surfeit of words too long suppressed. On entering into certain details of his recent life, he frequently repeated the phrase: "This I am telling you alone, because there is no one else I can trust." He listed off the servitudes of Power, the many disappointments he had suffered, the impossibility of having friends when one intended to command. "They will tell you I used a hard hand, hard indeed, in Guadeloupe and even in Rochefort. I had no choice. Revolution is to be *waged*, not debated." While he talked relentlessly, only pausing to solicit a *no?*, a *don't you think?*, a *don't you see?*, a *didn't you know?*, a *didn't they tell you?*, or a *do people know elsewhere?*, Sofía noticed a number of obvious changes in his person. He was quite fatter, though his sturdy frame bore it well, and it appeared like muscle. His expression had hardened, despite the new fleshiness filling out his face. His somewhat earthy complexion still harbored the determination and health of other times . . . The doors to the dining room opened: two maids had placed candelabras on the table with a cold dinner, served in silver dishes so heavy they could only have come from the fleet of a Viceroy of Mexico or Peru. "Good evening," Victor said to the servants. And in a more intimate tone: "Now, tell me about yourself." But Sofía could think of no worthy tale, no interesting event from her own life, sadly impoverished compared with his, which was full of clamor and furies and feats with men who had given their name to the era. She had a merchant brother, a pusillanimous cousin whose counsels struck her as so hollow against the grandeur now before her that she preferred to conceal them from a sense of pity. Even her marriage was a lamentable affair. She had been a housewife, but hadn't found God in her pots and pans like the nuns of Avila. She had waited. That was all. The years had passed, indifferent, unmoving, from an Epiphany without kings to a Christmas without meaning in the impossibility of picturing the Great Architect lying in a manger. "Well, then?" Victor said, encouraging her to speak. "Well, then?" But a strange, indomitable stubbornness kept her silent. She forced a smile; she stared into the flame of the candles; she scratched the tablecloth with a fingernail; she stretched her hand out to a glass, but left it sitting there. "Well, then?" And Victor went toward her. The lights had changed; there were shadows where she felt him grasp her, squeeze her, with a hunger that rekindled her adolescent yearnings . . . They returned later to the table, sweaty, hair in disarray, stumbling, laughing at themselves. They spoke the language of before: the one they had spoken in the port of Santiago, contemptuous of the mariners' prying, when they fled the heat and the stench of the bay for a narrow cabin between decks, between boards that smelled of fresh varnish, like the ones in this very house. The breeze, rising on the coast, filled the room with a breath of sea. Water ran audibly in a nearby weir. The house was a ship, thrashed by waves of trees that crashed against the window.

XLIV.

Sofía marveled at the discovery of her own sensuality. Her arms, her shoulders, her breasts, her flanks, her knee pits began all at once to speak. Lofty in submission, her body became aware of itself, in thrall to impulsive generosities and cravings that neglected to seek the mind's consent. Her waist was delighted to be taken prisoner; her skin shook and tautened at the mere hint of an approach. Her hair, let down on nights of joy, was given to him who clutched it in handfuls. A supreme munificence emanated from this gift of the entire person; from the *What can I give that I haven't yet given?* that in hours of embraces and metamorphoses delivered a human being to the extreme poverty of feeling *nothing* in the sumptuous presence of the other; so affluent in tenderness, in energy, in delight, that the mind seemed to melt in fear of failing to reciprocate these splendid gifts. In returning to its roots, the lovers' language returned to the naked word, to the muttering of a word anterior to all poetry—a word of thanksgiving before the blazing sun, the river overflowing the tilled soil, the seed gathered in the furrow, the ear of grain swollen like the weaver's spindle. The word was borne of tactility, elemental and pure, as was the activity that gave rise to it. With physical rhythms coupled to the rhythms of creation, a sudden rain, a blossoming of plants in the night, a change in the course of the breeze, the blossoming of desire at dawn or twilight sufficed for the bodies to seem to find themselves in a new clime, their embraces resurrecting the radiance of their first meeting. Everything was the same, the forms were present, and yet everything was eternally different. That night—the night beginning just then, still indecisive and laggard—would have its own pomp and exultation, and was not the night of yesterday, and would not be the night of tomorrow. Outside time, abbreviating or lengthening the hours, the two bodies lying there perceived as permanent, everlasting, a *now* externally manifested in what their senses, committed to the boundless task of understanding themselves, perceived in a remote and contingent manner; in the weight of a storm, the persistent cawing of a bird, the jungle scent borne on the morning breeze. It may have been just a gust, a whisper, a breath; but the presence of grace, between the ascent to ecstasy and the descent into slumber—joyous repose— seemed to last the entire night. The lovers recalled an embrace of hours, growing closer to the rhythm of a tempest, but they realized, when they awoke, that they couldn't have heard the wind blow more than a few minutes, when the tree limbs trembled next to their window . . . In the light of the everyday, Sofía felt a supreme self-possession. She wished everyone could share in that blessing of love, contentment, sovereign calm. Flesh sated, her thoughts turned to people, books, things, with a quiet mind and an admiration of the *intelligence* of physical love. She had heard it said that certain oriental sects considered the gratification of the flesh a necessary step in the ascent to Transcendence, and she believed this on noticing in herself an unsuspected capacity for Understanding. After years of voluntary confinement among walls and objects she'd grown all too used to, her spirit was pouring outward, finding a motive for reflection in everything. Rereading classical texts that before now had spoken to her in the voice of fables, she discovered the original essence of myth. Casting aside writings steeped in the rhetoric of the age and the lachrymose novels so beloved of her contemporaries, she turned to texts that had fixed in enduring traces or symbols the profound ways Man and Woman lived together in a universe fraught with hostile predicaments. She made her own the arcana of Lance and Chalice that had been obscure cyphers for her before then. She felt that her being had become *useful*; that her life, at last, had a path and meaning. It was true that she let the days, the weeks, flow past, cleaving blissfully to the present without thinking of tomorrow. But she did not, for that reason, cease to dream of great endeavors she would one day commit with the man she had bound herself to. So powerful an essence—she thought to herself—could not endure long without a majestic undertaking to commit to. But his actions depended greatly on events in Europe. Things were happening so quickly that by the time the newspapers reached Cayenne, the information in them was well out of date, and occasionally even contrary to what was happening at the moment of reading. Bonaparte seemed little concerned with revolution in America; more immediate problems occupied his attention. For that reason, Victor Hugues spent the better part of his time on administrative tasks, ordering irrigation works built, opening up roads, signing commercial treaties with Suriname, and developing agriculture in the colonies. People called his government paternal and sensible. The old planters were satisfied. The winds of prosperity were blowing. Since the abandonment of the ten-day week and the return to the Gregorian calendar, the Leader went to the city on Mondays, returning home on Thursday or Friday. Sofía devoted several hours to the household each morning: giving orders, putting the carpenters to work, beautifying the gardens, having the Swiss businessman, Sieger, bring her tulip bulbs from Paramaribo. The rest of the time she spent in the library, where there was no lack of excellent works amid the annoying abundance of Treatises on Fortifications, the Art of Navigation, Physics, and Astronomy. Several months passed this way, and when he returned each week, Victor never brought news that might disturb the peaceful, flourishing life of the colony.

One day in September, Sofía went to Cayenne to make a few purchases, in a rare break from her discreet country retirement. Something strange was happening there. The shrill bells had been ringing in the chapel of the sisters of Saint-Paul-de-Chartres since dawn. Other bells chimed in, unknown, not yet hung, concealed, perhaps in attics and warehouses, pounded with hammers, with firebrands, with horseshoes across the entire city. Nuns and friars disembarked from a newly arrived ship. A motley army of the Faithful seemed to descend on the population, in habits, Flemish veils, black cloths, Carmelite, gray, filing down the middle of the streets, hailed by the passers-by, bearing forgotten adornments of rosaries, pious medals, scapularies, and missals. Passing priests blessed the curious who peered from their windows. Others tried to shout down the uproar with the verses of canticles, but their voices combined only poorly. Baffled at this spectacle, Sofía walked to the House of Government, where she was supposed to meet Victor Hugues. But his office was empty apart from Sieger, who was sunken in an armchair, with a bottle of tafia nearby. He greeted her with cheerful motions, buttoning his tailcoat: "A beautiful parade of Capuchins, indeed, my lady! A priest for every parish! Nuns for all the hospitals! The time of processions is upon us once more! We have a concordat! Paris and Rome have embraced! The French are Catholic again. A great thanksgiving Mass will be said in the Chapel of the Grey Sisters. All the lords of government will be present there in their finest uniforms, bowing their heads to the ecclesiastical Latin: *Preces nostrae, quaesumus, Domine, propitiatus admitte.* And to think that more than a million men died to destroy what's been restored today . . . !" Sofía returned outside. Travelers were still stepping down from the Ship of Friars, opening big red and green umbrellas while black porters piled bundles and valises on their heads. In front of Hauguard's inn, several priests were sorting their luggage and drying their sweat with large checked kerchiefs. Then something strange happened: two Sulpicians, the last to disembark, were greeted by their colleagues with furious shouts. "Jurants!" the others shouted to them. "Judases! Judases!" And they pelted them with pineapple skins pulled from the gutter, with stones and other rubbish. "Out of here! Go sleep in the jungle! Jurants! Jurants!" The Sulpicians, not intimidated in the least, tried to enter the inn, throwing punches and kicking, and a menacing storm of black habits engulfed them. The priests who had sworn loyalty to the Revolutionary Constitution were hurled against a wall, and gave confused responses to the charges leveled against them by the *insubmissives*, the *true priests* the Concordat had suddenly ennobled as Soldiers of Christ, resisters of persecution, men whose clandestine worship made them fitting descendants of the Deacons of the Catacombs. Guards came and dispersed the churchmen with blows from the butts of their muskets. Order appeared reestablished when a young priest emerged from a nearby butcher's and threw a bucket of fresh blood from a recently slaughtered cow at the two Sulpicians, who stood now haloed by a large spot of red that had broken on their bodies and struck the tavern's white wall, leaving behind fetid clots and splatters. Again the bells tolled deafeningly. After hearing the thanksgiving Mass, the regally dressed Victor Hugues left the Chapel of the Grey Sisters with his officials . . . "Have you heard?" he asked Sofía when he found her in the House of Government. "It's all quite grotesque," she responded, telling him what had happened with the Sulpicians. "I will have them sent back to the ships; here people will make life impossible for them." "It seems to me it's your duty to protect them," Sofía said, "you must think more highly of them than of the others." Victor shrugged his shoulders: "Even in France, no one cares anymore for the jurant priests." "You smell of incense," she told him . . . They returned to the estate, not talking much during the journey. When they arrived, they found *the Billauds*—as they called them— installed there since midday, along with their faithful hound, Patience. For several days, they had known they would turn up there uninvited: "Once more, Philemon and Baucis are here to abuse your hospitality," the former Terrible One said, using an image he had been fond of ever since marrying his servant Brigitte. Sofía had noticed in recent months that Baucis's influence over Philemon was increasingly evident. Craftily, the negress coddled Billaud-Varenne, with loud, affected declarations of her admiration of his every word and deed. Detested by the neighbors of his country house near the coast of Orvilliers, the ex-President of the National Convention had for a time been subject to sudden fits of melancholy. In the evenings, anonymous figures in the colony sent him newspapers from Paris; now and then, he saw his name mentioned there with revulsion. When this happened, he would fall into despair, shouting that he was the victim of dreadful calumnies, that no one understood the historic role he had played, that no one sympathized with his sufferings. Brigitte, seeing him desperate and weepy, had a phrase at the ready, which comforted him like none other: "How, my lord, after conquering so many dangers, do you let the writings of these vermin upset you?" The smile would then return to Billaud's face. And that smile would allow Brigitte to make and remake the farmhouse in Orvilliers, to act haughty with the staff and authoritarian with the farmhands, to keep a keen and critical eye on everything, Mistress of a domain whose bounties she oversaw astutely . . . Sofía found her in the kitchen giving orders for supper to be prepared, just as if she were in her home. Her dress was as fine as any to be found in Cayenne, and she wore gold bangles and filigreed bracelets. "Oh, dear," the negress exclaimed, dropping the wooden spoon she had just brought to her lips to taste a sauce. "You're just radiant! How could he keep from falling in love with you more every single day?" Sofía responded with an evasive grimace. She didn't care for Brigitte's familiarities, which cast her as little more than the consort of a powerful man. "What will we be having?" she asked, employing, despite her esteem for *la petite Billaud*, the tone of a mistress addressing her cook. In the salon, Billaud-Varenne had just heard of the Concordat and that morning's events in Cayenne: "That's just what we needed," he shouted, pounding his fists in time with his words on the table of English marquetry. "We're sinking into shit."

XLV.

Like the long and dreadful summer thunder foretelling the cyclones that blacken the sky and level cities, the brutal news rang out across the Caribbean, provoking shouts and blazing torches: the Law of 30 Floréal, Year X had passed, reestablishing

slavery in France's American colonies and abrogating the Decree of 16 Pluviôse, Year II. The landowners, estate holders,
and planters were quickly informed—indeed, the news had
outrun the messenger ships—and rejoiced at the auspicious
news, particularly when hearing the colonial system that had
prevailed before 1789 would be restored, putting an end, once
and for all, to the humanitarian caviling of the goddamned
Revolution. In Guadeloupe, in Dominique, in Marie-Galante,
this intelligence was received with salvoes and fireworks, while
thousands of *ci-devant* free citizens were taken back to their
former barracks beneath a rain of lashes from whips and blows
from sticks. The White Lords from before hastened to the fields
with packs of dogs to find their erstwhile serfs, who were then
handed over to foremen with chains around their necks. Fearing they would be swept up in the savage hunt, many freedmen
from the monarchist era, owners of shops and small holdings,
gathered their things with the intent of fleeing to Paris. But they
were soon thwarted by a new Decree, that of 5 Messidor, that
forbade all persons of color from entering France. There were
too many negroes in the mother country already, Bonaparte
had decided, and he feared that their great numbers would taint
the blood of Europe with *hues that had spread through Spain
since the invasion of the Moors* ... Victor Hugues heard all this
one morning, in the office of the House of Government, in the
company of Sieger. "The exodus will be tremendous," the businessman told him. "We won't give them time," Victor replied.
And he immediately sent urgent notice to the militia chiefs and
owners of nearby estates that a secret reunion would take place
the next day. They must act first, making the Law of Floréal
public only after slavery had been brought back de facto ...
Tracing a plan in the midst of exultation on the verge of spilling
over into excess, they waited for night to come. The gates to the
city were closed; troops occupied the region's farmhouses; and
with the thundering of a cannon fired at eight o' clock in the
evening, the negroes freed by the Decree of 16 Pluviôse were
surrounded by masters and soldiers who arrested them and
drove them to a small plain situated on the banks of the
Mahury. By midnight, several hundred negroes were packed

together there, trembling, frightened, unable to imagine the reason behind that forced concentration. Whoever tried to pull away from the sweating, frightened mass was shoved, kicked, battered with the stock of a musket. Finally, Victor Hugues appeared. Standing on a barrel, surrounded by torches so all could see, he slowly unrolled the paper where the text of the Law was transcribed, and read it in a solemn, deliberate tone. Translated quickly into dialect by those who had heard it most clearly, the words passed from mouth to mouth until they reached the edges of the field. Those present were then told that all who refused to return to a state of servitude would be punished with utmost severity. The next day, their former owners would come and take possession of them, returning them to their respective farmhouses and estates. All who went unclaimed would be sold at public auction. A vast, convulsive, exasperated cry—a collective cry like the strident ululation of threatened beasts—emerged from the blacks, while the Authorities retired amid a deafening battery of drums . . . But already, shadows were sinking into the night, seeking shelter in the jungle and the underbrush. Those who escaped the first raid ran to the mountain, stole boats and canoes to take to the rivers, half-naked, without weapons, to return to the life of their ancestors in places where the whites couldn't reach them. Passing through the more distant farms, they told their families what was happening; then ten or twenty more would abandon their labors, deserting the fields of indigo and clove, joining the groups of Maroons. A hundred, two hundred men, followed by their wives, who carried the children, took to the jungles and forests in search of a place to found their settlements. As they fled, they threw barbasco seeds into the rivers and creeks to poison the fish, which would rot and infect the water with their miasmas. Beyond this river, beyond that mountain draped in waterfalls, a new Africa would be born; they would return to their forgotten languages, to their rites of circumcision, to the adoration of the First Gods, far older than the recent Gods of Christianity. The brushland closed over men who turned their backs to the course of History, reverting to the time when Fertile Venus, with her grand udders and swollen belly, had ruled over all

Creation, adored in deep caverns where the Hand would vaguely trace the first figuration of the duties of the hunt and the feasts devoted to the stars . . . In Cayenne, in Sinnamary, in Kourou, on the banks of the Oyapec and the Maroni, the people lived in horror. Insubordinate or rebellious negroes were whipped to death, quartered, decapitated, subjected to unspeakable tortures. Many were hanged, with hooks through their ribs, in the public slaughtering grounds. All over, men were hunted, to the joy of good marksmen, while huts and scrublands were incinerated. Where countless crosses marked the graves of men deceased in exile, the sinister shape of the gallows rose up against sunsets made redder by the flames spreading from the houses to the fields—gallows or, worse, leafy trees with groups of cadavers hanging from them like clusters of fruit, vultures lighting on their shoulders. Again, Cayenne had fulfilled its destiny as a land of abominations.

Sofía was horrified when she heard on a Friday of the barbarities committed the Tuesday before. Everything she had hoped to find in this progressive redoubt of new ideas had turned to an intolerable deception. She had dreamed of being useful among men daring, just, and firm, who had abandoned gods because they no longer needed Covenants to reign over a world that was their birthright; she had thought she would labor alongside titans, unafraid of the spilled blood great undertakings demanded, but instead, she was witnessing the gradual restoration of all that seemed abolished—of all that the finest books of the time had taught her *must* be abolished. The Trammeling of the Enchained had followed the Restoration of the Temples. And those who had the power to stop it, on a continent where what was lost across the Ocean could yet be saved, refused to pursue this destiny in consonance with their principles. The man who had trounced England in Guadeloupe, the Commander who had not flagged before the danger of war between France and the United States, had been subdued by the abject decree of 30 Floréal. He had shown a tenacious, almost superhuman zeal for abolishing slavery eight years before; now he was no less zealous in reestablishing it. She was astonished a man could do

Good or Evil with the same consummate coldness of spirit. He could be Ormuz or Ahriman; reign over the shadows or reign over the light. Depending on the tenor of the times, he could turn suddenly into his own contrary . . . "You rather act as if I were the author of the decree," Victor said, hearing a string of harsh reproaches coming from her for the first time, and remembering with slight remorse how much of his eminence he owed to the noble law of Pluviôse 16. "It seems you have all turned your back on the Revolution," Sofía said. "The same one you once boasted you would bring to American soil." "Perhaps I was still influenced by the ideas of Brissot, who wished to export the Revolution to the ends of the earth. But if he, with the means at his disposal, could not even convince the Spanish, I shall not presume to take the Revolution to Lima or New Granada. He who has the right to speak for all of us already said it." And he quoted, as he pointed to a portrait of Bonaparte that now presided over his office: "*The novel of the Revolution is over; it is time for us to make it History and to consider only that which is real and possible in the application of its principles.*" "It's pitiful, beginning that history with the restoration of slavery," Sofía said. "I'm sorry. But I'm a politician. And if bringing slavery back is a political necessity, I must bow to that necessity." Their argument continued; the ideas, irritations, impatience remained the same, as did Sofía's contempt for the shameful moral capitulation; and on Sunday, Sieger appeared, interrupting their bitter dispute: "It's unbelievable, but it's true," he shouted from the door in the uncouth tone of a biscuit vendor. He removed the thick winter overcoat he wore on rainy days, its fur sweaty, its leather collar moth-eaten—and it was raining, sheets of rain were now coming down from the Highlands, perhaps from the unknown distances where the Great Rivers originated and rocky monoliths man had never reached lay hidden behind the clouds. "It's unbelievable, but it's true," he repeated, closing an enormous green umbrella that seemed made of leaves of lettuce. "Billaud-Varenne is buying slaves. He owns Cato, Tranche-Montagne, Hippolyte, Nicolas, Joseph, Lindoro, and more than three women for house servants. We're making progress, yes sir, we're making progress. Obviously, once you've been President of the Convention, you can find a justification for anything." And he began, imitating the haughty accent of the person in question: "*I've more than realized that the negro, born with an abundance of vices, lacks both reason and sentiment, and can understand no law save that imposed upon him by force.*" The Swiss laughed, thinking he'd done a clever impression of the voice of the erstwhile Terrible One. "I'd prefer we not talk of that," said Victor, ill at ease, requesting the building plans Sieger had brought in a pigskin portfolio . . . And soon, perhaps in accordance with these same plans, the Great Works began. Hundreds of negroes brought to the hacienda, harried by the lash, began to plow, dig, till, hollow, refill lands stolen from the forest in grand extensions. Over the ever-expanding borders of humus fell the trunks of centenary trees, their crowns inhabited by birds, monkeys, insects, and reptiles, like the symbolic trees of Alchemy. The giants exhaled smoke, burned by fires that scorched their entrails but left their bark intact; the oxen trod from the busy fields to the recently constructed sawmill, dragging the long corpses of wood still full of sap, of juice, of shoots emerging from their wounds; rolling huge roots that clutched the earth, dismembered beneath the axe; dragging limbs that yearned to cling to something. Flames, pounding, working songs, curses enveloped the trains of haulers, whose horses, weary from the effort of felling a quebracho, emerged from the tumult sweaty, shimmering with foam, their collars hanging aside, nostrils sinking as they trotted across the furrows. When there was wood enough, scaffolds were built: walkways and terraces rose above timbers smoothed by machetes, announcing obscure structures, the nature of which remained unclear. One morning a strange circular gallery appeared, still skeletal, suggesting an eventual rotunda. There was a tower destined to an indeterminate task, left undefined by the contour of its crisscrossing beams. The negroes stood among the water lilies in the river, filling in the pylons for a dock; they howled with pain when stung by a sting ray, when a torpedo shocked one and sent him flying through the air, or when the maws of a gray moray latched down on their genitals. Embankments, stairways, aqueducts, arcades emerged from a

nearby bed of coarse-cut stone, drawing blood from the hands
of the drudges, who were constantly returning their chisels to
the forges because they chipped after ten strokes of the hammer.
Braces and girders, brackets and joists, hoisting and nailing
multiplied on all sides. They lived amid dust, plaster, sawdust,
sand, and filings, and yet Sofía never managed to understand
what Victor had in mind with those multiple projects constantly
modified without warning, ignoring the plans traced out on the
rolls of paper that poked from every pocket of his suit. "I will
tame this country's nature," he said. "I will raise statues and
colonnades, trace out roads, stock ponds with trout as far as
the eye can see." It disgusted Sofía that Victor was wasting such
energy in the vain attempt to create, in this jungle that extended
without interruption to the sources of the Amazon—to the
shores of the Pacific, perhaps—an absurd re-creation of a royal
park, its statues and rotundas to be absorbed by the undergrowth as soon as attention lagged, a prop, a temptation for the
immeasurable vegetation perpetually upsetting the stones,
cracking the walls, fracturing the mausoleums, annihilating
whatever had been built. This Man aimed to impose his negligible presence over an extension of green that stretched from
Ocean to Ocean, like the image of eternity. "Ten rows of radishes would make me happier," Sofía said, to the Builder's an-
noyance. "It's as if I'm listening to the Village Soothsayer," he
responded, burying his face in his plans.

XLVI.

The work went on amid mud and dust. Weary of the sound of
pickaxes and saws, pulleys and mallets echoing to the edge of
the estate, Sofía shut herself up behind newly hung curtains,
shawls spread across windows, and screens serving as walls and
partitions, in a home overrun with sentinels and guards since
the bands of negroes with their confusion of dialects had arrived. Sitting atop a stepladder, lying on a carpet, reclining over
the cool mahogany of a table, she had read all the literature
there was in the library, casting aside treatises that said nothing

to her with their algebras, geometries, and illustrations with overwrought scientific allusions, with characters shouldering the A or a B in a theorem describing the trajectory of stars or portentous electrical phenomena. For this reason, she was thankful to the young officer De Sainte-Affrique, who sent frequent orders for interesting novelties to the Parisian bookseller Buisson on her behalf. But nothing of note had come from France for her recently, apart from a few travel chronicles—about Kamchatka, the Philippines, the fjords, or Mecca—and tales of discoveries and shipwrecks whose popularity must have owed to people's weariness with all those polemical, moralizing, admonitory texts, apologetics, memoirs, panegyrics, and true histories of this or that which had been published in the past few years. Unimpressed by the squat columns, the arched bridges over artificial streams, the little temples in the Ledoux style now covering the surrounding fields—which failed to impose themselves on a rebellious vegetation hostile to any architectural styles obedient to proportions and canons—Sofía traveled in her imagination aboard the ships of Captain Cook and Le Perouse when not following Lord Macartney on his wanderings through the deserts of Tartary. The rainy season, good for shutting oneself up with books, soon passed, and the season of sumptuous twilights returned, open to the mystery of the remote jungle. But now the twilights weighed too heavy. Their final glimmers marked the end of days without progress or purpose. De Sainte-Affrique said that beyond these grueling lands stood marvelous mountains covered in water. But there were no roads to reach them, she knew, and the undergrowth was full of hostile peoples restored to their original state who fired arrows with steady hands. Transported by a longing for action, for a full and useful life, she had ended up in reclusion among the trees in the most vain and benighted spot on the planet. All she heard talk of was business. The Age had arrived triumphally, raucously, cruelly, to an America that just yesterday still resembled the old image of a place filled with viceroys and captains-general; the Age was dragging it forward, and those who had carried the Age on their shoulders, disposing it, imposing it, not shying before the Shedding of Blood that had been required to affirm it, hid their noses in account books to forget all that had occurred. The game proceeded among lost rosettes and stained dignities, played by men who seemed oblivious to their mighty, tempestuous past. This past—some said—had been a time of excesses. But those excesses would vouchsafe the memory of men whose names were now too splendid for their frail figures. When it was said that Holland or England might attack the colony any day, Sofía wished for it to happen soon, so something, however cruel, would shake from their slumber those gorged on trade, harvests, and profits. Elsewhere, life went on, altered, aggrieved, or exalted, bringing changes to the styles, tastes, customs, and rhythms of existence. But here they lived again as they had a half century before. It was as though nothing had happened in the world. Even the fabric and cut of the best-off settlers' clothing was the same as it had been a hundred years ago. Sofía dwelled in an awful, stationary time—one she already knew well—with today equal to yesterday, equal to tomorrow.

Summer passed, creaking, laggard, its heat stretching into an autumn similar to any other autumn when, one Tuesday, in response to the bell struck to call the negroes to work, the silence was so prolonged that the sentinels walked to the barracks with their whips held high. They found the cabins deserted. The guard and bloodhounds lay poisoned in the foam of their last vomit. The cows, freed from the stables, stumbled like drunken beasts and collapsed. The horses, their bellies swollen, had their heads sunk in the mangers, blood draining from their nostrils. Soon people arrived from the neighboring farms: all over, the story was the same. Traveling down tunnels dug in the night, taking nails from walls so stealthily no one heard a single noise, distracting the guards with fires started here and there, the slaves had run off into the jungle. Sofía remembered the pounding of many drums in distant trees the night before. No one paid attention, thinking it might be Indians in the midst of some barbaric ritual. A messenger was dispatched immediately to Victor Hugues in Cayenne. In their fear of the growing shadows that swelled with affliction and menace, the colonizers fretted that a week should pass without the Agent returning; but one afternoon, a prodigious squadron of canoes, small ships, and light barges appeared on the river, loaded with troops, provisions, and arms. Victor Hugues went home to speak with those who could inform him of recent events, taking notes and consulting the few maps at his disposal. Surrounded by officers, in consultation with his General Staff, he gave orders and assigned punishments to be carried out ruthlessly and with haste against the Maroon settlements multiplying unacceptably in the jungle. From the doorway, Sofía saw a man who had recovered his vanished authority, clear in his explanations, sure in his proposals, once more the General of other days. But this General had placed his will, his rejuvenated drive, at the service of a contemptible and cruel enterprise. A look of scorn on her face, she left for the gardens, where the soldiers, who had refused to lodge in cabins that smelled too much of negroes, had set up their camp and bivouacs in the open air. Those soldiers were different from the meek, bovine men Sofía had encountered before. Sunburnt, arrogant, with scars across their faces, talking loud, stripping her naked with their eyes, they were a new sort of warrior whose insolence pleased her with its virile and brash self-possession. Alarmed at seeing her among that rabble, the young officer De Sainte-Affrique came to escort her, and he told her these men, survivors of the plague of Jaffa, had been sent to the colony after the Egypt campaign. Some were still in a bad state, but they were believed well-suited to the climate of Guiana, which was killing off the Alsatians in ever-increasing numbers. She looked now with astonishment at those soldiers come from a land of legend, who had slept in tombs carved with hieroglyphics, who had fornicated with Coptic and Maronite prostitutes, who boasted of knowing the Koran and of having laughed at the jackal- and bird-faced gods whose statues still stood in temples with colossal columns. They exuded a breath of Adventure from across the Mediterranean, from Abu Qir, from Mount Tabor, from Saint-Jean d'Acre. Sofía never tired of asking one or another what he had seen and thought on that strange quest that had taken a French army to the foot of the Pyramids. She wanted to sit with them

in their canteens, to share the soup ladled generously into their
bowls, to throw dice over the drum where the bones struck like
hail, to drink the strong waters each of them carried in flasks
marked with Arabic letters. "You shouldn't be here, ma'am,"
said De Sainte-Affrique, who for some time had acted the part
of Sofía's jealous, protective *cicisbeo*. "These men are loud and
vulgar." But the woman remained drawn to their stories and
heroic deeds, secretly flattered—and she was not ashamed of
it—to find herself craved, denuded, pawed at in the minds of
those men rescued from a biblical affliction, embellishing their
exploits to make her remember their boorish faces. "So you're
a serving girl now?" Victor asked, when he saw her return. "At
least a serving girl has something to do," she said. "Something
to do! Something to do! It's always the same rubbish with you.
As if a man has any choice but to do what he must . . . !" Victor
came, went, gave orders, set objectives, issued instructions concerning the positions of the troops along the river. Sofía almost
came to admire his energy, until she remembered he was orga-
nizing a vast slaughter of negroes beneath his roof. She hid
away in her room to conceal a sudden access of fury, and soon,
she had broken down in tears. Outside, the soldiers of the Egypt
Campaign burned tiny pyramids of dried coconut to ward off
the mosquitoes. And after a night too full of noise, of laughter,
of uproar, the morning reveilles were heard. The squadron of
canoes, barges, and light ships moved upriver, dodging whirlpools and torrents.

Six weeks passed. And one night, beneath the loud, heavy rains
that had been falling for three straight days, a number of boats
returned. Men stepped forth from them, exhausted, feverish,
arms in braces, muddy, stinking, wrapped in silt-colored bandages. Many were carried on litters, having been shot by Indian
arrows or skinned by the negroes' machetes. Victor came last,
dragging his feet and trembling, his arms around the shoulders
of two officers. He fell into an armchair, and kept asking for
more blankets to bundle up in. But his shivering continued despite the layers of woolen coverings and vicuna ponchos. Sofía
saw that his eyes were red and oozing pus. He struggled to

swallow, as if his throat were swollen. "This is no war," he said finally, in a hoarse tone. "You can fight against men. You can't fight against trees." De Sainte-Affrique, whose stubble cast a blue shadow over his ailing, greenish skin, spoke with Sofía alone after draining a bottle of wine in anxious swigs: "A calamity. The settlements were empty. But every hour, we ran into an ambush. They'd kill a few of our men, and then they'd disappear. If we returned to the river, they shot at us from the banks. We had to walk through swamps with water up to our chest. And still worse, the Egyptian Disease." And he told how the soldiers who'd overcome the Jaffa Plague had brought back with them a mysterious ailment that had now infected half of France and was laying waste to the population. It was like a malignant fever, with pain in the joints that rose through the body, exploding through the eyes. Pupils grew inflamed; eyelids swelled with humors. Tomorrow more sick men would arrive, more wounded; more men bested by the trees of the jungle and by prehistoric weapons, darts of monkey bone, cane arrows, peasant's machetes and picks, that had faced down modern artillery: "Shoot a cannon into the forest and nothing happens. You just find yourself buried in an avalanche of rotten leaves." In discussion with the cripples and men hacked with blades, it was agreed that Victor would be taken to Cayenne the next day, along with those casualties in need of better care. Overjoyed at the expedition's failure, Sofía gathered her clothes. The young officer De Sainte-Affrique helped her pack them in woven baskets that smelled of vetiver. She had the feeling she would never return to that house again.

XLVII.

The Egyptian Disease arrived in Cayenne. The Hospital of Saint-Paul-de-Chartres had no space for all the sick men. Prayers were said to Saint Roch, Saint Prudentius, Saint Charles Borromeo, always recollected in times of plague. The populace cursed the soldiers who had brought the new pestilence back with them from God knows what underground passage filled with mummies, God knows what land of sphinxes and embalmers. Death made his appearance in the city. He leaped from house to house, and his brusque, disconcerting entrance incited a dreadful proliferation of rumors and myths. It was said that the soldiers of the Egypt Campaign were furious at being called away from France, and meant to exterminate the population of the colony and take it over for themselves; they had compounded salves and liquids, macerated oils with filth, to mark the houses where they intended to spread the contamination. Every stain became an object of suspicion. If a man laid his hand against the wall, leaving behind traces of his sweat, passersby would pelt him with stones. A group of people keeping watch over a body beat an Indian to death with sticks one morning because his fingers were too black and sticky. Despite doctors' protestations that its consequences were in no way comparable to the plague, all persisted in referring to it as *the scourge of Jaffa*. In expectation of infection—which would come to all, sooner or later—fear became the handmaiden of lust. Bedrooms were opened to all comers, bodies sought out on the verge of death throes, balls and feasts thrown amid pestilence. A man spent in a night what he had amassed through years of peculation. The self-declared Jacobin who had hoarded golden louis threw them down on the baize. Hauguard poured out his wines for the ladies in the colony, who waited for their lovers in the rooms of his inn. While funeral bells tolled throughout the town, orchestras played at dances and feasts until dawn, and the benches and tables set out in the street had to be pushed aside for the wagons, carts, and carriages that came past at daybreak carrying coffins oozing tar from the cracks between their boards. Two Grey Sisters, possessed by the Demon, prostituted themselves on the quay, while a former Acadian, his devotion to Isaiah and Jeremiah only growing as the flesh withered from his bones, shouted in squares and on corners that the hour of God's Judgment had finally come.

Victor Hugues, eyes sealed with thick bandages soaked in an infusion of mallow, walked blindly through his chambers in the House of Government, grabbing chair backs, stumbling, groaning, feeling around for objects. To Sofía he looked weak, fretful, frightened by the noise of the city. Despite a high fever, he refused to stay in bed, afraid of sinking forever into a denser, second darkness that would settle over the darkness of his bandages. He touched, fingered, weighed everything his hands discovered, simply to feel himself live. The Egyptian Disease had invaded his organism with a tenacity comparable only to the strength of the man struggling against it. "No better and no worse," the doctor said every morning after examining the effects of some new medicine. A cordon of troops watched over the House of Government and impeded access to unknown persons. The servants, the guards, the functionaries had been sent away. Sofía was alone with the Leader—who complained of stiffness in his bones, of pains, of an unbearable burning in his eyes—in a building of walls pasted with edicts and proclamations, watching funeral processions pass through the windows. (*Ils ne mouraient pas tous, mais tous étaient frappés*, she recited to herself, remembering how Victor Hugues had read her La Fontaine at her home in Havana to improve her French pronunciation.) She knew that her presence there was useless temerity. But she endured the danger to convince herself of the substance of a loyalty of which in fact she was far from certain. She grew as she observed Victor's fear. At week's end, she felt sure the disease wouldn't affect her. She was proud, with a sense of fate, imagining Death, lord of the land, had bestowed his favor upon her. In town, prayers were now said to Saint Sebastian, adding one intercessor more to the trilogy of Roch, Prudentius, and Charles. *Dies Irae, Dies Illae.* A medieval sentiment of guilt had wormed into the minds of those who remembered all too clearly their indifference to the horrors of Iracubo, Conanama, and Sinnamary—and because he reminded them too much of it, people chased the old Acadian through the streets with clubs. Victor, sinking deeper into his armchair, searching for objects in the night of his blindness, spoke already the language of the dying: "I wish to be buried," he said, "in my suit as Commissar of the Convention." And he felt around for it in the armoire, pulled it out, showed it to Sofía, then threw the jacket over his shoulders and placed the plumed hat over his bandaged forehead: "I always believed myself the master of my fate. And yet it took fewer than ten years for the others, for *those* who make and unmake us, even if we do not know them, to take me from one stage and place me on another, and so on and so forth until I no longer know on which I am meant to stand. I have worn so many suits, I no longer know which one fits me." He struggled to expand his thorax and accommodate the flood of syllables: "But there is one that I prefer to all others: and it is this one. It was the gift of the only man I ever put above me. When they overthrew him, I ceased to understand myself. Since then, I have ceased to try and understand anything. I am like those automata that play chess, walk, blow the fife, or tap the drum when you wind them up. There is only one role I have not yet played: the blind man. And now I am doing so." Then he added softly, counting on his fingers: "Baker, merchant, Mason, anti-Mason, Jacobin, war hero, rebel, prisoner, absolved by those who killed my champion, Agent of the Directory, Agent of the Consulate . . ." And his enumeration passed the sum of his fingers, fading into an unintelligible murmur. Despite the illness and the bandages, Victor, a half-dressed Commissar of the Convention, regained something of the youth, strength, hardness of the man who had one night pounded the door knockers at a certain house in Havana. The man present became the man past—the rapacious, cynical governor, unsettled now by the breath of the grave, eschewed useless riches, the vanity of honors, sounding like a priest uttering a Mass for the dead. "It was a beautiful suit," Sofía said, smoothing out the feathers on the hat. "It's out of date," Victor responded. "Now it's only fit to be my winding cloth." One day, the doctor tried a new remedy that had worked wonders in Paris for those afflicted with the Egyptian Disease, applying slivers of fresh, bloody beef to his eyes. "You look like a parricide in an antique tragedy," Sofía said, thinking of Oedipus, when she saw him return from the chamber where they had treated him. For her, the time of pity was over.

Victor woke without fever and asked for a glass of cordial. His dressings of bloody meat fell away, leaving his face bright and clear. The world's beauty astonished, even dazzled him. He walked, ran, leaped through halls of the House of Government, joyous after his descent into the night of blindness. He stared at trees, creepers, the cats, objects, as though they were newly created and, like Adam, he was tasked with naming them. The Egyptian Disease was claiming its last victims, who were taken quickly to the graveyard without handbells or funerals, their risible burials brought quickly to an end. Lavish Masses were uttered in praise of Saints Roch, Prudentius, Charles, and Sebastian, though the impious, forgetting their prayers and entreaties of before, began hinting that a strand of garlic around the neck had done more than any appeals to the saints. Guns saluted two ships entering the port. "You were sublime," Victor said to Sofía, ordering preparations made to return to his country home. But she looked askance at him, picked up a book of travels to Arabia she had read the previous days, and showed him a paragraph from a Koranic text: "The plague was devastating Devardan, a city of Judea. Many of the inhabitants took flight. God told them: Die! And they died. Years later, they were revived at the pleading of Ezekiel. *But all preserved on their faces the mark of death.*" She paused. "I'm weary of living among the dead. It matters little that the plague has left the city. You've all worn the mark of death on your face for some time now." And she turned her back to him—painting a dark silhouette over the luminous rectangle of a window—and talked a long time of her desire to leave. "You want to go home?" Victor asked, astonished. "I shall never return to a house I left in search of one better." "Where is this better house you're looking for now?" "I don't know. Wherever men live differently. Here everything stinks of corpses. I want to return to the world of the living; of those who believe in something. I can hope for nothing from men who hope for nothing." The House of Government was overrun with servants, guards, functionaries, who were busy again ordering, cleaning, attending. The light coming through windows with their curtains pulled aside raised a tiny cosmos of dust, which floated up through slanting columns of light. "Your army will return to the jungle," she said. "It can be no other way. Your post demands it. Your authority requires it. But I refuse to stand by and watch this spectacle." "The Revolution has changed more than one of us," Victor said. "That, perhaps, is the great achievement of the Revolution: to change more than one of us," Sofía said, beginning to take down her clothes. "Now I know what I must reject and what I can accept." Another ship—the third that morning—was greeted by cannonfire. "It's almost as if I'd sent for them," Sofía said. Victor struck the wall with his fist: "Take your shit and go wherever you damned well please!" he shouted. "Thank you," Sofía said. "I prefer seeing you like this." Grasping her arms, he hurled her through the room, bruising her, throttling her, finally dragging her off into bed. He fell on her, clutched her without encountering resistance: she offered him a body cold, inert, and distant, acquiescent to anything so long as it would soon end. He looked at her as he had before when they were done, eyes so close to hers that the image of them blurred. She turned away. "Yes, you'd better go," Victor said, rolling over, still panting, unfulfilled, invaded by enormous sorrow. "Don't forget my safe conduct," Sofía said placidly, sliding away from the bed and approaching the writing table where the forms lay. "Wait, there's no ink in the inkpot." She smoothed out her leggings, arranged her disarrayed garments, found a fresh bottle, dipped the pen inside, and handed it to Victor. And she went on gathering her things while she waited for his hand, quivering with rage, to finish filling in the papers. "This is it, then?" he asked. "There's nothing left between us?" "There is. A few images," Sofía responded. The Leader walked to the door wearing a dreadful, conciliatory smile. "You won't come?" When she didn't speak, he concluded: "Bon voyage." And his steps echoed down the staircase. A carriage was waiting below to take him to the harbor . . . Sofía was left alone with her dresses strewn about. Past the garments of satin and lace lay the uniform of the Commissar of the Convention that Victor was so anxious to show her in his blindness. The tailcoat with the tricolor sash lay on the back of a tattered armchair. With the breeches below it, the hat resting against absent thighs, it recalled one of those relics—an empty suit without skeleton or flesh—that families kept in frames to recollect a departed ancestor who had been notable in his day. All over Europe, the attire of illustrious figures from the past was displayed in this way. Now that the world was so changed, that memoirists' *once upon a time* had been replaced by the phrases *before* and *after the Revolution*, museums had become very popular. That night, to ease her return to solitude, Sofía gave herself to the young officer De Sainte-Affrique, who had loved her with Wertherian modesty since her arrival to the colony. Once more she took possession of her body, closing with a willful act the long cycle of self-estrangement. New arms would embrace her before she boarded the ship that would set sail for Bordeaux the following Wednesday.

CHAPTER SEVEN

XLVIII.

And, behold, there came a great wind from the wilderness, and smote the four corners of the house, and it fell upon the young men, and they are dead; and I only am escaped alone to tell thee.

JOB 1:19

The sound of heels tapping in concert to the rhythm of guitars emerged from the upper floor as the traveler stretched a frozen hand from the folds of the Scottish blankets that enveloped him and lifted the heavy knocker in the shape of a sea god adorning the immense door that opened onto the Calle Fuencarral. Despite his knocks, like shots from a blunderbuss, the noise upstairs only intensified, with the ragged voice of a succentor trying in vain to catch the tune of the "Polo del Contrabandista." His hand, burned by the frozen bronze, went on pounding. With feet shod in heavy boots, he kicked the wood of the door, knocking morsels of wax onto the icy stone of the threshold. Finally, there was a creak, and a servant opened, bathing the traveler's face in the light of an oil lamp. Seeing that the stranger resembled a portrait hung upstairs, the servant, startled, let through the fearsome killjoy, outdoing himself in apologies and explanations. He hadn't expected the gentleman so early; had he known he was coming, he would have waited for him at the Casa de Correos. It just happened that, being the First of the Year, his Saint's Day—his name was Manuel— some acquaintances, good but boisterous people, had surprised him in bed after he had prayed to God for the gentleman to be safe in his travels; they wouldn't listen to reason, and had started chanting and drinking *whatever they had with them*, but that was all, *whatever they had with them* and nothing more. The gentleman should wait a few moments while he ran the rabble down the service stairs. Pushing the servant aside, the traveler climbed the broad staircase to the salon. The furnishings had been moved, the carpets piled against the wall, and in the middle of the floor, Madrid streetwalkers and young men of dubious aspect were frolicking brazenly, dumping full glasses of wine down their gullets and spitting left and right. To judge from the number of bottles and flasks lying empty in the corners, the party must have been at its high point. One woman was hawking warm chestnuts, though there were none to be seen; a *maja* on top of a divan was shouting the "Song of the Marabou"; farther on, another woman groped a man, while a chorus of drunkards pressed in around a blind man whose throat was frayed from shouting *soleares*. A thunderous *Get out!* disbanded the merrymakers, who grabbed what bottles they could on their way at the sight of a distinguished-looking head emerging from the bundle of Scottish blankets. Stringing together inept laments, the servant hurried to return the furniture to its place, stretching carpets and taking away bottles with utmost diligence. He threw logs on the fire, which had been burning since morning, and brought brooms, feather dusters, and cloths to wipe away all traces of merriment from the armchairs, the floors, and the lid of the grand piano, which was stained with a liquid that smelled like brandy. "Good people," the servant moaned, "People who would never dream of stealing a thing. But unpolished. Here it's not like in other countries, where everyone learns respect . . ." Shedding the last of his blankets, the traveler walked over to the fire and asked for a bottle of wine. When the servant handed it to him, he saw it was the same sort the revelers had been drinking before. But he pretended not to notice. His eyes fell on a painting he knew well. It depicted an *Explosion in a Cathedral*, cured, if deficiently, of the long wound it was dealt one day by glues that rippled the canvas where it had been torn. Walking behind the servant, who held up a large candelabra with new candles, he walked into the next room, the library. Beside the bookshelves stood a panoply crowned with helmets and morions of Italian manufacture, but several weapons were missing, taken down with violence, to judge by the twisted hooks that had held them. Two armchairs were pulled close, as if for discussion, on the two sides of a narrow coffee table, where evaporated Malaga wine had left colored streaks in the glasses. "As I had the honor to communicate to the gentleman in writing, not a single thing has been touched since that day," the servant said, opening another door. The traveler entered what appeared to be the untidy room of a woman just awakened. The sheets were still thrown aside where she had stretched out in the morning; the nightgown on the floor and the disordered garments torn from the wardrobe gave a sense of the haste with which she had chosen the apparel that was now missing. "It was a tobacco-colored dress, with lace," the servant said. The two men stepped out onto a broad gallery whose outer windows were whitened by frost. "This was his room," the servant said, searching for a key. The stranger was shown a narrow chamber furnished with almost austere sobriety, its sole adornment a tapestry hung on the wall opposite the bed, with a droll concert of monkeys playing claves, viol, trumpet, and flute. On the nightstand stood bottles of medicines, a water pitcher, and a spoon. "I had to dump out the water, it was putrid," the servant said. Everything was clean and orderly, as in a barracks: "He always made his own bed and put away his things. He didn't like the servants in here, not even when he was ill." The traveler returned to the salon. "Tell me what happened that day," he said. But despite his evident inclination to help, hoping to turn attention from the party and the wine with a flood of words interlaced with abundant praise for the kindness, the generosity, the nobility of his masters, the man's tale was very dull. The details were familiar from a letter the servant had already sent him, written out by a public amanuensis who, though ignorant of the case, had added annotations in his own hand; the hypotheses these put forth were far more illuminating than the scarce facts remembered by the lackey who, in a word, could tell him nothing. On the morning in question, caught up in the enthusiasm that filled the streets, the servants had left the kitchens, laundries, pantries, and coach houses. Some returned later; others did not . . . The traveler asked for pen and paper, noting down the names of anyone who, for whatever the reason, had had dealings with the masters of the house: doctors, purveyors, hairdressers, booksellers, upholsterers, apothecaries, perfumers, merchants, artisans ... He overlooked neither the fan seller who had come often to show her wares, nor the barber who kept his shop nearby and knew any and everything about the people who had lived in the Calle de Fuencarral during the past twenty years.

XLIX.

So it happened.

GOYA

With information turned up in stores and workshops; with the talk in a nearby tavern, where the heat of brandy refreshed many a clouded memory; with the accounts of people of every class and condition, a story came together in traces, with lacunae and paragraphs cut short, like an ancient chronicle reborn from an assemblage of scattered fragments. The House of the Condesa de Arcos—according to the account of the Notary who, unwittingly, was prologist to the cento—had stood empty for a long time, being the setting for strange and scandalous occurrences involving phantoms and apparitions. Time slipped past, but still, the noble mansion remained abandoned, isolated by its own legend, and the merchants of the neighborhood missed the days when its masters held feasts and soirees that had required substantial purchases of adornments and lamps, fine delicacies and exquisite wines. For that reason, the afternoon when lights appeared in the windows was greeted with excitement. The neighbors approached curiously, watching the drudgery of servants carrying trunks and bundles from the coach house to the attic and hanging new chandeliers from the smooth ceilings. The next day came painters, paperers, and plasterers with ladders and scaffolds. Cool air blew through the rooms, dispersing the spells and enchantments. Bright curtains enlivened the bedrooms, and a liveried stable hand brought two splendid sorrel horses to the stalls, which smelled again of hay, oats, and grass peas. Word spread that a woman of Spanish blood had rented the mansion, not one to be intimidated by tales of sprites and phantoms . . . The chronicle passed now to the lips of a lacemaker from the Calle Mayor: Soon the lady of the Casa de Arcos became known as *the Cuban*. She was pretty, with big, dark eyes, and lived alone, receiving no visitors and never bothering to meet with the people of the *Villa y Corte*, as the metropolis was known. Constant worry shadowed her gaze, and yet she sought no consolation in religion: it was a known fact that she never attended Mass. She was rich, to judge by the number of her servants and the ostentation of her housewares. And yet, she affected sober dress, though when she did buy a kerchief or a bit of lace, she demanded the best, with no concern for price . . . As the lacemaker had nothing more to say, he turned to Paco, the jocular barber and guitarist, whose shop was thought one of the city's premiere gossip mills: *the Cuban Lady* came to Madrid with a delicate mission: seeking a pardon of a cousin of hers who had been jailed years before in Ceuta. *Her* cousin, it was said, had been a conspirator and Freemason in the Americas; a Gallophile, a devotee of Revolutionary ideas, a printer of subversive writings and songs meant to undermine royal authority in the Overseas Domains. *The Cuban Lady* must have had something of the conspiracist and atheist about her, too, living in isolation as she did; she was indifferent to the processions that passed before the Casa de Arcos with the Holy of Holies held high, and never bothered to peek at them from one of the mansion's many windows. Some alleged the impious pillars of a Lodge had been raised in the Casa de Arcos, and even that Black Masses were held there. But the police, apprised of these rumors, surveilled the mansion for several weeks, and reported that it could not be the site of any reunion, whether of conspirators, Freemasons, or the godless—indeed, no one gathered there at all. The Casa de Arcos, once a house of mystery on account of its hobgoblins and ghosts, remained a House of Mystery in the possession of this beautiful woman highly coveted by the men who saw her on occasion when she stepped out to a nearby shop or to buy, for the Christmas holidays,

marzipan from Toledo in the vicinity of the Plaza Mayor . . .
Word passed now to an old doctor who had frequently visited
the Casa de Arcos for some time: he had been called on to treat
a man of formerly vigorous constitution whose health had been
ravaged by his imprisonment in Ceuta, a place he had just returned from after being freed by royal pardon. His legs bore the
marks of shackles. He suffered from intermittent fevers and
from occasional asthma that had tormented him since childhood, though his crises abated when he smoked cigarettes rolled
with petals of Angel's Trumpet that he ordered from Cuba
through an apothecary in the Tribulete neighborhood. Submitted to a revitalizing regimen, he had slowly recovered his health.
The doctor wasn't called to the Casa de Arcos again . . . Now it
was the turn of a bookseller: Esteban had no interest in philosophy or the work of economists, or any writings that examined
the History of Europe in recent years. He read travel books; the
poetry of Ossian; that novel about the sorrows of Young
Werther; new translations of Shakespeare; he remembered the
young man's enthusiasm for *The Genius of Christianity*, a work
he qualified as *simply extraordinary*, and had ordered bound in
velvet covers with a tiny golden lock, to keep secret the personal
annotations he made in the margins of the text. Carlos, who
had read this book by Chateaubriand, could not grasp why Esteban, man devoid of faith, had taken such an interest in a text
frequently blustering, lacking in unity, and unconvincing to
those who lacked true faith. Looking all over, Carlos found one
of the five volumes in Sofía's room. Leafing through it, he noted
with surprise that this edition included, in its second part, a sort
of novel-like tale entitled *René* that didn't appear in the other,
more recent copy acquired in Havana. Most of the pages were
free of notes or marks, but there was one series of phrases, of
paragraphs, underlined in red ink: *This life, which at the beginning had so enchanted me, was not long in growing unbearable. I became weary of the same scenes and the same ideas. I
plumbed my heart and asked myself what it was I wanted . . .
Without parents, without friends, and without, so to speak,
having yet loved on this earth, I was overwhelmed by a super-
abundance of life . . . I descended the valley and climbed the*

mountain, calling with all the strength of my desire to the ideal object of a future flame . . . You must recall she was the only person in the world I had ever loved and that all my feelings came to be mingled in her with the pain of the memories of my childhood . . . A movement of pity had brought her toward me . . . A suspicion formed in Carlos's mind. He questioned a waitress who had served Sofía for some time, with oblique overtures that might lead her to reveal some confidence while concealing his interest in the case: There was no doubt Sofía and Esteban cared greatly for each other, and lived in a quiet and tender affection. On the harsh winter days, when the fountains of the Retiro froze, they would have their meals in her room, pulling their armchairs close to a brazier. In summer, they took long carriage rides, stopping to drink horchata at the stalls. They were seen more than once at the Feria de San Isidro and found the people's capers highly entertaining. They held hands in the way a brother and sister might. She didn't remember ever seeing them quarrel or argue heatedly. Never. He called Sofía by her name, and she called him Esteban, that was all. The wagging tongues—which are always present in kitchens and pantries—had never suggested any untoward intimacy between the two of them. No. At any rate, no one had ever seen anything. When his illness made the nights hard for him, she had more than once remained by his side until dawn. For the rest, they were just brother and sister. It did surprise people that a woman of her beauty would not resolve to marry. Had she wished to, there would have been no lack of well-bred and attractive suitors . . . "Certain things we can never learn the full truth of," thought Carlos as he reread the phrases underlined in the red velvet book, which could be interpreted in so many different ways. *An Arab would say I was wasting my time, like a person searching for the tracks of a bird in the air or of a fish in water.*

He still had to reconstruct the Endless Day; the day when two existences apparently dissolved into a tumultuous and bloody All. Only one witness to the initial scene of the drama remained: a gloveress who, not suspecting what would soon happen, had gone early to the Casa de Arcos to deliver to Sofía several pairs of gloves. She was surprised to observe only one old manservant in the mansion. Sofía and Esteban were in the library, leaning out the open window, listening attentively to what was coming to them from outside. A frantic uproar was filling the city. Though nothing seemed out of the ordinary on the Calle de Fuencarral, a handful of stores and taverns had suddenly closed their doors. In back of the houses, in the adjoining streets, a dense multitude was congregating. Suddenly, chaos broke out. Groups of men from the village, followed by women and children, appeared on the corners, shouting "Death to the French." People left their homes armed with kitchen knives, boards, and tools: anything that could cut, wound, harm. Gunfire was audible all over as the human mass, driven by inner impulses, poured toward the Plaza Mayor and the Puerta del Sol. A vociferating priest, walking at the head of a group of *manolos* and brandishing a razor, turned back every now and then to shout: "Death to the French! Death to Napoleon!" The entire population of Madrid had taken to the streets in a sudden, unanticipated, and devastating revolt, with no need of printed proclamations or rhetorical artifices to provoke them. The faces; the yammering and shoving of the women; in the unrelenting instinct of the collective march; the universality of rage—these were eloquence enough. All at once, the human tide seemed to pause, as if trapped in its own whirlpools. The musket fire worsened, and for the first time, severe and thunderous, the voice of a cannon rang out. "The French have brought their cavalry," some shouted, retreating, already wounded, with saber wounds on their faces, their arms, their chests from the first skirmishes. The blood, far from frightening those who advanced, drove them toward the place where the artillery and musket fire was thickest . . . It was then that Sofía turned away from the window: "Let's go!" she shouted, tearing down sabers and daggers from the panoply. Esteban tried to stop her: "Don't be a fool! They're firing muskets. You won't do a thing with that scrap of metal you're holding." "Stay if you want! I'm going!" "Who are you fighting for then?" "For those who have taken to the streets!" Sofía shouted. "We have to do something!" "What?" "Something!" Esteban watched her leave the house, impetuous, inflamed, one shoulder bare, hoisting a blade with unprecedented force and determination. "Wait for me," he shouted. And he grabbed a hunting rifle and hurried downstairs . . .

That much could be known. Then afterward, the furor, the roar, the tumult, the chaos of collective convulsion. The mamelukes charged, the cuirassers charged, the Polish guard charged at the multitude that fought back with knives and clubs, at the women and men who ran to the horses and sliced their flanks with razors. Platoons emerged from four streets at once, and surrounded, the people went inside or ran, jumping over walls and across rooftops. Firebrands, stones, and bricks rained from the windows; cauldrons and pots of boiling oil were dumped over the attackers. The cannoneers fell one by one, but the guns went on firing, wicks lit by raging women when there were no more men left to do it. An atmosphere of cataclysm, of telluric disturbance, reigned across Madrid—with fire, iron, steel, all that cut or exploded, now turned against the masters—in a tempestuous *Dies Irae* . . . Then came night. A night of grim slaughter, of mass executions, of extermination in Manzanares and Moncloa. The rifle fire had grown thicker, less diffuse, concerted in a fateful rhythm that responded to orders against the sinister ulcerated backdrop of walls reddened by blood. That night in early May, the hours swelled, their passing clotted with blood and horror. The streets filled with corpses—with wounded beings who wept and were finished off by patrols of bleak myrmidons, their ragged dolmans, lacerated braid, and torn shakos bespeaking the disasters of war in the light of a timid lamp, carried alone across the city in the impossible search for the face of a single body among countless other bodies . . . Neither Sofía nor Esteban ever returned to the Casa de Arcos. Not another trace of them or their final resting place was ever found.

Two days later, after learning what little there was to learn, Carlos ordered sealed the crates where he had placed certain objects, books, and clothes which, by their shape, their scent, or their folds, still spoke to him of the existence of the departed. Downstairs, three carriages were waiting to take him and his luggage to the Casa de Postas. The Casa de Arcos would be returned, again empty, to the hands of its owners. One after another, the keys turned in the locks of the doors. Night moved into the mansion—night fell early that winter—as the fires inside died down, and the half-burnt logs were pulled away from the rest and doused with water from a pitcher of gilt red glass. When the last door was closed, the painting of the *Explosion in a Cathedral*, forgotten—perhaps willfully—ceased to matter, and erased itself, leaving a shadow on the dark carmine of the brocade dressing the walls of the salon, which seemed to bleed where damp had marked the fabric.

Guadeloupe, Barbados, Caracas
1956–1958

Concerning the History
of Victor Hugues

As Victor Hugues has been almost ignored by the history of the French Revolution—which is far too occupied with describing the events that took place in Europe between the days of the Convention and 18 Brumaire to turn its gaze to the remote domains of the Caribbean—the author of the present book believes it useful to clarify certain matters concerning the historical truth behind this figure.

It is known that Victor Hugues was from Marseille, son of a baker—and there are even reasons to believe he had distant ancestors who were black, though this would be far from easy to prove. Drawn by a sea that has been—particularly in Marseille—an eternal summons to adventure since the times of Pythias and the Phoenician captains, he set sail for America, as a cabin boy, voyaging several times to the Caribbean. Rising to the rank of navigator of commercial vessels, he traveled through the Antilles, eventually leaving the wanderer's life behind to open a large general store—a *comptoir*—in Port-au-Prince, with diverse merchandise acquired, gathered, collected, through trade, smuggling, or barter, exchanging silks for coffee, vanilla for pearls. Such places still exist in abundance in the ports of that luminous, glimmering world. His true entry into history dates from the night when Haitian revolutionaries burned this establishment to the ground.

From this moment, we can follow his trajectory step by step, just as it is narrated in the book. The chapters concerned with the reconquest of Guadeloupe follow a precise chronological schema. All that is said about his war against the United States—what the Yankees of the day called the *Brigands' War*—as well as the action of the corsairs, with their names and the names of their ships, is based on documents the author has consulted in Guadeloupe and in libraries in Barbados, as well as on short but instructive references found in the works of those Latin American authors who mention Victor Hugues in passing.

Concerning Victor Hugues's actions in French Guiana, abundant information exists in memoirs of the deportation. In the period after this novel's end, Victor Hugues was brought before a military court in Paris to answer for handing the colony over to Holland, following a surrender that was, in truth, inevitable. Absolved with honor, Victor Hugues turned back to the political realm. We know he had dealings with Fouché. We also know he was in Paris when the Napoleonic Empire collapsed.

But here his trail goes cold. Some historians—the few who have looked into his case by chance, in addition to Pierre Vitoux, who dedicated to him, more than twenty years ago, a still unpublished study—say he died near Bordeaux, where he "possessed some properties" (?), in the year 1820. Didot's *Bibliographie Universelle* places his death in 1822. But in Guadeloupe, where the memory of Victor Hugues remains very present, people say he returned to Guiana after the Empire fell, taking possession of his properties once more. It seems—according to researchers in Guadeloupe—that he died a slow, painful death, of an illness that may have been leprosy, but that evidence indicates was most likely some form of cancer.*

What was the end of Victor Hugues? We still do not know, just as we know very little about his birth. But there is no doubt that his hypostatic action—firm, sincere, heroic in the first

---

Author's note: These pages were already published in their first edition in Mexico when, finding myself in Paris, I had the opportunity to meet the last living descendant of Victor Hugues, who possesses important family documents concerning him. He informed me that the grave of Victor Hugues lies not far away from Cayenne. In one of the documents I examined, I came upon a remarkable revelation: Victor Hugues was loved faithfully for years by a beautiful Cuban woman who, even more shockingly, was named Sofía.

phase; wavering, contradictory, predatory, even cynical in the second—presents the image of an extraordinary man whose behavior reveals a dramatic dichotomy. For this reason, the author has seen fit to reveal the existence of this neglected historical character in a novel that has, at the same time, the whole of the Caribbean as its subject.

A.C.

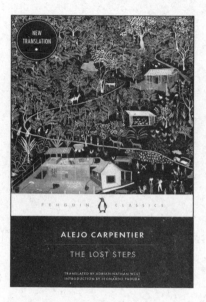